MW01118335

JIM VARNADO

BIG IRON

BASED ON THREE BALLADS
BY MARTY ROBBINS

TATE PUBLISHING
AND ENTERPRISES, LLC

Published by Tate Publishing & Enterprises, LLC
127 E. Trade Center Terrace | Mustang, Oklahoma 73064 USA
1.888.361.9473 | www.tatepublishing.com

Tate Publishing is committed to excellence in the publishing industry. The company reflects the philosophy established by the founders, based on Psalm 68:11,
"The Lord gave the word and great was the company of those who published it."

Book design copyright © 2014 by Tate Publishing, LLC. All rights reserved.
Cover design by Rodrigo Adolfo
Interior design by Jake Muelle

Published in the United States of America

ISBN: 978-1-62902-942-9
1. Fiction / General
2. Fiction / Westerns
13.02.13

DEDICATION

I wish to dedicate this work to *Marty Robbins...*

For it is truly upon his genius that I stand.

I also wish to co-dedicate this work to my wife *Kathy Varnado*.

She lived with me, tolerated me, and greatly assisted me for

The eight plus months it took to translate my thoughts into these words.

ACKNOWLEDGMENTS

Benelli USA Corporation
17603 Indian Head Highway
Accokeek, MD 20607

The color photos are of fully functional handguns as used by the Ranger and Texas Red; these are not photos of replicas. My thanks to Benelli for their courtesy in allowing us to use these exceptional photos.

Barbara Garner
Interior designer and decorator
Oklahoma City, Oklahoma

Barbara wrote almost the entire scene where the ranger was looking around Texas Red's mansion, as well as other scenes of the mansion and guest house. Barbara ensured the description of the interior of Red's mansion was period correct and accurate for the time.

Kathy Varnado (my wife)

I searched for two hours trying to find the contact info to obtain a license to use the three Marty Robbins ballads in my concept for a western novel to no avail. Kathy found them and e-mailed them and received a reply all within twenty minutes. I cannot count the number of 2:00 a.m. readings and editing in our *writer's cave* at home or the hours of reading and editing at Jimmies Egg while having breakfast. I thank her especially for the encouragement, strength, support, and enormous help, ideas, changes, and assistance

Kathy gave. She even knew when to tell me to go to bed and when to go to work.

At least 95 percent of everything Kathy did was after a major, crippling stroke on December 27, 2012. She spent a month and a day in the hospital, and she could not speak for over a month, but boy howdy she could communicate. I am immensely proud of her, impressed with her, and in love with her.

Blake Lawrence (my attorney)
Hall, Estill, Hardwick, Gable, Golden & Nelson, PC
100 N. Broadway, Suite 2900
Oklahoma City, OK 73102

Good people exist in every strata of human endeavor, and Blake is one of them. There were no problems, disagreements, arguments, or trouble of any kind. Yet I am still far better off with a professional such as Blake handling my contracts, licensing, and paperwork.

TABLE OF CONTENTS

Lyrics

THE RANGER'S BIG IRON

Designed and made for rangers is this 1847 .44 caliber Colt Walker nine-inch round barrel. From 1847 to 1934 when the .357 magnum was released, it was the most powerful factory-made handgun on earth. It is still the most powerful black powder handgun ever made.

TEXAS REDS HANDGUN

Purchased by Texas Reds mother is this 1851 .36 caliber Navy Colt with a seven-and-a-half-inch octagon barrel. In its day, it was the most popular Colt revolver ever made, sold, and fired, mainly because of its extensive use by both sides in the civil war.

FOREWORD

BY MARSHALL TRIMBLE

I was in Oklahoma City in the spring of 1979 attending an event at the National Cowboy Hall of Fame when I checked into the host hotel headed for an empty elevator. I pressed the button and just as the door was closing the legendary Marty Robbins stepped in. l always make it a practice in the presence of famous people to give them their space, probably because I fear making a fool of myself. I pulled my hat down and humbly starred at the floor. Next thing I knew a face was peering at me from under the brim of my hat.

He grinned, stuck out his hand and said, "Hi, I'm Marty Robbins."

I'd heard he was one of the most popular members of the Grand Ole Opry, now I knew why.

"Yep, I know who you are," I replied then blurted out, "I used to see you on local television in Phoenix and I know your wife's name is Marizona because she was born in Maricopa County, Arizona."

"How'd you know that?" he asked.

"I wrote a book on Arizona history and the two of you are in it."

"How about you and me go to dinner," he said.

And that's how I came to meet Marty Robbins.

We spent the next two hours talking about gunfighters and his ballads about gunfighters. He told me about how he came to write "El Paso" while returning from a family visit in Texas. Marty had deep roots in the Texas and Arizona history. He was the nephew of "Sandy Bob" Heckle, who was featured in Gail Gardner's famous cowboy poem, "*Sierry Petes*" or "*Tyin' Knots in the Devil's Tale.*" It told the story of two drunken cowboys who were accosted by the Devil on their way back to the ranch after a wild night on Prescott's "Whiskey Row."

Instead of the Devil gatherin' in their souls "Buster Jig" and "Sandy Bob" roped him, notched his ears, de-horned and branded him, tied knots in his tail and then rode off leaving him necked up to a blackjack oak tree.

Marty could sure tell a good story and that's what he did with his ballads about gunfighters. Jim Varnado has taken those lyrics and created a literary postscript to three of Robbins' best-known western ballads, "Big Iron," "Feleena" and "El Paso," blending them into an intriguing novel packed with action and romance that spans two generations.

He's remained true to the lyrics in the ballads and expanded the story of the young cowboy who dies in the arms of the beautiful cantina girl, *Feleena*. We learn how the notorious *"Texas Red"* evolved from an eastern college boy into a ruthless killer. One of these two gunmen who meet on the street in the town of Agua Fria at twenty past eleven is the son of the young cowboy and Feleena, the young senorita who dances at Rosa's Cantina in El Paso. I'm not going to give anything away so you're going to have to find out for yourself.

I'm reminded of Bobbie Gentry's haunting and mysterious ballad *"Ode to Billie Joe"* that went to the top of the charts in 1967 and around the country the hot topic of conversation was what did Billie Joe and his girlfriend toss off the Tallahatchie Bridge. Everybody had a different guess and we still can only speculate on what happened up there on Choctaw Ridge.

Like *Ode to Billie Joe*, Big Iron is chock-full of wherefores and whys. Some questions are answered and some left for the reader to decide. I think they will enjoy the creative way Varnado has taken Marty Robbins' ballads and turned them into a gripping narrative.

Stay tuned 'cause Jim is already working on a sequel.

—Marshall Trimble
Official Arizona State Historian

BIG IRON CONCEPT

The "Big Iron" story develops, enhances, and combines the stories and lives contained in these three ballads into one homogenous story that spans two generations. There exists a common theme, connection, and life within these three ballads that actually lend themselves to be completed and told and can easily be melded into one story—a story that seemingly ends with the Arizona ranger and Texas Red with forty feet between them, in what turns out to be the final gunfight for both men...albeit for far different reasons. This is a story that never truly ends; it is simply retold by different characters, in different places, at different times.

QUESTIONS

Why was it decided to have a gunfight at 11:20 in the morning? Never in the annals of Western gun-fighting, leather-pulling, or fast-draw gunfights has there ever been a gunfight at 11:20 a.m. Who set the gunfight for 11:20 a.m. and why?

How could the jealous cowboy in the ballad "El Paso" be guilty of murder when the handsome young stranger who was sharing a drink with Felina made the first move?

> I challenged his right for the love of this maiden,
> Down went his hand for the gun that he wore.

How did the posse in the ballad "El Paso" know exactly when and where the cowboy who loved Felina would return to El Paso? That he would return for Felina was a certainty—but how did the posse know exactly when?

MAJOR CHANGES

ONLY THREE MAJOR CHANGES FROM THE LYRICS WERE REQUIRED

In the ballad "Faleena," the cowboy and Felina are together for only six weeks. This was expanded to ten months to allow enough time for them to have a son.

In the ballad "Faleena," the cowboy returned to Rosa's Cantina the very next day; this is expanded to five days.

In the ballad "Big Iron," the Arizona ranger is in town for only a few hours. This was expanded to eight days to maximize development of the characters and how their lives were shaped and molded. Far from being hated, Texas Red is beloved by *his* town, and he makes the town a better place to live. Texas Red was a robber of stagecoaches and even a few trains but never close to home. But at the end of the day, Texas Red is indeed *ruthless and a killer*, fatally flawed by his own internal burn, bloodlust, and temperament.

INTRODUCTION

1882

I n the small town of Agua Fria, New Mexico, history wrote a new page and a legend was forged. Two of the fastest, most deadly, and most feared gunfighters alive, Texas Red and an Arizona Ranger, were pacing off the final steps that one of them would ever take. Within minutes, a fatal bullet would be—must be—fired. Only one will survive. There was eighty feet between them as they walked toward each other on the wooden boardwalk on either side of the street. They had not yet stepped out of the shade and onto the dirt street that would soon claim and absorb the blood of the second fastest.

As they paused for a moment to await the appointed time, both men tipped their hats ever so slightly to the other and nodded with the last remnants, the last vestiges, and last thoughts of friendship or respect. The past week of their lives must now be forgotten and pushed aside. It is time to kill.

They know each other's greatest strength and greatest weakness. Both men know they have just cause to fear for their lives, and both know without question that the other man could win this gunfight. They know that they may well lose their life, and both gunfighters are too skilled to risk mercy and aim for an incapacitating wound. They *must*, and they will, aim for an instant kill.

One of them has a draw so blindingly fast that gun-fighting legends refer to it as an *invisible draw*—a draw so rare there has never been two such elite gunfighters alive at the same time. However, this master gunfighter has attained such legendary speed at a potentially fatal price. An erstwhile secret injury, openly known since just last night, could render the fastest gun alive as helpless as a child. They resumed their slow but fatal walk to death. With sixty feet between them, they stepped out onto the dirt street, at the appointed time, to take those final steps that one of them would ever take. With fifty feet between them, they could no longer see the other as human, nor could they see anything except what was directly in front of them as both men were so intensely focused, their sight compressed into a tight scope of tunnel vision.

Texas Red chose the appointed day, and the ranger chose the appointed time. It was exactly 11:20 Saturday morning, and there was forty feet between them when they stopped to make their play.

Both men reached for their guns at exactly the same instant. There were two gunfighters and two guns, but there was only one blast from a single gunshot, and there was only one tongue of flame, and there was but one cloud of blue-white smoke. The second fastest gunfighter now lay in the dirt street, dying by the second. He has perhaps two minutes to live, and he lives them with the ultimate humiliation feared by all gunfighters—the dying gunfighter never cleared leather.

An Arizona ranger named Kyle Lawton came to Agua Fria eight days ago to arrest, or kill, the outlaw called Texas Red, who has killed twenty men in fast-draw gunfights. In addition, he has robbed stagecoaches, banks, and even trains, resulting in a number of additional deaths. The ranger was packing a customized Big Iron that was one of a matched pair. The other Big Iron belonged to his brother, a Texas ranger who also faced Texas Red. The ranger's brother was one of the twenty notches carved deep into Texas Red's gun handle. Although Texas Red was barely twenty-four years old, he is already a vicious killer, and he was forced to flee El Paso and live in New Mexico territory because of the very first notch on the handle of his six-gun; the notch was for a deputy sheriff in El Paso.

Before he was Texas Red, the six-foot, two-inch, 240-pound outlaw was William, William Travis Jr. He has genius-level intellect and is an exemplary college graduate with a master's degree. Moreover, he was a greatly feared member of his college boxing team, and he is every bit as tough and strong as he looks. Texas Red has flaming red hair, a soft voice, and a disarming baby face smile and equal charm. He is very charismatic, but the angelic face and boyish charm can turn into a raging demon from hell within a single heartbeat. Texas Red aches inside to become famous, more so to become legendary. Others can see this in part, but no more than a tenth of it. Like a dangerous iceberg, 90 percent of the danger remains hidden. It is a hunger and emotional starvation he has felt all of his life. It was relatively easy to hide while in college, but now his internal demon is too powerful to contain and has been unleashed. His hunger and ache to be legendary overwhelms all else, and when it comes to a final choice, even his beloved sister, Lynda, is second.

The incident with the deputy in El Paso did not transform William Travis into Texas Red. The incident was the triggering mechanism that unleashed the outlaw that was already there, and Texas Red would have soon emerged in any event. Although killing the deputy in El Paso was arguably justified, it was the gateway for Texas Red to justify every act, crime, and murder for the rest of his short life. The incident gave Texas Red a guiltless excuse to commit the crimes he would have committed anyway. Eventually, William would have transformed into Texas Red under any circumstances. The incident with the deputy simply made it sooner rather than later.

1876

Accepted by his college to begin studies on a new degree program called a PhD, which has only been available for fifteen years in the

United States, William returned home to El Paso to tell everyone the good news and then quickly returned to college.

Three months into his studies, William realized he had not received a letter from Lynda in over a month. He had many friends, and he mailed letters to several people he knew, and after yet another month, there was no response from anyone.

Then William sent a telegram telling them he was on his way home, and he asked very pointedly and almost threateningly, "I strongly suggest a response. What is wrong?"

The only response to his telegram was anonymous, short, cryptic, and worrisome.

> Lynda will survive, but she is not well. We fear for your life
> if you take action.

Two weeks later, William burst into the house and shouted for Lynda. She was in a corner of her darkened bedroom crying and shivering and tightly grasping William's eighteen-inch, hunting knife. Lynda was catatonic, and it was long and difficult for him to convince her that he was her brother William. Then she dropped the knife, grabbed William, and held him as tight as she possibly could. She cried uncontrollably and could not speak. Then William turned up the light, and he froze in horror and could not believe his own eyes.

It took long seconds of staring at Lynda for William to realize what had happened. He saw Lynda's misshapen face, viciously and violently beaten and broken from more than one beating. William begrudgingly thought she was lucky to be alive as he looked at the fist and knuckle marks permanently indented into her face and skull.

It was an hour before Lynda could tell the story.

It was the deputy. He made lewd advances toward her and demanded an enormous amount of money for his *protection*. When she refused, he broke into their home, late at night, and beat her senseless and raped her repeatedly as she lay unconscious. He also committed unspeakable acts. Although he returned time after time and despite being observed and followed, Lynda was able to hide and escape all but twice more. When he caught her those times, he now demanded the money and also threatened to kill William while she watched if she did not comply. However, Lynda staunchly refused and unwaveringly withstood the beatings, torment, threats, and rape. She would not give up one dime of their money, and she spat on him and cursed him. The third time was by far the worst beating of all but was fortunate in that this beating required hospitalization where she was out of the deputy's powerful reach and out of his sphere of influence. The deputy had no concept of the enraged beast that would instantly ignite within William. Everyone thought of William as a...*gentle* giant. However, the deputy thought of William as a spineless, weak college boy with a soft voice. His misconception would be excruciatingly painful... and fatal.

William was enraged beyond the ability of words to convey. His rage went beyond the wild, screaming, loud rage of verbal threats and mindless actions. Outward, William seemed almost calm. His rage was the quiet, cold, unemotional, calculating rage that went to the marrow of his bones. Someone...was going to die. The deputy showed no mercy; now he would receive none. Not even a quick death.

Lynda mercifully went to sleep on the couch and enjoyed her first real sleep since the nightmare began. She knew in her heart that William would make everything all right.

William went to his room and found *the gun*. It was a six-gun his mother bought for 5 dollars from a man named Reno when she ran away from home at seventeen. The six-gun was a .36 caliber Navy Colt with modifications Reno made for gun fighting, and the gun has a long, tragic history in William's family. When he was about fifteen, William bought a black, leather holster custom-made especially for this six-gun, and he became quite proficient at drawing it. William's hand speed is so fast that in boxing, his hands always wore the blood of his opponents. This is how William actually got the nickname Texas Red, not because of his red hair. Ironically, he thought the source of the nickname was too violent and refused it. Now his extreme hand speed could easily mean the difference between life and death. However, William does not care about his own life, as long as he fires two bullets into the fat deputy's belly before he dies.

William went to a friend of his named Saul who owns a gun shop. Saul oiled the holster, cleaned the Navy Colt, and made a batch of carefully measured cartridges with close attention to detail.

Saul then took William out back to practice and taught William everything he could in an hour. After an hour, Saul told William that he had the speed but wondered if William had the nerve to pull the trigger when facing a man rather than a target. Saul was amazed at William's speed, and if William could pull the trigger knowing his bullet will kill a man, this gunfight was already over. Saul continued to shake his head at William's speed, and William wanted more practice, but Saul knew William would soon become slower rather than faster because of fatigue. William had to go with what he had.

William made certain that Lynda was watching as he called the deputy out into the street. Surprising to some, he did not want to come out, and even from a distance, he could see the look of a killer in William's eyes. The deputy immediately realized that William did not care about his own life, and William wanted only to avenge his sister, at any cost. The deputy called out that Lynda was a lying whore and he had nothing to do with her beatings. In fact, the deputy claimed he put a stop to them. The whole town then knew the deputy was a coward as well as a liar.

William asked him how he knew this was about Lynda. Then he called out that the deputy was indeed a champion among women and then challenged him to try his skills against a man. William said many things that drew a crowd and generated laughter. It got to the point where the deputy would be an ineffective laughing stock throughout the city if he did not come out and face William. Moreover, everyone knew what the deputy did to Lynda, and everyone knew he prevented her from leaving town. Then the deputy got an idea and finally opened his door and walked out onto the street.

The deputy drew first, long before either man was supposed to draw. Another deputy who was to count down to the draw had not even started. Even at that, the deputy barely touched his gun before two gunshots blasted two holes in his lower abdomen, and the bullets simultaneously bent him double and knocked him backwards. He screamed for mercy with a mouthful of dirt, but it was already too late. The only mercy available to him at this point was a gunshot to the head. He did not know that the teenage William had anticipated exactly what the deputy would do. The deputy was a lifelong bully and tyrant but never a skilled gunfighter. The deputy's name remains unspoken in order to prevent the tainting of others with a name he made too evil to speak.

William started walking toward the slowly dying deputy, but by the time he got there, William was Texas Red. He then put a bullet through each of the deputy's shoulders and each of his knees. Then Texas Red mocked the deputy and told him that it was going to be excruciatingly painful for anyone to carry him to the doctor's office. Perhaps he should walk. The shooting was arguably justified, and the gunfight was more than fair considering the deputy's early draw. However, such a deputy could not exist without equal corruption and support from higher-up. Not to mention that, corrupt or not, he was a legal deputy sheriff and therefore afforded a measure of latitude by law.

Warned by friends that the deputy was the sheriff's first cousin, William and Lynda knew they could not wait until the deputy died; they knew they had to leave El Paso now, and they had to leave El Paso forever. Fortunately, the hospital knew what had happened to Lynda, and they kept her as long as they could. The point being that Lynda's face has healed more than enough for her to travel in a hurry.

As they feared, within an hour, friends warned them of their impending arrest and near-certain death from hanging or death from manufactured excuses, such as shot while trying to escape or while fighting *law officials* for a gun. William and Lynda had to leave El Paso, and they had to leave immediately. Since almost all of their money was outside of Texas, their immense wealth was safe and secure. Unfortunately, nothing within Texan borders was either safe or secure, especially their lives.

The doctor was able to slow the deputy's internal bleeding but could not stop it. It would take two days for the deputy to die, and there was very little the doctor could do for the pain. From the instant William's second bullet slammed into the deputy's body, he was on the wrong side of a deathwatch.

Back in their El Paso home, William and Lynda quickly grabbed the things they needed most. William walked into her room, carrying a small travel bag containing not much more than his gun and holster, and he asked her where she wanted to go. Lynda told him they have much of their money in a Santa Fe bank. And since it is over three hundred miles from El Paso, Lynda suggested they return to their childhood home. William agreed and then told her from that moment forward, he is no longer William. He is now Texas Red. Lynda quickly informed *Texas Red* that he has been William all of her life, and he would continue to be William for the rest of her life. As they walked down the stairs to leave, she still fussed at him and informed him that he was her brother, William, and she would call him by no other name…not politely, anyway.

As they got into their buggy to leave, they heard the last voice on earth they wanted to hear.

It was the sheriff. "Hold up a minute. We need to talk here."

The sheriff walked up to the horse and laid his hand on the back of the horse, and then he pets the horse. He took a deep breath and looked long at Lynda's face and then looked at Texas Red. "I'm not doubting what your sister claims. I know what he can be, but he is my cousin. At least he is for the next day or two. The doctor says my cousin doesn't have a chance. If you had killed him quick, I could wrestle with this thing a lot better. But you shot him twice with no intentions of him dying right off, but you made sure he would die. I look at your sister, and I can see some of that, but he's still my

| 24 |

blood, and she is still alive. Why does he have to die while she still lives? That's the hardest part of what I'm wrestling with. I am really wrestling with this thing, young man. I'm wrestling hard with it, and a lot of it won't go down. You gut-shot him, and then shot him in each knee and shoulder. That's vicious, young man, pure vicious. You knew the man was going to die, and you knew your sister was going to live. But you still turned as vicious as a meat ax. This is some powerful poison that you want me to swallow."

Then he looked at Lynda and nodded. "It's a sure thing that you have suffered enough, and there will be no more on you. But I do ask that you stay out of the way if the fighting starts. But to tell you right, I am split right down the middle on this thing."

Then he looked back at William. "So what I am going to do is split your chances of getting out of here alive right down the middle. I will give you what I think is a fifty-fifty chance to survive. That way, we are leaving this thing in the hands of higher powers to decide who lives and who dies. Here's the deal...I am coming after you with full intentions of killing you. I am going to give you a two-hour head start, and then me and two other cousins are coming after you. You can go in any direction and use any means of travel."

Then he glared at Texas Red with the coldness of death. "Don't let me catch you, boy. If we catch you, your sister is going to see things she ain't ever going to forget."

Texas Red nodded. "Are you saying that if I had shot your cousin between the eyes, it would have watered down and diluted the poison we're passing around here?"

The sheriff nodded, "Oh yeah. It would have made a huge difference."

Texas Red pulled his gun out of the travel bag with blinding speed and shot him right between the eyes. "You mean like that?"

He grabbed the sheriff and put him in the buggy and positioned his arms like he had been shot in the shoulder. They took off in the buggy and yelled at everyone to get out of the way. When they got to the doctor's office, Texas Red put the sheriff over his shoulder and easily carried him into the doctor's office and put him down on an operating table. The doctor looked at the sheriff and quickly looked at Texas Red. "What the…"

Texas Red pressed his gun against the doctor's body as hard as he could to muffle the gunshot and pulled the trigger. Lynda was in the buggy and never heard the gunshot. Texas Red put the doctor in his chair at his desk and even put a book in his hands. Then he got in the buggy and simply rode out of town like nothing had happened. Lynda never knew that William killed the doctor.

As his father had done before him, William, who has now transformed into Texas Red, had to flee El Paso for his life, perhaps Lynda's as well.

They would soon settle back in the small town they grew up in on the outskirts of Santa Fe. A small town named Agua Fria.

1882

Arizona commissioned a ranger, who had been a US Marshal for ten years, to extract an outlaw in New Mexico Territory. Texas Red settled down too close to Santa Fe, therefore territorial officials requested help from the newly organized second formation of the Arizona rangers in 1882. This request was not surprising because New Mexico and Arizona were the same undivided territory less than twenty years ago, and they were still accustomed to being citizens of the same territory.

The US marshal was Kyle Lawton, who for ten years extracted outlaws so dangerous that no one else could face them and take then down. No one else could work alone and do what he did. He was now an Arizona ranger and proud of it. In fact, he prefers the title ranger to his own name. Strangely, he had never felt that way about his title of marshal. At thirty-one years old, the ranger is tired of the ceaseless traveling to Godforsaken places and dangerous little towns. He mocked himself within his own mind that he could call more rattlesnakes by name than he could people. Although proud of his ten years of service as a US marshal, and proud to be a ranger, he is beginning to have fleeting thoughts of settling down and having a family. However, for now he can still brush such thoughts aside, albeit with increasing difficulty. He could have easily gone after Texas Red as a US marshal, but he resigned to become a ranger, and for now he cannot figure out why. The ranger did not yet realize that by resigning as a US marshal and becoming an Arizona ranger, he has taken a very large step toward abandoning his fraternity of rattlesnakes and living among people.

The ranger stands about five feet, ten inches tall and weighs perhaps 180 pounds, but he is a pure gunfighter. Gun fighting was all he did, all he thought about, and all he had ever known. He was the best of the best and well known among outlaws as the fastest gun alive. No man he ever faced so much as cleared leather, and most never got a firm grip on the gun handle. Moreover, Kyle's reputation as a US marshal was such that many outlaws, who faced criminal charges they could hang for, declined to draw against him. They figured it was better to die later rather than sooner, and they figured they had a much better chance of escaping from jail than escaping from the feared marshal. In addition, he could almost *smell* an ambush, and in ten years, he was never wounded or so much as marked by a bullet.

With all of that, the ranger is indeed the best. However, he has a fatal secret—a secret injury that is not fatal to his opponents but fatal to himself. An injury that is getting worse and will not heal, and it is an injury that he carries with him to face Texas Red. This injury destroys his ability to defend himself and is an injury that awakes and sleeps according to its own timetable and strikes without warning. In less than a heartbeat, the ranger can plummet from the best gunfighter to the most helpless gunfighter. Most of all, there are no warning signs whatsoever.

He was not exceptionally close to his brother, named Henry, who faced Texas Red and lost. Nevertheless, Henry was his brother, and Kyle swore on Henry's grave to avenge him and kill Texas Red.

That is when Kyle resigned as a US marshal and became an Arizona Ranger. His timing was such that he had a unique choice to either fight Apaches or to accept a commission to New Mexico territory as an Arizona ranger to extract an outlaw. An outlaw called Texas Red. He could have easily become a Texas ranger, like his brother, but Texas rangers do not go into New Mexico territory and, as a rule, neither did Arizona rangers. The ranger could have gone after Texas Red on his own as a civilian, but after being a US marshal for so many years, he was not comfortable with that in the least, because it was too close to being a vigilante. He has seen far too many innocent men at the end of a vigilante rope. He also had too many powerful ingrained memories that generate and create nightmares that he aches inside to erase.

The second formation of Arizona rangers was formed exclusively to fight Apache's within Arizona Territory. However, Kyle was the best man to send to Santa Fe to help them with a dangerous and feared outlaw. He was the right man, at the right time, for the right job. When presented with his options and choices, Kyle wondered if he was dreaming. However, one thing is now certain, and that is, he will never again go out on the trail as a US marshal. He is done with it.

Kyle Lawton is the Arizona ranger whose gunfight with Texas Red became a timeless legend. Texas Red forced the ranger to wait over a week before they drew leather, which gave Texas Red time to build the gunfight into legendary status. When the week was over, the ranger's life had changed in ways that he never dreamed possible when he first rode into Agua Fria looking for Texas Red. A lesson the ranger thought he thoroughly learned years ago was etched further into his mind, and this time, it etched deep into his soul—the good guys are not always good, and the bad guys are not always bad. Nevertheless, with all said and done, that's the way the cards will fall.

The ranger never met an outlaw like Texas Red, and Texas Red has never met anyone like the ranger. The ranger never met an outlaw as intelligent, as wealthy, as educated, or as helpful. Yet when talk ends and actions begin, Texas Red is a vicious killer who must be extracted.

All of this, and Texas Red is but a youth of twenty-four.

THE RANGER ARRIVES IN AGUA FRIA

1882

The ranger rode into Agua Fria from the south side early in the morning. As is customary of the times, most town saloons are open day and night. The ranger walked into the saloon and, looking around carefully, chose a table and sat down with his back to the wall.

When Sam, the barkeep, asked if he wanted drink or food, the ranger slowly shook his head and remained quiet and ominous. The ranger remained silent long enough to size up the town and his situation. Meanwhile the town soon buzzed with excitement and speculation that the stranger among them was an outlaw who was loose and running and was here to do some business with his artistic but lethal Big Iron. When the ranger finally spoke, he openly and clearly stated that he was an Arizona ranger and he has come to take the outlaw called Texas Red back to Arizona…dead or alive, it didn't matter.

Within the hour, word reached Texas Red that a ranger is looking for him and is sitting at the *gunfighters'* table in the saloon. The gunfighters' table gives a clear line of sight from the table to anyone who enters or leaves the saloon, as well as everyone inside the saloon. The ranger realized the position of this particular table was not an accident.

Assuming the ranger was a *Texas* Ranger, Texas Red scoffed to the men around him. "This is the third ranger they have sent for me. Texas must have more rangers than they can pay, and anyone due for a raise has to bring me in." Then Texas Red laughed. "Maybe they have an overly severe punishment detail." Twenty men have tried to take Texas Red, and all twenty are dead. He shows no mercy nor grants leniency to any man who dares face him.

Texas Red chose the time of his arrival at the saloon carefully. It was three hours before he opened the swinging doors of the saloon and then stood in the middle of the doorway. Texas Red was very much aware of what time of day the contrast between the darkened saloon and him standing in middle of the bright sunlit doorway would be near blinding to the ranger. Texas Red was surprised to see the ranger sitting calmly at the table with both hands clearly in view on top of the table. "I hear that you are a Texas Ranger and that you are looking for me." Texas Red fully intended to end this quickly.

The ranger nodded slightly. "You are partially correct, but I am an *Arizona* ranger. However, yes…I am here to arrest you and take you back to Phoenix to stand trial for multiple high crimes, including train robbery and murder. You are also wanted in El Paso." Again, the ranger's unexpected demeanor of total, unshakeable confidence put Texas Red slightly off balance.

"Arizona? There haven't been any Arizona rangers for twenty years."

The ranger's smile was decidedly unfriendly. "We just formed a new group of Arizona rangers a few months ago. I will be glad to explain it to you in detail on the trail back to Phoenix."

Texas Red chuckled and gestured toward the street. "We have our own courtroom and legal process around here, and it is right out there in the street, but there are no appeals. I have faced twenty prosecuting attorneys, and all have been found in contempt of court…my court." Texas Red's smile was sinister to the point of evil. "You are a man of the law. Do you dare challenge me in my court?"

The ranger looked straight at Texas Red and smiled with his own brand of confidence. "I was hoping you would say that." It was immediately clear the ranger had no fear of Texas Red. Many others had *acted* as if they had no fear of him, but the ranger is not acting. He has no fear of Texas Red.

While the ranger had surprised Texas Red and even put him slightly off balance, he had no fear of the ranger either. This was not about fear. It was about survival of the fastest draw in an arena where second place is a grave marker. Texas Red held his gun hand out, palm up, and motioned with his fingers. "Come on, ranger. The court is waiting, and you and I are our own judge, jury, and executioners." Texas Red stepped to one side of the saloon doors, no longer blocking the entrance. The saloon quickly but quietly began filling with patrons eager to see who lived and who died. Texas Red and the ranger both ignored them as they conducted their fatal business.

The ranger had read a thick dossier accumulated over a period of five years on Texas Red's actions, tendencies, and behavior. The ranger quickly understood that what looked like an unusual level of fairness in Texas Red was actually arrogance. Texas Red was convinced he was the best gunfighter in the world, and he felt so confident that he could afford to be fair. What difference would it make? Fair fight or not, he was going to win either way, so he might as well make himself look good, and up until now, he was right. The dossier also recorded that Texas Red was willing to take surprising risks to increase his recognition and grandeur as he climbed his way up to become a legend, which is what he truly ached for, at any price and at any cost.

The ranger stood up, still keeping both hands in clear view. Both men sized up the other, and it was obvious to anyone with eyes that the ranger could not possibly match Texas Red in a fistfight, hand-to-hand combat or virtually any fight without guns. Texas Red stood six feet two inches tall and weighs a solid 240 pounds, while the ranger is barely five feet ten and perhaps 180 pounds. Furthermore, Texas Red is clearly well muscled and moves liked the superb athlete that he is. Texas Red can kill a man with his fists almost as quickly as with his gun.

The supremely confident Texas Red looked at the ranger and smirked. "Hand speed and aim, ranger. It's all about—" Texas Red stopped instantly and froze for a moment when he saw the one-of-a-kind, custom-made Big Iron. He looked at the gun and then at the ranger. "I've seen that gun before. As I recall, it was another ranger carrying it, and he *was* a Texas ranger. Must have been someone kin to you, huh, ranger?"

The ranger nodded slowly and answered with a deceptively calm voice yet with unmasked vengeance in his eyes, "Yeah, he was my only brother, and you killed him awhile back."

Texas Red shrugged and then almost nonchalantly challenged, "Are you saying or claiming it was not a fair gunfight with your brother? Has anyone told you it was not a fair gunfight? Has anyone told you that any of my gunfights were not fair with both of us packing loaded guns? Do you have any evidence whatsoever that any of my gunfights were less than fair?"

The ranger was very surprised at the thought of his brother losing a fair gunfight and was unprepared for Texas Red's questions. Although he was in no mood to explain anything to Texas Red, he did explain one thing, "Our Colt Walkers are a matched pair but not identical. His gun was buried with him, and the one I'm packing will bury you."

Texas Red allowed some time to pass to dissipate the fire in the ranger's eyes and then spoke with his deceptively soft and disarming voice as he looked at the ranger, "That Big Iron weighs about four and a half pounds and is the most powerful handgun ever made. It is a great weapon for a shootout, and many other things, but it is almost suicidal for a fast-draw gunfight." Then Texas Red added almost involuntarily, "My handgun is a .36 caliber that weighs an ounce or two shy of two and a half pounds, so why are you stacking the deck against yourself by pulling a Big Iron, ranger?"

The ranger's only response was to calmly gesture toward the street with his right hand. Texas Red turned toward the swinging doors and the street, but then he stopped and then turned to face the ranger.

Something happened inside of Texas Red. There was an internal burn and an overwhelming bloodlust that was very different from the other gunfights. His bloodlust has never been this powerful before. This ranger is different. The mere thought of two rangers, who were brothers, coming after him with a matched pair of exquisite custom-made Big Irons made his heart pound. It was intoxicating, and Texas Red decided that he must savor every moment of this historic, once-in-a-lifetime gunfight. He could become famous, perhaps a living legend with a lifetime of fame and glory ahead of him. All he has to do is kill yet another gunfighter and yet another ranger.

To a small town like Agua Fria, and even to Texas Red, this truly was a once-in-a-lifetime gunfight. Texas Red decided that this gunfight, more than any other, would be his defining moment.

To be honest with himself, Texas Red was growing tired, even bored, with the loud mouths and the arrogant half-baked gunfighters who would challenge him and then simply die before his eyes and then fall to the ground with their pistols still in their holsters. However, Texas Red already knew this ranger was the best he would ever face. Being around the ranger for just a matter of minutes made him realize just how incompetent and unskilled the gunfighters he had faced were. It was a fateful warning sign to Texas Red, but a warning he chose to ignore.

Texas Red also realized that the deep, internal burn he had developed for putting himself in imminent danger and the bloodlust for gunfights would never go away. He simply could not help himself—not after El Paso.

Texas Red scoffed at his own thoughts, "You know something, ranger? You just might be the best gunfighter I have ever faced. This time, there will be *two* gunfighters in the street. We will have our gunfight, ranger, but what is the hurry? Let's take some time to savor the experience."

The ranger never took his eyes off Texas Red, and he could see that he was working something out in his mind, something serious. However, the ranger was unprepared for the words Texas Red had just uttered. The ranger shook his head. "What in the hell are you talking about, Red? This is when we step out into the street to see who lives and who dies."

Texas Red slowly shook his head and answered, "Not yet, you are too good to kill so quickly. I grow weary of the quick, meaningless kills. I am tired of fighting children who think they are men. I am tired of fighting men who are dead before they hit the ground and die with their guns still in their holsters. You are different ranger, and you will be treated different."

The ranger was stunned, "Red...I am here to arrest you and take you back to Phoenix, where you will account for a deputy sheriff you killed in El Paso, and you will probably be extradited back to El Paso. Either way, you will be charged with multiple crimes in at least three states, several of which you may hang for. Tell me what there is to savor about such an...experience. This is a life or death situation. I am a specially trained and skilled gunfighter sent out to extract outlaws whom no one else can face. You say packing a Big Iron is suicidal, but I assure you, Red, I am very good with it, *very* good."

Texas Red looked down at the ranger and spoke with more than a little anger, "Yes, I assure you that one of us will live and the other *will* die. However, I will not allow you to arrest me and take me back to Phoenix, nor will I allow you or anyone else to extradite me to El Paso. End of discussion, ranger, end of discussion."

Not wanting the situation to escalate, both men broke eye contact and said nothing. They walked toward a crowded part of the bar that cleared before they got there. Sam owned the saloon, and he knew that neither man wanted alcohol, so he fixed a bland but nonalcoholic drink without them having to ask.

To help defuse the situation, Sam chuckled, gestured at Texas Red, and then looked at the ranger. "Do you realize that you are the only man in town who dares to call this man Red? You are the only man in town he tolerates calling him Red. I've never seen that before."

Texas Red looked at Sam. "The ranger called me Red?"

Sam nodded. "He has called you Red several times."

Texas Red looked at Sam and shook his head. "I did not even realize it. I guess I can't shoot the ranger for it now, so I will have to shoot the next person who calls me Red, twice." When the ranger looked away, Texas Red looked around at everyone with a harsh, unyielding glare.

Then the ranger took a deep breath. "When will—"

Texas Red held his left hand up to stop the ranger. He had no concern or care for the ranger whatsoever, but he wanted to appear to be heroic and merciful, although he was incapable of true mercy. His gunfights were fair only because of his arrogance, not because of mercy. He craved attention and glory, whether real or imagined, and with the power of an overwhelming drug, he craved the very thought of fame and becoming a legend. He then looked around and made sure there were plenty of witnesses, although Texas Red already knew the ranger's answer before he even asked the question.

"I am going to give you not one but two fair chances to live. You can walk out of here right now, get on your horse, and ride back to Arizona unharmed. This is your one and only chance to walk out of here alive. However, even if you do not accept my offer of safe passage, I will give you another fair chance to live. I will choose the day, and you choose the time for us to meet in a fair and equal gunfight to the death."

Texas Red chuckled. "Although it cannot truly be a fair gunfight with you pulling that huge Big Iron, but that is your choice. Let me show you what you are up against."

Texas Red then did something that would have been shocking only minutes ago. He took out his six-gun and handed it to the ranger. The ranger looked it over and quickly began looking at it in close detail. Texas Red cleared his throat and gestured with his eyes toward the Big Iron the ranger was packing. Despite the situation, the ranger chuckled. "Oh, of course." The ranger then hesitantly handed the cherished Big Iron to Texas Red.

Texas Red immediately began examining the artistic harbinger of death as closely as human eyes would allow. "I thought so. This is an 1847 Colt Walker in mint condition and heavily engraved and inlaid by a master craftsman. A .44 caliber six-shot revolver weighing slightly over four and a half pounds with a nine-inch barrel and is the most powerful handgun on earth. But according to the laws of physics, it is impossible for you to pull four and a half pounds, perhaps a few ounces more, from your holster as fast as I can pull my two and half pound Thunderbolt. I am much bigger and stronger than you are, and it is simple math and gravity, ranger. I have been to Africa, and this weapon can easily kill animals the size of a lion. But, ranger, you simply cannot match me in a fast-draw gunfight when you are pulling nearly twice the weight."

The ranger nodded. "I am impressed with both your knowledge of firearms as well as your life experiences." Still looking at Texas Red's six-gun, the ranger noted, "This is an 1851 Navy Colt .36 caliber six-shot revolver with a seven and a half inch octagon barrel that weighs just over two and a half pounds, although this one feels a bit lighter. Your Thunderbolt has been heavily tuned and lightened. You've done extensive work to it, but it is work intended to be functional rather than decorative or artistic." The ranger hefted the very light weapon. "You're right. It certainly is easy on the draw. However, I warn you, Red, I am what some call a gunner, and I only go after the best, or the worst, depending on how you look at it. I am now an Arizona ranger, but I was a US marshal for over ten years, and I tracked down and faced highly skilled outlaws who thought they were the best of the best. I have faced over thirty men, and I had to kill almost half of them. I killed twelve, wounded ten, and ten did not draw. Six or seven others surrendered on sight. However, I have to admit to you that I am very surprised and appreciative of your warning about the laws of physics and gravity." The ranger chuckled. "You sure are dead set against me pulling a Big Iron in a fast-draw gunfight…"

Reflecting William more than his Texas Red persona, he shrugged. "I do not know why I said that, but I also appreciate your warning, as well as your impressive résumé. One thing is for sure, ranger, and that is you are different and you are right. I am certain the Big Iron you are packing is going to get you killed. It is just too heavy to pull fast enough." Texas Red thought about using the ranger's brother as an example but quickly thought better of it. In fact, the unspoken thought passed through both men's mind.

The ranger handed the Thunderbolt back to Texas Red, and he returned the treasured Big Iron. The ranger thought for a moment and then decided to ask, "I am curious about something, Red."

"Okay, ranger, what is on your mind?"

"I still use a Colt Walker black power handgun because in my opinion it is the best, most reliable, and certainly the most powerful handgun on earth. However, why do you still use an old 1851 Navy Colt black powder handgun? I can think of several modern alternatives to your '51 Navy that are more powerful, just as light and with much better ammunition."

It was very much an unexpected question, and Texas Red took a few seconds before he decided to answer it. He figured out an answer that would magnify his glory and his status as a legend. On further thought, Texas Red was glad he kept and used the reliable old handgun, and the more he thought about it, the more excited he got about the matchless, tragic story and history behind his six-gun. Texas Red had not yet holstered his weapon, so he held it out for the ranger to see and then displayed it around the room for everyone to see.

"My mother bought this six-gun for five dollars when she ran away from home at the age of seventeen. What's more, this is the very gun my father used in his jealous rage to kill a young cowboy who was sharing a drink with mother, and this is the same handgun Mother used to kill herself after father died in her arms. And this is the only gun I have used in my exploits since turning what some call outlaw. However, to answer your question, ranger, I cannot possibly part with it."

Everyone looked around at each other in silence. They now felt closer to Texas Red and somehow felt an emotional link with him. Suddenly, the famed outlaw with the huge mansion was a man just like everyone else. And his six-gun that was held in awe because it bore twenty notches was now much more than just a weapon.

Texas Red was absolutely glowing inside at the growing thoughts of the legend he would now certainly become. He was very quickly becoming obsessed with becoming a legend, and it was totally blinding him to the reality of the ranger's skills and experience. To Texas Red, the mere thought of losing to the ranger was not even a possibility, and in his mind, the ranger was already dead and buried. The only thing certain at this point is that it will indeed be a fair gunfight, even if only for the sake of the growing legend.

The ranger took a deep breath and sighed. "Red, we are intense men who live intense lives…short lives but very intense. Okay, Red, when?"

"I will give you one last chance to change your mind, ranger. Do you realize that if you do not leave town within an hour, you cannot change your mind later? If you try to leave town later, my men will hunt you down and kill you where you stand, sit, or crawl. And do you realize that if you stay, then your only chance to live will be to face me in a fast-draw gunfight?"

The ranger shrugged. "I understand the situation clearly, Red, but do you understand that I must either arrest you or shoot you? I will take you back to Arizona either sitting on your saddle or tied to it. The choice is yours, but I am here to take you back…dead or alive."

Texas Red was glowing inside, but he realized he needed time for this once-in-a-lifetime gunfight to build and grow into legendary status. Yet it could not wait too long, or everything could fall apart, and the gunfight could be in the wrong place at the wrong time with no witnesses. Texas Red looked down at his bland drink and pushed it aside. "Let's have a real drink, ranger. Like I said, I will choose the day, and you choose the time…I choose next Saturday."

"You mean tomorrow?"

"No, I mean a week from tomorrow. One of us only has a week and a day to live, so let's live it." Then Texas Red looked at the ranger. "What time?"

The ranger shrugged, and his answer was more of a question than a statement. "High noon?" On the night before the gunfight, the ranger will change the time. If an angel from above and a demon from hell both told the ranger why he would change the time of the gunfight from high noon to the very unusual time of 11:20 a.m., the ranger would not believe either one of them.

Then the ranger became noticeably and surprisingly uneasy. "A week…a full week? Why so long?"

Texas Red thought for a minute and then scoffed. "You are not used to being in one place very long, are you? The idea of being in the same place for a whole week makes you nervous." Then Texas Red laughed. "It is funny that you have the courage to pull a four-and-a-half-pound Big Iron against me in a fast-draw gunfight, but the idea of sleeping in the same bed in the same room for a whole week makes you nervous. Now that is one for the books."

"You are enjoying this, aren't you, Red?"

"Yes, indeed I am."

"Do you have a college degree, Red?"

Texas Red nodded and then stopped and shook his head. "Not really, it was the other guy who got the degree."

"The other guy? You mean the man you were before you became Texas Red?"

"Touché, ranger, I am impressed. You probably have a degree yourself, perhaps a degree in law and disorder."

The ranger shook his head as Texas Red laughed. Two of the deadliest men alive were almost becoming…friendly. Then again, both men were supremely, unshakably confident whether the gunfight was tonight or in a week. Moreover, nothing, but nothing, will break or affect their focus and concentration when the appointed time comes for them to step onto the street.

The ranger chuckled and started to say something, but he stopped, and both men then looked around. They had been oblivious to the growing number of men and even women filling the saloon. Texas Red looked in one direction, and the ranger looked in another. They saw well over fifty men and a number of women staring at them intently, hanging on every word and every syllable the two men exchanged. After the two combatants focused on them, the saloon quickly began clearing out, and one very excited man spoke loud enough for everyone to hear, "Someone telegraph the big-city newspaper in Santa Fe. This is gonna make history and gonna make the winner a legend. This will be the granddaddy of all gunfights and will be the gunfight to compare with all others. This will put our little town on the map."

Texas Red glowed inside and began thinking this is going to work even better than he expected.

The ranger looked around and then back at Texas Red. The ranger was somewhat incredulous. "I guess this is a lot more fun when you don't have to look down the barrel of a loaded gun that is designed to splinter your skull."

Texas Red absentmindedly took his hat off and laid it on the bar, exposing his flaming red hair. The ranger chuckled. "Glad to meet you, Texas *Red*."

Both men drank as much as they dared, which was not a lot, but it was enough to loosen their tongues. Besides, neither man had ever met another they considered an equal, and both men quickly considered the other as a potential equal, a feeling both men were uneasy with. There was growing respect for each other. Besides, both knew the gunfight was a week away, so they could relax a bit and talk some.

Texas Red sighed. "My hair is not how I got the nickname Texas Red. I was on a boxing team back east in college. My hand speed is so fast I always had my opponent's blood on my hands, so they called me Texas Red." Texas Red then leaned against the bar and spoke so that only the ranger could hear. As Texas Red intended, his secretive talk to the ranger started several rumors, all glorifying the winner of the historic gunfight. "Here's another one for the books, ranger. I would not allow anyone call me Texas Red because I thought the source of the nickname was too violent."

The ranger whistled and then asked a question no other man would dare ask. No one, but no one dared to so much as speak the name "El Paso" around Texas Red. "That *is* one for the books. Tell me something, Red. What happened that turned you from a respectable college graduate to a greatly feared outlaw and gunfighter? Was it the incident in El Paso?"

Texas Red glared hard at the ranger for a long moment, and then he sighed and rubbed his left hand through his hair. "El Paso was a large part of it, but only a part. My father had hair as red as mine, and it comes with a bad temper and a self-destructive temperament. At least for us, it did. My father's name was Will, and my mother's name was Felina. They met in El Paso at Rosa's Cantina where my mother worked as a dancer. My father was very, very good with a gun, but he had no passion for gun fighting. All of his intensity and passions focused on Mother. They both died on the same day because my father killed a man, actually a nineteen-year-old kid, while in a jealous rage. My downfall will be in a gunfight. I know that, ranger, but my father's downfall was his uncontrollable, insane jealously over my mother. They loved each other intensely, but it was a love that destroyed them. They did not know how to share life with someone they loved. That is probably why I have no steady woman. I guess I feel the same way about a steady woman as you feel about staying in one place too long…makes me a bit nervous."

The ranger shook his head. "You mentioned how your parents died, but how did they come to die on the same day? What is the story behind that?"

"My father fled El Paso for five days, which was as long as he could stay away from Mother, even with his life at risk. Father knew they would shoot him on sight, so he planned to come in fast, get mother, and then leave before anyone even knew he was there. However, an ongoing adversary, named Oliver, who hated my father, saw father on his way back to El Paso and rode as fast as he could to inform the sheriff. A posse waited for him, and they killed my father almost on the back doorstep of Rosa's Cantina. Mother expected him to try to get her, so she was waiting for him, but when he died in Mother's arms, she grabbed his pistol, the same pistol I carry now, and shot herself through her heart. There were twenty men in that posse, ranger. Twenty men gunned down my father, who was all alone and never drew his weapon, even with all of them shooting at him. All he wanted was the woman he loved and his two-month-old son—me. They would have never gone back to El Paso. My father made a huge mistake by killing a young cowboy who was sharing a drink with my mother, to be sure, but not that big. The young cowboy looked to be wearing a loaded gun. But forgive me, ranger, I don't want to get into that right now."

Texas Red looked at his hands for a long moment and then looked at the ranger. "My birth parents, as well as my adopted parents, were very wealthy, and Mother made sure I went to college back east. My adopted mom was my mother's absolute best friend, and since Mama was sixteen years older than my Mother, they became like mother and daughter back when they were saloon girls and dancers. I was glad to have them as long as I did, but my adopted parents died by the time I was eighteen. Mama Phebe died of typhus when I was sixteen, and two years later, a mining accident killed Ben, my adopted dad. Sadly, he was never the same after Mama died, and Ben was more dead than alive even before the accident. And I have taken care of my sister, the best I could, which was not…"

A look of regret crossed Texas Red's face when he spoke of his adopted sister, a look that was not lost on the ranger. The ranger gestured back toward the *gunfighters' table*, and they walked over to it and sat down as before.

The ranger took a deep breath and let it out slowly, and for the first time, he was slightly hesitant. "I am extremely curious and fascinated about your parents and how they came to die on the same day and how your life took such a huge drastic turn and what happened in your life that changed you so drastically and so quickly."

Texas Red shook his head insistently, but it was a ploy. He was already doing everything he could to distract the ranger and get the ranger to let his guard down and soften up. Most of all, without being able to leave town, the ranger had no place to practice and maintain his gun-fighting skills without Texas Red watching his every draw and every move. One thing for sure is that the ranger cannot hide the thunderous sound of his Big Iron, which precludes any practicing in private.

Texas Red was still shaking his head as the ranger spoke. "You're the one that set the gunfight so far away. If we can't kill each other then we might as well talk, huh Red?"

The two men locked eyes, and the ranger shrugged. "Well?"

Again, Texas Red was begrudgingly impressed with the ranger's demeanor and unshakable confidence. Texas Red scoffed at the ranger within his mind. *If confidence was armor, this ranger would be bulletproof. I cannot wait to see his face pale in horror and terror when he catches a bullet before he even clears leather with that huge Big Iron.*

Now the entire town could sense and feel it. It was all everyone talked about, and the legendary status of the gunfight between Texas Red and the ranger was growing stronger by the hour.

No one gave the ranger a chance.

TEXAS RED'S LIFE STORY

exas Red nodded thoughtfully and looked the ranger squarely in the eyes. Still meeting the ranger's unblinking gaze, Texas Red thought for a long moment and then nodded to himself. "Okay, ranger, I'll tell you about my parent's lives and my life, and I'll even tell you what happened between college and outlaw."

Nothing Texas Red was saying was for the ranger's benefit. Texas Red craved attention beyond description, and craved being the center and focal point of everyone's attention. Not only is he the center of his own life, he psychologically trespasses and bullies his way into being the center of everyone else's life too. He was well aware of the people gathering around, focusing on him and intently listening to every word he said. Texas Red had never talked about his youth, or life before, and he now wondered to himself why he had not done this a long time ago. It was a completely new surge of power and superiority.

"I never knew my father or my mother. I was only two months old when they both died on the same day. In fact, I do not even know what my father's real name was. He became wealthy when he rode into a rather large town on his way to join a cattle drive and was mistaken for a tall, red-haired beneficiary of a fortune from an uncle my father didn't have. A beneficiary no one had actually seen. A few months later, someone figured out it *was* an uncle my father didn't have…it was a mistake, but my father took full advantage of it.

"Mama Phebe told me that Father was very confused when he tied his horse and people started pointing at him, shouting that he had to buy them a round in the saloon, and everyone called him

Charles. Father was even more confused when a smiling sheriff and an attorney met him. However, Father hid his own feelings and confusion, and he just played along. Next thing father knew, he was signing papers in the attorney's office, and they told him he was inheriting cash, land, houses, cattle, and a few buildings. The attorney offered to liquidate all of the physical property into cash for a *small* fee. Father could not believe his luck or the fact that the attorney wanted to move as fast as Father did with the liquidation. For an additional fee plus various service charges, the attorney gave Father cash up front instead of waiting to sell the properties. The total inheritance was enormous, and my father rode out of town with $475,000 dollars deposited in a bank account in San Francisco, accessible only with a secret code. Within a few weeks, Father divided the money into five bank accounts in three states. Father figured when they discovered the mistake, they might get some of their money back, but they weren't going to get all of it back. As it turned out; the attorney was less than honest, and in order to protect himself, he had to protect the identity of my father and protect father's San Francisco bank account. The attorney was able to contact Father because Father had left a small sum in the San Francisco account, and both agreed that secrecy, and Father staying far away from the town was the best course of action.

"However, Father still protected himself just in case. He traveled a lot and changed his name several times before he finally moved a thousand miles to El Paso to visit his dying father. In El Paso, Father changed his name to Will Travis, after the famous colonel at the Alamo, but he could never change it again. That's the name that he had to stick with because that's the name he gave Mother."

"I look too much like my father to go out searching where he came from and what my family name really is. At six foot four, my father was two inches taller than I am, although Mama Phebe told me that I weigh twenty to thirty pounds more, and I am a lot stronger. Furthermore, except for our age difference, we would look like twins. My father was very good with a gun, and we both have a natural talent for gun fighting, but my father did not have the passion for guns or gun fighting that I do. Father had everything figured out. He was young, financially set for life, and was in full control...until one night he walked into Rosa's Cantina. He saw the most beautiful woman on earth dancing, and by the time she threw him a rose an hour later, they were already etched into each other's heart.

"My mother was a dancer in Rosa's Cantina, and she just turned twenty years old and was at the peak of her goddess-level beauty. The instant she saw Father walk in the door, she knew in the center of her soul that he was *the* one. When my grandfather died, Father bought some new clothes that cost two months' salary for a cowpoke and went to town. At twenty-five, Father was also at his peak...at least Mother thought so."

"They had no idea, ranger...they had no idea whatsoever that both of them had less than a year to live." Texas Red had heard his parents' story so many times and read it in diaries and journals so detailed that he felt like he was there.

1857

Will walked through the swinging doors of Rosa's Cantina and, holding the doors open, stopped to look around, just to be sure no one there was looking for him and equally as much to attract attention to himself. Felina glanced at the open doors and froze. She drew in her breath with an audible sound, which the background noise covered well, and her heart started pounding in her chest, and she felt like her stomach was swarming with butterflies. Felina never had such feelings before. How could this be happening to her? Her fleeting hesitation went unnoticed by all, except the tall handsome stranger still towering over the doors looking like an Adonis.

They had never seen each other before, and they had not so much as spoken to each other, but it was already too late.

Then Will saw it; it lasted a mere fraction of a second, but he saw Felina's eyes meet his own, and he saw her smile at him with power available only to a goddess—a smile that overpowered his senses, smashed through his survival instincts, and instantly owned his soul. Will tried desperately to stop a fleeting thought from forming in his helpless mind, a dangerous thought that he could not control or contain. *I would take a bullet for that woman.*

His resistance was crumbling by the second; then, she looked straight into his eyes with all of the power and passion she possessed. Will was instantly smitten and helpless before this beautiful Mexican maiden, and he would willingly lay his life at her feet. Will had no way of knowing that she was as helpless before him as he was to her.

As of yet, they had not even spoken to each other…at least not verbally.

Three brothers, Oliver, Edwin, and Francis sat at the table closest to Felina's dancing. Will grabbed Oliver, the man with the best seat, threw him on the floor, and sat down. Oliver jumped up, grabbed Will, and drew back his fist. However, when Will stood up, the hapless Oliver realized that Will was pretty close to being a foot taller and a half-ton heavier. With Oliver's fist still drawn back, Will placed his hands on Oliver's shoulders, smiled, and said, "I am not looking for trouble. I am looking for a good seat."

Oliver feigned equality and then gestured with his hand toward the prized chair. "Why don't you join us, stranger? After all, the next round is on you." Will smiled and nodded. Then he turned his focus totally on the captivating goddess who had smiled at him.

Felina continued dancing but subtly watched the drama quickly unfold, and Will's actions only increased his overpowering grip on her heart. As her heart pounded anew, she thought to herself, *The man had no fear of three. It was as if they were children…and he got his way so easily, they couldn't even slow him down let alone stop him.*

With a smile created by her glowing heart, a glow she had never experienced in all of her saloon dancing days or in her life, Felina danced close to Will's table. Then Felina threw Will a rose and then pointed to her private table with her black, spellbinding eyes.

To her surprise, Will instantly bolted to his feet and quickly walked over to Felina's private table and sat down. No one had ever dared sit at her table without being personally escorted. A large man almost Will's size walked toward the table to challenge Will, but a fierce, aggressive glare from Will caused the large man to think better of it.

Then it happened, before they even so much as spoke to each other, Will saw smiles from Felina cast in the direction of other men, which immediately began stoking the inferno of Will's soon-to-be uncontrollable, raging jealously.

Looking away from Felina's smiles cast at others, Will felt a soft touch on his left shoulder, and as he looked up, he heard the voice of an angel. "My name is Felina."

As he stood up, he answered, "I'm Will, Will Travis."

When Will stood up next to her, he stood as tall as his six-foot-four-inch frame would allow. Felina almost swooned. She saw that he was a big man, but she had no idea just how tall and muscular he truly was, and his chest was so thick.

Will held up the rose Felina threw him. "Thank you."

Again, Felina smiled and spoke softly with all of the sensuous power she had, which was considerable. However, with her heart pounding and her mind spinning, she reverted to her native language, "Eres muy bienvenido," which is to say, "You are very welcome."

Will removed his hat and set it on the table, clearly showing his flaming red hair.

Felina gasped and almost involuntarily stood up on her tiptoes, reached up, and ran her fingers through his hair. "I love your hair, and I've never seen hair so red before."

Will smiled. "My mother has—"

"If she is still alive, we must go see her so I can properly thank her."

Will looked down at her and slowly shook his head.

"I'm sorry, please forgive my manners. Won't you sit down?

They barely took their eyes off each other as they spent the evening talking, asking and answering many questions ranging from the simple to the serious. Of course, there were frustrating intervals when Felina had to dance. The other working girls were amazed; no one had ever seen Felina act like this before. Suddenly, everything about Felina was different. Her smile, her tone of voice, and the way she moved, even the way she danced was different; she had never kept her eyes only on one man as she danced before. Most of all, Felina giggled and spoke in soft, warm tones that no one had heard before. The other girls who worked in Rosa's Cantina kept looking at Phebe, Felina's most trusted friend, but all Phebe could do was shrug and shake her head. Even a half-drunk cowboy, Levi, who was a regular patron looked at Phebe for an answer but got the same unknowing shrug. Several times, Phebe approached Felina's table but warded off by subtle yet frantic gestures that went unseen by Will.

Will and Felina's conversation soon reached the point where they could no longer talk as they would like. Besides, Felina did not know how much longer she could dance while looking only at Will without causing problems, and there was now too much noise and too many distractions for the things they wanted to say. They agreed that when they got off, Will would escort Felina and Phebe to their rooms across the street, and they agreed to meet at the very table where they were sitting tomorrow afternoon a couple of hours before the saloon began filling with nighttime patrons. The saloon never officially closed, and the doors were always open, but it did get quiet and empty at times.

It was past daybreak as they stepped through the swinging doors onto the wooden boardwalk. Phebe looked up at Will and then looked at Felina. "It's a good thing I already have a man, Fela. Otherwise, I would steal this one from you right now." Before

Felina could explain that Fela was a nickname only Phebe could call her, they heard a voice behind them.

"Where're ya goin, big man?"

They turned around to see the three brothers who were sitting at the table Will appropriated so he could be closer to Felina. Oliver was doing the talking.

Already known is Will's fatal weakness with uncontrollable jealousy for Felina. However, facing three half-drunk cowboys singlehandedly is not a weakness to Will. It is a game long enjoyed.

Will smiled and nonchalantly pointed across the street. "I am escorting these fine ladies to their rooms across the street."

Oliver mocked. "Fine ladies? How can you call them saloon girls fine ladies?" He smirked and then laughed.

"Well, the sun is up."

"What in the hell does the sun got to do with it?"

"Sunlight means there is no drinking and no dancing. With no drinking or dancing, they are not saloon girls. They are two fine ladies."

Felina and Phebe knew what was coming next, and they already knew who was going to win this one. They stepped to the side out of the way and smiled within themselves.

Oliver was genuinely unsure. "Are you tryin' to make fun of us? Are you tryin' to make us look like fools?"

Will chuckled in disbelief. "No, sir, I am not trying to make you look like fools in the least. You are doing a real fine job of that by yourselves. You do not need my help at all."

Edwin was the closest, and since he used his fists, he made the smallest mistake. Edwin threw half a dozen punches at Will with everything he had. Will laughed and answered with half a dozen punches of his own. Edwin's jaw was broken in two places, and he had a concussion.

Francis pulled a knife and lunged at Will, who acted as if the knife didn't exist. He punched and hit Francis as if it was just a fistfight. Francis was swinging and flailing the knife wildly but could not even come close to cutting Will. In frustration, Francis backed up and held the knife up so that Will could not miss it. "I have a knife here. Ain't you afraid of a knife?"

Will's tone of voice and facial expression became very serious and very threatening. "Use it or run…decide."

Francis again lunged at Will with the knife, but this time, Will grabbed his wrist, straightened out his arm, and then hit the back of his elbow with the palm of his left hand so hard it sounded like snapping a large, dry twig in the dead of winter.

Edwin was unconscious, and Francis was screaming and running toward Doc Edward's office. Oliver then scoffed with supreme overconfidence and said, "Looks like *I'll* havta take care of ya myself." Then Oliver squared his body toward Will and held his hand almost a foot above his gun.

Will could not help himself and laughed at Oliver's ridiculous posture. Oliver dropped his gun hand, but before he even touched his gun, there was a loud gunshot. In panic, Oliver slapped his chest, stomach, arms, and the tops of his legs. Then he looked down and did not see any blood or feel any pain. Then Oliver reached for his gun again, but it was gone, and his holster was empty. Oliver started scampering around in small circles looking for his gun, his eyes darting everywhere.

By now, Will and the women were laughing so hard they couldn't stand up straight. Will had shot Oliver's gun right out of his holster. Oliver finally found his gun and picked it up, but damaged beyond repair, Oliver quickly dropped it before Will shot him.

Will contained his laughter long enough to gesture with the barrel of his gun and say, "Put your hands up." Not knowing what else to do, Oliver hesitantly put his hands up. Another gunshot rang out, and Oliver instantly dropped to his knees clutching his right hand and gasping in pain. Will had shot Oliver in the center of his gun hand.

Will stopped laughing and leveled an ominous glare at Oliver. "You can still work and earn a living, but you will never draw a gun again for the rest of your life. In fact, I may have just saved your life."

Will pulled the hammer of his gun back with an ominous click and pointed the gun right at Oliver's head. "Now get out of here."

Again, Felina almost swooned.

Will then escorted Felina and Phebe to their rooms and then went straight to the sheriff, Dan Alders, to report and to explain the entire event. A small number of eyewitnesses that had gathered confirmed Will's story. Sheriff Alders then went to Doc Edward's office, and all three brothers were still there. Two of the brothers confirmed Will's story, and only Oliver gave a different version. Sheriff Alders looked at Doc, and Doc shook his head at Oliver's version. The eyewitnesses unanimously told the sheriff that Oliver was very lucky to be alive. A man came at Will with his fists, and Will beat him senseless. Another man came at Will with a knife, and Will disarmed him and merely broke his arm. Another man tried to pull a gun on Will, and all Will did was shoot him in the hand. Sheriff Alders decided that he liked Will Travis, and Will was welcome in his town. The sheriff then fairly and thoroughly examined and considered all of the evidence and statements for several hours, and only then did he close the case.

Felina woke up in her bed and wondered if it was all a dream; it was so surreal.

How a man such as Will could have true, lasting feelings for her, feelings in the daylight? She was a lowly saloon girl, a mere dancer, yet Will was an overwhelming Adonis to men and women alike. So many men had been so close and so promising to her in the dark of night but were so very far away in the light of day. From afar, Felina had seen so many weddings, heard excitement of newly betrothed, and heard many tears of joy because of a newborn child. However, for her, men were unreachable in the light of day. So close, yet so far.

Before Felina was fully awake, she already knew that if this tall, handsome man among men was like the rest; she would be utterly devastated, and her shattered heart would never recover. She was helpless before him. Will could have her any way he wanted her, any time he wanted her, and for as long as he wanted her. As Felina rose and fixed herself up for the man of her dreams, she decided that no matter what he asked, she would tell him the truth…all of it. She would not risk losing Will to a lie. Her bright lights, partially fulfilled dreams, and more than a little wealth had all come at a hideous price. Then Felina's heart beat in fear. Would he even be there at her table?

The main doors of Rosa's Cantina were open and latched back, leaving the swinging doors open to all. Felina hesitantly walked up to the doors and stopped. It was quiet inside.

Then she heard something, almost like a growl. Felina quickly, but quietly, stepped into the saloon and looked over at her private table. Her heart nearly leaped out of her chest. Felina was an hour early, yet Will was already sitting at her table, but…but that damn man had his boots on top of her prized table. As she walked toward him, she heard the growling sound again. It was Will snoring. Not only was he there to see her and talk to her and spend time with her, he had already been there for quite awhile waiting for her. Will was asleep, stretched out with his boots on top of her private table. Felina quickly thought to herself, *The hell with the table. I've got a real man in the daylight.*

Felina touched Will on his left shoulder, and when he stirred and looked up, she repeated the first words she spoke to him, "My name is Felina."

Will stood up and held her hand tightly between his own. He beamed with joy, and his smile reflected it as he said, "I was so afraid you would send a friend to tell me you were sick or something. I am…I am so glad you came, but I want to tell you something right up front."

Felina returned his warm smile and nodded as Will continued, "I want to spend time with you and talk to you and take you places where nice girls and fine ladies go."

Felina chucked at the memory of the last time Will used the term "fine ladies." Then she asked, "Is something wrong?"

Will started to answer but stopped. He thought for a moment and then shook his head and then blurted out his words as if driven by pressure, "I am not proud of everything I have done, but I will not risk losing you. Felina, I want you to know that if you ask me tough questions, I will not lie to you, and I will not take the chance of losing you because of a lie. What I'm trying to say is, please forgive me if I would rather not answer a question right away, but I cannot...I will not...take a chance on driving you away because of lies and deceit. You can know right now that when I tell you something, explain something, or answer your questions, there will be no surprises in the future. Am I making sense?"

Felina grabbed Will and hugged him tight for a long time. When she looked up at him, she had soft tears in her eyes. "I will not lie to you either. I was so afraid that *you* would change your mind about meeting me here for our first date. I will not lose you to lies or deceit either. I want you to hear the things I will say, I want you to take me to those nice places you mentioned, and I want you to spend time with me, and Will...I want you to want me both day and night." Felina looked down and spoke in a soft, almost pleading, voice, "I want you to want me...during the daylight. Do you know what I mean?"

Will wrapped his arms around her and returned her long hug. He looked down at her and brushed her tears away and then bent down and kissed her on the forehead. Felina's entire body tingled, and she ached for him. Will looked into her black, enchanting eyes. "Let's start right now."

"What do you mean?"

"Let me take you to breakfast so we can talk."

"It would be a lot more private here, and Rosa won't be here for three or four hours. She is letting us have the place to ourselves for a while."

"Then I will go across the street and bring breakfast here."

Before Felina could respond, they heard a soft, feminine voice at the swinging doors that both of them instantly recognized as Phebe. "I'll do it. I will bring you breakfast from the Round Up café across the street. And when I get back, I will be so quiet you won't even know that I am sitting at the next table."

Felina answered in a singsong voice, "Men *ain't* the only ones who shoot troublesome, irritating, obnoxious people."

Phebe responded, "I am offering to buy both of you breakfast, and here you are threatening to shoot me. I am so hurt."

Felina smiled. "Not as hurt as you are going to be."

"What do you two want for breakfast?"

The three settled on scrambled eggs, bacon, and grits with toast and coffee.

Will chuckled. "You two love each other like sisters, don't you?"

Felina smiled. "We had some rough times back in Santa Fe, and I don't know if either of us would have made it without the other. Then we started making enough money so that we could keep some of it. You know the old saying that It's not how much you make, its how much you keep. And I am so glad she found a good man."

"Where is her man?"

"Ben is on a cattle drive that will give them enough money to set up a good homestead and settle down. I thank God Phebe can get out of the saloons forever and have her own home. I will tell you a little secret if you promise not to get me killed."

"Is there any money involved with this secret?"

"No, but it is a matter of life and death. You must swear to me you will not tell anyone."

"Okay, I will take your secret to my grave."

"Phebe is carrying Ben's child."

Will stopped smiling. "She really does need to get out of the saloon business. Maybe we could help them out."

Felina was glad Will offered, but she shook her head. "They won't accept it. I've tried several times, even before Phebe became pregnant."

Phebe came back and saw them transfixed with glowing smiles they could not hide. Again, Felina felt waves of tingling sensations sweep through her entire body.

Phebe set the plates on the table, and then she looked back and forth at them and uttered, "Uh-oh."

Will smiled at Phebe and asked, "When is your baby due?"

Phebe's anger was feigned, and the tone of her voice belied any real disapproval. "I knew it. I knew she was going to blab to the whole town. I will never speak to you again, Fela, and I will never tell you anything again, and I will take Will's gun and shoot you right in the ass…yes, I will. I will shoot you right in the ass, and that will kill you instantly."

Will chuckled and shook his head. "How will shooting her in the ass kill her instantly?"

Phebe pretended to be shocked. "It will kill her instantly because that is where her brain is. Yes, it is. I know this woman. Her brain is in her ass, and shooting her there will kill her right now on the spot."

Even Felina laughed. Will chuckled. "I'm starting to like her."

After a moment of laughter, Felina looked at Will. "You are probably wondering why we are dancers and how we got here. I will tell you if you want me to."

Will nodded as he looked at her. "Please do, I would very much like to hear it."

Phebe pulled up a chair, sat at the table, folded her arms, and looked at Will.

"I'm here to make sure she tells it right."

FELINA'S CHILDHOOD

elina took a deep breath and looked at Phebe, who smiled and nodded her encouragement for Felina to share their life stories with Will.

"I was born in New Mexico territory one night during a severe thunderstorm. My parents told me that as soon as I cried, the thunder and lightning stopped, and the sky cleared so the golden moon and stars could shine again. They always believed this was a heavenly sign that I was sent to them. Yet I was always so different from the rest of my family, even my mother. So many times, I tried to talk to my mother so I could understand the feelings inside me and the overwhelming desire to quench some inexplicable hunger and to live unspoken dreams. However, my mother never understood what I was saying or what I was feeling. Mother tried, she really did, but she could never understand me or the feelings and desires inside my heart and soul. She could only tell me that it was a phase and that I would *soon* outgrow it. Yet the desires within me grew stronger instead of weaker. I did not outgrow them. They kept growing within me and kept getting stronger.

"I started crying myself to sleep by the time I was six or seven years old, clutching my rag doll ever so tight. I cried quietly and alone because I was the first of six children children and did not want to disturb anyone. Papa was smarter than most, so he made more money and took better care of us than most families, but even as a child, when I looked at the mountains, it was as if something I could not understand was calling me. I knew that I did not belong where I was, and I knew that my real life was somewhere on the other side of the mountains that seemed so far away, so vast, and so far beyond my reach. "

Felina looked away, and her voice trailed off. "I was so young when it started…"

1845

Mama ran as fast as she could to where Papa was building a water sluice for the cattle about a hundred yards from the house. "Papa… Papa…I can't find Felina anywhere. She's gone."

Felina was only eight years old, but she could already feel the irresistible pull of some unknown life that was calling to her from beyond the mountains.

Papa immediately stopped working on the sluice and spoke as he mounted his horse, "Where was the last place you saw her?"

Mama pointed back in the general direction of the house and exclaimed, "On the other side of the goat pen. Please find her, Papa."

Papa spoke as he rode away, "How long has she been gone?"

Mama cupped her hand at the side of her mouth and called out, "About an hour, please, Papa…"

Mama already realized that she would never understand the fire that burned so soon and so deep within her little girl's soul. Mama only knew that within her own heart lived a full measure of a mother's love for her oldest daughter. Tragically, Mama had no way of knowing that she would endure one of life's greatest and most hideous perversions—when a parent outlives a child.

Papa felt the all too familiar but powerful pangs of guilt that would grow stronger with each heartbeat until he saw his little Felina safe and sound. Although only eight years old, this was her third and most serious attempt to run away; this time, there was no warning.

Papa knew the direction and even the path little Felina would take, but there were rattlesnakes, loose rocks, sharp rocks, and steep hills to climb, and all of these dangers started at the very beginning of her path to quench her unknown longing. Papa knew all too well that an hour was more than enough time for little Felina to be in danger.

This time, fate was with Papa, and he found little Felina within fifteen minutes, and all was well except for a scrape on her left knee. Then a deep stab of fear pierced Papa's heart when he realized that Felina had traveled over a mile from home.

After dinner, both tucked the children in bed, and Mama and Papa then talked about what they could do about Felina.

Papa shook his head. "Mama, we cannot talk to Felina like the child she is...not in this matter. Our little Felina was over a mile from home when I found her. She has determination that is born of the devil himself, and I feel it is an evil spirit that drives her away from us and her family. How else can such a small child be so driven to flee from her own family? She flees from her own blood. This is the devil's work, and we must protect her not only from the devil but from herself."

Mama shook her head in disagreement. "Our little girl is not of the devil. I do not understand what drives her and what secrets are within her little heart, but she is not of the devil, or I would feel it in my own soul. We must help her even if we cannot understand her. Help her, Papa, help her."

"How can I help her, Mama?"

"You are the head of our family. God be with you and help her, Papa. Remember the sign when she was born, the thunder and lightning stopped, and the stars shined when she first cried."

Papa remembered the sign at Felina's birth that he had not thought of for a long time, and he became deep in thought. "I will pray for wisdom and do whatever I am guided to do."

Mama nodded her agreement. "I will pray to the saints for you to have wisdom and help our child through her trial."

Papa stayed up all night, and he thought, prayed, and searched his mind for the wisdom to help their little Felina find her true calling and true path. Papa searched for understanding of what little Felina was feeling and enduring with none to help or understand her.

In the midst of a beautiful desert sunrise, Papa suddenly knew what to do. He now realized they could not fight Felina's longing, and they would never truly understand it. However, Papa now knew that he must support her and help her until she was old enough to seek her own path.

Papa told Mama what they must do, and Mama cried tears of joy. Papa said there was not a lot they could do, but they must do what they can to help and support little Felina.

After breakfast, Papa took Felina to the hill where just yesterday he found her struggling to reach the top but had only climbed a few feet.

Papa lifted Felina from the burro, set her on the ground, and then pointed at the top of the hill. "We cannot risk you falling or getting hurt with no one around to help you. I will make you a promise if you make me a promise, and we will bind our words with the very love in our hearts for each other. And we will swear to keep our promises to each other until the sun burns out."

Felina smiled and even said. "I will keep—"

Papa spoke quickly, "No, no. You must hear your promise before binding yourself to it."

"Okay, Papa, what is my promise to you?"

Papa smiled at her and answered softly, "Whenever you feel the mountain call to you, you must tell me and let me know this. Then as soon as we can, which I promise will be the same day or no more than two, I will bring you here and watch you climb, and if you get hurt, I will be here to take you home so Mama can take care of you. Be assured that you must climb all the way up the hill by yourself with no help. And you must promise me and swear to me that you will never come here alone until I see you climb the hill by yourself."

Papa knew it would be several years before Felina could make it to the top of the hill by herself. While he was not sure what would happen when she finally did, he would keep the sacred promise that he was about to make to her with his last breath and his last heartbeat.

"What do you promise me, Papa?"

It was much more difficult to speak than Papa thought it would be, so he spent several seconds shaking his head and nodding as if he was still in thought. "On the day...on the day you climb all the way up the hill by yourself...I will...I will give you a burro, a canteen full of water, and some money for you to find your dream that calls you from the other side of the mountain. I swear, on my love for you, that if you keep your promise to me, I will do this."

Papa ached inside hoping and praying Felina would soon forget the longing she felt and that she would soon forget about climbing the hill that might take her away from them.

Felina glowed inside, and her ever-so-young eyes shined with a sparkle that Papa had never seen before. He had never seen a child with such powerful emotions and such a powerful conviction before. Somehow, Papa already knew with all of his heart that Felina would never lose her longing for another life beyond the mountain, and she would not lose her personal quest to climb the hill by herself. To Felina, it was not merely climbing the hill but a path to discover her longing for a life she could not yet understand or explain, yet it was a longing she could not deny even if she tried.

Felina looked up at Papa and, beaming with a smile more fitting of an adult, vowed to her father, "I swear on my love for you, Papa, that I will keep my promise to you and will never come here alone until you see me climb all the way to the top by myself."

Felina knew without doubt that Papa would never break his word or break their sacred promises to each other. Felina now knew that one day she would be free to feed an inexplicable hunger and to live unspoken dreams

Felina was happy, and she surged with inexhaustible joy, hope, and energy. She attended school almost every day and now excelled in all subjects. She worked anywhere she could, doing anything that Papa would allow, to earn money that went into a special jar for the day she reached the top of the hill. She could already see in her mind's eye climbing the hill by herself with no help and with Papa watching over her making sure she was safe. Papa made her feel so safe and secure, even when she fell and scraped her knees, her back, or her elbows. He was there.

Then one day when Felina was fourteen years old, she came home from an afterschool job and found Mama crying hard. Felina panicked. "What is wrong, Mama. What is so wrong for you to cry so? I have never seen you cry like this. Is Papa okay? Please tell me. What is wrong, mama?"

Mama fought through the tears and sobs. "Papa has been in an accident." Mama's voice broke and failed her.

"What happened? Is Papa still alive? Mama, please tell me that Papa is still alive."

Mama nodded and spoke with difficulty. "I was waiting for you so we can go to the doctor's office together. Yes, Felina, Papa is still alive, but both of his legs were broken when a wagon wheel came off on his way to town. The wagon rolled over his legs and broke them. Papa lay on the ground with the wagon on top of his broken legs for three hours before someone came along and took him to the doctor's office. The doctor sent a man to tell me what happened and what his injuries are...and mainly that Papa is still alive. The... doctor...the...the doctor does not know yet if he will have to take one of Papa's legs...or both of them. He thinks one of Papa's legs will probably make it, but he won't know for a few days. There was a lot of damage done from Papa trying to get out from under the wagon. The people who saved Papa said Papa was delirious and didn't know where he was or what had happened...and the ride to town was excruciatingly painful."

Felina's head was spinning, and she became nauseous and had to sit down. "Give me a moment Mama, and I will hook up the buggy. I will do this in a minute."

Mama shook her head. "That's okay, darling, the man who brought the news hooked up the buggy for us. It is ready for us to go."

The doctor met them outside of his office on the wooden boardwalk. Fear turned into terror at the deathlike expression on the doctor's face. When the doctor saw the deepest of fears in their faces, he shook his head. "Your Papa is still alive, very much alive, and at this point and for the moment, I do not fear for his life.

"However, I fear for his left leg. We can save his right leg with surgery if we can fight off and prevent infections, but I do not think we can save both legs. It may be too much of a strain on his bodily systems, especially his healing mechanisms. His left leg is much worse, and trying to save it may very well prevent us from saving his right leg. If we do not make the right decision, he could lose both legs and worse. His body may have the strength to heal one leg but not both."

The doctor then took a deep breath and sighed. Mama looked at him. "What is wrong that you do not want to tell us? What is it?"

"Papa does not want me to take his leg. He said he would rather die than be half a man, and he said he cannot face his family as such. If I do not take his leg, he does not have much time left. We have a little time to see if his right leg will heal, but we must take his left leg now. But he refuses."

Felina started toward the doctor's front door, but he stepped in front of her and blocked her from getting to the front door. "You do not want to see your Papa now."

Felina made a very quick move that easily got her around the concerned doctor. Then she walked heavily into the critical care room where Papa was.

Papa's eyes got big. "No, Felina, you cannot see me like this. Go back with Mama."

Felina looked around and picked up a very large knife, and then she held it up for Papa to see. "If you do not let the doctor take your shattered leg, then I will do it myself."

"You do not understand that I cannot live as half a man. I cannot face you, Mama, or anyone as half the man I was. You do not understand."

Papa has never seen such fire in Felina's eyes, nor has anyone else. "If you lose your leg, then you will no longer love us? A man can beat me or do despicable things to me, and you will not care or protect me?"

Papa bolted up and grabbed Felina by her shoulders. "Don't ever say that again."

"What difference does it make if you are only half a man? If you lose your leg, you will no longer love us, no longer protect us, or provide for us? If you lose your leg, will you have no wisdom? Will you no longer remember anything you have learned? As half a man, will you no longer remember how to speak, build things, or fix whatever breaks down? Will you lose all of these things and no longer remember them, or as half a man will you still have half of your love for us and half of your wisdom? How do you halfway ride a horse? Will you see with only one eye?"

Papa tried to say something, but Felina would not allow it until she was finished.

"Your love of Mama and me is not in your legs." Felina patted her chest hard. "Your love for us is in your heart, so which half of your heart will the doctor remove? Your wisdom and goodness are not in your legs...but in your mind. Will he cut out half of your brain? You swore to me. You vowed to watch me and help me if I get hurt climbing the hill. Is half of your vow to me gone? If I get hurt climbing the hill, will you only take me halfway home? Papa, you swore to me that you would take me to the hill when it called me, and you swore by the very power of your love for me that you would do this, and you swore to me that your promise would last until the sun burned out." Felina walked quickly to the window, snatched the curtain back, pointed with her hand, and outstretched arm at the sky. "The sun is still shining, Papa...by the power of your own unbreakable promise to me, the sun is still shining."

Felina again displayed the large surgeon's knife to Papa. "You have already lost your leg, Papa. Now who do you want to remove it, the doctor or me?"

Papa could not possibly speak, and he reached for Felina with his arms open. Felina fell into his arms and hugged Papa so tight and kissed Papa all over his face, and they cried.

With tears streaming down his face, Papa looked at the doctor and spoke with a breaking voice, "I…choose you…to take my leg. And please take that evil-looking knife away from my daughter."

Mama and Felina stayed at Papa's side during the surgery. The doctor warned them the surgery would be ugly and very intense but, mercifully, very quick. Mama and Felina decided that sometimes life is ugly and sometimes life is so ugly that all we can do is hold onto something closest to our heart and endure. They chose to hold onto Papa, and Papa chose to hold onto his family and their love for him, and somehow, the surgery wasn't quite so ugly.

Papa's right leg healed better and quicker than expected; he was getting around surprisingly well, and all during his healing and adjusting to his new artificial leg, Felina would go to the bottom of the hill. Yet she would get no closer than a hundred feet from the base of it. Papa kept his word, and Felina kept her promise that she would not climb the hill alone. Her heart ached when the mountain called, but she would not, she could not, break her promise to Papa. Felina waited patiently; over the months, she visited the hill often but never approached it too closely.

One day, she went to the hill and spoke to it, "I will soon climb to the top, and I will then answer the calls you send me from beyond the mountain. I will find the unknown life that waits for me on the other side. I promise you and the mountain, it will not be much longer."

Felina turned and was startled as she almost ran straight into Papa; then she shrieked with joy. Papa was standing there on his new leg and supported by two crutches. "How long have you been standing there, Papa?"

"I've been here long enough to know that the hill and the mountain do not have a chance of holding you much longer. You are close to climbing to the top of your dream and finding your own path for a new life. My heart breaks and shatters at the very thought of it."

"I have to go, Papa. When I am ready, I have to go. I have no choice. The call is too strong, but I will always love you and Mama and my brothers and sisters. I will always love my family."

"Perhaps all of this time, your climbing the hill has been symbolic or a warning, a warning of how close I am to losing you to your new life. The hill is large, rugged, and high, and it is more of a small mountain than a hill, but you are getting bigger, stronger, and a better climber every day. Every attempt you make to climb the hill, you come closer with each effort."

Felina nodded as she looked up at the hill. "It is a true test, Papa, and I am beginning to understand why you chose this hill and this path for me to climb."

"What do you mean by true test?"

Felina smiled. "Every foot higher is tougher and more difficult than the last. You chose this one because it is the hardest to climb and will take me the longest."

Papa smiled. "If you never make it, then you will grow old with us in our home."

Felina laughed. "In that case, I will dig myself through the hill rather than climb over it."

They laughed together, but Papa noted the unwavering determination.

FELINA'S ACCIDENT

1854

As Papa said she would, Felina grew stronger, bigger, and a better climber. She was about a year from reaching her childhood goal of climbing unaided to the peak of the hill…as well as the peak of her dreams. It was then that Felina had her first, her last, and her only major setback—a setback that will take her a full year to recover from, which then puts her on schedule to reach the top of the hill several months past her seventeenth birthday.

Felina was climbing well when she made a rare error. She reached up and pulled on a rock without testing it, and the rock instantly gave way. Felina fell and rolled down the hill and almost immediately slammed her left collarbone into a large immoveable rock. Then she continued falling and tumbling down the hill. Then she saw an even more dangerous rock that she could not avoid. She was going to slam into the rock with her face but barely raised her left arm in time to save an already beautiful face. Felina and Papa both heard her arm snap, and Papa was already frantically climbing the hill to reach her and stop her from falling and rolling down the hill any further. Papa moved as fast as he could, and he was able to stop Felina's fall at least fifty feet short.

Felina's head was spinning, and she was extremely nauseous, but she stopped herself from throwing up and forced herself with sheer willpower to contain the dizziness and nausea. Papa quickly but carefully put Felina on the burro and headed home for the buggy.

As soon as they got home, Felina's oldest brother, Miguel, spoke quickly to Papa, then got on his horse, and headed to the doctor's office to tell the doctor that Papa and Felina were coming. Miguel told the doctor as much as he could, which was as much as Papa had told him. By the time Papa and Felina arrived, the doctor was well prepared to treat bruised and broken bones as well as deep cuts, lacerations, and possible internal injuries. Miguel had saved the doctor many precious minutes.

Papa and Miguel stood back as the doctor checked Felina carefully. Then the doctor smiled at them. "She is going to be fine. She has many bruises, including a bruised collarbone. She needs a few stitches here and there, and she has a large bump on her head. For the next week or so, every square inch of her body will be sore and painful.

Papa and Miguel glanced at each other and then at Felina and then looked back at the doctor, and Papa spoke, "There is something more, no?"

The doctor nodded. "Felina does have one significant injury…a serious injury. Her left arm is broken midway between her wrist and elbow. It is not a clean break, and it will be awhile before she climbs her hill again and…"

Felina flashed a concerned look at Papa and then the doctor. "How long?"

Papa stopped her. "Un momento, little one, the doctor has more to say, and I do not believe it is good news, eh, Doctor?"

The doctor nodded in agreement with Papa. "She is young and strong, and she will probably make a full recovery. But there are some problems here…and there will be a lot of pain and suffering for the next few months, and her full recovery could take a year."

Papa shook his head. "I had a broken arm, and it healed in two months. Why so long for my precious, Felina?"

The doctor looked at Papa and then at Felina. "Her arm is broken in more than one place. It is broken in two or three places. I cannot be sure, but it may require special surgery that I cannot do. We can have a skilled surgeon here in about a month. But…"

Felina took a deep breath and nodded as she looked up at the doctor. "Thank you for giving me time to know I have a serious injury, but please tell us what we need to hear."

The doctor looked at Papa, and Papa nodded his approval, as did Miguel.

The doctor sighed and focused on Felina. "When the surgeon gets here, he will rebreak some or all of the healing that occurs from now until he gets here. He will reset the breaks in your arm so your arm will heal and grow straight. When all of this is over, you could be as good as new, but there will be a lot of pain. And it will take about a year for complete healing and recovery."

The doctor looked at papa and shrugged. "God has given you one more year with your daughter. There should be no, or very little, permanent damage. You are a good man, Papa, and we all love little Felina as if she were a daughter to us all. Pay what you can, and we will pay the rest."

In an increasingly hoarse voice, Felina then asked, "What can we do now?"

"I will put your arm in a splint so the breaks in your arm can heal as best they can. The surgeon will leave what he can and re-break what he must, which means the healing process starts all over again for what he must break."

As the doctor set the multipart wooden splint on Felina's left arm, Felina sat there with tears of pain streaming down her face, yet she made no complaint, made no outcry, nor did she utter a sound. Neither the doctor nor Papa could have been more impressed. Each of the two men secretly wondered if they could do as well. Suddenly, Papa realized that Felina was much like a fledgling eaglet with only days left before it flies from the nest for the final time. Only her injury has delayed Felina from leaving her nest within a year. Once the doctor told Papa there should be no permanent damage, Papa was grateful for the additional time he would have with Felina but very saddened by her pain.

Then Papa smiled at her with a smile that made Felina both suspicious and nervous. Papa looked at her and said, "There is one more thing." The tone of papa's voice increased Felina's apprehension.

Tilting her head, she cautiously asked, "What is it, Papa?"

"I get to remove your splint." Then Papa held up the same large surgeon's knife that Felina once held up to Papa when he had his leg amputated.

Despite her pain and fears, Felina laughed and looked at the doctor. "Will you please take that evil-looking knife away from my father?"

Even the doctor laughed.

Yet things were different now, and Papa had mixed emotions about Felina's healing and recovery. The better and stronger she got, and the more she healed, the closer Papa was to losing her. Papa knew deep inside of himself that Felina might be gone the very day she reached the top of the hill. He clung to a waning hope that she would change her mind.

Papa and Mama had very long talks about Felina, and they cannot even begin to understand the drive and the yearning she has felt all of her young life. They cannot understand what power calls to her and pulls her away from them. They know it exists within her, and they know some force compels her to seek unspoken dreams beyond the mountain, but they cannot begin to understand what it is or where it comes from. Is it an angel within her or is it a demon from hell? They know not whether to bless or curse this power. They only know that whatever this power may be, it lives within her and calls to her. However, they cannot understand it, for they have never felt such a calling or longing in their lives.

In a month, the surgeon came, and the doctor had done well; the surgeon only had to re-break one place in her arm, but as the doctor had said, the healing then had to start over again.

Even while she healed and recovered, Felina grew taller and increased in strength. Papa now accepted the inevitable. Felina will make it to the top of the hill very soon after her recovery, perhaps even on her first attempt.

Felina celebrated her seventeenth birthday by having her final splint removed in the doctor's office. Despite the taunting and threats, Papa did not remove her splint. Nor did the doctor use the huge surgeon's knife. The doctor made several quick, small cuts, and the multipieced splint came off within seconds. Felina…was free. The doctor, as well as Papa, was stern enough to convince Felina not to attempt climbing the hill for a few months. However, the doctor did give Felina some exercises that would build the strength back up in her left arm.

Knowing the time was at hand, Papa spent as much time with Felina as possible. They talked about her future, the places she wanted to go, and things she wanted to do.

Papa took her to the hill, and as they stood at the bottom looking up, Felina wrinkled her brow and had a puzzled look on her face. She drew in a breath with an audible sound.

"Papa, what happened? How could it have changed so much?"

Papa nodded. "What do you mean? How did it change?"

Felina shook her head. "It's…the hill is smaller, and the top no longer looks unreachable. The hill has changed, and it is not so big anymore.

With tears in his eyes, he hugged Felina and held her tight. "It is not the hill that has changed my precious. It is you that has changed."

"Me? I don't understand, Papa."

"The last time you faced this hill, you were still a girl…but now you face your hill as a woman, and you can see and feel that the hill has lost its power over you. The hill can no longer restrain you. You are no longer a girl, Felina. You are now a woman, and you see your hill, and you see life no longer as a girl but as a woman."

Felina became very excited. "Yes, Papa, I understand. I can climb this hill right now, and I can be free…today."

Papa nodded in agreement, but he asked one last thing of her. "Please do not try to climb your hill today."

"Why not climb it today, Papa?"

With tears Felina could not yet understand, Papa answered, "Give me one more week to spend with my precious daughter who was a little girl but who has now become a woman. I will bring you back here one week from today, and I will watch you climb your hill with my own eyes, and that, my precious, will fulfill your promise and your vow to me. The moment I see you reach the top of your hill, all of your obligations are fulfilled, and then you will be free."

Felina looked up at him. "A whole week?"

Papa chuckled. "Yes, my precious, a whole week, just for me."

"Well, if it's for you, Papa, but you and Mama are the only ones worth waiting a whole week for."

For the next week, Felina went to the same places, talked to the same people, and did the same things she has done all of her life. Yet suddenly, everything and everyone was different. Somehow, the adults she looked up to and she respected so much are still respected, yet somehow, they were different, and they had lost something akin to a godlike awe.

Felina kept asking herself how everyone and everything could have changed so much almost overnight.

True to his word, Papa brought Felina back to the hill one week later, almost to the minute. Papa looked up at the hill and looked at Felina, and she looked at him. Then she walked over and hugged Papa and cried; she could feel deep inside that her life was about to change. Everyone and everything had changed so much, but she was secretly so glad that Papa had not changed. He was still Papa. Everything was smaller, and everyone was shorter…except Papa.

Felina took one last look at Papa, and she saw him smile at her with so much pride in her that his heart was about to burst.

Felina then looked down and focused. Then she started up the hill, faster and then a little faster and then a little faster. Felina was amazed and shocked. Every time in her life she had ever climbed this hill, every foot higher was tougher than the last. Now, somehow in some mysterious way, every foot higher was easier and faster. What she could not accomplish in hours, she now accomplished in mere minutes with ease. When she finally looked up at the top of the hill, she froze for a moment. The top of the hill was no more than ten feet away, and she was barely breathing hard. Only in her mind has she ever climbed the hill this fast and with so little effort.

She stood at the top of the hill, fully absorbing the moment and what this meant to her. She yelled down, "Can you see me, Papa? Can you see where I am?"

"Yes, I can see you, and you are standing on top of your hill."

"How could I do it, Papa? How could I climb the hill so fast and so easy?"

Papa yelled back, "A little girl is no match for this hill, but this hill is no match for a woman. You are not a little girl anymore, and you never will be again. You are a woman, Felina." Felina then took a moment to look around at the beauty that can only been seen from the top of the hill. Then she came back down, and she grabbed Papa and held him tighter than she ever had in her life, and she cried and cried at length.

Papa and Felina were silent all the way back home.

Felina hugged and kissed Mama without a word and then went to her room. Then for the first time, Felina counted the money she has been saving for almost ten years. She gasped at how much she had saved, and long before she was finished counting, she realized that she could support herself with nothing else for a full year. Then she realized that she was not the only one putting money in her savings jar. For all of these years, she has had help. Last summer, Miguel had worked very hard on a dangerous job on a county dam for two solid weeks with no time off and little sleep. Miguel had agreed on five dollars, but his work was so exemplary and so needed, they give him ten. Now Felina is looking at a ten-dollar bill in her savings jar. Felina cried softly and kissed the ten-dollar bill, making sure her lipstick was thick and somewhat sticky.

Deep in thought and barely aware of her actions, she spoke to Mama and told her in detail about climbing the hill with Papa watching over her. Mama did not want to hear about Felina climbing the hill. It gave Mama a knot in her stomach, a knot of fear, fear that her little girl was going to leave, but Mama could not understand why Felina would leave her family and all that she loves. However, there was no hurry, and Mama talked to Felina and asked her to stay home for just one more month, and then she could stay at the boarding house in town for a few months so she could be on her own but still close to her loved ones. Mama was certain that Felina would change her mind.

"Mama wants me to stay here for another month," Felina heard herself say she would stay home for one month as if someone else was speaking with her voice.

Papa felt as if his blood was turning to ice, and more than anyone else he knew, he knew Felina had to leave, but even Papa believed she would change her mind and come home. Papa just *knew* within a short time, Felina would come home, no longer tormented by this inexplicable hunger to seek her unspoken dreams. Not even Papa could truly understand.

The next morning, Mama was cooking breakfast, and Papa and Miguel were talking about the day ahead of them, and as usual, Felina slept late. It was difficult for Felina to get up early in the morning, just as difficult as it was for her to go to bed early. She would stay up every night reading, thinking, and dreaming. She tried in vain to fit in with the rest of the family but could not, but the family did note her efforts. The family could not understand why she could not simply lay down and go to sleep as everyone else does.

Mama and Papa could not read or write, and Miguel had a letter in his room he needed to read to them. Papa told him to get the letter and read it.

It took longer than Papa expected. "Miguel? What is taking so long?"

Miguel came back with a stunned, shocked expression on his face, and he was almost pale. "She's gone, Papa...she's gone."

Papa was just as stunned. "Felina is gone?"

"Yes, Papa, Felina is gone." Miguel handed papa three monetary bills that were stuck together. There were two five-dollar bills with another bill in the middle. Papa gently separated the bills, and there were two five-dollar bills with a ten-dollar bill in the middle. On each side of the ten dollar bill was Felina's lipstick, which lightly stuck the bills together.

Miguel explained that he put the ten dollars he earned at the dam in Felina's money jar.

Papa shook his head. "You showed all of us the five-dollar bill you earned working at the dam, and I remember that was what you agreed to work for."

Then Miguel shook his head and explained his boss gave him a bonus for working so hard on the dam and the five-dollar bill he showed everyone was five dollars he had saved up. Then Miguel held up his left hand holding a note from Felina. Then they heard Mama shriek from Felina's room and cry out, "She's gone. Felina has run away. She has run away from us. All of her favorite things and her best clothes are gone, and Felina is gone. Papa, go find her and bring her home as you always do. Please, Papa."

Papa nodded and looked at Miguel. "Let's go to town and see what we can find out."

Miguel said, "Yes, sir," and stuffed Felina's note in his pocket.

When they arrived in town, one of the first things they noticed was their family burro tied up in front of Jose's blacksmith shop. Since Papa promised and swore to give her a burro when she climbed the hill, Papa wondered if she had sold it to Jose. However, Jose quickly explained that she bought a horse and asked him if he would watch the family burro until her Papa came to get it.

Jose turned to go back into his blacksmith shop, but he stopped and spoke without turning around. "Everybody in town knows and loves Felina. I sold her the horse for half of what it is worth. I sure hope I didn't do anything wrong or cause you any problems. Oh, another thing…she has a lot of money on her, so I told her to keep her money in three or four different places so that when she buys something, it doesn't look like she has so much money."

Papa shook his head although the blacksmith could not see him. "I thank you from my heart for helping our precious Felina, and I thank you for watching our burro, but how can I possibly thank you for your words of wisdom that may save her untold grief? I am heavy in your debt."

Jose turned around. "No, you are not the least bit in my debt. She is running away, isn't she? I was just trying to help her, and it was only after she left that I realized the meaning of what she said. And for what it's worth, she left about five hours ago."

Papa shrugged his shoulders. "Yes, she ran away. But what could she say that held so much meaning?"

"Everybody in town knows that Felina has been trying to climb that hill since she was eight years old. It wasn't what she said as much as the way she said it, but she said that she had finally climbed the hill with you watching her...and now she is free."

Papa hesitated and then asked, "Yes, I saw her do it. Do you have any idea where she is going?"

The blacksmith thought about it for a moment and then shrugged. "She bought enough oats to feed her horse for five days, and then she took the north road out of town. There are a hundred places she can go, and that's if she stays within the territory. And with the money she has, she can pretty much go anywhere."

Then Papa thought of something. "By the way, did she buy a saddle?"

The blacksmith glanced at Papa and scoffed. "I forgot to take it off the horse. I guess that is my loss."

Papa looked at Jose and shook his head, "If you ever need anything just let me know."

Jose shrugged. "We all love her, but thank you very much. Are you going after her?"

Papa shook his head. "No...it wouldn't do any good even if we caught her. She is free now, and Felina is free to find her unspoken dreams. Besides, we don't have a horse or enough money to catch her."

With heavy hearts, they returned home and explained the situation to Mama. Felina has ran away, and they had no way of knowing that she would never come back to stay. Nor did they have any way of knowing that Felina only had three years left to live.

They would see her only one more time for a very few, and very precious days.

Then Miguel remembered the note and took it out of his pocket, and when everyone gathered around, he read the short cryptic note.

> Miguel, I cannot accept what you put your life in danger for, although you made me cry happy tears. Mama and Papa, I will carry all of your love the full distance of the path that is now before me.
>
> Your Felina

FELINA'S BEST FRIEND

1857

Felina sobbed and cried softly, but she cried at length. She did not simply retell the story of her childhood; she has just relived it. As Felina's mind refocused to the present, she saw Will and Phebe, and she realized they were in El Paso sitting at her private table in Rosa's Cantina. She smiled at them as they quietly gave her the time she needed to rejoin them.

Felina looked at her arm that was broken and rubbed it. "I was...I was back at the hill I climbed, and I was...I was back in the shack where I grew up in New Mexico Territory. I saw Mama and Papa and my brothers and sisters, and I lived my childhood all over again."

Felina leaned back in her chair, looked up, and closed her eyes. "Oh God, in my heart, I had to leave home all over again. I had to do it again...it broke my heart the first time, but..."

Phebe had tears of her own. There was much that Felina just told them that Phebe was not aware of. "But what, Fela?" Fela is a nickname only Phebe can call her. The privilege was well earned.

Felina looked at Will and then Phebe. "But...but time does *not* heal all wounds. It hurts just as bad if not worse as I grow older. I do not miss them any less. I miss them more, but I can't go back home, and I can't go back to the mountains or the shack I grew up in or even my hill. I love them so much, but I just do not belong there."

Will leaned over and kissed Felina on the forehead. "You are a very special woman, and I am so glad we met."

Felina beamed inside, and her face glowed. "Hearing you say those words to me makes all of the bad times worth it. All of the loneliness, fears, broken dreams, bad men, everything."

Within seconds, Felina's words fueled Will's jealousy almost to the boiling point. Will wondered what Felina meant by bad men. *How many?* Phebe saw a powerful darkness cross Will's face, and she could sense the quiet power of an awakening demon, an awakening demon Phebe immediately feared.

Before she met Felina, Phebe saw a man who was enraged with jealousy kill another man over a woman he had met barely an hour earlier. Phebe saw the same darkness and the same rage in Will's face that she saw that night, much smaller to be sure, but still there like a tiny rattlesnake that can do nothing but grow. However, like Felina, she decided to ignore it. Phebe decided that as Felina fills the emptiness in Will's heart and as they grow together, love and happiness will replace the demon. She pushed the dark memory aside and convinced herself that Will is different, and his darkness was that of loneliness.

Despite her denial, from that moment, there was a cold fear in the pit of Phebe's stomach that would not go away, and she would soon fear Will more than she has feared any man in her life.

Felina was glowing and radiant inside and out. The powerful, irresistible attraction to a tall, handsome man who wants to be with her in the daylight provides her with enough emotional power to ignore any warning signs. Besides, if there are any problems, her feelings for him that are growing like a windblown wildfire will change him.

However, Will's charm and sincerity made it easy for them to love and trust him, each in their own way, but despite small nagging doubts, they trust him wholeheartedly. Surprisingly, Will has never felt such powerful feelings and emotions for any woman before. Will was not totally convinced that a blazing, overwhelming, life-changing love even existed. He knew there was love, and that it is powerful, but nothing like this. Will has never chased a woman in his life. Women have chased him, quite often, but he never did the chasing, until now, but he was willing to chase Felina to the ends of the earth if necessary. Will was falling for Felina as if he fell off a cliff. In a different way and with a different kind of love, he was beginning to love Phebe as well.

Will pushes it to the back of his mind, but he knows how Felina and Phebe earn their living, and he is all too aware of what they have to do to earn the kind of money they make, wear the jewelry they wear, and buy the very expense clothes they wear.

Yet two things Felina said are too strong and powerful for him to completely push to the back of his mind or brush aside. The thought is already twisting his insides at how many *bad men* she has been with, and it eats at him what she said about finding a man that wants to be with her *in the daylight*. How many men has she done unspeakable acts with in the dark of night? What unimaginable acts has she done with these panting, sweating, grunting men, and how many times has she done them?

Felina and Phebe looked at each other with growing concern. They were not staring at Will, but they could see a powerful darkness in his thoughts, and they knew that his thoughts were not good, and they had a good idea of what his thoughts were.

Phebe touched the side of Will's face with her hand and broke his darkened thoughts. Will tried to smile his way out of denial and nonverbally attempted to convince them his thoughts were of other things but to no avail. They were very young women, to be sure, but in many ways, they are far beyond their years. Both of them knew that such thoughts and painful questions would occur, but Will's darkness was too powerful and too soon.

Phebe looked at Felina and with slight gestures and facial expressions and, with her eyes, asked Felina a nonverbal question. Felina looked down as she nodded for Phebe to take charge of the situation. Felina realized that Phebe had some tough questions and statements herself. Will knew the score, and he met Felina in a saloon. It was time to face reality.

Phebe likes to laugh at life and even laugh at herself. She is bold, is humorous, loves to tell jokes, and does not take herself or others too seriously nor does she apologize for her station in life or for what she did. She made her decision, and she lives with it. Phebe jokes that she made her own bed, and now she has to sleep in it...quite often in fact. Will was aware of some kind of unspoken communications between them but did not know what it was. The look in Phebe's eyes was beginning to make Will feel uncomfortable, and for the first time, he is seeing the strength of Phebe's mind and her near-invincible logic and wit. Will is fully convinced and certain of two things: Felina has already made herself vulnerable to him, and Phebe has something to say, and she is about to say it.

Phebe looked at Will, and she was not smiling, laughing, joking, or kidding around. Phebe was as serious as the situation, and she was well able to match the seriousness of the situation.

Felina moved her chair until it touched Will's. Though she could not look at him, she buried her face in his shoulder. "Please don't hate me, Will, please don't hate me. I would rather you shoot me than hate me."

Will smiled confidently. "It is not possible for me to ever hate you, and even though it has never happened to me and I have never seen it, I believe that love at first sight does happen. And, Felina, I already believe that we can have a future together."

Phebe moved her chair around until it was almost across from Will. The intent was clearly adversarial. Then Phebe nodded. "Things are happening so fast with you two that perhaps it really is love at first sight. I am open to that, but, Will, I must be what is called the devil's advocate here. I love Felina so much that I would die for her, and I will help her in any way I possibly can. I like you, Will, and I think you could well be the man for which Felina aches. I hope so much that you are her man, but I am sure you have painful doubts and questions. Ben had very painful doubts and questions. He was so hurt that I was a whore, and he agonized over how many men I have been with and what perverse and sordid things I have done. There was a part of Ben that felt like I was unclean."

Will flinched slightly, and his eyes opened at how easy Phebe used the word whore and how open she was about her lifestyle and what Ben thought about her. This was deeply personal.

Phebe continued, "And Ben was so scared that I would always be a whore and that I couldn't help myself, so we faced our doubts and questions, Will. We faced everything that bothered him, hurt him, or made him doubt me. We brought everything out in the open and dealt with it. I answered every question he asked me and answered every doubt he had in his mind and in his heart. However, don't think that I did not have some very serious and tough questions and doubts about him too."

Again, Will looked at her with eyes opened in surprise. He had not considered that Phebe would have serious doubts and questions too. He assumed that she would feel lucky to get any man she could get. Will liked Phebe very much, and now he was learning to respect her as well.

Will hesitated and then asked, "Is it okay if I ask you a question that I am very curious about?"

Phebe nodded. "Yes, you certainly can ask me a question. I may not answer it, but I won't fault you for asking."

"Why isn't Ben here?"

Phebe laughed. "Oh boy, if you could have only heard us hash that one out. We actually argued over that one for several hours. Our arguments were nonviolent but forceful, and neither of us likes to back down. Ben is stubborn in certain ways, and he would not compromise about the money. Well, I wouldn't compromise on a few things, so I let him have this one. Ben knows that I have a lot of money. I did some investing with the money I made, and it went very well. I have a very nice sum of money. However, Ben did not want us to use any of my money until he could make a significant amount of money himself. It didn't have to be as much as I had but enough to be substantial, so he signed up for a very long cattle drive, which included a return cattle drive halfway back that would make him a *lot* of money. I gave Ben my word, and I swore to him that I would be waiting for him when he gets back, so when he gets back in a few months, we will combine our money and live as we see fit. And my pretty little ass will be out that door, and I will be gone, as Fela's papa would say, until the sun burns out."

Felina did not look up but kept her face on Will's shoulder as she spoke, "Tell Will what you and Ben did to face your doubts and questions."

Phebe sighed. "I realize we can't change the world in six months and can't change ourselves as much as we would like to, but there is so much that we *can* do in six months. As you know, I am carrying Ben's child. The first question *some* people ask me is how do I know who the father is? Go ahead, Will, ask me how I know."

Will hesitated and then asked, "Okay, how do you know Ben is the father of your child?"

In an instant, Phebe had fire in her eyes, "Because I haven't been with another man in over six months. I will sing, dance, share drinks, smile, and even laugh at stupid half-drunken and fully drunken jokes that I have heard a thousand times, but I will no longer lie on my back for any man in this world except Ben. Something you really need to understand, Will, is that I do many of the same things that I have always done, but they no longer *mean* the same thing. If they want to laugh and joke and share a drink, fine, but it goes no further than that—no birthdays, no divorce anniversaries, no celebrations, no special occasions, and no exceptions. I am no longer available."

Will nodded. "And within a few months, Ben can trust you enough to go on a long cattle drive, and he knows that you will be waiting for him when he gets back. But most of all, he feels so secure about you that you can still work in the saloon while he is gone. How did you accomplish something that seems to be impossible?"

Phebe shook her head. "I couldn't accomplish it. The answer is we accomplished it together."

Will nodded. "Okay, the answer is that we must do it together. We must do something, in a powerful way, to build such a bond and such trust. How did you and Ben do it?"

Phebe took a deep breath. "What worked for us may not work for you and Fela. The point is that you must face and conquer your demons together in a way that works for you. If you do what we did, it could destroy you. It came very close to destroying us."

Will nodded. "What did you do?"

Again, Phebe took a deep breath. "We spent a week in a cabin, and we are very lucky we didn't kill each other. There were no holds barred, and nothing was sacred. I answered every question he asked, more like demanded, and every detail he wanted to know. I told him about everything, everywhere, and everyone. We argued, yelled at each other, and I got so mad at him that I even locked him out of the cabin with snow on the ground. He was so mad at me that he wouldn't even ask me to open the door because he swore that he would never speak to me for the rest of his life. After a whole week of this, we were exhausted. Our bodies, our minds, and our hearts were exhausted. We couldn't fight anymore because we had nothing left. Our bodies, minds, and emotions were all spent."

Will let out a long breath, "That's when it was all over and settled?"

Phebe giggled mischievously. "No, that's when I nailed his ass to the wall. I reached down inside myself and found something extra, and then it was *my* turn to demand some answers. No man has ever talked to me like that in my life, even Ben isn't going to talk to me like that without paying his rent, and on that day, he paid his rent in full. I started in on him just before sunup, and I didn't stop until just after sundown. The light of that day did not give Ben one minute of peace, and he was already exhausted before the day started. When that day was over, Ben was closer to being dead than alive. And it was the only time he, sort of, hit me."

Felina jerked her head up and glared. "Ben *hit* you? He *hit* you?"

Phebe's shoulders sagged, and she was sheepish. "I kind of jumped on top of him while he was still asleep, and I commenced to beating and whaling on his chest and shoulders. He thought he was being attacked by a wild animal, so he defended himself. He only hit me once before he realized what was going on, and it wasn't a hit as much as Ben trying to push me away vigorously. But I wasn't about to let him apologize. I wanted blood, and it was my turn to do the talking. But Ben was right about one thing."

Still emotional at the mere thought of Ben hitting Phebe, Felina pointedly asked, "What was he right about?"

Again, Phebe giggled. "He *was* being attacked by a wild animal, me."

Will rubbed the back of his head and was a little hesitant. "What answers could you demand of him?" Will wondered what he himself was facing.

For the first time, Phebe smiled her warm smile. "Most of the day was silent, but that cabin was filled with my anger and hostility, and I made sure Ben did not relax for a minute or have one minute of peace. If he so much as looked like he was peaceful or relaxing, I glared at him until I was sure there was no relaxing going on. He was so exhausted, and I was on fire. It got to the point where he ran from me from one part of that small cabin to another. We couldn't go outside because we were snowed in. Finally, he locked himself in the bedroom, and I yelled at him through the door. I was in the midst of collecting Ben's rent, and after a week of hell, it was *my* turn. I was crying so much that I could barely see, but nothing was going to stop me or slow me down. I still don't know where the energy and strength came from, but I wasn't going to waste it."

Phebe's mind drifted back to the cabin that started out as a week from hell and ended as the most beautiful and wonderful moment of her life.

"Who in the hell do you think you are? I have never explained myself so much to anyone in my life. How dare you make me explain my actions one hour or even one minute before we met? From the moment we met, I became your woman, but how dare you demand explanations of my actions before we met? How dare you demand of me to explain my past in so much detail? You have no right to demand such explanations of me. I made the decisions I made. I did what I did, and nothing can change that. You were not there. For this whole week, you have made demands of me, and you wanted explanations of everything I did, how I did it, who I did it with, and when I did it. You have forced me to relive memories that I despise and detest. You have demanded that I relive my worst nightmares and the worst parts of my life. How dare you do this to me? Who in the hell do you think you are?"

Phebe leaned her head against the silent, closed door, and cried. She knew all too well that the door might never open to her. However, she said what she had to say, and if that is what happens, then so be it. However, she had one last thing to say to Ben.

Her voice softened as she took a deep breath and talked to the man she loved, "Ben? Haven't you wondered or ask yourself why I have endured the torment and hell of this last week? Don't you want to know why I have told you the heartbreaking agony of my secrets? Don't you realize how utterly humiliating it has been telling you the most intimate parts of my life? Why have you done this to me? Don't you care for me at all? Don't you feel anything for me?"

The silence behind the closed door was agonizing.

"I did it because I love you, Ben. I love you so much that I have humiliated myself before you, and I have answered questions and explained myself unlike anything I have ever done in my life. I did it all because I love you so much. Why do you think I am still here? I would have died in the snow before I endured this with any other man. Our demon is dead, Ben, and now it's only us."

Finally, there was a voice from the other side of the door. "Our demon is dead? What the hell is that supposed to mean?" Phebe could hear sounds like Ben was packing, and her heart fell through her stomach. Ben could get out if he really wanted to.

"There are no more surprises, and there is nothing left to tell you. If someone came to me and demanded a thousand dollars or they would tell you my secrets, I can laugh in their face now. No one can tell you anything. There are no secrets. Our demon of secrets is dead, and I stand before you far more naked than I have ever been in my life. I have never given my heart to any man before, and no other man has so much as seen my soul, but I have given both to you and to you alone. I offer you all that I have and all that I am. I love you, Ben."

"I have fears too, Ben, fears that you will throw every secret I've told you in my face every time we fight or argue, fears that you will get mad at me, throw me aside, and call me a whore, and fears that you will mistreat me and then blame it all on my past."

Again, there was a welcomed sound of Ben's voice. "I hear all of the things you've said, and I have thought about us, Phebe, I have thought about us a lot more than you know. How can you think and worry that I would do such things to you because of your past? How can you even think I would do that after what we have endured here? How can we ever have such fire and hell again? Have I blamed you or blamed anything about your past or what you have done? If I were going to do anything like that, wouldn't I have already done it here and now? The heat, fire, and hell we have endured have burned all of that out of me. There is nothing left to blame you with or to blame you for. The hell, fire, and heat have burned all of your past into a pile of ashes. Phebe, why do you think I am still here after this week? It has been hell for me too, and I have endured as much as you have…well, almost as much. No matter what the situation is, Phebe, when you hurt, I feel the pain too. The fact we are both still here tells us something, but I had to know it all, Phebe, and I had to know it all so that our demon will *stay* dead for the rest of our lives. I had to come to terms with it, Phebe, and I didn't know any other way to do it, and I don't know what else to say right now."

Phebe spoke softly but with conviction, and her voice became louder as she spoke, "I know *exactly* what to say, Ben. Either give me a gun so I can shoot myself dead or give me a ring so that I can make the rest of your life so miserable it won't be worth having." Phebe then hit the door moderately hard with her fist.

Ben opened the door, looked her in the eyes for a few seconds, and then handed Phebe a gun. She grabbed the gun, turned it around, and pointed it at Ben and pulled the trigger. The surprisingly loud dry snap startled her and made her jump. She squealed and dropped the gun.

Ben's smile melted Phebe's heart, and then he gently put his arms around her and said, "I might be a little bit out of my mind right now." Ben shrugged. "Okay, I might even be a lot out of my mind right now, but I am still smart enough not to hand you a loaded gun."

Then Ben backed up a few steps and held his closed hands out to her. "Pick a hand."

Phebe was incredulous. "What? I am not in the mood for—"

"Pick a hand."

An irritated Phebe jabbed his right hand with her forefinger, and he turned his hand over and opened it. There was nothing in his hand. "Wrong hand. Pick the other one."

"Ben, I am going to find a knife and—"

"There isn't a knife anywhere in the cabin. I made sure of it several days ago."

"Then I will find a rusty nail in a loose board, and when you go to sleep—"

"You must pick the other hand before you can go looking for rusty nails to commit unspeakable crimes with."

Phebe touched his left hand and was a bit sarcastic. "Is it possible this is the correct hand?"

Ben's smile made her heart beat faster, the kind of smile that was too much to hope for, and as he opened his hand, Phebe started crying and gasped. Then Phebe actually jumped up and down. "Oh my God, this isn't possible. It's a ring…a blue diamond ring…I… oh…Ben."

Then Ben bent down on one knee. "Since the gun is empty, will you—"

"Yes…oh yes I will, oh, Ben. It sounded like you were packing, and why did you take so long before you opened the door?"

"Can I keep that a secret, a *special* secret?"

"Not after what we've been through this week. Why so long opening the door?"

"I wasn't packing. I couldn't find the ring, so I kept looking for it."

Phebe rolled her eyes. "You made me stand outside of that door with my heart bleeding pure agony because you couldn't find the ring?"

"Yes, I did, but didn't I tell you that I was thinking about us a lot more than you know? Besides, I wanted to delay it as much as possible."

"Delay giving me the ring, delay opening the door? Delay what?"

"No, I wanted to delay the rest of my life that is going to be so miserable that it won't be worth having."

They laughed at length, then hugged and kissed, and as much as a man and woman possibly can, they bonded in not only a powerful love but also an equally powerful trust. Love and trust forged from a week in hell, but love and trust that would last them a lifetime. Their demon was truly dead. Then they curled up together and slept the precious deep sleep reserved for the utterly exhausted, and sleep reserved for those who have found the greatest of treasures.

As she drifted into a deep, dreamless sleep, Phebe kissed the most precious engagement ring in the world.

PHEBE QUESTIONS WILL

1857

P hebe's focus and attention returned to Felina's private table at
the Cantina.

Phebe looked at them and revealed one more secret. "Ben
and I made love all through the night, and Ben did things to me
that no other man has ever done to me before. Can you imagine
that? If that's not a sign from God, then what is?"

Will got up quickly, walked over to the bar, and got something
from a shelf behind the bar. Then he came back to the table, held
up a chalkboard, and then held a piece of chalk to the board ready
to write. "Exactly what did Ben do?"

They laughed and Phebe answered, "I don't know. I was
unconscious. Ben had to tell me about it, but just the telling of it
made me swoon again."

Will put the chalkboard and chalk back behind the bar. Then he
stood at the empty bar for a few minutes thinking while the girls
chatted and laughed and giggled. Then Will walked back over to
Felina's table and sat down. Phebe looked over at Will and smiled.
Will nodded and said, "I think she is worth it, Phebe. I really think
she is worth anything, so let's do it right."

With one major exception, Will is anything but a liar, and his
sincerity is unquestionably real. Will is a great guy, and he is a good
man. In addition, save for that one exception, he is as honest as the
day is long. However, Will has a dangerous flaw of which even he is
unaware. Tragically, this one flaw…is lethal.

Phebe smiled at him. "I was hoping you would say that, and I totally agree with you."

Will shrugged, shook his head, and looked at Phebe. "What you and Ben did at the cabin was very intense, and you two risked everything, and both of you have an overload of guts. I can easily see how a couple working out their problems by spending a week in a cabin all alone can destroy them. How do you think Felina and I can take a slower and less intense path?"

Phebe did not hesitate. "We simply talk, and we can talk about Santa Fe. Fela and I met and worked in Santa Fe a year ago, maybe more. It was the first saloon Fela ever worked in. It is where she learned to dance and where she learned about saloons and where she learned about life. I warn you that it is very difficult to be in love with a saloon girl. We attract men like magnets at night, but they are to be seen nowhere with us during the daylight. Daytime and night are two vastly different realities for us. We cannot go, visit, or be where nice girls or nice people go. We have fewer rights and less protection from the law than the drunks who stagger out of our saloons early in the morning. We have real babies, yet they do not accept us as real mothers or real parents. We have real hopes and dreams, but they consider us inferior and below such desires. If we want our children to attend school to learn to read and write and become educated, we have to put them in a school at least a hundred miles from where we work…sometimes further. The sad part is that sending your child so far away guarantees that the child will be split from his or her mother at a very early age and for a long time."

Will looked at both of them and was apologetic. "Most men… including me, never think of saloon girls as having a real life. It's almost as if we think saloon girls disappear at sunrise and then reappear at sundown and are pretty much nonexistent in between."

Felina glowed inside, and she felt a surge of warmth and passion for Will. She has never heard a man talk like that. Will is very different. Felina got up and walked to the swinging doors, and then she turned around and blew Will a kiss.

Then Phebe smiled at Will in such a way that he asked if something was about to happen that he might not live through. Phebe did not exactly answer his question, and he found that a bit irritating. Then he asked, "Are we about to draw swords and cross sabers?"

Phebe nodded, "Perhaps, but Fela asked me to talk to you, and she told me to tell her only what I think is important for her to know. I am truly honored to help her."

Phebe smiled and looked at Will eye to eye. "You can ask us questions, and we will answer and explain your questions and fears in as much detail as Felina is willing to share. Let's get all of your doubts and fears out in the open and deal with them...but the torment, painful thoughts, doubts, and malevolent questions *must* be resolved. And something I can guarantee you before we even start and that is your questions will contain more doubts and pain than the answers...*if* you let go of them. Will, you will ask adult questions that will assault and inflame the most private and intimate memories possible, memories that Felina does not want to relive, and I must warn you..."

Phebe hesitated, and Will knew Phebe's hesitation was for a valid reason, but he was ready. "Your warning?"

Phebe took a deep breath and looked away for a moment. "My warning is that your adult questions will have adult answers. And don't forget for one second, Will, I love Felina more than life itself, and there will be some tough, adult questions for you to answer as well."

Will shrugged, laughed, and shook his head. "There is no question that you can possibly ask me that I need to fear in the least."

Phebe looked straight into Will's eyes with a look akin to a glare. "Do not say that to me again, Will, please."

Will scoffed and held his hands out level with his shoulders, then put his hands back on the table. "There is no question that you can possibly ask me that I need to fear in the least."

Phebe shook her head. "Are you sure? Because this particular conversation is not about Felina, it is about *you*."

"Yes, I am sure, and I am positive. You may fire at will."

Phebe locked eyes with him. "Will, what is your *real* name…how did you really get your wealth…and how long were you in prison?"

Phebe then looked at Will with an unmasked threat in her eyes. "Another warning to you from the heart, Will, don't even try to lie to me. I am significantly older than I look. And for every lie you have heard in your life, I have heard a thousand."

If Will had been standing up, he would have fallen to the floor. He paled and felt a wave of numbness. Will was stunned; he froze unmoving in his chair, his heart pounding, and his own mind turned against him and shut down. However, as Will's mind began to function again, he decided to challenge her and test her.

"Even if I had been in prison, there is no way you could possibly know that. Please correct me if I am wrong."

"Okay, Will, I will correct you. We have at least six or seven regular patrons who have served serious time in prison for a number of different high crimes. Three of those men have come to me to warn me that you have served some amount of time in prison. Not a lot, to be sure, but you have been there. Please correct me if I am wrong."

Will shook his head and looked at Phebe with vastly increased respect and perhaps a bit of fear. His shoulders sagged, his mouth slackened, and he looked away with unsure eyes. Then Will stalled to give himself a few precious seconds to clear his head, but he did not correct her. "Sorry, but I have to ask, just how old are you? You look like you're only twenty-eight or twenty-nine years old."

Phebe shook her head but smiled and quickly patted him on the shoulder to encourage him. "Nice try, Will, but this conversation is still about *you*, not Felina or me."

Will looked straight up and closed his eyes, and then he looked over at Phebe. "This is only my third day here. How could you possibly know about me changing names? I haven't told anyone about that…ever."

Phebe hunched her shoulders apologetically and shook her head. "Yes, you did tell someone. You told *us*."

Will stood firm but now showed due respect to Phebe. "I respectfully disagree with your statement that I told you and Felina that I changed my name a number of times."

Phebe partially stood up, leaned over, and kissed Will on the cheek. Phebe does not intend to embarrass him, but she *will* have her questions answered about the man her emotionally adopted daughter is falling in love with, even if she has to crawl through the pits of hell.

Phebe is beginning to like Will a lot, and Phebe especially likes that Will is not spouting what she politely refers to as idiot-level excuses nor is he burying himself in denial.

Phebe explained, "Will, the three of us have been talking a lot to each other for over two days now. And during our conversions…you have…well…you have referred to yourself by three different names."

Again, Will was stunned, but he responded quickly, "I can't lose her, Phebe. I cannot lose the woman of my dreams…at least not to a lie. Okay, *Mama*, I will be straight with you. To explain it as simply as possible, I rode into a large town on the way, like Ben, to join a cattle drive, and everyone in town mistook me for a tall red-haired beneficiary of an uncle I did not have. Phebe, I simply could not resist such a staggering amount of money. The inheritance was so much that my part was just over $475,000. The attorney thought I was the right man, but he was not on the level either. For a small fee, he agreed to consolidate all of the physical holdings, such as cattle, land, houses, and such. There was a lot of property. I kept track of everything he said in my mind, and the total inheritance was well over two million dollars."

Phebe again smiled at Will and told him he was doing well.

Will continued, "Then for a much larger fee, the attorney offered to pay me cash for the entire inheritance right there on the spot. I hesitated and argued a bit and talked him up on the price, but I agreed somewhat quickly because I did not know how much time I had before someone figured out that I was the wrong man. Yet it was still an enormous amount of money, especially since it was not mine to begin with. I signed all of the papers, and he gave me a fortune in cash. In addition, he said when they settled everything, he would send more money to a special account in San Francisco. Then I got a room in a hotel that was on the very edge of town. I kept to myself for a few days, and I told everyone I was grieving. Then after the memorial service, as soon as it got dark, I left town and never looked back. I made sure there was no reason for anyone to look for me. I traveled a lot, and I changed my name as often as I needed to, but I did not want to change it too often. I kept the money in five or six bank accounts in several states. My thinking was that if they caught me, they might get some of the money back, but not all of it. If they caught me, I planned to say I gambled most of it away. I came here to El Paso with thoughts of maybe settling down and putting down some roots. They tell me I don't have to change my name anymore, but I am not totally sure about that, so when I got here, I used the name Will Travis after the famous colonel at the Alamo."

Phebe asked, "Who told you that you don't have to change your name anymore?"

Will was now relaxed and completely open with Phebe. "It gets a little complex, but as soon as I could, I checked the bank account in San Francisco. I was very surprised to find that the attorney had sent a thousand dollars to the account and left a message for me to contact him because he said I could make another twenty thousand dollars."

A very serious Phebe then asked, "Is that why you spent time in prison?"

Will looked at her and nodded. "Yes, ma'am, it is. I served a year and a day to keep my money, and I got a fifty-thousand-dollar bonus and a clean slate to boot. All for one year in a soft prison where the guards were not armed, and they called us by first name."

Phebe seemed to know the answers before she asked the questions. "Clean slate? Changing names or not, you still went to prison for a year. I wouldn't exactly call that a clean slate."

Will nodded. "Yes. They gave me a clean slate in the sense that no one will be looking for me to get the money back. The family finally discovered the mistake and that the wrong man got the money. There was about to be a huge investigation that could have put the attorney and a couple of others in not-so-soft prisons for a very long time. So the attorney offered me twenty thousand dollars to sign a carefully worded confession that included gambling, wasting money, women, being robbed, bad investments, and giving it away or otherwise disposing of over a million dollars that is lost and is irretrievable. But knowing the inheritance was almost two million dollars, I talked him into making the bonus fifty thousand instead of twenty. For which, I would keep the money I had, and another fifty thousand dollars paid in advance. Plus a judge the attorney knew who would give me only a year because of no prior crimes and because I cooperated and was instrumental in resolving the case."

Phebe laughed. "How could you have been *that* cooperative?"

Will also laughed, "By signing the confession and doing away with well over a million dollars that can never be accounted for or retrieved."

Phebe started to say something, but Will interrupted. "I almost forgot the best part. The attorney convinced the true inheritor to sign away all future litigation rights in exchange for *recovering* 25 percent of the inheritance—an overvalued 25 percent at that."

Phebe then said, "It sounds to me like you really don't have to change your name anymore, especially since you did not go to prison as Will Travis."

Will nodded. "Well, I sure would like to keep the name that I gave you and Felina, but tell me how you could know so much about me and about what happened?"

"Actually, you did it yourself. Usually when someone is in a lot of trouble or has a lot of explaining to do, it's self-inflicted. The first time you referred to yourself by another name, I was very uncomfortable with it, but most anything can happen once. The second time it happened, I knew something wasn't right. By this time, two of our patrons had warned me that you had spent some amount of time in prison. About this time, you referred to yourself by a third name. Scott, I think it was. Then about the same time, a third patron warned me that you have served some amount of time in prison. Not very long, to be sure, but you had been there. Since there was very strong evidence you had served time in prison, and since you referred to yourself by three different names, it was only common sense to doubt the source of your wealth. Even if your wealth was legitimate, you still had two very serious questions to answer. I couldn't lose by questioning the source of your wealth. By this time, the odds were against you, by a lot. It's like my mama always use to say, every time people open their mouth, it's incredible what they tell you… all you have to do is listen. On top of that, I have learned that the longer you listen, the more they tell you. And they don't even realize what they are saying."

Phebe got up from the table, walked over to the window, and spoke tenderly, "I do not love Fela as a sister, Will. I am thirty-eight years old, and she is twenty…I love her as a daughter. Will, I really believe you are telling me the truth, and you may well be the man of her dreams who will make her dreams come true. "

Will then smiled as he realized. "That explains everything. It's not a sister relationship between you two. It's a mother-daughter relationship." Will chuckled. "Beware of mama bear." Then Will laughed and grinned at Phebe. "Does this mean you could be my mother-in-law?"

"Don't make me hurt you, Will. I will hurt you real bad."

At a subtle gesture from Phebe, Felina rejoined them, hugged them, and then sat down.

Felina drew in her bottom lip, slightly biting it as she looked at Phebe almost in desperation. "Okay, Phebe, do we kiss him or shoot him?"

Phebe talked almost as if Will was not there, and she looked only at Felina. "He didn't lie to me, Fela. He didn't even try, and I believe everything he told me was the truth, and he did not try to insult my intelligence with any of what I politely call idiot-level excuses. I'll tell you what, Fela. You kiss him and see where it leads, and if necessary, then I will shoot him. I like him, Fela, and I think you have a good man. And he even looks good in the daylight." Will tipped his hat and bowed slightly from his chair.

Felina was a little disappointed and taken back at the lack of glowing praise and especially by Phebe's tone of voice. Felina was concerned. "Now *you* tell the truth. Is there something wrong or something you are concerned about?"

Phebe shook her head and smiled. "No, Fela, I am just very tired." This was the first and the only time Phebe ever lied to Felina. Phebe did in fact feel, or sense, a strong, ominous foreboding. However, she could not identify it or put it into words. It was only a gut feeling, but it was a very powerful one. However, there was not enough for Phebe to voice her feelings, and she would not risk Felina's future and happiness on a *feeling* without substantial evidence or proof. Yet Phebe did vow to herself to be alert for anything that threatened Felina's happiness. Phebe decided to keep her foreboding to herself, at least for the time being.

Phebe kissed Will on the cheek and then held Felina's hand. "Fela, the only negative thing I can say about your man is that he is not perfect."

Felina let her hand fall and slap the top of the table with flair, and the tone of her voice matched. "Damn, Phebe...we just let three perfect ones go last month, and now you tell me that Will isn't perfect? Maybe I should just shoot the both of you, and I will be done with it...can I have all of the money?" Will and Phebe understood Felina's nervous humor.

Phebe took a few minutes and told Felina how Will got his wealth, why he changed names so often, and why he spent a year and a day in prison.

Phebe was content with Will's answers and explanations, but she did not tell Felina about her instinctive apprehension or ominous foreboding. After all, Felina still has that six-gun she bought from Reno for five dollars, and she still knows how to prepare the cartridges, load the cylinders, and shoot straight.

Felina knew Will did not have an easy time of it, and she knew Will had some explaining to do that was serious enough to include some amount of time in prison. Felina did not want to know the details of what Phebe and Will said, and she did not want the details of his answers. All Felina wanted was Phebe's advice and approval after she thoroughly grilled him. Felina was content with, and trusted, Phebe's judgment and conclusions.

Will then looked at them, shrugged, and said, "Let's talk about Santa Fe."

Felina nodded. "Okay, Will. When I left home, I had no idea where I was going or what I was going to do. Even after my expenses, I still had enough money to support myself for six months. I had six months to figure out a lifetime, and I was only seventeen years old. I was still four months away from turning eighteen. Within a matter of hours, I was further away from home than I had ever been in my entire life. I was further from home than I had ever been, yet I was just starting my search for the inexplicable desires that called to me and led me to seek my unspoken dreams."

Will shook his head. "How on earth did you travel so far without some man trying to pick you up...or worse?"

Felina smiled. "I dressed myself so that even at a short distance, I looked like a man, or at least a boy. I also took a piece of canvas and a broom and shaped it to look like I was carrying a rifle in a scabbard. No one bothered me, so it must have worked, or so I thought."

Will then asked. "How did you end up in Santa Fe?"

FELINA RUNS AWAY

1854

F elina nodded. "I stopped in a small town and went to the general store to get more oats for my horse and to buy more provisions and food for myself. I was much too close to the storekeeper to hide the fact that I was decidedly not a young man or boy. The storekeeper saw that I was girl, and then he asked me about my *rifle* in the scabbard. When I told him it was just a piece of canvas over a broom to scare people off, he got upset. He told me that my canvas and broomstick looked too real and if anybody came after me, they would be prepared and ready to face a man or boy with a rifle. He told me since they would shoot first and assume that I was good with my *rifle*, I could get myself killed long before they realized I was a runaway girl packing an unloaded broomstick. When I asked how he knew I was a runaway, he explained that young girls traveling by themselves packing canvas and straw rifles aren't packing a family. Besides, he has seen enough runaways to spot me a mile away. He told me the best thing I could possibly do is turn around and go right back home."

"When I explained the calling and yearning and that I had to follow my dreams, he told me that he had heard that story many times before, too many times. Then he said if I wasn't going back home, then as pretty as I am, I should be dancing in a saloon making a lot of money. He told me that saloons are not safe places, but a saloon is by far and away safer than the path I was following. He said I wouldn't last a week out there alone and that I was lucky to be in one piece as is was. He scolded me and told me there were many dangerous animals out there, some with four legs and some with two. Either way, he said my broomstick lacked the firepower to protect myself."

Felina's mind drifted back two years, or maybe more, and she relived an unforgettable bittersweet experience.

"I thought it was going to be so easy. I thought my hopes and dreams would simply jump out and grab me at any moment, and then everything would be happily ever after, like the end of a fairy tale."

Felina naively asked the storekeeper. "Is there a saloon around here where I can learn to dance?"

The storekeeper shook his head. "No, the nearest decent saloon, as saloons go, would be Lu Lu's Saloon in Santa Fe. It's about 150 miles from here, and it's a three-day ride, maybe four, depending on animals, Indians, and the weather."

"Thank you so much for all of your help. My name is Felina. What's yours?"

The storekeeper froze for an instant and then shook his head. "They call me Reno."

"Is that why you know so much about two-legged animals, saloons, and unloaded broomsticks?"

Reno chuckled and rubbed the back of his head. "I guess so, little one, I went down that path a bit myself at one time...a very long time ago."

"Is that why you own a general store now instead of shooting bad guys?"

Reno laughed. "Some people said I *was* the bad guy. However, you are right, and that is exactly why I own this general store. A year ago, I became something I never would have lived to see if I hadn't slowed down and bought this store."

"What did you become?"

"I became a grandfather."

Felina paid her bill and started walking out the door. "Thank you so much for your help, Mr. Reno. I think I can make it to Santa Fe without stopping."

Reno closed his eyes and sighed. His thoughts were not good or positive. "Wait just a minute, girlie. There's one more thing we need to talk about."

"Okay, what is it?"

"We need to talk about your safety and well-being."

"Didn't you say saloons are a lot safer?"

"Yes, I did, but first, you have to get from here to the saloon in one piece, preferably alive."

"Okay, what do I need to do?"

Reno is doing exactly what he swore and vowed he would never do again, and that is to get involved with anyone, under any circumstances, going the wrong way that refused to listen. However, he never counted on running into a seventeen-year-old girl named Felina. "Felina, what caliber is your broomstick?"

"I don't know. I didn't know they came in—"

Reno rubbed his forehead in frustration. "Never mind, never mind."

Reno reached down and pulled up a large box and opened it.

"Judging from your horse and the things you bought, you are not hurting for money."

"Yes, I'm okay."

In the box was a six-gun. Reno picked it up, twirled it around, and did a number of impressive spins, including spinning it sideways. "This is the gun I used to carry. It's a twenty-dollar gun. Do you have five dollars?" Reno lied. It was a customized two-hundred-dollar gun bare minimum at wholesale.

Felina looked down at the gun and then looked at Reno. "Yes, I have five dollars. What is it?"

"It's a .36 caliber, 1851 Colt Navy six-gun. It weighs two and a half pounds and has a seven-and-a-half inch octagon barrel. And this gun has been customized and fine-tuned for shooting two-legged animals as well as four."

Felina shook her head and frowned. "It has an octagon barrel?"

Reno nodded. "Yes, that means the barrel has eight sides instead of being round."

"Oh, that's pretty. I like it, but didn't you say it's an 1851 six-gun?"

"Yes, I did, and yes, it is."

"Then it's almost five years old. Does it still work?"

Reno rolled his eyes, looked up, and laughed. "Yes, it is still in perfect operating condition. Guaranteed or your money back."

"Oh, thank you, Reno."

Reno thought to himself, *I am delivering a young, innocent soul to the very doorstep of the devil himself. Does that mean I am doing the devil's work...again? Is it possible that this precious, young girl is already beyond help? Whether she is or not, she desperately needs to learn how to defend herself. She is still alive, unmolested, and carrying four different pouches of money...there really is a God.*

Reno decided to spend an hour with Felina teaching her how to prepare the cartridges, how to load them, and how to replace empty cylinders with loaded ones. Three hours later, Felina got it right for the first time. Then another one, and then another. After five hours, Felina went through the entire cartridge preparation and loading process and changing cylinders ten times in a row without error. Reno had decided to give her an hour or two of shooting practice, but after five hours of reloading and changing cylinders, Reno decided that Felina needed a minimum of two or three days of firearms training and instructions just to keep from shooting herself and to remember which end of the gun the bullet comes out of. Reno checked her into a good hotel and made sure she was safe.

The next three days were very productive, and Felina learned how to handle a gun very quickly. Up to fifty feet, she became reasonably proficient, and Reno was convinced that Felina would at least come closer to hitting what she aimed at than herself or an innocent bystander.

After what turned out to be four days of practice and training, Felina was very excited, and Reno was proud of her. Reno told her good-bye and that she would probably end up shooting herself, but that was the best he could do. He wished her good luck and Godspeed.

Just over halfway to Santa Fe, Felina suddenly realized that someone was following her. Whoever it was, was barely within sight and was following the tree lines. Felina actually fired two warning shots and shouted at them. A lone man rode slowly toward her with his hands raised. She could not hear exactly what he was saying, but she could tell from his tone of voice that he was cursing. When he got closer, Felina recognized his voice. Then she recognized the man; it was Reno. He had followed her to make sure she was safe. Reno didn't talk much, and he seemed grim and solemn, much more so than he was back at his general store. Felina could not know that being out on the trail brought back bad memories, and Reno decided not to explain it to her, she had enough worries. About an hour out of Santa Fe, Reno started talking a bit.

Felina noticed the closer they got to Santa Fe, the less Reno looked at her, even when he was talking to her. When they got to the outskirts of Santa Fe, Reno gave Felina directions on how to get to Lu Lu's Saloon, and he gave her the name of the saloon's owner.

They stopped their horses, and Reno looked away from Felina. "Do you remember what I told you about me becoming something I never would have been if I didn't slow down?"

"Yes, sir, you became a grandfather about a year ago."

Reno nodded. "Yes, I did, and it was a girl. I had a granddaughter, but when she was three months old, she died. We don't know why or what happened. She just died in her sleep."

Tears formed in Felina's eyes. "I don't have the slightest idea of what to say. I can't even imagine such a horrible thing."

Reno nodded but still looked away. "What you just said was about as good as you or anyone else could have said. If you ever get into trouble or need a place to stay, just find your way back to the general store, and Grandma and I will help you out the best we can."

Reno turned his horse toward home, but then he stopped, and then he looked straight into Felina's eyes. "Our granddaughter's name was…Felina."

Then Reno turned and rode back home without another word.

FELINA AND WILL TALK

F elina's focus returned to Rosa's Cantina and Will. Will is now the center and the focus of her every thought and action, the center of every heartbeat. He is the center of her life and everything in it. In a mere four days, everything in her existence has changed radically and has changed her life and has changed her, forever.

Will shook his head. "Is that the six-gun you have been carrying around all this time?"

Felina nodded. "Yes, it is one of my most valued physical possessions. Would you like to have it? Will you hold me close to your heart as long as you wear it?"

Will slowly shook his head, very slowly. "Reno did not sell you that six-gun. He gave it to you as a gift, and I wonder if it was one of his personal treasures. We will send him a telegram to thank him for such a sacrifice and for such a gift. How can—" Will had to look away.

Felina was very concerned by the tone of his voice. "How can what?"

Will had to fight to keep his voice from breaking. "How can a baby just up and die for no reason? How can that happen? There was no injury, no sickness, no disease, no fever, no animal attack, insect, or snakebite. How can that happen?"

Will sighed deeply and looked away. "We don't even know what makes stars shine or what power or force holds a bird up in the air, so how can we possibly have answers about life and death? I will never believe, and I refuse to believe, that some God goes around killing babies. I believe the baby Reno named Felina died for a reason, and something caused the baby to die. We just don't know what the reason or cause is. It could be the devil, to be sure, but not God."

Felina looked at her beloved man with a new level of respect and awe—a new level of love. However, her only answer for Will's thoughts was a shrug with open extended hands and shaking her head with no answers or words to offer.

They sat there, looked at each other for a few moments, and looked away. Then Will smiled and spoke, almost forcing his humor. "Okay, lady, how much do you want for your six-gun?"

"It is very expensive…very, very expensive."

"You only paid five dollars for it. What do you want for it?"

"I want the rest of your life."

"That's an awful lot for a mere six-gun."

"For you, the gun is free. The other thing is what's so expensive."

"What is the other thing?"

"The gun has an attachment."

"What kind of an attachment?"

"Me."

"Sold."

Felina took the Navy Colt out of her handbag and set it on the table in front of her. Then she looked at Will and slowly pushed her most cherished and prized physical possession over in front of him. Felina then spoke the most prophetic words she ever uttered in her life. "This gun has the power to kill us, Will, but it does not have the power to kill our love."

Felina became lost in thought and stared with unseeing eyes through the window at the activity and the people outside busily walking back and forth. She wanted Will to know about her past, and like Ben and Phebe, she wanted to get all of it out in the open and deal with it so they can get it all behind them. Oh, how she wished this day was already over.

Felina spent a year in Santa Fe where she met the only person she can trust and the woman who became a strong mother figure. It was Phebe, and in Santa Fe, they referred to themselves as the dancing *sisters*. They did not want anyone to know Phebe's true age, which was thirty-five.

After a year in Santa Fe, they both yearned for brighter lights and the life that would escape them if they did not seek it out. Then one night, a cowboy passing through told them about El Paso, with many bright lights that glowed all night, and where money flows like whiskey, a place where you have to run as fast as you can just to stay even.

Felina's thoughts were interrupted as Will looked at the six-gun she put in front of him. He hesitated and looked at it, even spun it around, but he would not pick it up. She smiled at him warmly, picked up the gun, pressed it into his right hand, and then firmly squeezed his hand with both of her own. It was now *his* six-gun. They could not know, they had no way of knowing, that this very six-gun would have a long, tragic history for them as well as for the son they would bare.

Felina slowly looked around the saloon, and everything was different now, so very different. She will continue to do many of the same things as before, but they will no longer *mean* the same thing. A few days ago, a smile could have become more than a smile, and a flirt could have become more than a flirt. All of that is now gone; a smile is only a smile, a flirt is only a flirt, and never again will they mean anything more. She might *do* the same things, but they no longer *mean* the same things. More especially, Felina no longer *feels* the same.

Is there a heaven? It no longer matters. Felina already has her heaven here on earth, with all of the joy and happiness possible. Tragically, Felina's heaven revolves around a raging demon, a demon with the power and the motivation to kill.

Felina was preparing her mind and her heart for the most private and intimate interaction in her life. At the same time, Will was wondering if he should just ask Felina a few questions and lay everything else aside. Then Will quickly looked around the room; something was bothering him, but he could not figure out what it was. As he looked at Felina, she was experiencing the same feeling.

Then a flash went through his mind, and he suddenly realized what was wrong.

Phebe was still sitting there with them, but she had not spoken a word in over an hour, and the expression on her face was dark and ominous.

Felina was scared. "What's wrong, Phebe? Why are you looking like that? What has happened?"

Phebe shook her head. "I don't know. I just feel like something bad has happened, but I don't know what it is. I am so scared that something has happened to Ben."

Will shrugged and asked, "Could it be something related to carrying a child? Could it be something that is different within you? Plus it's only natural for you to worry about Ben while he's on such a long cattle drive."

Phebe seemed relieved and nodded. "Yes, that must be it. I've never had a baby before, and I haven't learned all of the details yet, and I do miss Ben so terribly. You are so right, Will, I worry about him every waking moment." Phebe smiled, but it wasn't quite her normal smile, and she was somewhat pale.

Felina got up from the table, went over to Phebe, and hugged her tight. "All of that plus you work. You must be exhausting yourself, Phebe. Maybe you should take some time off to make things easier on yourself and the baby."

Phebe winced. "I don't know if that's a good idea. If I don't keep myself busy and active, I would go nutty in an empty room by myself all day with nothing to do. I can afford it financially, but I don't know if I can afford it emotionally. I don't know if I can pay that kind of rent."

Will laughed. "What if you are already nutty to begin with?"

Phebe laughed too but then scowled. "You are going to pay your rent for that one, Will, and you will pay your rent in full."

Will held his hands up defensively and to indicate he wanted to ask a serious question. "Just to be sure I understand this correctly, what does it mean to pay your rent?"

Phebe was surprisingly serious. "It can mean to face the consequences of your actions or to bear unavoidable punishment, or it can mean you simply have to do whatever it takes no matter how hard or difficult it is. When we were in that cabin, Ben got to say anything he wanted to say and ask me anything he wanted to ask, and he voiced his opinion any way he wanted to voice it. However, when he was finished, he had to pay his rent...in full."

He nodded. "It can mean several things. That's what I thought, but I wanted to make sure."

Then Will became hesitant and looked over at Felina. He took a deep breath and let out a long sigh, and looking away for a moment, he was obviously in conflict with himself. Then Will became uncharacteristically serious and subdued.

Phoebe recognized the internal struggle. "Will, it's a lot better if you just come out and say it. Would you like to be alone with Fela? If my presence is causing difficulty, I will understand you wanting to be alone."

Will shook his head slightly and thought to himself, *I'm not as ready for this conversation as I thought I was.* Then he looked at Phebe. "No, it's not you, Phebe, it's me."

Phebe nodded her understanding.

Felina put her hand on Will's forearm and spoke softly, "What bothers you the most, Will?"

Will tried to smile but was not very successful, and he looked at his hands in front of him on the table. "You said there were so many men who were so close during the night but are nowhere to be found in daylight. What do you mean by that...and...how...and how many men were there, Felina?"

Felina did not hesitate or dilute her answer. "A hundred...two hundred...there were a lot, Will, an awful lot...far too many. The worst ones were at the beginning before I learned the ropes, so to speak. They would sweet talk me and make me think they were going to take me out of the saloon and give me an honest life. They were so sweet and charming, and oh they were so convincing. They made me feel important, and for a while, I actually believed that I could be any man's wife, any man I wanted. I actually believed all of those men wanted me for who I was, not *what* I was. However, in the morning, those horrible dream-shattering mornings, I would always wake up in the daylight, alone...and they were gone. And they always took my hopes and dreams with them. When I saw one of them during the day on the streets or a store, they would glare at me as if they hated me, and I swear that some of them would have shot me if I got any closer. Yet as soon as it got dark, they would come staggering right back, and do it all over again. I hate myself, Will, and I hate what I've done. Most of all, I hate what I have become."

Felina stopped as her voice broke. Then she looked at the six-gun she had just given to Will. "You have no idea how many times I loaded that gun and thought about putting it right up against my heart and pulling the trigger. I've been told that some men have lived for hours after being shot in the head, perhaps even survive. However, I've always heard that nobody survives a bullet through the heart. You just make sure you put the bullet right in the middle of it, and I know exactly where that is."

She looked straight into Will's eyes and spoke as she cried, "You see, Will, that is not a six-gun I gave you. It is not an heirloom or a prized possession or a gunfighter's creation. When I squeezed that gun into your hand, it is my hopes and dreams I was giving you, not a gun. You do not hold my gun in your hands. You hold my future in your hands...and you...you hold my life in your hands."

Felina looked away and again looked through the window. "If you are going to shatter my heart, use the gun, Will...don't use promising words that create counterfeit hopes and dreams. Don't use words that cause so much pain and so much emptiness and so much heartache."

Felina shook her head in disbelieve and again looked at Will. "I cannot believe that I trust you so much so quickly, and I am overwhelmed that I have made myself so vulnerable to you within a matter of hours...within hours, Will. How could that have happened? Who are you that you can walk right through my barriers and guards and my protective walls? How could you make me so helpless so quickly? Who are you, Will? I am so scared of you, and I am so scared of how helpless I am before you."

Felina scoffed and continued to shake her head in total disbelief as she looked down. "You come crashing into my life through those swinging doors, waltzing in and flashing your red hair, beating up three men as if they were children, and then you sweep me off my feet and turn me into a little puppy that follows its master wherever the master goes. All of us girls are looking for our own personal Adonis. You are my Adonis, Will, and it doesn't matter what other men have done to me. I cannot resist you, nor do I want to, but I am so scared of you."

Felina then looked up at Will and looked him straight into his eyes. "Again, I tell you, Will, if you are going to shatter my heart, have mercy and use the gun to shatter it, not empty words. When others shattered my heart, I healed, but with you, I would die."

Will's face was expressionless, but he was torn apart inside. A hundred? Two hundred? She is scared of *him*? What about how scared he is of her? He knows within himself that he is hopelessly in love with her and cannot resist her. For the first time, but far from the last, Will wonders if Felina is casting a spell on him that makes him love her against his will. There were several severely errant beliefs Will relentlessly clung to and refused to let go. One was that Felina was *blaming* him for some unknown and unspecified offense, and she was openly trying to make him look like a bad guy. His mind defectively interpreted Felina's heartfelt expressions of love as somehow blaming him for something. The loneliness and void in Will's heart was being filled with the counterfeit and dangerous emotion of jealousy. And worse, his growing and expanding jealousy was fast coming to a boil. He decided that he would watch her dancing and her eyes much more closely from now on. Tragically, another error of Will's thinking is that Felina does not truly love him, as he loves her, and that she is trying to manipulate him for some unknowable reason. And for that, he felt anger, an errant, baseless anger that was impossible to resolve but certain to grow and strengthen.

Will looked at Felina with a look she had not seen before, a cold look that put an icy knot of fear in the pit of her stomach. Will was about to utter words that would have shattered their fledgling relationship, but fate intervened.

They were severely startled when someone came crashing through the swinging doors.

BEN IS SHOT

1857

The swinging doors were thrown wide open and slammed against the inside of the wall.

"Miss Phebe! Miss Phebe!"

The three of them bolted from their chairs, and Will instinctively reached for his gun. Phebe reached over and grasped Will's right arm to stop his draw. Will has seen the very young man a time or two but does not know who he is. Phebe and Felina instantly recognized him as Josiah, the eighteen-year-old son of the telegraph operator. They quickly told Will who he was.

The boy raced across the floor almost instantly and was out of breath. "Miss Phebe. It is Ben...he...there was some kind of shoot out...Bandolero's...stealing cattle...Ben has been shot... more than once. We did not get the entire message, and some of it was garbled...but there will be a series...of messages, and we have requested they resend this message."

Phebe sat down hard, silenced by shock and disbelief. She thought to herself, *This can't be real. Ben can't be dead. I believe I'm going to have a little girl, and she is going to be a daddy's girl, and she is going to wrap Ben around her little finger. He has to be alive because he is going to spoil our little girl, and I will fuss at them for it, and when I fuss at them, they will go behind my back, and he will spoil her even more. We will love each other dearly, so he can't be dead."*

"Miss Phebe, you have to come with me to the telegraph office to see the messages."

Will stepped in and took charge. "No, Phebe needs to stay here with us. Bring the messages to the back room as they come in, and we will read them here."

Josiah shook his head. "I can't do that. She has to come to the office."

Will handed him a ten-dollar bill, and Josiah looked at it as if it were a thousand. He tried to hand it back to Will. "I will do this for Miss Phebe, sir. I don't need money because she is such a good person. I like her."

Will then handed him another sawbuck. "Here, keep it, you deserve it. Go get the messages."

"Yes, sir." And Josiah was gone.

While waiting for Josiah to return, Will and Felina stood in a silent vigil, and Phebe's agonizing sobs were heartbreaking. Never have the three of them felt so helpless.

Josiah quickly returned and handed a telegram to Will. Will read it the best he could, but it was mostly garbled.

> Something attacked and something Ben something alone and shot something times. He is...

Will crumpled the telegram in his hand. "What the hell is this, Josiah? This doesn't tell us anything. This is worse than nothing. What is this?"

Josiah shrugged and said, "Unfortunately, sir, this is the telegram business. Except in emergencies like this one, when we are having problems receiving, we wait until we have a completed message before delivering it. The only other thing I can tell you is that Dad told me there will be a series of messages."

Then Josiah looked at each of them almost apologetically. "Someone has something very important to tell you."

Josiah was very young but experienced, and he anticipated their next question. "We know the lines are still up because we are receiving parts of the message. If the lines were down, we would only get random, meaningless signals, and sometimes not even that. There is probably a thunderstorm, and our signals are being garbled by lightning. The interference could last for minutes, hours, or even days. Most likely, it will only be for a few hours."

Then Josiah left so quickly it was almost as if he disappeared, and within two minutes, he returned with a complete first message. He handed the telegram to Will with no explanation.

Will read it immediately.

> Ten Bandolero's attacked herd caught Ben guarding herd alone and shot him three times. He is…

Josiah started to leave but stopped and did not turn around. "Normally, telegrams are as short as physically possible, but whoever is sending this is not taking the time to do that. These will be longer telegrams and very expensive. What they are saying is urgently important to them." Then he was gone.

It was a long, agonizing thirty minutes before Josiah returned with another message and handed it to Will.

Again, he read the message immediately without reading it to himself first.

> Ben shot cow and used body for cover. Ben fought ten Bandolero's alone 15 minutes. Ben killed 6 wounded 2 last 2 shot off horses fleeing when help arrived.

Will shrugged and looked at Josiah. "That's it?"

"Yes, sir, we still don't know if Ben is alive or dead."

Just as Josiah's father was about to request Ben's survival status, another telegram came in and was sent over to the saloon and handed to Will.

Again, he read the telegram.

> Details unclear, much unknown, Ben in hospital but conscious, severely wounded, survival unknown, will inform when known.

Another long excruciating wait for the next message ensued, but this time, Josiah rushed in with a smile on his face. Phebe burst out crying more than ever. "I knew he was alive. I knew it."

Josiah was a step quicker and almost pushed the telegram into Will's hand.

> Private stage tomorrow, need Phebe, Ben uncooperative with doctor. Urgent Phebe be here immediately. Three men escort Phebe. Ben hero but not with doctor. Escort Jessie will explain.

Phebe stood at the window looking out but again without seeing. "Just for a little while, the whole world went dark. Everything was so black and hopeless and ever so cold. Who am I to be granted a life with Ben when so many other women live in loneliness and despair?"

Felina scoffed. "Who are you? I told both of you that I loaded Will's gun many times and thought for a long time about pulling the trigger...on myself." Felina walked over and put her head on Phebe's right shoulder. Phebe quickly turned around and hugged Felina. "Without you, I would have pulled the trigger long ago, and I think you know that. You kept me alive until I could meet Will."

Phebe nodded slowly and spoke softly, "And you kept me alive long enough to meet Ben. You see, Fela, I would not have made it either. Felina, you have been the daughter that I now hope to have, and if it is a girl I'm carrying, I do hope she is like you, her big sister."

The private stagecoach was very early and arrived at midnight. All three of them were still awake and unable to sleep. The cattle company Ben worked for rented a stagecoach from a company in El Paso who outfitted it with food, water, and supplies for Phebe to travel several hundred miles. The three men escorting Phebe walked in the saloon and soon found them in the private room in the back.

A burley, tough-looking man faintly smiled at them and tipped his hat to the ladies. "My name is Jessie, and I will do my best to explain everything I can before we have to leave. It will take about another twenty minutes to finish getting the stage ready, and then we need to leave immediately." He then looked at Phebe. "How long will it take you to be ready to go, ma'am?"

Phebe answered without hesitation. "I will walk through those doors right now. The only thing in my life that is important is waiting for me."

Jesse smiled. "Yes, ma'am, Ben feels the same way about you. He told us about a cabin you two stayed in. He won't tell us any details, but he said he learned to pay his rent in that cabin. Now whenever he gets mad at us, he tells us that he is going to teach us how to pay our rent. He tells everybody about you, and he even tells us that you were a saloon girl, but nobody better say a word about it. He says that all of the rent on that subject has been paid in full, and it is not open for discussion. He says he is too proud of you to hide it, and he says he will still love his wife three days after he's dead. One day he got so mad at a ramrod that he said he was going home to get his wife, and then he would put a gun in one hand and a whip in the other. Ben said after two weeks of you being the trail boss, they would never fear another man for the rest of their lives."

Phebe interrupted, "Please tell me what happened."

"Yes, ma'am. Your man Ben is known as a man among men. Nobody wants to fight him, draw down on him, or talk about his woman. Nobody wants any part of ole Ben. He was riding the east side of the herd alone when ten Bandoleros, who were waiting, ambushed him. Lucky it was dark, but they made a bad mistake by taking on Ben, and they made a worse mistake by not killing him with the first bullet. Ben grabbed his rifle and two boxes of ammo, slid off his horse, shot a cow for cover, and was shooting back at the Bandoleros all within about ten seconds. It takes longer for me to tell it than it took Ben to do it. We all saw Ben practice doing that very thing, grabbing guns, bullets, and falling off his horse. We kinda laughed at him…a little, but not too much. He told us we were coming into badlands and that we better be ready to fight at any time day or night, and if we didn't know how to get off our horses and start shooting, we could be dead before we even knew there was a fight. Well, ma'am, Ben sure was right."

A young escort nudged Jessie. "Ask her, Jessie, go ahead and ask her."

Jessie pulled away from the young man who was his younger brother. "No, not now, give her a chance to catch up on everything that's happened."

The young man rolled his eyes. "You've got to ask her, Jessie, we can't tell Ben."

Phebe put her right hand on Jessie's left shoulder. "What is he talking about? What is it that you want to ask me that you cannot tell Ben? This doesn't make sense. What is it?"

Jessie sighed and looked away for a few seconds. "Ben bought one of the cows, and he named her Lucy. Ben told everyone that he was taking Lucy home to give his daughter milk. When we asked Ben how he knew it was a girl, he said because if it's a boy he is going to send it back."

Jessie then became serious. "We counted almost a hundred bullet holes in the cow Ben shot for cover. What none of us want to tell him is that the cow he shot was Lucy."

Phebe's laugh and her glare were without humor. "So you want *me* to tell Ben that the cow he shot dead to give him cover and save his life was the cow he was going to bring home to feed our baby girl. Is that it?"

The only answer Phebe got was throat clearing and nervous glances at each other.

Phebe put the issue aside for the moment and shook her head. "I don't understand the urgency to get me to Ben, and the telegram said Ben was a hero but not to the doctor. What is going on?"

Jessie nodded. "Ben fought them by himself for over ten minutes. He killed six of them, which is a lot. He kept aiming about three feet behind the muzzle flashes. He wounded two more, and the other two were shot off their horses when help arrived, which was the three of us. Ben said we were good luck for him, so he figured we would be good luck for you. Funny thing is that the Bandoleros would fire everything they had until they ran out of bullets, and then they would reload and do it again. What's funny is that we could hear their rifles, and every time they reloaded and started firing again, there were fewer Bandolero gunshots, and we could hear Ben's booming .44 caliber rifle using his own nonstop load and fire idea. We nicknamed Ben *the Blacksmith* because he melted and warped several rifle barrels practicing how to load and fire. Ben is intense when it comes to figuring out ways to fight his way out of trouble so he can go home to you with enough money to retire. He is very intense about that."

"Me? He did all of that because of me?"

Jessie chuckled. "Yes, ma'am, he would fight a grizzly bear with his teeth to get home to you and his baby girl. All of a sudden everything was much more important to him, especially anything to do with you and the baby." Jessie stopped and looked down.

"Do you have something to say that I won't like?"

"No, ma'am, but if I asked real nice, do you think you could tell us a little of what happened in that cabin?"

Phebe smiled. "I won't tell Ben you asked, but there's not a chance in hell I'm ever going to answer that question. However, I want to ask you what load and fire means."

Jessie nodded. "Ben practiced for hours with his .44-caliber lever action rifle on how to hold a handful of bullets in his right hand in such a way that he could load a bullet in his rifle almost as fast as he fired. The Bandoleros fired everything they had and then had to reload. Ben would fire one and load one, fire one and load one, and he did this so fast no one could tell he was loading. The Bandoleros probably thought they were fighting two or three armed men. It sounded like his rifle held fifty bullets, but it only holds seven. And when he needs to fire faster than he can reload, Ben can reload all seven bullets in about five or six seconds. Ma'am, that man wants to come home to you."

Phebe then asked suspiciously, "What happened to the two Bandoleros Ben wounded?"

Jessie shrugged. "They...well, ma'am, they were shot while trying to escape."

Phebe tilted her head as she looked at him. "Where did Ben shoot them?"

"One was shot in the leg and the other through the side."

"Just how fast could they run?"

Jessie shrugged. "They couldn't run at all, ma'am, they could barely move."

"Yet they were shot while trying to escape?"

"Yes, ma'am, they *looked* like they were trying to escape, and they tried to kill Ben, and they tried to steal a lot of our cattle. There was no way those men were going to live to see the sunrise. They didn't kill Ben, but they tried awful hard, and to us, it's the same thing. If you shoot one of us, don't let another one of us catch you."

"Okay, Jessie, fair enough, but why is it so urgent that I be there, and what happened between Ben and the doctor?"

"Well, ma'am, Ben and the doctor almost got into a fistfight, and I put two dollars on Ben, but they didn't fight. Ben was shot three times, and one of the bullets hit him pretty good. The doctor pulled two of the bullets out almost without Ben knowing it, but the third bullet is deep and in a vital area. The doctor said that Ben should have died five or six times already, but *something* inside of Ben won't let him die, and all of us cowpokes think it's you. The doctor is fierce about getting that last bullet out immediately, but Ben says he is not complete without you, and he says that he is only half the man without you and that he only has half the strength without you. That may be true, but I don't think those Bandoleros would agree with that. Ben won't let the doctor take the last bullet out because he thinks he won't have enough strength to endure the surgery without you being there to strengthen him. Ben really believes that, ma'am. So we have to get you there as soon as possible so the doctor can get that last bullet out. Of course, the doctor says that Ben is trying to cheat death too much, and he says Ben won't live the three or four days it will take us to get you there. We are not out of the woods yet, ma'am."

Then Will asked Jessie, "Why is the cattle company going through so much trouble and expense to save one man?"

"Well, sir, Ben did a very brave thing, and he could have easily gotten away without a gunfight, but he stood and fought ten armed men who had the drop on him. Ben saved an awful lot of cattle from being stolen. And to be honest with you, sir, Ben set an example that the cattle company would like all of their hands to strive for. The rewards are the company's way of saying that every man should strive to be like Ben, and if you are like Ben, then there are great rewards." Then Jessie looked at Phebe. "By the way, ma'am, the company is going to double Ben's wages and pay his fare home as soon as he is able to travel."

Will seethed inside and thought to himself, "*A man among men.*" Will ached inside for someone to say that about him and give him such wide fame and a huge reward and a...and a...*private stagecoach.* Everyone in every cattle company in the west will hear about Ben. They will hear how Ben singlehandedly fought off ten Bandoleros and then refused to let the doctor remove a near-fatal bullet until his wife came and completed his strength. Phebe and Ben will easily be able to retire now. Not only are they very rich, but their grandchildren who haven't been born yet are already rich. Will cried out in internal frustration. "Damn. Damn. Damn."

On the outside, Will appeared to be calm, encouraging, and supportive of Phebe. On the inside, he was seething with incredible envy and jealously, especially about the private stagecoach.

Just as the stagecoach pulled up out front, Josiah came running in with another telegram. Will quickly reached for it, but Josiah, understanding that the stage was ready to leave, bolted out of the room and tried to get the telegram to Phebe in the stagecoach.

Will and Felina could hear the stagecoach driver shouting commands, and they could hear Phebe shouting back. The three escorts mounted their fresh horses and took their positions at each side and the back of the stagecoach. Phebe almost jumped into the stage and hollered for the driver to go, go, go. They heard the leather straps slap the backs of the horses, and they heard the sound of the stagecoach wheels picking up speed and hitting ruts. As the stage picked up more speed, they could then hear the thundering hooves of galloping horses and the sounds of the stagecoach creaking and rocking in addition to other expected sounds of a stagecoach in a hurry.

Seeing the stage leave, Josiah jumped on his horse and tore after the stagecoach. When he caught them, he shouted to the driver that he had a telegram for Phebe. The driver slowed down but refused to stop. Josiah got as close to the stage as he could and reached out to hand Phebe the telegram. But just as Phebe touched it, it flew out of Josiah's hand. He stopped his horse as fast as possible and found the telegram and picked it up without dismounting his horse. As he looked up, one of the escorts was coming toward him and reached for the telegram.

The escort shouted, "I will give it to her, son."

Josiah stretched out and handed him the telegram and then stopped his horse and dismounted to watch the stage until it was out of sight and out of earshot. As he stood there, he shouted out loud to the rapidly fading stagecoach. "Hang in there, Mr. Ben, don't die on us now. She's on the way."

Josiah rode back to the saloon to tell Will and Felina what the telegram said. When he faced them, he smiled. "The telegram had more good news, sir and ma'am. Miss Phebe hadn't left yet, but they told Mr. Ben she was on the way, and he got better that minute. He got stronger, all of the bleeding has stopped, and he went to sleep, a healing sleep. It looks like Mr. Ben is going to make it."

The exhausted youth then walked slowly out of the private room and went home to sleep.

Everything happened so fast. The stagecoach was gone, the escorts were gone, all of the noise and chatter were gone, Phebe was gone, and even Josiah was gone. All of a sudden, everything was so very quiet and empty. The room seemed much bigger now. There was so much activity, so much stress and tension that saturated the entire saloon. Now it was eerily quiet and, in a way, lifeless.

Will and Felina looked at each other and didn't know what to say. It was as if a stampeding herd of cattle stopped suddenly in the middle of the stampede and instantly became calm and quiet. The events of the past twenty-four hours were, to say the least, emotionally treacherous and psychologically destabilizing.

Their own emotions and feelings were temporarily swept aside as events came at them and hit them faster and harder than they could absorb. Will shook his head to clear his mind, and he muttered, "A *private* stagecoach. I've never…"

Felina sat in his lap and curled up against him and buried her head in his chest. "I don't even know what to think, let alone what to say."

Will held Felina close, looked up at the ceiling, and let out a long sigh. "Can you take a couple of days off?"

"I certainly can."

"Let's go somewhere."

"Will?"

"Yes, my love."

"Before all of this started, you were going to say something to me when Josiah slammed through the doors. The expression on your face and the tone of your voice terrified me. Were you about to throw me aside, Will?"

Will thought quickly; it only took a few seconds for him to reclaim the memory, and he truly was, to be sure, about to throw Felina aside and walk out of her life. Free at the moment from the raging emotional demon, Will spoke softly and loving to her, and he quickly apologized. He truly loved Felina, and she truly loved him, but…although they loved each other unlike they have ever loved before, their love was in vain. They are powerless to stop the fatal spiral that is already spinning out of control. Will has a fatal weakness that, tragically, is strengthened by the very love the fatal weakness will destroy. It was the most vicious of vicious cycles. The power of his deepest love can change and transform between heartbeats into the raging demon. As the love that binds them to each other's soul grows stronger and more powerful, it also empowers the demon that much more. For the demon is fueled by the very power of the love they cling to and cherish, the demon is the other side of their coin of love and passion. They can no longer stay away from each other, nor can they survive without each other. Within a few hours, Will has lost the power to leave Felina or to cast her aside. Their fate is now inevitable.

Yet he does love her to the bottom of his heart and soul as he explained, "No, I can't leave you, Felina. I was a little angry, but it was entirely my fault. My emotions for you have not settled down yet, and I overreact sometimes. I love you, Felina, just tolerate me for a little while, and I will become halfway civilized."

Felina beamed and smiled at him. "Halfway civilized? Is that all?"

"Yes, halfway. For me to even attempt to become totally civilized would be a hopeless task requiring multiple lifetimes."

Felina laughed with an easy heartfelt laugh. Ben will survive his three gunshot wounds, and Will cannot leave her. It was one of the best days of her life. However, even though there are no other men in her life in the slightest way, Felina cannot yet quit the saloon. Her heart has been shattered and scarred too many times. It will take a long time for her to build the confidence and the courage to leave her only source of security and the only life she has known since she left home. By three months, Felina is twenty years old; she has been on her own for almost three years.

Will was thinking about many things, and just when he was about to ask Felina where she would like to go, he heard a soft, gentle, feminine snore. He smiled, gently held her a little tighter, and thought to himself that this is about as good as life gets. Will sat there holding Felina for a long time. His arms and back ached but never in his life had he felt such pleasurable pain, nor has he ever felt as protective.

Then he spoke softly to exhausted, unhearing ears, ears of a woman who found much comfort in his strong embrace. "Words cannot carry enough meaning for me to tell you how much I already love you. I told you the truth when I said that I can no longer leave you or throw you aside. If I was going to do anything like that, it had to be before now. No matter what our path and life may be, and no matter where we go or what we do, I love you more than life itself, and I always will."

Felina roused with a glowing smile. "What a way for a woman to wake up."

THE RAILYARD RESTAURANT
AND LODGING

Will looked at Felina with a warm smile. "Would you like some breakfast? I know I do. I've had a rough night. Besides, today is a very special day."

Felina let out a breath as she playfully slapped Will on the shoulder. "We were right in the middle of it, weren't we?"

"Uh-huh…I wonder how long it will take Ben to heal. I only met Ben that one time at their wedding, but I doubt if he remembers very much. I would like to get to know him better."

Will shook his head. "I can't get used to us being alone all of a sudden. I mean, we were sitting here talking and had everything planned out when all of a sudden Josiah comes busting through the door hollering for Miss Phebe. Then we heard that Ben was shot three times and a private stagecoach was hauling Phebe off to God knows where to be with her critically wounded husband. Honey, I think it safe to say that I've never had a night quite like this before. I guess I am still trying to catch up to things that have already happened, if that makes sense."

Felina nodded in agreement, "Same perspective of things over here, love."

Then she looked at Will and batted her eyes several times. "Are you going to feed me, or do I have to fall on the floor and flop around like a fish?"

Then Felina slapped her forehead with the palm of her hand and laughed out loud. "Oh God, now I sound like one of Phebe's jokes."

Will chuckled. "Falling on the floor and flopping around like a fish sounds like one of her jokes? Are you serious?"

Felina nodded and grinned. "Oh yeah, I'm as serious as a hangman's noose. She loves to tell jokes, and she has a joke about a nonexistent saloon girl named Marylou, who is the easiest woman in the world for any man to get."

Will shrugged his shoulders and chuckled. "Okay, how easy is she?"

"Everything there is to do and everything that can be done, Marylou has done it, and she has done it for half the price. All a man has to do is snap his fingers and point down, and Marylou will flop around like a skinned catfish on a plate of salt. And that is some serious flopping."

Will laughed hard and at length. "Now that is funny. In my mind, I can picture her so clearly telling that joke."

Will stood up. "Okay, I decided to feed you so you won't have to do the floor act."

Felina fell into his arms. "Wise decision. Where are we going for breakfast?"

"I was thinking of the Amanecer."

Felina did a double take. "I thought we were going across the street...the what?"

Will shook his head. "No, not across the street. I want to take you to the nice places, places you deserve to be."

Felina looked up at Will. "There are a lot of those nice places I am not supposed be in."

Will smiled at her. "Not any more. If anyone gives us any trouble, we will buy the place and fire everyone who says anything bad about you and give raises to those who are nice to you." Felina was still shaking her head. "The Amanecer? That word means sunrise, but I've never heard of a restaurant...are you sure about the name?"

Again Will smiled. "You can get used to nice places because that is the way it is now. I will take you to the nicest and fanciest places in town. And you can feel free to quit the saloon any time you want. Either of us has enough money to retire on, let alone both of us together."

At the mention of quitting the saloon, Felina felt a powerful jolt that spread shock waves throughout her entire body. The mere thought of quitting the saloon terrified her, and it caught her totally by surprise and was completely unexpected. Felina herself had no idea she would react this way to the mere thought of quitting the saloon. She knew the saloon has become her safe house and her security blanket, but she did not realize how much so until Will said she could quit.

Will could see her hesitation and the expression of fear on her face. He understood that it would take some time before she could break free of the saloon. He had no problem with that, not as long as he could be there every night and as long as Felina did not move an inch toward the upstairs rooms, and no more full body hugs and no more kisses.

His smile was warm and encouraging. "I don't mean for you to quit now, but when you are ready. We can talk about this another time, when the time is right."

She looked up at him, obviously relieved. "I didn't realize…"

Will held her close to him yet did not say anything. She returned his hug in equal silence and stood there feeling more secure and more comfortable with her man with each passing heartbeat. Then she closed her eyes and savored the moment.

Will chuckled, "If we don't get something to eat soon, I will be the one flopping around on the floor."

Felina laughed and stood unmoving and folded her arms. "That would be worth waiting to see. I could sell tickets for that. And where is this restaurant you are talking about? I never heard of it."

Will feigned a look of surprise. "You mean the Amanecer?"

"Yes, where is it?"

Will gestured to the swinging doors with an outstretched arm. "It's right outside, and it's waiting for us. Take a look, honey."

Felina was puzzled, but she walked over to the swinging doors and looked outside and saw a beautiful sunrise. "Other than a beautiful sunrise, all I see is a sleeping town and a dirt street."

Felina looked back at Will and giggled. "Are we going to make mud pies for breakfast?"

Will chuckled. "You've been hanging around Phebe too much. No mud pies, but this beautiful sunrise is just for us, and this is our first sunrise with just the two of us alone. Every amanecer for the rest of our lives is for us and for our love. The restaurant where we are going to breakfast is the Railyard, but it is the glow of this sunrise, a sunrise just for us, that now lights our world."

It was only then that Felina realized with Phebe and Ben gone, they were truly alone. But she did not feel alone, nor would she ever feel alone again.

They decided to take a buggy for the one mile jaunt to the Railyard and enjoy the very special sunrise. But as they got closer, Felina became nervous. "That is such a nice restaurant. What if they won't seat us?"

Will fired a harsh look at her that was obviously not meant for her. "Honey, after the night we had, there is a very big part of me that wishes and hopes they won't. But it is very early, and there shouldn't be more than a handful of people there, and there should not be a problem. However, to answer your question, if they refuse to seat us, if they say or do anything to embarrass you or try to humiliate you, they will have a very big problem on their hands—me."

The maitre d' instantly recognized Felina but nodded politely as they walked in the door. "We have a lovely view of the sunrise with a large window or a view of the street and the awakening activities of the town. However, I would have a word with the gentleman."

Will shook his head. "This lovely lady is my fiancée so anything you need to say to this gentleman applies equally to her." Will quickly put aside the real purpose and reason he brought Felina to the Railyard. He was angry, and the hair on the back of his neck stood up.

The mention of being Will's fiancée sent a different kind of shock wave all through Felina's body—endearing, happy, wonderful shock waves, shock waves of joy and most of all…the long sought after and fervent desire for acceptance.

Will then noticed the maitre d' focused his eyes on Felina.

Will followed his eyes to Felina's bare ring finger and did not give the maitre d' a chance to question her about a ring. "The ring has been ordered and will be here in a few days. We will be glad to come back and show it to you."

The maitre d' smiled but was smug to the point of arrogance. It was his best shield against feelings of inferiority. "I doubt that very seriously, sir, but as you wish. However, the word I would have with you is that we will allow you to be seated, and we will even serve you. Nevertheless, I must insist that you finish your meal and vacate the premises by 8:30."

Two hours was plenty of time for breakfast, but it was the principal of the thing.

Will scoffed at the maitre d' and smiled mockingly as he spoke, "Since you doubt the ring so much, how about a free dinner during regular dinner hours when we show you her ring?"

"That would be quite out of the question, sir."

"Why? You all but called me and my fiancée liars, but when challenged, you seem to turn tail and run. You can run your mouth pretty good, but you seem to be a little short on actions, and you don't seem to be able to back up your words."

The maitre d' was becoming frustrated; he was not accustomed to being challenged and certainly not accustomed to explaining himself for what he said. "Sir, and I use the term loosely, this is your final opportunity to be seated and served or else."

"Or else? What are you going to do, hiss at us, or insult us in three languages? Or else what?"

"We have rather burly gentlemen who specialize in the removal of undesirable clientele, which you are rapidly approaching."

Will looked around. "Oh, pray tell, where are they? I wish to speak to the stoutest of these burly gentlemen and ask his opinion on this matter of you calling us liars."

The maitre d' snapped his fingers, held up one finger, and motioned for security.

Big Jake swaggered over with a little bit of smile and a lot of smirk on his face. "Got a problem, boss?"

The maitre d' also smirked. "I don't think so, but this gentleman has a question to ask you about your opinion of my mannerisms."

Will was at least four inches taller, but Big Jake was a bit heavier. Jake scoffed at Will and shook his head. "I don't have an opinion on your mannerisms, boss. I just take out the trash whenever you call. I don't have opinions. I have duties. If you tell me to seat them, I will offer the lady my arm. But if you tell be to remove the big man here, I can do so with about the same amount of effort."

Will looked around at everyone as his chuckle transformed into a scoff and then a grunt of contempt. "What did you say?"

Jake put his hands on his hips and put his face within a foot of Will's face. "I said…"

Two short, lightning fast, and powerful punches put Big Jake on the floor. The smacking sound of Will's punches could be heard fifty feet away. There was sunlight from the new day shining on Jake's face, but his internal lights were out, and all he saw was blackness.

Will glared at the maitre d'. "Maybe there is something you should know about us, little man, and now would be a good time to tell you. We can easily pay cash for this establishment and turn it into a livery stable and not be the poorer. If you do not believe me, have your banker contact our banker and verify what I am saying. You've seen me in here before, several times in fact. My name is Will Travis, and our banker is James over at the West End bank."

The maitre d' paled with shock and responded almost involuntarily as if to himself. "James is my banker too."

Will then became serious. "This establishment is owned by a corporation in St. Louis."

The maitre d' was a bit more hesitant. "That is common knowledge, sir."

As Jake got back up on unsteady legs, Will chuckled at the maitre d'. "We wish to be seated now. Why don't you send your boy here to perform his duty and run over to the bank and ask James about what I just said. The bank is not open yet, but James is already there. Then you can join us, but what we will discuss with you at the table is *not* common knowledge."

The maitre d' was stunned that this man knew James so well, and he nodded at Jake. "Go check with James about what Mr. Travis just said."

Jake shrugged and looked at his boss with a blank look. "What did he say, boss?"

The maitre d' walked Jake to the door rapidly giving him instructions on what to say and do. As Jake was about to walk out of sight, he stopped and looked back at Will and Felina. When he gained their eye contact, he nodded his respect to Will and tipped his hat to Felina.

The maitre d' walked back to them. "We shall see about the boast you made, but in the meantime, I will personally seat you."

Will smiled. "You already know we're telling the truth. You have a knack for reading people, my compliments."

"Thank you, sir. However, until I receive official notification otherwise, I still make the rules and regulations by which we operate."

Will chuckled. "What are you saying? Are you still kicking us out at 8:30?"

He took a deep breath. "I have decided to extend leniency…you have until 9:00."

Felina smiled at the maitre d'. "You are so brutal. We only have two and a half hours to eat breakfast."

Will noticed several times that the maitre d' almost glares at Felina when he looks at her. It was almost subconscious.

Will came right out and asked him, "We have seen you at Rosa's a number of times, and yet I notice that you have a lot of negative feelings toward Felina. You glare at her almost every time you look in her direction, and that bothers me. I am asking you straight out…what is it?"

The maitre d' thought for a moment and decided to answer. "Nature hands saloon girls a free gift of beauty and attractiveness. The girls do not have to spend years developing it. Nature hands it to them without them having to earn it."

Will nodded. "There is a measure of truth to that. She makes her living with her beauty, her dancing, and by understanding the desires and lust in men who seem so respectable during the daylight. You make your living with your knowledge, years of education and training, and professionalism. And since you are the maitre d', you must be capable of solving many varied problems very quickly. To me, this explains your deep-seated hostility and resentment of Felina and explains why you feel inferior to her."

The maitre d' turned red in the face from anger mixed with embarrassment. "How could you possibly think that I could ever feel inferior to a *saloon girl?* How could anyone think that? Now I am asking *you* straight out to give me one good, solid reason to remotely think I could possibly feel inferior to a saloon girl?"

Will shrugged his shoulders. "Money is a great equalizer, and Felina makes more money in one night than you make in a month. A lot of girls make a lot more than Felina because she is semiretired, and she is no longer what is called…active. And I think her income bothers a man like you who invests so many years of your life to become an educated, trained, and experienced professional. I think it bothers you a lot."

"Perhaps it is small of me, but yes, it bothers me a lot. Our incomes should be reversed."

Felina shook her head as she spoke, "Give me a day and a night of your life, and you will never say that again as long as you live. Give me one Friday and one Friday night."

At that time, Jake came back from the bank. And walking over to their table, he reported to his boss. "Are you ready for this, boss?"

"Yes, what did James say?"

"He said that whatever Mr. Travis and his new fiancée want, you better do it twice, and you better do it right. It is true that either one of them can pay cash for this establishment at any time of their choosing."

The maitre d' looked at Will. "Are you who I am beginning to think you are?"

Will nodded. "I probably am."

The maitre d' shook his head dejectedly. "Then the rumors are true. I am so isolated from the corporate structure out here that it is very difficult to know what is true and what is rumor."

Will looked at him. "I won't keep anything from you. When Felina and I leave here, we are going to see James, and from what James told me yesterday, an announcement may be in order. If so, we will have a dinner meeting here tonight, and I will explain everything to you and Jake. Then you two can inform everyone else as you see fit. Do you have a wife?"

The maitre d' shook his head. "I am wedded to my profession."

Will then looked at Jake. "Do you have a wife?"

"Yes, sir, I do."

"Okay, if an announcement is in order, both of you are invited for dinner here tonight, and all five of us will talk. "

The maitre d' was very scared as he glanced at Jake and then looked squarely at Will. "We behaved badly today, sir…we would truly offer you our most profound apologies. However, at this point, I fear such apologies would be offensive to both you and your fiancée."

Then Felina looked at the maitre d'. "We would like a sunrise view with the large window, please."

The maitre d' bowed at the waist. "As you wish, my lady." Then he walked them to an extra large table with a gorgeous view of the sunrise. The window was made of a darker than average glass to keep the sun from being blinding yet did not detract from the sunrise.

Felina looked around at everything she could see. "Oh, Will. This is such a nice place. It will be our favorite, and I would like to come back soon."

The maitre d' quickly looked at Will and started to speak but Will put his left forefinger to his lips and the maitre d' smiled knowingly. Felina had no idea what was really going on, but Will had it all planned out, and it started with the sunrise and saying they were going to the Amanecer.

The maitre d' whispered to Will, "I am fully responsible for Jake's actions, and he was only doing what he was told, and he has a family to support." Will nodded in understanding and agreement. The maitre d' has heard fearful rumors for months now, each worse than the last. And after his ill advised earlier actions, he is certain that his career is over. But he is a professional and will do what he can. He has been under an enormous amount of stress and has been trying to do far more than any one man can do. And he now realizes that his supreme efforts to save his career may well have cost him his career.

Felina giggled and snuggled against Will for a brief moment and then moved away from him a foot or so. She made sure her actions were proper and polite.

Some time had passed since the maitre d' told them he would bring them an extensive menu. Will was looking at Felina when her mouth dropped open, her eyes got very big, and she drew in a breath with an audible sound. Will turned around, and what he saw made his own eyes grow to maximum size, and he also drew in a breath with an audible sound.

Will shook his head, twice. "What the…"

The maitre d' and Jake were pushing four food carts loaded with every menu item the Railyard has to offer.

The maitre d' bowed at the waist. "Since we did not take your order, we simply brought two of everything we have. Madam, please enjoy, and, sir, this is, of course, on the house."

Felina looked at the maitre d' with new respect, and she was starting to like the guy. "You did not apologize with words, but you have indeed apologized with actions and substance. I am very impressed, and I thank you."

Toward the end of breakfast, Felina motioned for Jake, and he quickly joined them, as did the maitre d'. But it was Jake that Felina looked at and spoke to. "Jake, there are some people a mile or so from here." Jake was nodding before she finished.

Jake smiled. "I will be glad to take care of it, ma'am. You have been very wealthy for a long time, yet you still think of the poor while you are in the midst of plenty. My deep respect to you, ma'am."

Felina shrugged. "We can't save the world, but we can give some of those close to us a good day."

"When you come here alone and if you have any problems with anyone, just call out for me and I will be there." Jake looked at Will. "I personally guarantee her safety, sir."

Felina laughed. "What if the problem is Will?"

Jake chuckled. "In that case, we will take him on together, ma'am."

Will was still puzzled. "What about the poor? What did you mean?"

Jake answered. "Your fiancée wants me to take the remaining food to some poor people who have no homes and little to eat."

Then Felina looked at each one of them eye to eye. "An hour ago, we were lucky to get a seat, and then we were fighting fist to fist. Then the three of you talked about rumors and secrets and having the same banker, and Jake made an early morning trip to see James. Then we get the best seat in the house, and we get four carts of food, on the house. Then Will says we might have a dinner meeting this evening. Who is Will to call a dinner meeting? Then we end up talking and respecting each other. Will someone please tell me what in the world is going on here? What could I have possibly missed that can explain all of this?"

The three men looked at each other, stammered and hesitated, and cleared their throats.

Then Jake looked at Will and spoke, "I have a suggestion, sir."

Felina blurted out, "Do you see what I mean? Jake has a suggestion, but who is he looking at?" Almost in frustration, Felina asked, "Why is Jake looking at Will, and why does this seem normal all of a sudden?"

Felina glared at Jake. "What happens when Will and you both are the problem?"

Jake nodded. "In such a case, we would have to check you for weapons."

Felina shook her head. "Don't try to change the subject. What is your suggestion?"

Jake glanced at Will who nodded quickly, and Jake answered, "Perhaps James is the person most able to explain the current situation."

"Oh? Is he going to check me for weapons?"

Jake chuckled. "He will if we can get in touch with him in time."

Felina then looked at Will. "Okay, boss. Now I am the one with a suggestion."

Will nodded. "Sure, what is it?"

"I suggest that you and I go see James right now with a delay factor of zero."

Libby Myers was sitting within three tables of them. She heard every word spoken and saw everything that happened. Miss Libby is the matron of society, and she is not there by coincidence.

Will and Felina went to the back door of the bank. Will knocked on the door, and James returned the knock.

James spoke low and asked, "How much do you want Felina to know?"

Will answered so she could hear, "I want her to know everything. She is the love of my life, and she is my fiancée."

James smiled. "Okay, you're the boss…"

Felina sighed. "Not you too. It seems like everywhere we go, Will is the boss. We went to the Railyard for breakfast, and it started out with a fistfight and ended up with Will as the boss. When I asked what in the world was going on, Jake suggested that perhaps you are the person most able to explain the current situation to me."

James nodded. "Perhaps, and it is very simple to explain. But first of all, I must check you for weapons.

Felina moved her forefinger back and forth in front of her and chuckled. "You've been talking to Jake, or the maitre d', but don't even think about it, bucko. It's time to acknowledge the corn."

James looked at Will. "Acknowledge the corn?"

Will nodded. "It means face the truth. I guess it's time to explain what's going on and to reveal all secrets."

James took a deep breath, looked at Felina, and shrugged. "Long version or short version?"

Felina was thoroughly enjoying this, and she has ached inside for years for a fraction of the attention and acceptance she has received in the last few hours. Felina has long had money, but Will has made her feel important and made her feel like she is somebody, somebody better than a lowly saloon girl. Within a week, Will is fulfilling her deepest and most secret desires.

Felina grinned like a child at Christmas. "Spill it, James, the long version."

Both men laughed, and James chuckled as he answered, "Okay. A few weeks ago, Will decided to stay in El Paso for a while, so he transferred some cash to my bank. He did not gloat or act superior because of his money, and he seemed to be just a nice guy who is rich. Realizing that Will had a lot more cash than he was transferring, I told him a corporation in St. Louis wanted to quick-sell the Railyard Restaurant and Lodging. I also told him this would be an excellent investment for someone who had the cash. Will asked me to contact the corporation on his behalf and see what happens. Fortunately, I know of their banker, and he knows of me, so it was agreed that if we could come to terms quite quickly, there would be no need for attorneys or complex negations, which would do little more than drive the price and cost up. I had a local attorney read the final terms and agreement on our behalf, and they had a secondary attorney, someone's brother-in-law I think, read the final terms and agreement on their behalf to make sure all was legal."

Felina scoffed. "Sounds to me like the corporation is going to be dissolved and someone in St. Louis is taking one last opportunity to pocket some cash. But then, I am just a helpless little girl."

James chuckled. "Will got some expert, competent advice in the person of Phebe, and she said the same thing you just said. However, after looking it over, she advised Will to grab it."

Felina grimaced and looked at Will. "May I ask a delicate question?"

Both men laughed, and James answered, "St. Louis is bearing the cost of my commission and fees. The El Paso side of this deal is for gratis."

Then Felina put the palm of her hand to her forehead. "Of course, how brilliant. St. Louis can't cheat you out of anything because you are transferring the money. But how did a restaurant get the name of Railyard. Isn't a Railyard for trains?"

James nodded. "Yes, normally the name or term Railyard is for trains, but the original name was the Grassland. Right after it was bought by St. Louis, an executive was here and overheard a patron make a comment to a bellhop that this place was as busy and complex as a Railyard. Well, the executive liked the term, and the Grassland was renamed the Railyard."

James put the telegrams, there were only four, on his desk in the order they were received. Felina picked up the last one, which was received this morning. So much meaning in just two words—*deposit confirmed*. Then James handed Will the signed paperwork inside of a nice leather case with straps.

James looked at Felina. "Will Travis is now the official owner of Railyard Restaurant and Lodging. And it is completely and totally free and clear."

Felina giggled and responded, "And here I thought he was just a poor boy picking cotton."

As they walked out the door, Will laughed. "You've been hanging around Phebe too long."

Will and Felina went back to the Railyard and told the maitre d' and Jake the dinner meeting was on schedule for 6:00 that evening, and everything would be explained and discussed. The maitre d' told Will there was a private room for meetings and he would set everything up in the meeting room. But in his mind, the maitre d' was already job searching, and he was hoping he still had a career somewhere.

Will and Felina looked around and then sat at a small table out of the way. It was difficult to believe everything that had happened in just one day. Then Felina remembered Will saying earlier it was a very special day. Now she understood what he meant.

Then Jake came up to their table and was very somber. "Sir, I understand the boss talked to you and took full responsibility for my actions, and he told you I have a family to support. Well, sir, I am not a child or a slave. I am responsible for my own actions, and I am a grown man, despite behaving so poorly. But whatever I did, I did as a man, not a child. So whatever fate the boss must face, I will share it with him as a man."

Will nodded and started to say something but Jake had to walk away to avoid becoming emotional, which Will well understood. They would talk again later.

Will and Felina talked for several hours and periodically would take a moment to look around at everything, still having a hard time digesting it all. Every now and then, they would notice people looking at them and were obviously talking about them.

Then they noticed it was getting very busy and there were a lot of people in the dining room even in the off hours. When Will asked the maitre d' about the number of people present, he responded that word was getting out that the Railyard has been sold, and many people were curious about the new owner.

At 6:00 p.m., everyone was sitting down in the private dining room and ready. Jake introduced his wife, Hannah. The maitre d' was fidgety for several reasons, not the least of which was someone else doing his job and making his decisions, even if only for the evening. But he did not even know if he still had a job.

Before anyone could speak, Felina held her hands up at shoulder height and looked at Will. "Boss, I really need to ask a question that has been bothering me all day long."

Everyone chuckled at her calling Will boss. "Certainly, you can ask more questions than you yet realize."

Felina shook her head. "I'll figure that one out later. But right now, I would ask the maitre d' a very simple question."

The maitre d' nodded. "Yes, ma'am?"

"What the heck is your first name? I have been here almost all day, and when I wasn't here, you still came up in many of the conversations. But not one person has called you or referred to you by name, just your well-earned title of maitre d'."

He smiled faintly. "I much prefer being called by what you graciously referred to as my well-earned title. And I thank you from the heart for that supreme compliment. But to answer your question, ma'am, my name is John...John Isaac Wilson. And I do thank you for asking."

Then Will casually asked Felina. "What do you think of John?"

"John has been under extreme stress about rumors he could not confirm and questions he could not answer and a future clouded in doubt. He has been under heavy stress and trying to make sense of ever-changing rumors about his very livelihood and his future and his career. Everything that he is, is now at stake here. He behaved errantly, but even his errant behavior was focused on his establishment, and this establishment is indeed part of John, so in a real way, it is and always will be his establishment. If we shoot everyone who makes a mistake, then who will fire the last shot?"

John chuckled, which was a rare thing.

Felina shrugged. "What is it?"

John smiled, which was also rare. "I know the answer to that question."

Felina laughed. "Okay, I will restate the question, and you answer it. If we shoot everyone who makes a mistake, then who will fire the last shot?"

John looked around at everyone. "The person who fires the last shot will be…the biggest liar."

Everyone laughed.

Felina looked at Will. "I like John, and I hope you keep him."

Will shrugged. "It's not up to me. It is your call. You are the real boss, not me."

Felina shook her head. "What are you talking about? I was there when you signed the papers. I saw the telegram that confirmed the bank deposit and that you are now the owner."

Will shook his head. "There was one document I signed that you did not see."

Felina shook her head smartly. "All of that can wait. Are you saying that it is up to me whether John keeps his job and his career?"

Will was very serious. "It is totally up to you."

Felina shrugged and gestured to John with her hand. "I've heard nothing but good about this man everywhere we go. James said we have the best maitre d' in the entire state of Texas. And I like him, and my instincts say he is a good man. So if it's up to me…"

Felina shocked everyone when she spit in her right hand and held her hand out to John. "Put her there, partner, you're in."

Tears were forming in John's eyes, and he had to spit twice to hit his right hand, and he quickly, but gently, clasped Felina's outstretched hand. "Count me in, boss."

Felina smiled at Jake's wife and became serious as she asked Will, "I would like your opinion of Jake."

Jake's wife had not dared to speak. She was almost trembling and so scared that Jake would lose his job and be tagged with a horrible job reference.

Will nodded. "Okay. Jake did two things that erased everything else."

Will then looked at Hannah and nodded. "You picked a good man, ma'am."

Will looked at Felina and kept his eyes on her. "After our disagreement, Jake stopped as he was leaving and looked back at us, and then he tipped his hat to you. That was the highest of all respect, and it was directed at you, and the meaning of that is hard to put into words. Then John told me that he was responsible for Jake's actions and that Jake was only doing what he was told. Then Jake came to me and told me that he was not a child or a slave. Jake took full responsibility for his own actions and then Jake told me that he would share his boss's fate."

As Will, Jake, and Hannah looked at one another, they heard Felina spit. Jake quickly returned the gesture and gently clasped her hand as she spoke, "Put her there, partner, you're in this too."

Then Will asked Felina, "Why don't you tell everyone what happened at the bank today so they will know what is going on?"

Felina told them everything that happened and everything that was done. She especially told them about the telegram confirming the bank deposit.

Then Will handed a document to John. In a few seconds, everyone saw John's eyes get big, and he lowered the document and looked at Will. "Are you serious?"

Will nodded. "As Felina would say, I'm as serious as a hangman's noose."

John handed the document to Jake and then Jake handed it to Hannah.

Hannah's eyes grew wide. "Does Felina have to sign this for it to be active?"

Both Will and John nodded to affirm.

Hannah got up clutching the document close to her and walked quickly around the table and put the document on the table in front of Felina. "Quick, sign it. Don't even look at it, just sign it."

Felina read it and was shocked, and it was the last thing on earth she expected. It was a document transferring ownership of the Railyard from Will to her, and Will has already signed it. Felina signed the document, and Hannah and John were the two witnesses required to make it legal. Felina is now the sole owner of the Railyard Restaurant and Lodging.

Speaking through tears, Felina spoke to Will, "I don't know how to thank you...I can't."

Will looked around at everyone. "That's okay, honey. Just don't cast me aside now that you are rich and famous."

Felina grinned mischievously. "Don't worry, my love, you will always be my favorite slave." Then she put her right hand on Hannah's shoulder and pointed at Jake. "You can have that one if you want."

Hannah laughed. "I will give him a fair chance and see what happens."

They all laughed heartily, and they all had so much to look forward to. And while the waning light of a magical day and a golden sunset still glowed, it got even better.

A short and portly gray-haired woman, obviously of means and social graces, stepped out from a small enclosure meant for the servants to await the preparation of food.

John, Jake, and Hannah immediately bolted from their chairs and stood up.

Although at a slower pace, Will and Felina stood up, and Will nodded and bowed from the waist in respect, while Felina executed an excellent curtsy.

John was incredulous. "Aunt Libby?"

By her normal standards, her entry was undignified. "I am Libby Myers, a widow, and some consider me the matron of El Paso higher society. I saw and heard everything that occurred this morning. I was informed the new owner was on premise, and I did indeed eavesdrop on your current dinner meeting. For the snooping and eavesdropping, I sincerely apologize from my heart. Normally, I am above such things, but John is family, and I will do everything in my limited power to help him. While there is little I can do directly, there is much I can do in certain indirect areas, such as societal influence."

Felina shook her head and held Miss Libby's hand with both of hers. "Forgive my manners, Miss Libby, and please honor us by taking a place with us. And you are most certainly invited to join our conversation, especially anything regarding John."

Miss Libby shook her head and did not take her eyes off Felina for a second. "I will join you, but I have already heard and seen all that I need to. With my own eyes, I have seen a fistfight grow into a gathering of near-family. I needed to see and hear the real things, not the different things you would say and do because of my presence. You have dealt most fairly and extended mercy to my nephew, and you did the same to Jake, who has been John's best friend since childhood. I heard the things you said to Hannah, and you set her in a high place with high regard. Instead of anger, you spit in your hand and offered that hand in friendship. As you have dealt with my family, my blood, so now will I deal with you and extend what fairness and mercy I am capable of. And I will now do all in my modest power to grant you one of your greatest desires."

With tears, Miss Libby looked around at everyone and spoke softly, "I would ask that no one say a word and we all maintain silence. It is not a rule of etiquette or any such thing. It is simply my way of things. Do we have a packed house, John?"

"Yes, ma'am, some are sitting, and many are standing, but all are waiting."

Miss Libby smiled broadly. "Good, then let us give them something to talk about for a while."

She locked arms with Felina, and they led the others as they walked into the restaurant from the private room.

The silence in the restaurant was total...and nearly instant.

They stood in the most visible location in the restaurant, and Miss Libby stood at length, locked arm and arm with Felina. Many, if not most, of the patrons recognized Felina and knew who she was. But with Miss Libby standing in a highly visible restaurant with arms locked, it no longer mattered who Felina *was*; it was now who she *is*.

Miss Libby took a few steps back from Felina and looked around at everyone. "I have seen the legal paperwork with my own eyes, and it is truly my honor to introduce you to the new owner of Railyard Restaurant and Lodging. Congratulations, Felina."

Then she gestured toward Felina with her hand and applauded Felina.

With gloved hands, she applauded with the highest regard by tapping the palm of her left hand with the fingers of her right hand. It was a quiet applause, but it was life changing. Those who sat, stood up, and those who were already standing stood up straighter, but all gave Felina a standing ovation.

With the applause still ringing in Felina's ears, Miss Libby stepped up and hugged Felina for a long moment, and the applause increased.

Felina has attained her greatest desire. She was not merely tolerated or treated with politeness; she was welcomed, and most of all, she was accepted.

FELINA IS WITH CHILD

1858

Will woke up, or more accurately, recovered from his coma of sheer exhaustion. Yesterday was a day unlike any other in his life, except the day he blundered into his wealth. Will had to fight for clarity, and it was not an easy battle. The darkened room was confusing for many seconds rather than a few. But he could see well enough to light the lantern. He realized the bed was empty and the room was quiet. As he looked around for Felina, he saw a note pinned to the door.

I have gone to work. Come on over, breakfast is on the house.

Will thought, *What?* Still clumsy with sleep, Will fumbled for his watch. *She's already gone to work at 5:00 a.m.?* Then with a wave of remembrance, Will smiled and spoke aloud, "Oh yeah, I give her an entire restaurant, and I get breakfast on the house. I'm going over there and demand a do-over."

Will decided to walk, but he was halfway to the Railyard before all of his brain parts were roped together.

When he walked in the doorway of the Railyard, Will was struck by the brightness of the lights and the beehive of activity, which was in stark contrast to the dark, quiet room he left just minutes ago.

Felina and John were discussing a list of things she needed to know and things for her to learn. Then Felina asked him, "Do you stay in the same room or do you change rooms periodically?"

John was stunned. "No, ma'am. We would lose our jobs if we stayed here without paying."

Felina wasn't sure if he was serious or joking. "What? How many rooms do we have?"

John decided to answer more than she asked, "We have four floors. On the first floor is the restaurant, gift shop, entry and desk area, main office, and several utility closets. And we have sixty-three rooms on the top three floors, with twenty-one rooms on each floor. We have three different size rooms: queen's room, king's room and crown suites. The queen's room accommodates two or three persons comfortably, the king's room accommodates at least five, and the crown suites are more for luxury than number of persons but would easily accommodate perhaps eight persons."

It was obvious that Felina was working something out in her mind. "Thank you for the extended answer, but how often are all of the rooms taken at the same time?"

John shook his head. "It is very rare. We reach a peak of between fifty to fifty-five rooms several times a year. But the only times we have filled all sixty-three rooms was for infamous hangings or special fraternity meetings, political conventions, and such."

Felina nodded. "Okay, how often do we fill all of the rooms?"

John thought for a moment. "I can check the records and give you a more accurate answer, but we fill all of the rooms about once every five or six years."

"Was there a reserved corporate room?"

"No, ma'am, no one from corporate ever came out here after the inspection tour when they bought it. They inspected it, bought it, and renamed it from the Grassland to the Railyard, and that is all we have seen of any corporate entities. And that was over ten years ago."

Felina nodded. "From now on, we have sixty rooms with a couple of rooms reserved."

John did not understand. "Sixty rooms from now on? Reserved rooms?"

"Yes, sixty rooms. Will and I get first choice, then you, and then Jake and Hannah. The reserved rooms are for visiting family and guests. Would you like a room to live in?"

John was amazed. "Yes, I certainly would. We have not had a salary increase in five years. But besides everything else, our plumbing was upgraded six months ago, and we now have what is called Plunger Closets, which is a type of indoor plumbing invented back in 1777 by Samuel Prosser. Indoor plumbing is currently the rage in Europe, especially the British. The Railyard is one the very few establishments with this feature. It is so much cleaner and more sanitary than the Earth Closets. We were astonished at how much better the entire area smelled. My point being that in no other way could I otherwise live in such a modern environment."

Felina nodded. "Thank you for the information on our modern advanced plumbing. I did not know about that. But about the salaries, I know we make a good profit, so we will look into salary increases right away."

"Thank you, ma'am, and thank you ever so much for multiple reasons."

In the ensuing weeks, Felina quickly brought everyone's salary up to scale according to trade standards, their experience, and individual efforts. John was indeed wearing too many hats but with wages brought up to scale, much of what he was doing was delegated. Jake became head of security. One troubling thing was that Felina still visited Rosa's Cantina quite often. On the outside, Will smiled and stated he hoped she would soon stop going there. On the inside, he was coming to an emotional boil.

When she went back to the Cantina, Will wondered if she was being drawn back to stay.

Will stayed in the background watching Felina ask questions and make decisions like an experienced professional. He was so proud of her. But one man kept looking at Felina and smiled. He would look away and hang his head, but he always looked back at Felina. Will quickly grew intense, and anger narrowed his vision.

Finally, Will walked over to the man, picked up a chair, and turned it backward and sat down glaring at him. The man looked at Will and smiled as if they were long acquainted friends.

"Excuse me, sir, but the woman you keep ogling at is my fiancée, and it would be a real good idea if you stopped staring at her."

"I am not staring or ogling, sir, and I mean no disrespect."

Will scoffed. "By my reckoning, you are doing both. Now I am not asking you…"

The man ignored Will's remarks and threat. He seemed all the world to be a man with no fear of death. He again looked at Felina and then looked back at Will and smiled with hollowness. "I lost my Sarah to cholera."

Will looked at him suspiciously. "Sarah?"

Again, the man looked at Felina, and Will then grabbed him by the throat. "I said I am not asking. I am telling you to get out of here right now." Then Will spoke low but with the threat of death. "If you have a gun, then maybe you should pull it."

"I carry no gun, but your lady looks so much like my Sarah. Your lady even moves and walks like Sarah. But she can't be Sarah. I lost my Sarah to cholera six months ago." The man looked at Will with gaunt eyes and hopelessness in his flat, emotionless voice. "My Sarah died, and she's not here anymore. I miss her something terrible, but she died, and she's gone." Then in a whisper, he said, "She left me."

Will instantly let go of the man and looked around. Somehow, what had just transpired went unseen and unheard. Also unknown is that Will had his hand on his gun, and the thought crossed his mind to pull it.

Will asked himself what was wrong with him. He has never acted like this in his life. Why is he acting like this now? Why is he feeling this way now? Not all witches are ugly, some are beautiful. A fleeting thought crossed Will's mind that Felina must be casting a spell on him. Was she taking control of his heart and his mind? Since he has never acted this way or felt this way before, it must be something Felina is doing to him. It did not occur to Will, nor would he accept, that he has never been in love before, and he has never cared so much about a woman before. And the power of his love inadvertently fed and unleashed an internal demon.

Will went to Felina and asked that the grieving widower not to be charged.

Felina smiled at Will with love, and she thought him a hero. She had no idea of what really happened and, more especially, what *almost* happened. Will came within a whisker of beating the man senseless. Also unknown to Felina is that Will has been overwhelmed by his jealousy more times than she knew, and on a few occasions, he has pulled his gun. In addition, the jealousy-fueled events are occurring more frequently and becoming increasingly violent. But instinctively, Felina's fear of Will's jealousy is growing stronger, and she knows something is very wrong.

But Felina holds fast to a false hope. With all their money, accomplishments, and paying cash for a modern major establishment, all they have to do is try harder, and everything will work out.

Will is in the woods, and he is being attacked by a vicious, wild animal. He tries to fight it off, but the attacking animal is too fierce. He tries to run, but the animal is all over him, and he cannot escape. Then he hears sounds of anger from the animal. Mercifully, he wakes up and realizes it is only a dream. Unmercifully, the wild animal is Felina, who is hitting and flailing on him as hard as she can. She is cursing him up one side and down the other in Spanish, which he cannot understand.

"Felina, wake up. You're having a nightmare. It's me, honey, it's Will."

"I know who the hell you are, and this ain't a dream. I am doing everything in my power to beat you to death, so get ready to meet your maker."

"Honey, what are you doing and saying? I love you, and what can I do?"

"Forget it, *honey*, you've already done enough, and if I'm going to suffer, then so are you."

"What's wrong? This doesn't make any sense. What have I done?"

"I am with child, and I am very, very sick with child. I just threw up everything I had, and then I heaved for an hour with nothing to throw up. I hate you, Will Travis, and I am going to make sure you know it."

Will shouted out, "We are going to have a baby? How wonderful is that?" Then he reached for her to hold her.

"Don't even try to touch me, Will Travis."

"But it doesn't matter if I touch you now. It's already too late."

"Look outside, Will Travis, quick, look outside."

Will rushed to the window and looked outside expecting to see some kind of commotion, but while all was peaceful outside, it was not so inside. "Everything is fine. What am I looking for?"

"The daylight, Mr. Travis, you are looking for the daylight."

"Okay, I see the daylight. Now what?"

"It is the last daylight you are ever going to see…I am going to strangle you, Will Travis, and it won't be quick, painless, or merciful."

Then Felina ran back to the Plunger Closet to throw up some more. Then Will said the right thing, but he said it at the wrong time.

"I sure am glad we have that new indoor plumbing. What did you call it, Plunger Closet?"

A glass came flying out of the closet that missed his head by a foot and smashed against the wall.

"Do you want me to leave you alone for a while?"

Felina said something, but it was too garbled to understand, but it was not nice or encouraging.

Felina heaved and then spoke sharply, "Don't even think about trying to leave this room or I will hunt you down and shoot you where I find you."

"I honestly thought you might want me to leave for a while."

She heaved again, and as soon as she could breathe, Felina shouted, "If you leave, I can't make your life is as miserable as mine."

Then Will got all excited and spoke as he opened the door to leave. "Honey, I have to go downstairs and tell everybody. This is big news."

"Don't you dare tell anyone. Since I get the misery, I get to tell them."

"Okay, then I will tell everyone that you have a big announcement to make."

"Don't you dare tell..."

She heard the door close, and she finished what she was saying in a whisper. "...Anyone to come up here."

Within minutes came the dreaded knock. But when Felina realized it was Hannah, she actually felt better and opened the door.

As soon as Hannah cleared the door, she rubbed Felina's tummy for good luck.

Felina looked at her and sighed. "I am actually glad to see you, Hannah."

"Well, Will is downstairs all puffed up like a bantam rooster, and he's glowing like a brand-new gaslight, and he says that you are as sick as a dog. The only thing on earth that fits that combination is a baby."

"Why did you rub my tummy?"

Hannah was regretful. "I'm sorry. You don't know the old custom that it brings good luck to rub the tummy of an expectant mother?"

Felina shook her head. "No, I've never heard that."

Then Felina laughed. "My mother had six children, and I never heard of that custom. Just think of all the good luck I missed."

Hannah shook her head. "I think any good luck you missed has caught up with you, with room to spare. You are blessed, Felina. You are truly blessed among women."

Felina hugged Hannah. "Thank you for saying that, because I still have doubts and concerns that will not allow me to *feel* blessed among women."

"If I may say something?"

"Certainly."

"It is not what we feel. It is what we have that makes us blessed. What we feel can be wrong, but what we have speaks for itself. That is why I say you are blessed among us all. And know this, Felina, I ache inside to have the wonderful future that you have. You are so young and so beautiful, you are wealthy and you own the Railyard. Not to mention your man. You have got it all, Felina, you have got it all."

Felina started to say something, but Hannah put her hands to the sides of her head and mildly shrieked. "Oh no, I almost forgot the most important thing by far. You must, you *must* tell Miss Libby in person, and if I know the people around here as well as I think I do, then you've got about thirty minutes to be the first to tell her."

Felina sat up straight. "You're right. I must be the first to tell her. Please get the buggy ready while I make myself halfway presentable."

Felina hurried to get herself ready, and Hannah had Jake get the buggy. Both were ready to go at about the same time. Felina asked Hannah to join her to see Miss Libby, but Hannah said she and Jake would drop Felina off at Miss Libby's, but it was too personal for them to join her and that Felina should go in alone. Miss Libby will get Felina back home.

Felina did not have to be told that it was a great honor to be received by Miss Libby in her bathrobe. But as soon as Miss Libby saw Felina, she gasped. "You look a fright, my dear. Please sit and comfort yourself. Any time you are in this home, feel free to relax and let any stress or worries dissolve into nothing."

Miss Libby gestured for her manservant, Andrew, to get a footstool for Felina, but being observant he was already getting one. Andrew also poured a bowl of water and brought a cloth for Felina's forehead. There are women in the fair city of El Paso who would kill to be in such a setting with Miss Libby. However, Miss Libby would kill *not* to be in such a setting with them.

Miss Libby made a fuss, and she felt of Felina's face and looked at her eyes and checked Felina over. "Tell me, my dear. Are you here to tell me you are with child?"

Felina shook her head. "Oh God, how could anyone have told your first? I am so sick in the mornings, but I had to rush over and tell you myself. Who could have beaten me here?"

Miss Libby shook her head. "No one beat you here, my dear, nor would I have received such news from anyone except yourself. But tell me, and I do not wish to tax you, but what is one plus one?"

Miss Libby's question did not make sense, but Felina did not care. "One plus one equals two."

Miss Libby shook her head. "If one plus one equals two, then you would not be so ill. Actually, one plus one equals three, and that is why you are ill and why you are here."

"Sick or well, I do not understand how that is possible?"

"It is simple, my dear. Will plus Felina equals Will plus Felina plus baby. One plus one equals three. You can count on it."

Felina laughed and felt so much better. "No wonder I love you so much, Miss Libby. I feel better already. I always feel better around you."

"Trust me, little one, words like those do not flow in my direction very often. You are with child. You have climbed from the bottom of an earthen closet to the peak of the housetop, yet this is truly your greatest gift and your greatest achievement. I refused to have children because I did not have the time or inclination…until it was too late. Take heed, little one, it is my biggest regret in life. Perhaps you can be the daughter I never had."

Felina's smile was warm. "Part of me already feels that way. I don't know why, but I really do. It's almost natural, and I feel better when I am around you. But you might not want anything to do with me if you knew of the things I've done. It's true that I have a lot of money, but money doesn't clean a dirty soul, and I didn't waste any time making mine dirty. Miss Libby, I don't even know if my parents are alive or dead because I simply cannot face them. I feel like I would defile their home just by my presence. They live in a shack with dirt floors, but I feel like I would make it unclean with my footprints. I would build them a mansion, but they are proud and would not accept it, nor would they accept any money. I wonder about them, and I still love them, but I know in my heart that if I went to them, I would bring them nothing but grief."

Miss Libby shook her head and spoke softly. "No, you would not bring them grief. You would bring them news and the unspeakable joy of a grandchild. You would not bring them grief, little one, for they already grieve for you from not knowing where you are or what you are doing. You see, my dear, if you do not know if they are alive or dead, then they do not know if you are."

Felina stood up, and Miss Libby held her tight and cried with her. "You cannot know the emptiness and the unspeakable pain in their hearts from carrying the horrible doubts of not knowing where you are and if you are safe. They cannot express the sorrow of not knowing. Please go to them, little one, go to them while you have the most perfect reason to contact them with the greatest news you could give them…the news that you are alive and well and the news of an impending birth of their grandchild. Please, little one, do not do as I did, and do not create a lifelong regret that eats at your heart like an incurable disease. It is a pain that no doctor can remove. Do not let your heart die while your body still lives. Compared to me, little one, your soul can be no more than smudged. It is my soul that has achieved total darkness. Go to them, and we will talk more when you get back."

"Will you go with me to see my family?"

"No, my dear, this is your journey, not mine. This is a journey for the sake of your heart and for theirs. But we will talk again when you return."

"Do you promise?"

"Yes, I promise at the risk of my own blood."

"Then I will go to them, for I treasure your words…Mama."

Miss Libby felt a glow that she did not know existed. She saw fire in Felina's eyes, a fire that once burned so bright behind her own eyes.

Felina kept the private words locked in her heart, but she told Will that Miss Libby advised her to make contact with her family and tell them she is alive and well and for her to go to them and give them the good news of the baby. "I will be gone for two weeks."

Even Will feared the wrath of Miss Libby Myers. However, Will insisted that Jake and Hannah accompany her, Hannah for company and Jake for security. John was not really happy with this, so he insisted that Will stay behind to take up some slack. Will intended to stay behind anyway so the focus of the reunion would remain on Felina. But suddenly two weeks seemed like a very long time.

But first, Felina had to make sure they were alive and well, and then she had to find out if she was still welcome.

As they began preparations for the journey, Felina sent a telegram to her family, and she paid for their response in advance.

Is everything and everyone alive and well?

Two days later, Felina received a response.

Yes, we are all well. We ache to see you, come home, Felina.

Felina sent another telegram and again paid for a twenty-word response in advance.

Can you endure the presence of a lost one you once loved who is no longer fit to be permitted into your home?

Felina waited for confirmation that the message was received, which came quickly. Then as she was turning to leave, the telegraph clicked rapidly. A few seconds later, the telegraph operator asked her to wait a moment.

"What?"

"Ma'am, the operator who sent this to us just signaled me that your message is already being responded to. There will be an answer very quickly."

"How can that be?"

"The only way for that to happen is if someone sent the telegram and then waited for your response."

Within minutes, the operator chuckled. "There is no way this is bad news. It has to be good." Then in a bit of good humor and drama, he folded the telegram twice before handing it to Felina.

She looked at him with mild irritation for having to unfold the telegram before she could read it. Why did he fold it? But when she opened it, all else was forgotten. The telegram was a single word repeated twenty times, and that single word was…yes.

Felina cried all the way back to the Railyard where she pulled Will aside and grabbed on to him and held him as she cried as softly as she could. "They still love me, Will." Then she showed him both telegrams.

Will rubbed her silky, black hair with his right hand, and his voice was just as soft. "Does your family want you to come back home?"

"Oh, I'm sure they do. But, Will, my family is in New Mexico Territory, but my life is here in El Paso with you. When I ran away from home, I was a very unaware, naïve, young girl, but now I know that my life is with you, and wherever you and I are, that is where home is. Even if home is just you and me lighting a campfire somewhere on a trail. I may never get over the nightmares, Will, but I will never let go of our dreams either, nor will I let go of you."

Once again, Felina went back to Rosa's Cantina. She told everyone the news, and they all rubbed her tummy. There were hugs and congratulations, but the hugs were becoming more polite and formal. Rosa and the girls noticed that when Felina comes to the Cantina now, she no longer dresses, or acts, like one of them. They can see and feel a difference in her, and there were unmistakable changes even in the way she walked and how she talked. They knew it was only a matter of time, and they will never see her again, at least not in the Cantina. It is clear that Felina was no longer a saloon girl; she has reached the big time, but Felina is and always will be a welcomed guest. And while in Rosa's Cantina, she was still a sister. But all of them knew in their hearts that Felina does not yet realize how much she has changed.

Will stood with Felina beside the stagecoach as Jake and Hannah climbed in from the other side.

The driver was polite but firm. "Sorry, folks, but we are running an hour late, and we need to pull foot. We will load your luggage and leave in about five minutes." The driver and the shotgun quickly loaded the luggage and some gear for the stagecoach, such as leather straps, bridles, harness fittings, and grease for the wheels.

Will sighed and bit his lower lip. "I never realized or understood this before, but for the first time in my life, I feel loved. This may sound crazy, but your love has made me realize that I've never been loved before. I guess you have to experience real love before you can understand that you've never had it."

Felina reached up and kissed him modestly. Then she held him while the stagecoach hands finished loading the luggage. Jake and Hannah were seated and ready to go, and as they watched Will and Felina, both were secretly glad they did not have to be apart for two weeks.

Will thought for a moment and added, "There are things about your past that trouble me deeply, some of it I can't even discuss yet, but I will never let go of you either, my love. I know we've only been together a few months now, but I don't care how soon it's been or how quick things have happened. It's real, and it is there for us."

Will hugged her. "Okay, I guess I'm getting a little mushy because I will miss you a lot in the next two weeks. In fact, I already miss you. And I'm a little concerned about your family talking you into going back home.

Felina smiled. "They couldn't do that before I met you. It sure isn't going to happen now."

One minute Will was standing there talking to her, and the next minute she was riding off in a large cloud of dust. The cloud of dust was visible long after the stagecoach was out of sight. And Jake was already doing his job. Jake knew that by far the best seat inside of a stagecoach is under the shotgun position. It takes a bit of getting used to because riding backward sometimes produces feelings not unlike mild seasickness. But the seat is more restful as it has less than half of the bumps and jars the other seats have.

To be honest, Jake intended to give the best seat to Hannah, but Hannah also knew which seat is the best, and she figured Felina needed all of the rest she could get. The journey was over three hundred miles and would take three days, plus Felina is with child. Felina has not told her family what the important news is; she has only told them that she brings news so important that it is life changing. Jake is looking off into the distance and has suddenly become somber.

Hannah was concerned. "What's wrong, Jake?"

Jake took a deep hesitant breath. "There are a couple of things I need to explain just in case things go wrong. There are some things you need to know so you will understand what is happening. The first thing is easy to explain. I cannot guarantee that you will make it back home safe and sound. It doesn't work like that. But what I can guarantee you is that if you don't, then you will watch me die first. I will protect the two of you with my life, and that is my guarantee. And you can depend on that. I—"

Felina interjected, "Jake, you should hear Will talk about you. The way he talks, we are safe from the devil himself with you around. Will said that you made a rookie mistake and you made a young man's mistake. But Will says he would bet his life that you will never make that mistake again for the rest of your life. And

Will said that you learned from your mistakes and you are now at least ten times meaner than you were."

Hannah shook her head. "That's a compliment?"

Jake grinned. "It sure is."

Felina continued, "And Will also said there are only two other men in the whole world he would trust with guarding us, but both of them are dead. I think Will looks at you as a little brother or something."

Jake got quiet. "Now that is a supreme compliment."

Felina asked, "What was the other thing you want to explain?"

"Something I don't want either of you to see, but I really need you to know and understand that if things go downhill, I might have to get mean and very ugly. Perhaps even turn animal."

Felina looked over at Hannah with an unspoken question and Hannah shrugged. "I've never seen this."

Jake held his hands up and slowly let them down. "I hope you never see it. It's not pretty. But there are no Indians or bandits active in this area, and no one is looking for us. Everything should go well. But I just want you to know up front that any and all meanness I display is not directed in any way *at* you, but *for* you, and for your protection. And we do have to remember that New Mexico is a territory, not a state."

Felina looked at Jake. "Now that you put it that way, we need you well rested. Perhaps you should take my seat."

Jake shook his head and laughed. "A few minutes ago, you said something about Will thinking of me as a little brother. Well, if I took your seat, I'm pretty sure I would very quickly become an illegitimate brother."

Some barbarian was knocking on her door, and Miss Libby was outraged. No one she knew would dare knock on her door like they were using a meat ax. She had half a mind to answer the door with a gun. *After all, if we are not going to be civilized, then let there be blood to attest to it.*

Andrew walked briskly toward the door, but Miss Libby waved him off. "I will answer this one, Andrew."

Miss Libby opened the door smartly and was stunned. It was Will with his hat in his hand.

Will was obviously nervous. "Could I possibly speak to you for a few minutes?"

She shook her head gently as if to clear her mind of what she saw. "Of course I will talk to you. However, there is one condition."

Will shrugged. "Name it."

Miss Libby looked behind her. "Andrew?"

"Understood, Mum."

Andrew stepped through the doorway and stood beside Will, and she closed the door.

She heard Andrew's flawless knock on the door, followed by voices, and then another knock, an all-too-flawed knock. She shouted the word no, which was followed by another flawless knock and then voices of instructions and then a raw but acceptable knock. Miss Libby opened the door and said for Will to do it again to prove it was not an accident.

Then came half a dozen knocks from Will, and each successive knock was better than his last.

Miss Libby opened the door and smiled. "Welcome to my home."

For some inexplicable reason, he felt good about his accomplishment and Miss Libby's approval. But she had a way about her that made one feel that they needed her approval.

Will smiled. "I can now knock, in a civilized fashion, on any door in this city. Was that the one condition?"

Miss Libby looked up at him. "It was."

"Miss Libby, you are greatly respected and admired, not only in El Paso but in all of Texas."

Miss Libby was taken back. Will is fast becoming respected and admired himself. And everyone knows that he just laid out a huge amount of cash for an almost incomprehensible gift to his fiancée.

And most of all, according to no less than James, Will is none the poorer for it. In fact, Will got such a deal on the Railyard that it actually increased his wealth to buy it. Of course he gave it to Felina, but everyone reckons they will be combining their wealth soon enough.

Miss Libby looked at Andrew. "Andrew, we will receive our guest in the main sitting room, please."

Andrew stilled for a split second. "The main sitting room?" Andrew looked over at Will. "Perhaps you should show *me* how to knock on a door properly." Andrew shook his head and echoed, "The main sitting room?"

As they walked into the sitting room, Will looked around in wonder. It seemed that Miss Libby may have achieved perfection. The room was beautiful but not ornate. The couch and matching chairs were blue silk with patterns made of gold thread. The full width curtains contained matching patterns of near perfection although the curtains and couch were made centuries apart. The Persian rug blended into the walls, and the entire room centered on a pair of matched Roman vases that were two thousand years old. Nothing in the room was created within the same century, yet all looked so well matched it was as if all were created by the same craftsman on the same day.

Will looked around the room at length and then nodded and bowed to Miss Libby. "This room carries a powerful message if one but can read."

She smiled and nodded approval. "Will, what is the message that you read from this room?"

Will looked back and forth from Miss Libby to the room as he answered, "The finest things in life and our greatest achievements cannot be bought. They must be created. This room is created out of willpower and sheer determination, and it cannot be duplicated at any price."

"I am impressed, Will. Did you say you wanted to talk to me?"

Andrew looked down and shook his head and thought to himself, "*First, the main sitting room and then she calls Mr. Will by his first name. That man is halfway to heaven, and he's still alive.*"

Will was hesitant but determined. "Well, Miss Libby, it's about Felina and about—"

Miss Libby interjected. "It's about the things you imagine she has done with so many other men. You envision so many things she has done so many times and in so many ways with so many men. "

"Yes, ma'am, Felina has an awful lot of money, and there is only one way she could have earned it."

Miss Libby shook her head insistently. "No, my young man. Felina had three different sources of income. What I am about to tell you must remain unspoken outside of my front door. And for me to continue, what I am about to say must remain within these walls until the crack of doom."

Will understood and nodded. "I swear it, Miss Libby, I swear that I will take what you are about to say to my grave, and it will remain unspoken."

She looked at him firmly. "What I know about this I learned from a queen, I learned from Miss Phebe. Felina and I like the crowds and the noise and the attention, but Phebe likes to remain quite in the background. Phebe and I have spoken much more than is known."

Will asked, "Did you say Felina had three sources of income?"

Miss Libby sighed. "Will, if you cut all of your evil doubts and the thing you envision she did in half, it would still be more than there really was. Yes, she had three incomes. First was her normal income, then an income from investments that Phebe handled, and she is a genius at investments by the way, she even handles a significant portion of my money, and I am doing well. The third income was from what they call bonuses, which are things like charging patrons for services they were too drunk to do—double charging those too drunk to count, money dropped on the floor, and such things. Any more than this should come from Felina, but I want you to know that it was not as bad or as much as you fear. But this life was far worse than you can ever imagine for Felina. And there is something else that you *must* know and understand."

"Yes, ma'am?"

"In order to endure her life and to survive her experiences, she had to develop an outer personality, which she presented to her patrons and to others. This preserved her inner personality and kept her true self intact. Above all others, Felina has allowed you past her protective outer personality, and she has shown you her innermost heart and soul. In doing this, she has made herself so very vulnerable to you, and she has given you the power to love her...or to destroy her."

Will nodded. "Yes, but still there are visions of things I cannot get out of my mind no matter how hard I try."

Miss Libby became very concerned. "Do you see these visions with your eyes?"

Will chuckled. "Oh no, nothing like that. I envision them within my mind."

"I will think of this, and we can talk again if you wish."

"Yes, ma'am, I would like that very much."

"But I can tell you one thing for certain right now."

"Please do."

"Many of us, both men and women, who have attained and achieved our greatest desires, have much to regret. I will tell you a truth, Will, many of us are, in fact, saloon girls...or worse. Because saloon girls do not hunt you down like a predator and destroy your life."

Miss Libby had to stop for a moment, and then she asked Will, "Do you remember what you said a few minutes ago about this room?"

"Do you mean when I said the finest things in life and our greatest achievements cannot be bought, they must be created? And when I said this room is created out of willpower and sheer determination, and it cannot be duplicated at any price?"

"Yes, that is exactly what I meant. Now take those precious words, Will Travis, and apply them to you and Felina, to your life together, and to your marriage. Those are such precious words, Will. Now apply them not to this room but to Felina, and if you live them, you cannot go wrong. That is the greatest thing I can possibly say to you. But when it is right, we will speak again of such matters."

"Yes, ma'am, we will. And if you ever need us or need anything, just let us know."

Miss Libby had tears in her eyes and could not speak. Will stood up and hugged her, and then he left her in peace. And he left her to ponder words that she could speak so easily, yet they are words she could not live by or apply to her own life.

Felina's whole family was waiting for the stagecoach when it arrived. It was a happy reunion with a lot of tears and hugs. Jake could speak Spanish, but Hannah could not, so Jake translated the conversations for her. A rented buggy was waiting for them. Jake and Hannah were invited to join the family in the family wagon, while Felina, Papa, Mama, and Miguel rode in the buggy. Papa drove the buggy and Jake drove the family wagon.

Then Mama chastised Felina. "What is this nonsense about you not being fit to be in your own home? No matter where you claim to live, this is always your home, and you are always welcome here. You were born in this home."

Felina decided to be honest and forward with them right up front. "I was a saloon girl, Mama. For over two years, I was a saloon girl."

Papa frowned. "You were a saloon girl, and all that it means?"

"Yes, Papa, and all that it means."

Papa looked at Felina sternly. "Do you think that matters to us? Do you think that makes you unfit for your own home and not welcomed? Felina, do not ever think such foolish thoughts again. Living in the big city made you forget who you are, and mostly, you forgot who we are. Never again are you to forget who your family is and how much we love you, no matter what. Besides, Felina, look at your clothes and the buggy you rented. When was the last time you went hungry or the last time you were thrown out into the streets?"

"I have not done without food nor have I been without a roof over my head. When it comes to that, I have not been without nor have I been scarce."

Then Miguel spoke up, "Do you see, my sister? So many people go hungry and so many people have no roof, yet you took care of yourself and provided what you needed. So how can you not be welcome by your own blood?"

Then Mama spoke, "Okay, Felina, what is this life-changing news you have for us. Do you have a man?"

Felina giggled. "Yes, Mama, I have a man, and he is my fiancé, but we have not set a date, although he has given me a spectacular wedding gift."

Mama said, "Never mind that, what is the surprise? Is it what I hope it is?"

Felina was glowing inside and out. "I am with child, Mama, and I carry the first grandchild for you and Papa."

Mama clapped her hands and cried for joy. "Did you hear that, Papa? A grandchild and I hope the first one is a grandson so he will grow up and be like you. Oh, Papa, this is a happy day."

Papa had to fight back the tears to talk. "Yes, it is a happy day, and I too hope the first is a grandson. Felina, you will have to stay here until you have our baby, and then you can go home and leave him with us."

Felina laughed. Her family makes her so happy, and she was so afraid they would reject her. "I don't think Will, my fiancé, would like that. He might grumble a bit and come up here looking for his son."

Papa smiled. "Can I take him out behind the barn and thrash him?"

Felina shook her head. "No, Papa, he's too big and mean."

Papa looked at Felina and asked, "What is this spectacular wedding gift he bought you?"

Felina was almost embarrassed. "He bought me a four-story restaurant with three floors of rooms to rent. It's called the Railyard Restaurant and Lodging."

Papa slowly shook his head. "It has been long ago, but I have been in El Paso many times, but I have never heard of a place called the Railyard."

Then Felina asked, "Have you ever heard of the Grassland?"

Papa looked at her sharply. "The one with the marble floors, textured ceilings, brass beds and very expensive furniture, imported rugs, and rooms that cost a month's salary?

"Yes, Papa, that's the—"

Papa interjected, "The Grassland is a temple of decadence and evil. Stay far away from it, my darling daughter. Do not so much as leave a footprint on any part of it."

Felina giggled. "But, Papa, they changed the name from Grassland to the Railyard, and I own it, free and clear."

Papa stopped the buggy. "You own the Grassland, or whatever it is called now, free and clear?"

"Yes, I do, Papa, my fiancé paid cash for it, and then he gave it to me for a wedding present."

Papa acted as if he had said nothing, "As I said, it is a temple of splendor and beauty and a good place for a family to stay, as long as it's a wealthy family...a very wealthy family."

Papa lightly strapped the horse to get back on the road. Then he shook his head in disbelief. "One of us is dangerously close to becoming one of those people I have complained about for so many years."

Felina did not understand. "What kind of people do you mean, Papa?"

Papa let out a long sigh. "People with a lot more money than sense. I've always complained about them because I never thought for a moment that one of us would ever be one of them."

Miguel half spoke and half blurted, "Now we can get rid of the land baron who's after our land."

Jake was riding close to them and instantly responded, "Now that sounded interesting. Do we have a problem, Papa? My first priority and my main job is to protect the women, and the very next thing on the list after that is to solve problems. If you have a problem, Papa, I am here to solve it." Then he glanced at Felina and Hannah and then looked back at Papa. "And I'm a lot meaner than I used to be."

Mama crossed herself. "Mother of God, our prayers are being answered in our desperate hour. The one we feared lost has returned at the moment of our greatest hour of need."

Papa looked at Felina. "I have been told that the land baron knows of *something* that is going to happen that will increase the value of our land ten times more than it is now. So he is trying to take all of our land and everybody else's too. He has so much, Felina. He has many thousands of acres, but we have a meager five hundred acres. Yet he will fight to take what little we have away from us. I want to fight, my little one, but I have nothing to fight with."

Jake scoffed but was respectful. "You do now, Papa. You have a lot to fight with now."

Felina's chuckle was ominous. "Papa, did you not say yourself that this is my home too? Then I will defend our home against those who make themselves our enemies with all that I have to fight with. From the last drop of blood to the last penny I have, I will fight. And those who are with me are worthy of fear. Papa, you have done your part, you have resisted and kept our home long enough for us to get here. Now we will carry the torch and finish this fight."

Jake smiled and looked over at papa. "I like your family, sir. Can my Hannah and me be a part of it?"

Out of the corner of his eye, Papa could see Felina nod. "Jake, I bid you and your lady, Hannah, a welcome part of a family that is in need. You do us honor by joining us."

All of a sudden, Jake's, Hannah's, and Felina's eyes all lit up with the same thought at the same time. And as if with one voice they spoke the same word at the same time, "Railroad."

Felina spoke quickly and excitedly, "Papa, the railroad must be coming through here in a few years, and the land baron already knows about it. It's the only thing we can think of that would increase the land value that much. What is the land baron's name?"

Papa thought for a few seconds. "Welsh…Alexander Welsh. He thinks of himself as a modern Alexander the Great, and it is his right to steal all of the land he sees."

As fast as reasonably possible, they went into Santa Fe and Felina sent several urgent telegrams. One of them was written in code to James to thoroughly check out a land baron named Alexander Welsh and see if they could find a weakness, such as a banknote they could buy for cash or any financial papers they can buy out. Another telegram was also in code and was also sent to James to transfer a war chest of money to Santa Fe to fight with. Another was to Will.

Just as they cleared town heading home, they ran into five men on horses that spread out across the road and confronted them. Jake stopped the wagon, and then Papa pointed to the man on the far left. "That is Alexander Welsh, and he is properly named as he is a welsh and a robber baron who steals our land."

Jake sized up the situation and looked each one of them squarely in the eyes. Most folks would say it was suicidal to draw down on five men, but that is exactly what the five men are thinking; hence, it is the last thing on earth they expect Jake to do. However, Jake was sitting in the wagon, which was the wrong place and wrong position to even consider drawing down on them. So he did something they halfway expected, something almost normal, and something that was somewhat disarming.

Jake looked at each of them in the eyes, except the land baron, and scoffed and shook his head and grinned as insulting as he could. The five assailants glanced at each other and actually got nervous. When Jake looked at the boss, he nodded in respect and bowed slightly. Most of all, Jake kept his gun hand well away from his gun. But he continued to sneer and mock the four others.

Jake slowly got out of the wagon and took three casual steps to his left. Again, Jake mocked them. "Any of you boys care to act like a man and take me on?" Jake shrugged and moved slightly. "You boys got the guns, for sure, but do you have the guts?" Jake quickly looked up at the boss and again nodded. "No disrespect to you, sir." Jake kept moving as he continued to challenge them. But the boss didn't like what he was seeing. He couldn't put his finger on it, but something was wrong, and he didn't like it. Jake's actions were that of a brash, arrogant, young man, yet his voice and the look in his eyes inferred competence and that he knew what he was doing. All of the land baron's instincts told him this man was dangerous. He held his hand up to stop his men. And Jake stood still, but he was now standing in the exact spot he wanted. Jake had a clear view of all five men, and they could not possibly move an inch without Jake seeing them so much as flinch or take a deep breath. He even knew what to do if they tried to rear their horses up at him. Jake was ready; all he need was a half-second diversion.

The boss looked at Jake sternly and commanded, "Get back to the wagon. You have guts. I'll give you that, and you look like you could fight your weight in wildcats. But this is not the time or place for a fistfight. Now you…"

Jake held his hands out close to his body, palm up, with his right hand almost directly above his gun. Then he put the most surprised look on his face possible and quickly glanced around at all five of them. "Ain't you forgetting somethin'?" Then all five of them looked at each other, and not one of them was looking at Jake. Jake got his half-second diversion and perhaps a little more.

Jake pulled his six-gun and pointed it at the boss man's head, who was only ten feet away. To his surprise, not one man realized what Jake was doing until he pulled the hammer back and cocked the gun with a very loud click.

The boss man did not yet realize his precarious position. "I said you had guts. I didn't know you were crazy."

Jake shook his head and kept an eye on all five of them. "Better think again, boss man, and you better look at your situation real good."

"You've got ten seconds before I kill you."

"Is that right, boss man? Tell me how you're going to do it. Look at your men and look where my gun is pointing. Look how far your gun hands are from your guns. Look at all that, and then tell me what's going to happen if one of your men so much as sneezes. Now I want every one of you to fold your arms and put them on your chest, and don't even breathe hard."

Jake was able to watch all five at the same time, and all of them knew it. They couldn't touch their guns before two or three of them were dead.

Jake was surprisingly calm and confident. "Let me spell it out for you, boss man. You should have never, never let me get down from the wagon. I wouldn't have a chance if I was still up on the wagon, but you let me get off of it, and you let me talk and move around until I stood in the perfect spot. Would you like to rear your horse up at me?"

The boss man nodded. "The thought has crossed."

"Don't let it. If your horse reared up, you could not shoot me because your horse would block your view. The horse would also block all four of your men from even seeing me, let alone shooting at me. Take a look and see if I'm wrong. Plus all of you would be shooting while sitting on top of skittish, near-panicked horses while I would be standing on solid ground."

The land baron's lead man spoke, "Sooner or later, you are going to make a mistake, big man. And when you do, you will be dead before you hit the ground. You can't keep this up forever."

Jake scoffed. "Having this little informal meeting wasn't my idea. It was yours. But one of my options is to shoot all of you. And if you don't give me a choice, don't think I won't."

Click…click.

There was no mistaking the sound.

They all looked around, except for Jake, and saw Papa with a double-barrel shotgun he had transferred from the family wagon to the buggy, and he had two shirt pockets full of shells. And he has just pulled both hammers back. Jake could not look behind him. "What's going on? I can't take a look."

Hannah answered, "Papa has a double-barrel shotgun, and he just let everyone know it."

Mere seconds later, they could hear a softer clicking sound, but it was definitely metallic.

Papa told Jake, "I've got them covered, Jake. You can look."

Jake turned around to see Felina spinning the cylinder of a six-gun. "I have five loaded chambers and one empty chamber. But now I don't know which chamber is empty."

Jake smiled at Hannah. "I know you are packing, honey, my life depended on it. But I didn't expect papa and Felina to be armed."

The land baron scoffed. "What is your point, big man? Do you think you are going to catch us by surprise next time?"

Jake laughed. "You're the one who started this. You stopped us. We didn't stop you. Actually, you caught us by surprise. I wasn't expecting this, but I was prepared for it. But to answer your question, I have a few more tricks up my sleeve, such as preparing for a predawn attack. So if you step foot on Papa's land, you might want to be careful what you step on. It might hurt. So I ask *you*... what was your point in stopping us?"

"Unlike you, we were going to give you a friendly warning. That's all."

"All five of you are still alive and unharmed. That's as friendly as it gets."

The land baron shook his head. "I'm sure we will cross paths again, big man."

Jake scoffed. "Not a good idea, boss, not a good idea at all. Think about this, you are the one who planned this meeting, and we got the drop on you. Then what do you think will happen when we plan it? You were so convinced, and you believed so hard that the last thing on earth I would do is pull my gun against five of you. Well, look what happened. Likewise, you probably think the last thing on earth we would do is attack you at your greatest strength, your ranch house. But let me assure you that it would be an easy matter. And at 2:00 a.m., I could have you shooting each other within seconds."

The land baron barked the order at his men. "Let's get out of here." Then he looked at Jake.

Jake nodded. "Keep your hands away from your guns, boys, at least until you get out of sight."

Miguel helped the telegraph operator by cleaning up, sweeping the floors, and doing a small amount of painting while waiting for telegrams from El Paso. There were a couple of coded telegrams for the land baron, but a man was waiting in the saloon for them. Then the operator got a very strange non-coded telegram from El Paso for Felina, so he called Miguel and shook his head at great length. He read the telegram several times, still shaking his head in a combination of disbelief and not understanding.

Then he muttered to himself, "How in the hell can El Paso know what's going on in our backyard when they are over three hundred miles away? It must have something to do with one of those coded 'grams." Then he handed the telegram to Miguel.

Miguel couldn't help himself, and he read it. He shrugged and looked at the operator for an explanation. "This doesn't make any sense."

The operator smiled. "You got that right, Miguel. Maybe it'll make sense to Felina."

Papa came into the house and looked troubled. When Jake asked Papa what was wrong, Papa shook his head and gestured toward a hill.

"Perhaps nothing is wrong, but there is a man at the top of a hill nearby. He has dismounted and is sitting down leaning against a tree. He is staying in clear sight and is not causing any harm. It's like he is waiting for something."

Jake nodded. "Okay, I will check it out."

Jake rode up to the hill and dismounted. He then walked up to the man and noticed the man's gun belt and his holstered gun were still hanging on his saddle horn. Jake recognized the man as the only other man to speak on the road out of town.

Jake nodded, and as a token of respect, Jake used two fingers to slowly turn his gun around backward in his holster. "Howdy."

The man stood up, returned Jake's nod, and touched the brim of his hat. "Howdy back to ya."

"To us, it looks like you are waiting for something. You are making a point of staying in clear sight, and I see your gun belt hanging on your saddle horn. That's might respectful of you."

Jake reached out a hand. "I'm Jake. I think we met earlier on the road."

The other man chuckled and shook hands. "I'm Nathan, and yes, sir, we did meet earlier on the road. And you did right proud of yourself, Jake, right proud."

Jake nodded his thanks. "If you're going to be long in waiting, you might as well come on down to the house and wait there. It doesn't make any never mind if you wait here or down at the house, and it won't change what's going to be."

"Okay, we might even talk some. There're a couple of things I could say without gettin' the boss all riled up."

They came down from the hill, and everyone could see Nathan's gun belt on his saddle horn, and they could see the men talking as if there were long-ago friends. And as they got closer, everyone recognized Nathan.

When they walked in the house, Papa welcomed Nathan into their home, and while looking around at everyone, Papa said, "This man is important. We all recognize and remember him, but did all of you notice that he was the only man other than the land baron who dared to speak? And once he even cut in on the boss talking."

Nathan turned to Papa and touched his hat in respect. "Your son Miguel is waiting at the telegraph office for a very important telegram from El Paso. I have been instructed to wait until you receive this telegram, read it to everyone, and discuss it, and then I will take your response back to the boss."

Mama asked, "What do you know of this telegram?"

Nathan shrugged and smiled at Mama. "I honestly do not know who it is, but you have a very, very powerful person on your side. I have been told by the boss to tell you everything I know. And I can assure you that telling you what I know is not the boss's idea. One of the coded telegrams enraged the boss so much it put him in a cursing fit for an hour, and he even threw things up against the wall, valuable things. But first off is that all of the telegrams: to you or to us, from you or from us, coded, un-coded, sent, and received and all correspondence, agreements, and offers are being handled directly and personally by your banker, James. I have been working for the boss for twelve years, and I have never seen him blink or back off. Whoever is on your side has the power to make the boss both hesitate and to back off."

Nathan waited a moment for them to absorb all of this news. Then he spoke, "If I may ask, is your banker, James, powerful enough to reach across three hundred miles and make my boss hesitate and back off where the boss has never hesitated or backed off before?"

Felina, Jake, and Hannah looked at each other and nodded decisively in agreement. Then Felina answered, "Yes, James has that kind of power, and it would make sense for him to fully support us. And I would think there has also been direct contact between James and your boss's banker, some of it quite stern."

Nathan agreed. "Yes, there has been direct contact between the two bankers you just mentioned. I don't know the details of what the contact was. It was coded, but I do know there was direct contact, and the boss didn't like it."

Miguel rode back to the house as fast as he could, which at a gallop took him just under an hour. He could have made it in less than half an hour, but he was gentle with his horse and rested him a couple of times. The telegram would not change whether it took him ten minutes or two hours. He got back home a couple of hours or so before sunset.

Papa cannot read, but Miguel handed the telegram to Papa out of respect; then, it was up to Papa who would read it aloud to everyone else.

Papa handed the telegram to Felina and asked her to read it.

> A truce has been offered by me and accepted by Alexander Welsh. Please do nothing for three days or until further contact. Please take no further actions at this time. Do you agree with truce?
>
> Signed, James

Surprisingly, Papa asked Nathan his opinion of the telegram.

Nathan almost didn't know what to say. "Folks, this is a shock to me. In twelve years, I've never seen the boss in this situation before. But to answer your question, my feel is that it is almost a threat to my boss. I also get the feel that something is going to happen in the next three or four days, and whatever it is, my boss is doin' the listenin', and James is doin' the doin'."

Everyone in the family over twelve years old gets a chance to speak. And in their own words, they all agreed with Nathan that James was telling everyone what to do. But this time, eight-year-old Lydia spoke.

"Kids my age like to make mud pies and have fun. But the boss is a bully who wants to take everyone's mud pies away from them and keep all of them only for him. And he doesn't want anyone else to have any or make any more without him taking all the new mud pies away from us. The boss needs to learn that we all have to share, and he can't have all of the mud pies just for him."

Nathan looked around at everyone and then Papa. "It's sure not like this at the boss's house."

Then Papa decided and looked straight at Nathan. "The way I see it, if your boss doesn't do anything for three or four days and we don't do anything for three or four days, then nobody can make a mistake or do anything wrong. We accept the truce."

It was three and a half days later when a knock came at the door. Felina answered the door, and her scream echoed throughout the house and sent everyone scurrying. Jake pulled his gun and bolted for the door. Papa was going for his shotgun, and Mama grabbed a large knife before anyone realized her screams were for joy. She was talking incoherently and crying so hard she couldn't speak, and then they heard a voice that Jake and Hannah recognized instantly; it was Will.

He was actually, really here. Felina has been fighting hard to overcome an almost overwhelming urge to run home to the safety of Will's arms as fast as she could. She was so scared she would do the wrong thing. Now Will is there, and she was so glad to see him. Now it didn't matter about the land baron or agreements or truces. Will's mere presence meant one thing. It doesn't matter what Alexander Welsh says or does…the war is over.

When Felina calmed somewhat, Will told her that he knew what was going on and that everything was going to be all right. She no longer had to worry about anything anymore. Felina felt like a weight beyond measure was lifted from her shoulders. Nothing else mattered now, Will was here, and all is right with the world.

For the next few hours, Will and Jake got a tour of all Papa had to show. Everything from their three-floor barn to Papa's own sluice system of water distribution, to the hill that Felina climbed as a child. Papa was so proud. They had carried so much fear and grief over Felina's fate, yet when they could no longer solve their problems, she came back home like a beloved and powerful guardian angel.

In a brief moment of solitude, Mama told Felina, "The path you followed that called to you was no accident, nor was it your own choosing."

The next day when things settled down a bit, Will said they all needed to talk.

There was room for everyone at the large family table. Papa told the family that Mr. Travis had important news that he would like to share with them.

Will sat next to Papa and explained, "A deal has already been made that solves all of your problems, and everything has already been agreed to. No one, but no one, is ever going to take your land. If it seems that the land baron knows more about what is going on than you do, it is because it was necessary. When Felina sent her telegrams to El Paso, three very powerful people got personally involved immediately. James, the banker, knew how to go about buying the papers the land baron wanted to keep. I got involved because I am Felina's fiancé, and Felina is the only one who has enough money to buy some papers the land baron has and wants to keep. There is someone else involved who knows which papers to buy and where they are."

Papa frowned. "It would take much power to break the land baron's grip on our land, not to say about his grip on his own greed."

Will nodded in agreement. "You are wise Papa, and that power is money, which we have."

Will looked around at every member of the family as he spoke, "Your Felina is very wealthy, and she has more money than the land baron, and your Felina bought some very valuable and expensive papers that the land baron wants very much. But your Felina is too strong and too powerful, and she took the papers away from the land baron. And now we have to go to the land baron's home and make him sign papers that he will never try to take your land again, and we have a big surprise for Papa, and we have a big surprise for Felina."

Felina hugged Will, and the little ones laughed and giggled and said, "*Aw...*"

Then Lydia walked over and hugged Felina as tight as she could. "We already love you, Felina, but we love you even more for taking the papers away from the land baron, and we can't say thank you enough times for spending your money to save us. And I am so proud to be your sister."

Felina hugged and kissed each of the other five children, including Miguel, with tears as she told each of them they were so very welcome and she was so glad to do it.

Papa leaned over and spoke quietly to Will, "Felina has much, but she does not have the power or money to do these great things. So it is you who has saved our home."

Will looked at Papa and also spoke quietly, "Felina is my fiancée, and she carries my child. That makes me part of her family, and that makes your fight, my fight. Without Felina, I would not be here, so that means Felina is the one who has saved your home and land."

Papa looked at Will with respect in his eyes, which was a rare thing. "My Felina has chosen her man well, and I now know the child will be good. But there is a mystery here that I do not understand."

"I will answer anything I can, Papa, what is the mystery?"

Papa thought carefully. "How can Felina take these papers away from the land baron when he has already bought the land? How is this possible?"

Will nodded. "The land baron did not pay all of the money for the land. He paid a little money to start, and then he makes a payment every month. But he has only paid a small amount of the money he owes. As long as he owes the bank money, the bank can sell his papers for cash. The land baron does not have very much cash, but we easily had enough cash to pay the full amount, which means we could own all of the land he was paying for. So the robber baron, I mean the land baron made a deal with us so he can keep the papers and finish paying for the land."

Papa understood. "So he did not pay for all of it, and that is why my Felina was powerful enough to take his papers away from him. So why don't you kept all of the land since you paid for all of it?"

"First, if you take everything away from them, men like him are very dangerous, and there is no doubt he would kill many people, and he would come after you and Mama first. We don't want a range war or anyone killed. And we really don't want his land, not all of it anyway. We want your home and land to be safe and secure. Second, we did not pay for all of it yet. We paid the bank a deposit that was enough money so that we have the choice to make the land baron a deal or we can pay for all of it and own all of it if we want to."

"You are going to give his papers back just for leaving our home and land alone?"

Will chuckled. "No, no, no…he has to do some favors and earn his papers back. Besides, we know why he wants the land so bad, and he's not getting it all back."

"Another mystery is why he would want so much land."

Will nodded. "Good question. The railroad is coming through here, and they will start buying up the land in three or four years. People like him find out about this and buy as much land as they can before the railroad drives the prices up tenfold. He buys the land while it's cheap and makes minimum payments for a few years and then sells it to the railroad at an enormous profit."

"Si, this is how the rich get so much richer, but they really don't earn it. They almost steal it. And all of this is legal, no?"

"Not quite all of it. The land baron had to pay someone off for giving him the information about when the railroad would start buying land and where they will buy it. And that is illegal."

Papa shook his head. "I learned much today, but some of it I am not sure if I want to know about."

Will smiled at Papa. "Si."

Will, Felina, Jake, Hannah, Papa, Mama, and the children all rode out to the land baron's home.

As they pulled up to the hitching post in front of the ranch house, everyone seemed to be nervous except Will. He smiled as he opened the front door without even knocking.

As they walked into the house, Felina thought it odd that a swivel chair had its back turned toward the front door. She also found it odd that she would notice such a thing. An unarmed Nathan was checking guns. But Jake shook his head and refused to give up his gun. Will told him it was all right because he was keeping his gun. Only the land baron and Will would keep their guns.

Will walked over to the swivel chair, bent down, and spoke softly. Then Felina had fire in her eyes as she heard the unmistakable sound of a kiss. Felina bolted to the chair and turned it a quarter of a turn. Then she shrieked, "Oh my God, how is this possible?"

A woman got out of the chair and stood up. Felina grabbed her and hugged her for a moment and then backed up and put her nose in the air.

"Ma'am, do you realize *that* is my fiancé you kissed?"

She grinned with a rare grin and then wiggled her hips and said, "I only kissed him on the cheek, but if I was ten years younger, he would be *my* fiancé." Then she looked around. "Okay, twenty years younger."

Felina grabbed her and hugged her again. "How is this possible?"

Of all people on earth, it was Miss Libby. Indeed, how was this possible?

Will explained, "When you sent the telegrams, I went straight to Miss Libby and asked her what to do. She was stunned beyond words when she read the telegrams and saw who was causing the ruckus. Alexander Welsh is her first cousin, and they grew up together. She asked me to escort her here, and we came to the ranch house and worked things out. That's what we needed the three days for. We needed time to get here and time to work things out. Actually we started working things out before we left."

Jake looked at the land baron and then at Miss Libby and let out a breath. "I sure am glad to see you here, Miss Libby."

The land baron looked Jake over. "You handled yourself well, young man, and nobody got shot. But why are you so glad to see my cousin?"

Jake nodded. "Well, sir, situations like this can be mighty unstable, and things can go wrong inside of a heartbeat. I just feel a whole lot better with her here."

Hannah looked around at the ceiling, the walls, the art, and the carpet. "Is your wife still alive?"

The land baron was a bit surprised. "No, ma'am, I lost her a few years back."

Hannah glanced at him and continued looking at the room. "She was a very special lady. You can see it in her art and decor. She was a very refined lady who brought beauty and culture to the wilderness." Then she looked at a powerful and widely feared man and smiled warmly. "She was much too good for you."

He laughed. For the first time in a long time, Alexander Welsh laughed. "Hell, ma'am, everybody knows that." Then he looked around at the room as if refreshing his memory. Then he looked at Hannah. "Thank you for your words, ma'am, I truly thank you. For you to see Victoria in her art, you must have this same gift within yourself. It is a great gift. And if I may, you have chosen a good man. He is tough, smart, and scary. But he is also one of the most aggravatin' men I have ever met in my life. I would almost waste a bullet on him."

Hannah scoffed. "Aggravatin'? Try living with him. We'll shoot him with my gun. I think my bullets are cheaper."

The land baron snickered and chuckled, and then he looked over at Jake. "She is much too good for you."

Jake smiled. "Hell, Mr. Welsh, everybody knows that."

Alexander looked over at Miss Libby. "Let's get this over with, cuz', all of this niceness is making me ill and is diluting my toxic karma."

They sat at a very large conference table with a smooth, thick finish, and Alexander chuckled. "I never thought this table would ever hear these kinds of words."

Alexander remained standing as everyone sat down. "Before we proceed with the business, I would like to thank my men for keeping an order, a command, that I made some years back, and even Nathan and Libby have complied. But as I stand here now, it was a foolish command. And I now speak a name that I would not allow to be spoken in this house. Tomorrow I will go back to being my, as some say, evil self, and the powerful ones here will be gone. But today is special, and Miss Hannah has brought back a small part of what was lost. Miss Hannah has brought back good memories, so I would like to end a foolish command and dedicate this meeting, this day, and the fine things within this house to a fine woman who is lost but not forgotten. Not even forgotten to other fine people she never met. I dedicate all of this…to Victoria—the only woman I ever loved or ever will. And she is the only person, man or woman, who could prevail over the despicable part of me."

Alexander paused for a long moment. When he spoke, there was more conviction in his voice than hostility.

"The four of you are the first women to ever speak serious and binding words at this table. You are the first women who sit at this table as equals to all others who sit here. What you say is important, and it matters. One last thing before my cousin Libby explains the agreements to you, and that is this is the first time in my life I will come out on the short end of the stick in a business deal. However, I want it noted that Libby has taken Felina in as a member of our family, and by extension, that also makes Will, Jake, Hannah, Papa, and Mama extended members of our family. It is only the combined might of my own family that could have put this agreement on me. And remember this day well, for it will never happen again."

Will looked around at everyone and lightly applauded. "Well spoken…my brother. We take your words most seriously, and you are correct. It took the combined family, plus James."

Alexander nodded his respect and thanks to Will. Then he gestured to Libby, and she stood up and explained, "Mama and Papa's land will remain with them, and there will be no more attempts to take their home or land. Also, they will receive a parcel of five hundred acres that Papa has wanted for years because it would give Papa a good water supply. However, the five hundred acres are not helpful to Alexander."

Libby stopped and smiled at length at Papa and Mama. "One more thing. Papa and Mama will receive a tract of land to sell to the railroad to help them start a new life. This track of land is to be no less than fifteen thousand acres. Half of Papa's tract of land is to be sold first before Alexander sells any of his land to the railroad. In exchange, Will and Felina relinquished their rights to the banknote for the total tracts of land held by Alexander that now total seventy thousand acres. However, Alexander did not give them a refund for their option to buy the land. Alexander claimed he could not be perceived as weak. All of the agreements and land sales will be administered and supervised by James or his designate at the time of sale to the railroad. The penalty for noncompliance is 50 percent of current holdings."

Alexander hosted a rather nice dinner party, with vintage wine and fine cigars, to celebrate what Alexander refers to as an internal family matter. The family aspect made an immense difference to him. In fact, it was the difference between a range war and a dinner party. If he lost a rare battle to his family, then so be it, but losing to outsiders could not, and would not, be tolerated or accepted. How much or how little money he lost did not matter. It was the simple matter of losing that he could not tolerate.

Alexander went to his supply closet to get more cigars. After getting the cigars, he lingered. He could not hear the words being spoken by the overlapping voices he heard. But he could hear the laughter, the joy, and most of all, there were children's voices laced with a child's laughter where powerful men feared to stand. His home of bitter-sweet memories was now resounding with the sounds of a family... a family at peace. Then Alexander heard the unmistakable sound of a child's hand slapping the top of his table — a table where strong men were crushed by Alexander's wrath. A table that was symbolic of his power, and a table that was feared throughout the territory. Then Alexander thought to himself. *"There must be a God... no other power could have brought this about."*

An unexpected benefit occurred a month or so after everyone went back to El Paso. Alexander has never apologized in his life, and he never would, not for now anyway. However, he was doing a *neighborly act* of helping fix up the shack Mama and Papa lived in. But one day Papa had to repair a section of his sluice system, and one of the men helping fix up the shack went with Papa to help him. Later, the man raved to Alexander about Papa's water sluice system, and Alexander ended up paying Papa a lot of money for designing and building a system to Alexander's extensive needs. Alexander did not pay Papa what he was truly worth, but he did pay Papa a lot more than he would have if Papa was not family.

The peace agreement covered everything they could think of. Unfortunately, there was one thing they could not foresee, and that was the future. The railroad had indeed decided to buy the very land that Alexander and Papa owned. But powerful events, actions, and the growing rumors of secession from the union by a number of southern states convinced the top railroad leaders to defer new growth and conserve their resources for a possible, if not likely, conflagration in the east and south.

The captains of industry, especially the railroads, realized that all of their resources, material, and efforts may soon be focused totally, to the exclusion of all else, on war efforts. They also realized that any major conflicts would be focused in the east and south, far from the west. Many of the astute and elite realized that a major war, if not an all-out civil war, was already inevitable. There were far too many internal issues to be settled in peace. All planned growth, expansion, and land purchases in the west were indefinitely deferred. The captains of industry, the astute, and the elite are gearing up for war.

IN THE NEAR FUTURE

Two years before it even started, the civil war effortlessly shattered Alexander's hopes and dreams of an empire, which were the only hopes and dreams he had left. Alexander is a very bitter man filled with anger and saturated with hostility at the whole world. His normal feelings and emotions, his life, and his heart are as dried up as a drought-stricken riverbed. His anger and temperament were mere facades for the unspeakable ache in his empty heart. Several years ago, his beloved wife became very sick, and after two days, he rushed her to the doctor. But tragically, she died before they got to town. He blamed and punished himself for her death even though the doctor told him the disease she contracted was incurable. His growing aggression and guilt were directed at himself even more than at others.

But now even his empty and lonely world was shattered and devastated. All of his hopes and dreams of wealth and power were destroyed by fearsome thunderstorms gathering in the east and in the south.

Without hope and with no one to turn to, Alexander no longer had the strength to fight off the overwhelming depression and despair. He sat at his desk with a loaded pistol setting directly in front of him a few inches from the front of the top of his desk. He was seriously considering shooting himself. And he may well have.

Suddenly, he heard an extremely loud banging sound at his door, a sound he had never heard.

It was the most startled Alexander has ever been in his life, and he could not figure out what the horrendous banging sound was. It wasn't a sledgehammer; the sound wasn't right for a hammer. Then he remembered he had propped up a coal shovel against the wall next to the front door. And that was the sound. Some suicidal idiot was banging on his front door with the coal shovel.

Alexander snatched the pistol off the desk and bolted for the front door as fast as he could. The gun was loaded, cocked, and ready to fire. And live or die, he was in the perfect mood for gunplay. He grabbed the door handle and threw the door wide open.

Then he absolutely froze in his tracks. He was stunned and shocked into paralysis. He could not have moved if his life depended on it.

It was the last woman on earth he expected to see at his door; it was Hannah. She briskly walked past him, slamming into his left shoulder, but kept walking. What is wrong with her, and why in the hell was Hannah banging on his front door with a coal shovel? Alexander was so stunned it was difficult to think clearly.

Then, his first fleeting thought was that she has gone mad and something has driven her insane. Perhaps Jake has left her for another woman. Then for the briefest portion of a second, their eyes met, and then he knew; Alexander saw her gaunt, hollow eyes that reflected the full power of the unspeakable agony that has tormented every sliver of his own life. He now saw the same hopelessness that saturated his life in her beautiful but haunted eyes. He then saw the most hideous contrast in existence. Beautiful, young eyes bathed and immersed in the agonizing helplessness of death. Alexander no longer needed to ask her what was wrong; he already knew. Jake did not leave her for another woman. Jake is dead.

Alexander avoided eye contact as he walked over to a window and silently looked outside.

He spoke while still looking away, "How did Jake die?"

Hannah took a deep breath and steadied her voice. "He was shot in the back while in jail."

Alexander froze for an instant. This is an issue that would be addressed further at a later time.

"I'm not going to lie to you, Hannah. It is nice to see you, but of all places, why did you come here?"

Hannah cried for some time before she could respond. She slowly sank to the floor and buried her face in her hands and cried. Alexander waited ever so patiently for her. Then as she struggled to regain her voice, he spoke gently, "Take your time, Hannah, we have all day, and I mean it. We really have all day. So don't try to push yourself any faster than you can go right now. We will stay right here on the floor if you need to and for as long as you need to."

Hannah looked up to speak to him but was surprised to see that Alexander had sat down on the floor next to her with his legs crossed. She reached over and put her arms around his neck. "Please hold me, Alex, please just hold me for a minute."

Victoria called him Alex, and nobody, but nobody has dared to call him Alex since…until now.

He put his arms around her and held her. "I know you don't believe this right now, but everything will get better, ever so much better. It is going to be okay, Hannah, but I won't lie to you. Grieving is a nasty, vicious thing, and you can't go around it. You have to go right through it, right through the center of hell. I will help you all I can, but most of the fight is inside yourself, and I can only help so much. But I will help you, Hannah. I will help you as much as I possibly can."

Hannah sighed. "I was playing cards with Aunt Libby when all of a sudden I started ripping the cards into pieces and throwing them. She didn't know what to do, so she started yelling at me and telling me to get a hold of myself. I wanted to strangle her when she said that. I don't know why I do a lot of things I do now. I don't understand, and I really think I am losing my mind. Sometimes I think I am going mad. Then I thought of you and that you have been through this, and you really loved Victoria, so you are the only one who can understand my madness. Nobody around me understands this madness I have, and I don't know what to do or say. I'm afraid and scared they were going to lock me up, so I came here, hoping you would help me. I really thought Aunt Libby could help me, but she reacted so much different when George died than I am reacting, and she tells me everything I do is wrong and that I have to get a grip on myself. And most of all, Alex, I suddenly felt like I didn't belong anymore. It was like everyone I knew became strangers, and I didn't know them, and they didn't know me anymore. "

Alex nodded several times as she spoke, "You say what you feel like saying and you do what you feel like doing. I threw a hundred decks of cards in the fireplace, and I even threw a few glasses and plates across the room and up against the wall. Sometimes it just hits you all of a sudden. And there will be no more talk about being locked up or that you have a madness. You are not mad, nor will anyone ever lock you up or even talk about it."

"I'm not crazy?"

Alex shook his head sharply. "No, you are not crazy. You are grieving and in mourning, and it is an extremely difficult time. But you are not crazy. Life is crazy for taking Jake away from you."

"Aunt Libby said it's been two months now, and I should be getting better."

He glared at her in anger meant for Libby. "That comes a lot closer to madness than anything you've said or done."

"Alex, I can't tell you how much I need to hear that."

"You don't have to tell me. I already know." Then he smiled. It was almost as if he had a purpose in life and something important to accomplish. Suddenly, Hannah was somehow the most important thing in his life. Helping her survive the pits of hell was the most important thing he could do right now. And she sure wasn't getting any help anywhere else. Here she is drowning in agony, and everyone around her is throwing her anchors.

Then Hannah noticed that his gun belt hanging on a large hook by the front door had a holstered gun in it. Then she looked at the gun he was still carrying in his left hand, although he was carrying it backward for safety. It was immaculately clean and smelled of fresh oil.

Hannah was puzzled. "Why did you already have a gun in your hand? You didn't have time to get a gun. You were much too fast to the door. You already had a gun…"

Alex shrugged, "I was cleaning it."

Hannah wasn't buying it. "I can see from here there isn't a cleaning kit on your desk. You had the gun out lying on top of your desk."

She thought for a few seconds. "Alexander Welsh, what were you thinking?"

He spoke without looking at her; he knew she had figured it out when she called him by both of his names. He always knew he was in trouble when his beloved wife called him by both names. "You're timing is perfect, Hannah. Welcome to the kingdom of destruction."

"Okay, that makes me the queen of destruction, but nobody said you could go getting all depressed and think about doing yourself harm. There are too many people who need you, Alex. I have no other place to go, so you can't get all depressed and think such dark thoughts. I even have a little money to throw in the pot. It is pathetically little, but at least I have something."

Alex involuntarily chuckled. "Now you sound like Nathan. He tried to give me three thousand dollars to help rebuild."

Hannah looked at him in shock. "And you didn't take it?"

Hannah ran to the front door and hollered out for Nathan. Then she ran to the back door and hollered for Nathan. Someone hollered back, "Who's asking?"

Hannah found a fight she could fight, and she found a place to stand. "It's no never mind to you who's asking. Now get Nathan, and get him now."

Deep inside of himself, Alexander suddenly felt he was no longer alone, nor did he have to fight life alone any longer. Even in the midst of her raw, sometimes crippling grief, Hannah was a force to be reckoned with. He was becoming proud that she chose to come to him.

The man who had hollered back responded, "There ain't no woman gonna—"

Something hit the man so hard it knocked him flat on his back. That something was Nathan, and then he pulled the man straight off the ground and stood him up.

Nathan pointed at Hannah. "When that woman speaks, you don't try to think or figure things out or question her. When she speaks, you listen…got that?"

Not knowing what else to do, the man looked at Hannah and gestured toward Nathan. "Here he is, ma'am."

Nathan walked briskly toward the house and was grinning and shaking his head at why Hannah would be here. Then halfway to the house, he stopped walking, and he stopped grinning, and he looked at her and shook his head no. He saw her close her eyes, and she nodded her head yes. Then she saw Nathan mouth the words, "The world has lost a good man." She smiled back in thanks.

The three of them walked into the house, and Hannah led them to Alexander's desk.

Then she spun around and looked directly at Nathan. "Did you offer Alex…"

Nathan involuntarily but very noticeably recoiled at someone saying the name Alex. He was surprised.

Nathan smiled slightly and looked at the boss man. "It has been too long since this house has heard the sound of your name spoken by a woman's voice."

Alexander nodded in agreement, and then Hannah continued, "Did you offer Alex three thousand dollars to help rebuild a life here?"

Nathan's answer was to pull out a large roll of money from each pocket and set it down on Alex's desk, "Yes, ma'am, three thousand dollars, and I was going to talk to him again this afternoon. Plus I know the boss man still has a few thousand left."

Alexander shrugged, "I have four thousand, perhaps five."

Hannah emptied the entire contents of her handbag on the desk beside Nathan's money. Her handbag held a surprising amount of money mixed in with hairpins, makeup, a small mirror, and a number of other things that most men cannot identify.

Then she looked up at Alex. "Okay, boss man, here is just over 2,600 dollars more. Now, if the three of us can't take what we've already got and what we have here on the desk and if we can't turn it into a decent living, then we don't deserve food on our table or a roof over our heads."

Alexander chuckled at length. "Nathan, we may have to work a bit harder for a while, but I think we can come up with something good here. What do you think?"

Nathan shook his head. "Boss man, I'm allergic to work. You know that."

Hannah looked at Nathan suspiciously. "What? What do you mean you're allergic to work?"

Both men laughed as Nathan grinned and answered, "It makes me break out in a sweat."

Hannah looked around. "Where's that gun? Where's your gun, Alex…"

For the next forty-one years, they had good lives, lives worth having, and they lived them well.

These events will occur in the near future and will be shared and lived by Hannah, Alexander, and Nathan. Tragically, it is a future that will be constructed from Jake's death pyre, a future that would have been impossible without Jake's death.

At this point, the focus of the story returns to the present. Everyone is arriving back in El Paso from the family meeting and peace agreement with Alexander. Jake has eight months to live. Will and Felina have a month less, and all three deaths are directly interconnected. Life has been almost inconceivably fabulous for Will and Felina, but life will now become an equally vicious nightmare.

WILL'S AND FELINA'S FATE

1858

When everyone finally got back to El Paso, they gathered for lunch at the Railyard. Finding that John had done an excellent job and all was well with nothing to report, Jake and Hannah darted off to the stores and to have some fun just taking in the town. Will told them they earned it. "Have some fun." John was very happy and relieved that his bosses were happy, and things went well.

Will went upstairs to their new home and halfway lay down and halfway collapsed onto their very large bed. Felina said she wanted to see Miss Libby, who got back a day ahead of them. Will had no other plans or objections; he just wanted some sleep.

Felina sat in Miss Libby's parlor where they were drinking English tea. Miss Libby knew Felina had something important she wanted to discuss, and they were far beyond the need for small talk or introductory politeness.

Miss Libby smiled and spoke encouragingly, "What is it, my dear? What is troubling your mind?"

Felina shook her head, "Everything that's happened to me all of a sudden. Meeting Will and falling in love with him, and now I'm carrying his child. Then the enormous gift he gave me when he gave me the Railyard. Then you holding my hand and hugging me in front of everyone during a very busy time at the Railyard.

Everyone knows who I am or who I was. They know, but you erased
all of that. Miss Libby, in two minutes, you changed my life, and
now everyone accepts me because of what you did. You and Will
have so much power, yet both of you have used it to elevate my
life. My life is incredible because of the two of you. All of this is
really bothering me because I am not worth it, and I do not deserve
these things. It's not just being a saloon girl, and all that came with
it. There are other things that haunt me. I did vile things that I
cannot forget."

Miss Libby got up from her chair and sat down beside Felina on
the couch. "What do you mean, my dear? Please tell me."

"I robbed them and stole from them, as many of them as I
could get drunk enough to pass out or at least drunk enough not to
remember what happened. I would drink colored water while they
drank whiskey, and then I would take them up to a pleasure room
and steal their money or gold or rings, watches, or anything they had
of value, even a nice belt buckle. And I did this many times, Miss
Libby. I would deliberately get them so drunk, and then I would rob
them. And I would make them pay me for my services even when
they were too drunk to do anything. It was so easy for me to get
them so drunk because they were so willing. I would even steal their
six-guns if they were valuable enough. Then I would have security
men throw them into the alley with their empty holsters and empty
pockets. I am so low, Miss Libby, a saloon girl, a prostitute, and a
common thief. How can I be worth the things I have been given?"

Miss Libby hugged Felina. "How did you feel when you did
these things and while you were doing them?"

Felina shook her head and looked down. "I was so angry at
them, very angry. Sometimes I would…I would…I would spit on
them in anger. Some of them were so drunk they would give me an
extra dollar for spitting on them. So I would spit on them again…
for free."

Miss Libby chuckled. "Felina, you are a young woman of rare
beauty. A lot of men would pay you to spit on them, even sober
ones. But do you know why you were so angry at them?"

Felina nodded. "They lied to me. You may not believe this, but I expected them to treat me and care about me like Papa did. I had never been so used before, and I believed their lies and alcohol talk and promises at first. But I soon learned the most heart-shattering lesson I've ever learned. What men say in darkness evaporates in the daylight. Men are so easy to find at night but are nowhere to be found in the light of day. That's how I knew Will really cared for me and loved me, because he was still there, and he still wanted me in the daylight. I thought and truly believed that I could be any man's wife I wanted, but in reality, I could be no man's wife. I did not live a life. I lived an illusion and called it a life. I robbed them of money and things of value, but they robbed me of something far more valuable…my hopes and dreams. And that is why I was so angry at them."

Felina returned Miss Libby's hug and cried on her shoulder. "You are such an important person, and I am so low. How could you even give someone like me the time of day?"

Miss Libby scoffed and looked away. "You are low, but I am not? You are still living an illusion, my dear—illusions that you are low and have dirty hands but the rest of us do not. Do you really believe that you are the only one with dirty hands and a dirty soul? Let me tell you the greatest secret in life that I can give you. It is nigh onto impossible to reach the top of any human endeavor without sacrificing your soul to the devil. My sweet, you are somewhat justified to fear judgment day, but I have so much more to fear than you do. Your question is reversed. Actually, how is it that someone like *you* will give *me* the time of day? If you are low, I am far lower. You are flawed, my Felina, but I am evil. You have done bad things, but I have done evil things. I suppose in one way or another all of us who achieve much are saloon girls of one kind or another. You are so much the daughter I ached inside to have, but I would have destroyed your soul beyond repair."

Felina's laugh was dry, incredulous, and without humor. "What? How can you say those things about yourself?"

"Outwardly, I practiced and developed a refined but counterfeit demeanor of peace and culture. But inside I was a raving monster who destroyed everything I touched. I truly thought and believed there was some great reward waiting for me, but the reward that awaited me was not great. It was the total destruction of my own life and the life of my husband. George loved me with a love that I am not capable of, and for that, I destroyed both of our lives."

Felina was still shaking her head. "Are you saying this just to make me feel better?"

"In part, yes, I am confiding in you to make you feel better about yourself, for you are not lost, but every word of what I am saying is still true, nonetheless."

"How can you possibly be evil?"

Miss Libby rolled her eyes. "Oh, very easily, my dear. Some of your fresh and honest words sting like angry hornets. You are right about robbing people of hopes and dreams being a bigger sin than robbing them of money or belt buckles. And I did even worse. I did not rob people of their hopes and dreams. I crushed their hopes and dreams. I had a goal that burned inside of me, and I would not stop, and I would not let anything or anyone get in my way. If they did, I would go after them like a hungry predator. I would plant stolen items and illegal drugs on them to smear their name and reputation. And most of all, I would start vicious rumors about everything from questionable heritage to secret affairs and everything in between, none of which were true. I started well-placed rumors that could not be stopped. If it destroyed a marriage or two or destroyed a career or two, so be it. It got them out of my way. Many people have accomplished as much as I have without taking the low road, but I did it much faster. But to be brutally honest with you, deep inside of myself I *wanted* to take the low road. I liked being that way. But, my sweet Felina, I tremble in fear at the thought of you turning into someone like me. I saw you take the high road in New Mexico, and you can accomplish great things without damaging yourself or Will and without being like me."

Miss Libby had tears in her eyes. "George asked me and pleaded with me so many times for us to spend more time together, but I refused. I was on a mission of what I thought to be success. I always told George, 'Tomorrow. We would spend more time together tomorrow.' Then one night, George died in his sleep...and there was no tomorrow. I refused to have children, and now it was too late. Not having children and not spending more time with a man who loved me and supported me were by far my greatest mistakes. I am so glad and happy for you that you are carrying a good man's child. And I am so glad and happy that you and Will spend so much time together."

Felina shook her head. "Why are you telling me these things? I will love you and respect you until the day I die. But please do not say anymore bad things about yourself. You will never be evil in my sight, so please don't try to tell me that you are evil. Why do you say such things? I love you, Aunt Libby, and my children will look up to you, respect you, and love you. I have already decided that my children will look up to you as a grandmother. We have no grandmother on Will's side of the family, so you will be that grandmother."

Libby could not look at Felina nor could she fully control her voice. "Grandmother? How could I ever be worthy? But before any member of your family and especially before your children think one good thought about me, I had to tell you the truth of what I really am. I wasted my life chasing a lustful ambition that wasn't worth the chase. So don't be like me, and do not look up to me with respect, my sweet, for I am toxic and infected with the devil's blood. So don't say in my presence that you are low, for I am far lower, and my fear of judgment day grows stronger every morning I awake. It was only after losing my husband and after I achieved my goals that I realized I had empty, meaningless ambitions and goals."

Then Felina understood. "You want to say something to me but don't know how. What is it?"

Libby shook her head. "Far be it from me to try to give advice on life."

Felina asked, "If you could live your life all over again, would you do it the same way?"

Libby shook her head empathically. "Not one second of it would be the same."

"Then your advice is valid and welcomed...Grandma."

Libby was very hesitant. "Okay, then as a grandma, I want to say something to you. It is not for you or Will. It is for the child. I know of such things. But I would die inside if you never spoke to me again."

"Please, Aunt Libby, what is it?"

Libby took a deep breath. "I fully understand why you still visit the Cantina so much. It is a place of security and comfort, and the Cantina will always be a part of you. I have such a place myself. But, Felina, you must stop going to the Cantina, and above all else, you must stop flirting. Will does not handle jealousy well. It is a demon he must contend with and a demon that you must not feed. Very few things can truly threaten you and Will, but flirting and jealously are real threats to you. I plead with you...no, I beg of you, Felina. Stop going to the Cantina, and please, above all else, stop the flirting. I have shredded decency more than any saloon girl, and I have damaged lives, none more than my own. I know of such things. Please stop these dire threats before they grow too strong to control."

Felina nodded in agreement. "I love you, Aunt Libby, and I will always welcome your advice. You gave me the greatest gift you possibly could when you publically hugged me and gave me acceptance to all of society. Now I say to you that as long as we are together, you have never done an evil or sordid act in your life. In our home and establishments, you are clean and guiltless. You are our children's wise and loving grandmother. I realize I still flirt a little, but it no longer means the same thing. Before Will, a flirt could mean a lot. But now, a flirt is only a smile and an eye blink. Aunt Libby, I may still do some of the things I have always done, but they no longer mean the same thing. I am even careful about who I hug and how I hug them. I am no longer available to any man except Will. He will see this and understand that the things I now do no longer mean the same as before."

Libby slowly shook her head. "Okay, my dear. But I must warn you of things I see, and I can see a powerful demon within Will's soul. And this demon can be a terrible threat to you and your future. Please do not feed this harbinger of destruction."

"Okay, Aunt Libby, I will be careful, and I really appreciate the warning."

As they parted and Felina returned to the Railyard, Libby knew that Felina did not take her warning seriously. Libby knew that Felina would, at great risk, continue to feed a vicious demon without even realizing it.

Will was half asleep on the couch when some disturbing and dangerous thoughts began flowing through his mind. Something has been bothering him for a while now, and it is getting more and more difficult to keep it out of his mind. He knows that has never acted like this in his life. He has never been overly jealous or so emotionally erratic before and never so prone to violence in his life.

Will has wondered about something that just a short time ago made him laugh at himself and made him wonder if he was touched in the head or moonstruck. But now he wonders if it is possible that Felina really is casting a spell on him. Could she be in league with the devil? Does she have special magical powers over him? As long as they are together, his tormented thoughts are easy to contain, but when he is alone, the darkness of his thoughts grows and is getting difficult to control. Will knew he was hopelessly and ever so deeply in love with Felina, but is she wicked? Dare he even entertain the thought she could be evil. He is so confused. How can part of him be so happy yet another part of him so tormented? Is it possible, is it really possible that he has fallen helplessly and totally in love with a woman who is wicked and evil? Is he in love with a woman who possesses the powers to cast spells? What else could explain how different he is and the agony that churns inside of him? How can he be such a different person unless Felina is casting a spell on him? Every time Will ponders such dark thoughts, they carve themselves deeper into his heart and mind. And every time he exercises these dark thoughts and doubts, they become stronger and more real.

Will cannot understand, nor would he accept, the true source of his demons of darkness and doubt. The true source of his darkness, his doubts, and his torment is his own heart and mind. Will has never been in love remotely approaching his love for Felina. His love has never had the power to reach his innermost heart and soul before. He has never loved so much that he had so much to lose. He has never loved a woman strong enough to fear losing her. His love has never been strong enough to reach his fears and doubts, but now he feels love with the full power to reach every speck of his heart, mind, and soul. He has never had so much to lose before and horribly, the demons that threaten them are being fed by his very love for Felina that grows stronger by the day. And the stronger his love for Felina becomes, the stronger his demons become, and he is helpless to control them. Will cannot and does not believe that the source of his demons is himself. So he concludes his darkness and fears must be from Felina, and she must have the power to cast a spell on him. That is the only explanation he will accept. Tragically, Will is wrong...dead wrong.

In an attempt to clear his mind of the darkness, Will invites Felina for a night out on the town. They will walk the park and then watch a Shakespearian play, then go dancing, and then have a late dinner at the most expensive restaurant in El Paso.

It was a beautiful evening that drew Felina even closer to severing ties with the Cantina.

Felina was now clearly showing that she was with child. They never considered that their baby could be a girl. It was little William from day one, a son named after William the Conqueror because of his anticipated flaming red hair.

The restaurant was romantic and dimly lit with candles. Will's heart melted as he looked at Felina's beautiful face glowing in the dim, flickering candlelight. Will himself beamed inside, knowing that part of Felina's glow is from carrying his child. They talked and laughed and planned their future and little William's future. With two glasses of wine, they relaxed. They were very, very relaxed. Will totally let his guard down and was enjoying a magical evening. Even Will thought his demon was asleep.

Then a man, named Martin, walked up to their table and stopped. He smiled broadly and reached down and picked up Felina's hand and kissed her hand as he spoke, "You are so beautiful and so glowing. I hope…"

Felina smiled back at him, and even in the semidarkness, Will saw her wink at him.

A lot of things have been building up inside of Will, and before he knew it, he bolted up from his chair and hit the man as hard as he could. And as the man started to fall, Will hit the man again. As the man fell, he instinctively grabbed a tablecloth and pulled several glasses down with him that shattered when they hit the floor. The broken glass cut his face in several places, one cut was much worse than the others.

The man's wife screamed and cursed Will severely. She shoved Will, slapped him, and even tried to hit him with her cane. Will froze in shock when he saw that the woman was at least sixty years old. The man he just pummeled was sixty-eight years old. Literally within seconds, the lights were turned up and gas lights were lit. Felina sat in shock and stared at Will while shaking her head at the surreal situation. The instantaneous and totally unexpected change from such peace and happiness to such misguided violence was more than her mind could cope with. She just stared at Will blankly and said nothing. But for the very first time, Felina looked at Will with fear and dread. And for the first time, Felina is afraid of him.

The maitre d', whose name is Fredric, quickly ushered Will and Felina into his rather plush office and invited them to sit down. Felina sat motionless on a small receiving couch, and Will remained standing. Felina could only stare at the wall in front of her. Even by saloon standards, this was brutal. There are numerous fights in a saloon, to be sure, but few result in broken bones, and attacking a sixty-eight-year old man without extreme cause is unheard of. But for that to happen in such an elegant restaurant, it was shocking, and it was unacceptable, and it would not be tolerated. Will has not only greatly exceeded his bounds; he has committed a high crime.

It took Fredric only fifteen minutes to gather the facts and learn the extent of the injuries involved. After his assistant updated him, he leaned backward against his desk, folded his arms, and shook his head. Fredric is a small man standing five feet eight inches tall and perhaps 165 pounds, but words cannot describe the anger and the rage that was swirling in his mind like a severe thunderstorm.

Fredric glared at Will. "My mind is still struggling to cope with what you did, but more especially...why?"

Will glared back. "I don't have to answer to you, and I don't have to explain myself to you."

Fredric almost mocked. "You don't think so?"

Will stepped up close to the much smaller man and tried to intimidate him. "No...I don't."

Surprisingly, the smaller man then walked up to Will, touching him, and glared at him. "Don't think for one second I am going to back down from the likes of you or act like a frightened child. Now is the wrong time, the worse time, for you to act like a schoolyard bully and think you are going to behave like an animal and then simply walk away. You broke a very wealthy man's jaw in two places. He will need thirty to forty stitches in his face, and he has a deep cut only a fraction of an inch from his right eye. Don't you comprehend that you can serve several years of hard labor in prison for what you just did?"

Will shrugged. "I will pay the man's medical bills and give him $50,000. That should square it up."

Fredric laughed and shook his head. "Martin can burn $50,000 in his fireplace and not even miss it. Besides, do you think for one second that his wife Ada will agree to that? I think you have the wrong idea of what wealth means and what it doesn't mean."

Will scoffed and then mocked. "Let me straighten…"

Fredric looked at Felina, who was now visibly shaking but still staring at the wall, and he interjected, "Ma'am, would you like to know what Martin was going to say to you? Martin and Ada have three grandchildren, and they saw the two of you come in, and they noticed you are with child. So when Martin walked by your table, he stopped to say that he and his wife hope your child is healthy and strong."

Without a word, Felina looked at him briefly and then looked back at the wall.

Fredric renewed his glare at Will. "But Martin didn't get all of his words out, did he? A sixty-eight-year old grandfather stops to tell an expectant mother that he and his wife hope you have a healthy and strong child. And for that, he ends up with a jaw broken in two places and comes within a quarter of an inch from losing his right eye. This is a high crime for which you could serve many years in prison for, but you don't think you have to explain yourself?"

Will shook his head. "Little man, you are starting to wear a little thin."

Fredric shook his head patiently. "You committed a high crime within my establishment. You brutally attacked a favored and long-time patron and badly injured him. Now you think you are going to simply walk out? Is that what you think?"

Will nodded. "If that is what I choose, yes I will."

Fredric stepped behind his desk and knocked on the wall several time. Within seconds, four men briskly walked into the office. All four of them were Will's size or larger, and they had very serious expressions on their faces. They were all business and obviously well trained. They were wearing suits, and one at a time, they pulled their left lapel back to reveal they were well armed.

Will had legal authorization to wear his gun at all times, but the four men positioned themselves in such a way that it was impossible for one man to cover any two of them, let alone all four. The four men neither smiled nor glared but continued to look straight at Will. Then Will noticed that one of them was focused on Felina's handbag. They were leaving nothing to chance, and they were assuming nothing. They were prepared for the unexpected.

Fredric nodded at the four security agents. "I thank you, gentlemen, very much. It is obvious what would happen if I had to face this man alone, and I will be the first to acknowledge it. So I thank you gentlemen, and I am so glad to have you working here."

Then the four men smiled, but they fanned out into a slightly larger circle. Will looked at the four of them and asked them why they did that. Fredric nodded at the lead man to explain.

"We are trained for several automatic responses, and one of them is that anytime we feel relaxed, we automatically fan out as a defensive maneuver in case we are being set up. We train for this so much we don't even realize we do it anymore."

Will nodded in respect to the lead man. "I also noticed that the fourth man here kept a constant eye on my fiancée's handbag."

The lead man nodded vigorously. "He was watching her hands too. We watch everyone's hands, pockets, boots, any kind of handbag, hats, back scratching, touching shirt sleeves, and all nonchalant movements. We don't care what you are saying. We watch out for what you are reaching for. And we never ever forget that a woman is just as dangerous as a man."

For the first time, Felina responded. She chuckled lightly, and then with her thumb and forefinger, she very carefully reached into her handbag and slowly pulled out a very lethal handgun by the end of the barrel. Then she said, "Your point is well taken."

Even Fredric chuckled as the lead man shrugged. "See what I mean?"

Felina dropped the gun back into her handbag so her hands remained clearly visible. However, the butt of her gun cracked her favorite makeup mirror.

Will then asked, "Don't tell me. Let me guess. When you leave this room, you will actually go on a higher alert status in case we are setting you up by acting friendly."

The lead man again looked at Fredric who nodded approval for an explanation. "Normally, you would be absolutely correct, but we know who you are, and despite the severity of your actions, we know that you can be a very big problem, but you are not a killer. That is why we came into this room without our weapons drawn."

Will thought for a moment. "Your training and your methods are very familiar."

The lead man shrugged. "They should be, sir."

Will nodded. "Jake?"

The lead man nodded and then gestured to his men, and with a gesture from Fredric, they left.

Jake was now a recognized authority on security and survival situations. He made a lot of money and did well giving classes and training. Even the sheriff sought his training, advice, and help. Jake spent six years in the army and was part of a top secret unit that protected senators, cabinet members, and the president and vice president. He left the army after he met Hannah and realized he could support a family far better as a civilian than he ever could in the military. He loved his job in the military, every minute of it, but he loved Hannah far more.

One of the toughest things Will has ever done in his life was to admit his grievous error and lack of emotional control. It helped enormously that Fredric was twenty years older than Will.

Within his own mind, Will is now convinced more than ever that Felina is, to be sure, casting a spell on him. To his mind, nothing else can explain the radical change in his behavior. But with that conviction, he must also believe that Felina is wicked and perhaps evil. He finally decides that it doesn't matter if Felina is casting a spell on him or not. He will choose Felina at any cost, even if it means his life.

In part, to give himself a little more time before facing Fredric, Will asked him a question. "Where did you get so much fight? You are a much bigger man on the inside than you are on the outside. Where do you get so much fight?"

Fredric became quite serious. "The answer to that is Biblical, and some people are offended by that."

Will shrugged. "Truth is where you find it."

Fredric almost became a different person, and the tone of his voice changed. "The night Jesus Christ was arrested, he refused to fight on the grounds that this world was not his kingdom. He said if this world was his kingdom, then he and his servants would fight. But since this was not his kingdom, he would not fight. This establishment has been given to me as my kingdom to manage. Therefore I will fight for it. With the last drop of my blood and my last breath of air and my last heartbeat, I will fight with everything at my disposal to protect and fight for my kingdom. So to answer your question, I look beyond myself for the power and strength to fight for the kingdom that has been given and entrusted to me."

Fredric took a deep breath and let it out slowly but did not take his eyes off Will. "But at this moment, Will, you are the biggest threat to my kingdom."

Will did not make eye contact with Fredric, but he did glance at Felina. "I behaved badly, and there are no excuses. But I will do anything I can to make it right."

Fredric's eyes widened with surprise. "Well, that's a good start, and I am impressed. But where do we go from here? How do we make it right, Will?"

Will shook his head. "I don't know. I don't even know where to start."

Fredric looked at Will without sympathy. "Making wagers is incompatible with my belief structure. But if I were to make a wager, I would bet heavily that you and your fiancée will figure something out rather quickly. "

Will shrugged and looked at Felina. "Do you have any ideas?"

Felina glared at Will. "I've got a few thoughts but they are moving a bit slow right now."

Shaking his head, Will looked at Fredric. "We don't know them. We don't know what they need or want. Actually, they are the only ones who know what it will take to make it right."

Fredric smiled slightly but quickly. "I would have won a wager. That didn't take long at all, and that is an excellent answer. "

Felina looked at Fredric with much fear. "Would you be willing to act as a go-between to see if there is a way we can make this right?"

Fredric hesitated but nodded. "Yes, I would. In fact, if you had not offered, I would have insisted to be directly involved. But keep in mind that it is very possible that there is nothing they need or want badly enough to make this right. However, with that being said, I am impressed and somewhat pleased at your reactions and willingness to make things right. I am due at the doctor's office to receive a detailed report and speak to Ada."

Will shrugged. "We will go home to our room at the Railyard. We will wait for you to contact us, and if we are not in our room, we won't be far."

Fredric nodded. "Agreed."

Will and Felina barely walked into their room at the Railyard before there was a knock at the door. It was a message from Fredric. The message contained just one word—*urgent*. But it was enough.

Within minutes, they walked back into the office they had just left half an hour ago.

Fredric had to gather his thoughts for a moment. He shook his head as if to clear the confusion from his mind. He paced the floor and then spoke to himself as much as Will and Felina.

"This was totally unexpected, and I did not see this coming. I had no idea they have such a problem. In fact, I didn't even suspect it."

Fredric interrupted himself and looked at Will and Felina with a stunned expression on his face, and he focused his attention on Felina. "Ada wants to talk to you tonight…immediately. Apparently there is something Will can do that would, to be sure, make things right. I have no idea of what Ada will ask, but be forewarned that she is going to ask much. They are very wealthy, so she does not want money or your restaurant or anything like that. But she will ask much of you. And instead of me being the go-between, she wants you to be such."

Then he looked at Will. "Apparently, because of Miss Libby's acceptance and praise of Felina, Felina is now a person of note and one to be listened to and respected. However, Ada has no desire to see you or talk to you. There is something you can do for them, and all will be forgiven but decidedly not forgotten."

Will shook his head. "Okay, Fredric, what's the deal?"

Fredric steepled his hands and rubbed his chin with his fingertips. Then he sternly focused his gaze on Will, without compassion. "First of all, the name Will Travis has been added to our list of undesirables, and you can never come to this establishment again without invitation, which at the moment, you have. Secondly, if you solve their problem, there will be no actions against you, and all will be forgiven. And for the sake of your business and Felina, mostly because of Felina, this issue will be kept quiet and private. There will be no legal actions, law officers, or lawsuits, no arrest or repercussions of any kind. However, I have no knowledge or idea of what their issue is."

Will smiled weakly and then scoffed. "Sure you do, all three of us have a good idea of what they want. They want me to kill somebody."

Fredric and Felina both nodded in agreement, and Fredric answered, "That thought does occur. But tell me, Will, if that is the case, what will you do?"

Will shook his head. "I don't know yet. I need to know some details so I can think it over and plan it out. I believe in two kinds of work. Hard work that makes you sweat and smart work that makes you successful…and keeps you alive longer."

For the first time, Fredric was hesitant. "I have a morbid curiosity about this. If you do this, how would you do such a thing? How would you go about it?"

"If I did something like that, it would be all legal and witnessed. I would goad him into a gunfight and shoot him. But I would make it look like he was the aggressor."

"But that means you are putting your life on the line."

Will shrugged. "You put your life on the line every time you walk down a flight of stairs or get on a horse."

"Yes, but I am able to walk downstairs and get on a horse with minimal risk. But the skills to pull a gun fast enough to shoot someone are beyond me."

Will chuckled. "You said it yourself, Fredric, this is my kingdom, so I will fight. I would look like an utter fool if I tried to be a maitre d'. And you would be an utter fool to pull leather against me. I really like what you said, each of us has been given a kingdom, and that is where we fight. The more we stay within our own kingdom, the better our life is. I really like what you said about that."

Then Fredric looked at Will with renewed respect. "Have you ever killed a man?"

Will nodded slowly. "I have been in a dozen gunfights, and I had to kill three of them. The others were slow enough for me to wound or they changed their minds and walked or they simply dropped their guns and ran. I have a nice, little collection of six-guns."

Then Fredric realized something. "Now I understand what Jake meant."

That piqued Will's interest. "Oh. What did he say?"

Fredric shrugged. "He said that you are the only man in his adult life that he has ever feared."

Will laughed. "I whipped Jake because he made a big mistake. Jake doesn't make the same mistake twice, so I don't want a rematch."

For the first time, Fredric smiled. "He likes you too."

Then both men became aware that something was wrong. They quickly looked around the room and realized that Felina was gone. It was decided that Will would go home and wait for her, and

Fredric would go to the doctor's office and see if she was there. As it turned out, Felina was at Ada's home drinking tea, and they were discussing the situation.

Patience is not part of Will's kingdom, so he paced the floor nervously for the next hour.

When Felina got home, her face was ashen and laced with fear.

She handed Will a note written by Martin.

> I will kiss the hand that inflicted my injuries and count it a blessing if you will relieve our torment. I plead with you to make my wife smile again and laugh again without being afraid, for we live in great fear to answer our own door.

Will quickly burned the note and asked Felina what their problem was.

Felina shook her head. "Maybe Aunt Libby is right. Everyone who becomes successful is a saloon girl in one way or another. Does anyone make it to the top without double-dealing, lying, cheating, or stealing?"

Will shrugged. "You and Phebe come to mind, but you're the only two that I know of. As you well know, I had to lie and be deceitful to get *my* wealth. Plus I had to spend a year in a soft prison to keep it. But I'm not going to serve several years in a real prison, no matter what."

Will braced himself. "Okay, honey. What are we looking at?"

Felina took a deep breath. "You were right. They desperately need a man...a man...taken down. Apparently, Martin embezzled a lot of money from the company he worked for, over a long period. Martin worked for a company that designed and built customized steam-powered paddlewheels. When he retired, a junior executive named Edgar discovered the missing money purely by accident and correctly guessed who took it. Then Edgar kept the company records as proof. He has made his living by blackmailing Martin and Ada for many years, but that's not enough for him. He has tormented them and made them live in fear every day of their lives. He will even come knocking on the door at 2 a.m. just for the torment. And right when he gets to the point of pushing them too far, he will back off and get friendly for awhile. Then it's right back to the torment and fear. Edgar even threatened their grandchildren once, but only once, now he has a large scar on his left cheek from Ada attacking him. In retaliation, Edgar demanded more money, but Martin told him to accept what they agreed on or he will get nothing. Again, Edgar backed off for a while, but lately, Edgar has been telling them he has plenty of money saved up and won't need them much longer. But they have had enough, and they were ready to hire an assassin when we came along. And what I am telling you now is just a very small part of what he's done."

Felina's eyes were wide with fear. "Will, are you as good with a gun as you say you are?"

He shrugged slightly. "The truth?"

"Yes, the truth. For God's sake, Will, be honest with me."

"I'm better. I have a very strong natural talent for guns. And even more, I have an equally strong sense of who to pull leather against and who to slap on the back and buy a drink. I have the skills, but I have never been passionate about guns or gun fighting. It takes many thousands of fast-draw pulls every month to be an elite gunfighter, but I can take on anyone except the elite. But to answer your question straight out, although I am not among the elite, I am nonetheless very good with a gun, and that, my love, is the truth."

Felina sighed. "That makes me feel a lot better."

"And next time you see Ada, tell her Edgar is a two-bit liar about having money saved up. That is just a bluff to scare them. His kind is not capable of saving money, and he always needs more money, not less. And I need some information about Edgar."

"What do you need?"

"I need everything Martin and Ada know about this man. Approximate height and weight, where he lives, known strengths and weaknesses, girlfriend's names, where he's from and where he's been, and anything else they can think of, especially things like his favorite saloon and how often he comes to town to buy supplies, food, grain for his horse, and anything like that."

Felina scoffed. "That will be easy enough. He makes sure they know where he is almost at all times and when he shows up at their home half-drunk or more he talks a lot. He doesn't have anyone else to talk to."

Will shook his head and smiled. "Then I give Edgar an A plus in stupidity."

"What are you going to do, Will?"

"I don't know yet. All I know for sure is that I'm not going to prison for five or ten years, even if I have to shoot this guy. I can make it look like his fault, but I need that list of things they know about him, and we will take it from there."

Ada stayed up all night making a list that totaled five pages.

When Felina brought the list from Ada, Will looked through it briskly, searching for red flags. On page one, he found Edgar's favorite saloon and when he would be there. Then he found what he was really looking for on page three. Will smiled at Felina and pointed to a line on page three.

Edgar often claims to be the fastest gunfighter alive.

Will rubbed his chin. "His favorite saloon is the Blue Diamond, and I know when he will be there. And he claims to be the fastest gunfighter alive. That's all I need to know."

Felina sat in a corner at the Blue Diamond Saloon and remained silent. She was absolutely terrified.

Will's gun belt was too low and all wrong. The angle of his holster was wrong, and his gun was hanging loose in his holster and was much too far from his gun hand, and his holster strap wasn't tied to his leg properly. Will had all the looks of a buffoon, and he appeared to be the most incompetent gunfighter in the west.

Then Will kept a friendly smile and casually spoke so that only Edgar could hear, but he used words that he knew would enrage him. "You've been tormenting some friends of mine for too many years. Now I am ordering you out of town. I command you to take what you've got from them and get out...or else."

Edgar spit out his words. "Or else what?"

Will's mocking chuckle was infuriating. "Or else you will have to face me in a fair gunfight, and a yellow, gutless coward like you has no experience at doing anything fair."

Then the maggot among men grinned with insult and sneered at Will. Then Edgar spoke loud enough for everyone to hear. "I'm calling you out, mister, you and me right here and right now. And to show everybody I know how to fight fair, I'm even gonna let you draw first, dead man."

Will mocked him. "Please don't hurt me, mister."

Then Will quickly readjusted his gun belt, his holster, his gun, and properly tied his holster to his leg. Suddenly, as Will stood ready to fight, he did not appear so incompetent. Then Will mocked Edgar with the last words Edgar would ever hear.

"Ladies first."

Edgar now realized that Will has set him up. But he has said too much, plus he has openly challenged Will. He cannot back down now, which is exactly what Will planned.

Felina closed her eyes tightly, and fear gripped her heart so tight it was hard for her to breathe. Maybe this was a bad idea.

Edgar lied; he did not let Will draw first, but that was also part of Will's plan, a big part.

Martin and Ada's long-time tormentor clearly made the first move, but he barely gripped the handle of his gun and pulled his gun no more than a few inches from the bottom of his holster before a bullet ripped through the center of his chest and liquefied his blackened heart. Edgar was dead before the bullet exited his back.

The sheriff's investigation into the gunfight took about fifteen minutes. There were plenty of notable and distinguished witnesses who heard Edgar call Will out, and the same credible witnesses saw Edgar make the first move.

The gunfight solved a torturous problem for Martin and Ada, and it kept Will out of prison, but it also unexpectedly and significantly increased business at the Railyard.

Even Fredric was so impressed he sent Will a note of support and genuine respect. The gunfight went exactly as Will planned, except for one thing—Felina.

As things settled down over the next few weeks, Felina began to think and to ponder just how close they came to total disaster and ruin. It was only by a massive stroke of luck that they were spared utter destruction. Felina understood that such massive luck occurs only once in a lifetime, and she also understood that such luck was fleeting. The more she thought about it, the more concerned and fearful she became. This cannot happen again with any expectations of survival. But her darkest thought was to ask herself if there were any real signs or indications that it won't happen again. She had to answer to herself, and the answer was no. She did not see anything that suggested Will has changed or anything to believe that it won't happen again. She then realized that Will simply got away with a monstrous, life-shattering mistake.

She thought back at Will's explosion of jealousy and his instant and extreme response. No matter how much she tried to justify or excuse his actions within her own mind, most people just don't behave like that. The mere thought of Papa doing anything remotely like this is unthinkable.

She has seen similar actions and behavior at Rosa's, but they were strangers, and there was no emotional impact, nor did it affect her life. Besides, Will wasn't drunk; he was stone-cold sober when he exploded. His actions could have destroyed their entire lives, not to mention the impact on their child. The more she thought about it, the more she realized that Will's jealousy was far more powerful and far worse than she ever imagined. And the more she thought about it, the more she realized that Will's actions were unjustifiably irrational.

Will's own actions forced her to conclude that Will is nothing short of emotionally unstable and violently jealous. But Felina cannot help herself; she's carrying his child, and she loves him.

But on the other side of the coin, Will blames Felina for his irrational behavior. Will has never acted like this in his life, and he has never been so out of control and so quick with his fist. Now he is getting a little quicker with his gun. Shooting Edgar came easy, a little too easy. To his mind, Felina was casting a powerful spell on him. She must have powers that she won't admit to. Besides, how could a saloon girl captivate someone as powerful and influential as Miss Libby? It must be Felina, not himself, causing him to act the way he does. Will now believes even more that to some degree, Felina was wicked and evil. But he was hopelessly in love with her.

If Felina could know how Will truly felt about her inside of his own mind and what his thoughts really were, she would be shattered.

However, there was now a time of counterfeit peace and calm before the final storm. Will's jealousy faded, and he became more protective as Felina became heavy with child. And his demon slept as Felina's figure and form were temporarily lost to the form of bearing a child.

But a point of contention between Will and Felina was that he did not understand that while Felina may say the same things she did, or even flirt, they no longer mean the same thing. She still flirted and said nice things to men, but the meaning was totally different now. Much of the problem was that although Felina does not go very often anymore, Will has grown increasingly impatient with Felina still visiting Rosa's. But now even Rosa is telling her it would be best if she stopped visiting the Cantina for a while, especially after the altercations and shooting. Despite her insecurities, carrying Will's child gave Felina the strength to sever her bonds with Rosa's, saloons, and dancing. She decides to make a visit to Rosa's to say good-bye and to let everyone know it was her last visit until the baby was born.

SIX MONTHS LATER

Felina held her two-month-old son up as high as she could. Little William showed no fear as he flailed his arms, kicked his legs, and laughed. Felina lovingly lowered him into her arms and brushed his already ample red hair back with her hand.

Felina beamed and glowed as she spoke to her son. "William Travis Jr. That sounds like a good name for a president, or a senator at the least. Daddy and I are going to start your campaign for mayor next week, and Grandma Libby will help." It was a good day, not only for little William but for Felina. Phebe and Ben were back and almost settled in, and little William has been declared fit as a fiddle by the doctor.

But the biggest news was that Felina has finally decided to sever all ties to saloon life. Since the night she met Will, Felina has declined to be a saloon girl in the full sense, but now she will no longer dance, share drinks, or dress as a saloon girl. They have more than enough money to retire, and thanks to Phebe, they are making more money every day on their investments, especially the Railyard. Felina has overcome her fears, and she now trusts Will with her heart as well as the rest of her life. Little William has changed everything, and for the first time in her life, Felina has a man she loves who is as close to her in the daylight as he is at night.

Sadly, Will's jealousy returned within a few days of Felina delivering little William. She thought his jealously to be a dead demon, but it was merely asleep while she was swollen with child. But now that she has decided to sever ties with Rosa's and will no longer visit them, certainly the demon of jealously will be gone forever.

Felina wanted Phebe to be the first to know about her final break from saloon life. But unknown to Felina was that Phebe has something to tell her as well. In fact, Phebe was worrying over how to tell Felina about the ranch they just bought, and even more so, Phebe is fretting over how to talk Felina and Will into moving their family and their lives some 350 miles. Tragically, they never get to discuss it.

The final act of gratitude by the cattle company Ben worked for was to offer Ben and Phebe a large ranch house, named Casa Grande, with five large barns, dozens of windmills, and five thousand acres of prime grazing land, all for a pittance. Actually, due to several changes and growth, not to mention corruption, the ranch is a burden to the cattle company, and they lose money on it every day. They were glad to get any reasonable amount of cash for it and glad to be rid of the crippling operating expenses. Plus it gave them more publicity for their *kindness*, and it helped Ben, who is a company hero. Ben served his company well. Not only is he a legend within the cattle industry, but the company can now hire the best cowboys and the best trail bosses in the country. At every position, the company can now sign the best of the best. Every cowhand of note now wants to work for the company Ben worked for.

But Ben and Phebe are nobody's fools, and they already know what the problem is with the ranch and the dangers involved and how to solve those problems. They hired an expert to observe what was going on and to fill out a report that did not assess liability. There was rampant corruption and three times more ranch hands than needed. The surplus ranch hands, who were doing little or no work, were giving a large percentage of their salary back to the bosses. And there were 183 head of cattle where there should have been over 2,000, which made it obvious the corruption went much higher than just the ranch. However, there were some 250 horses left. The long-term corruption has left little to work with or make a profit on. The payroll was bloated beyond survival level, and the cattle were gone. Yet the ranch itself is in excellent condition. Ben and Phebe had the skills, the cash, and the desire to make the ranch profitable within a very short time. But they had to get the ranch, fences, windmills, and barns intact with no major damage. Ben has seen such ranches razed to the ground because the new owners decided to get tough and did not understand their vulnerability or understand human lust for destruction. However, Ben is neither weak nor stupid. If Ben was too strong, there would be reprisals, and if too weak, there would be laughter and disrespect. Either way, the ranch would be severely damaged or destroyed. Most likely, it would be burned.

As part of the deal on the Casa Grande, Ben asked the company to send the lead foreman who ran the ranch and made the day to day decisions to El Paso to meet with him. Some in management considered this unreasonable, but the district manager immediately understood that Ben wanted to make a private deal, most likely to keep the Casa Grande intact. The district manager informed the lead foreman to make the trip, and he told the foreman what he wanted out of the deal. Then the manager told the foreman to make sure he came to an agreement because the company was most anxious to get rid of the long-time money pit with the grand name.

Ben and the foreman met at the Railyard in El Paso. The foreman asked Ben what he had in mind. Ben said that rather than waste a lot time he would make his best offer right up front and be done with it. Ben admitted that his main interest was in getting the Casa Grande intact and in its current condition.

Ben offered to pay every man who resigned and walked away in peace a month's pay. The foreman, whom he was talking to, would get a year's pay, and his assistant would get six months pay. The foreman shook his head and told Ben the payouts would be several thousand dollars.

Ben did not want the foreman to know he and Phebe had a lot of money. So he passed it off as having good credit but said the cash would be no problem. He just wanted the ranch intact. Ben then asked if there was anyone else, possibly upstream, who needed a share. The foreman nodded and told Ben there were some problems with the fences, and it was possible the 250 horses could escape before the fences could be fixed. Of course there were no problems with the fences. The 250 horses were to pay off the district superintendant. Ben clearly understood this and nodded in agreement and told the foreman that would be acceptable.

Ben was about to warn the foreman that Ben held him personally responsible for the Casa Grande to be intact when he took possession. But the foremen spoke first and told Ben he would personally give Ben and Phebe a tour of the ranch and allow them to inspect everything with him present. Then upon their approval, they will meet at the bank where the signatures will be witnessed, legally documented, and recorded. The foreman will then give them the keys to the ranch and the prospective buyers will then sign off on liabilities, and then the foreman will provide Ben and Phebe with surveyor's reports, deeds, mineral rights, timber rights, grazing rights, and the transfer of ownership papers.

The money was transferred, everyone was paid, and all agreements were kept. All went according to plan including the horses *escaping*.

Thus is the history of the home Ben and Phebe bought to build their future and to rear and nurture their two children: their daughter Lynda and little William.

The Casa Grande is where little William would grow and mature into a young man. The Casa Grande is in New Mexico Territory three and a half miles from a small town, a small town called Agua Fria. Little William would grow to be a six-foot-two-inch, 240-pound man with genius level intellect, a college degree, world class boxing skills, reflexes like a cat, and flaming red hair—a young man who was no longer called *little* William. However, William was a gentle giant; he was polite, had a quick smile and a soft voice, and was always eager to help—that is, as long as Ben and Phebe were alive and before he and Lynda moved back to El Paso for a year.

However, while Ben was still convalescing from his bullet wounds, Felina all but forced them to stay in a deluxe suite at the Railyard, and they had fun squabbling over paying or not paying. Sadly, Felina never knew about the Casa Grande that was 350 miles away. Again, it was tragic that they ran out of time before they were able to discuss it.

Felina knocked on Phebe's door quietly so as not to disturb the sleeping babies. Felina told Phebe that she was making one last visit to Rosa's and say good-bye. Phebe was happy to watch little William.

As Phebe opened the door, Felina said. "I'm here to collect the rent. I'll settle for your firstborn."

They laughed, but Phebe noticed that Felina was somehow subdued. Her tone of voice and the look in her eyes was not the Felina she knew. Felina was fine that morning but was very different now.

Felina looked around the room. "Phebe, who could have possibly guessed three years ago that we would end up where we are now?"

Phebe shook her head. "I would be the last one on that list of names. Are you all right? Is something wrong?"

Felina looked at her with pleading eyes. "I feel…I have a strong sense of foreboding, like someone is going to die."

Phebe smiled but was unconvincing even to herself. "Sometimes having a baby will do that. It does things to your mind. You'll be all right…I promise."

They talked for a while and then decided to get together tomorrow and catch up on everything happening in their lives. Phebe especially wanted to know every detail of what happened in New Mexico with Alexander. And she wanted to meet Jake.

They talked and reminisced until it was past dark. As Felina got up to leave, Phebe hesitated for a moment and then forged ahead. "We think we have found a new home. But it's…"

Felina interjected, "Oh, that's great. I want to hear all about it when I get back from saying good-bye to Rosa and the girls. Let's go see it tomorrow."

Phebe cleared her throat. "It might be a bit too far for the babies."

"That's okay, we'll have Will watch the babies, and that will give us a chance to have a nice, long talk on the way out there."

Phebe nodded and rolled her eyes. "You got that part right."

Felina hugged her. "You made me feel a lot better, my dancing sister. Now I will finally go say good-bye to Rosa and the girls. I'll be back soon." And with that, she walked out the door. As she closed the door, Felina heard the last words Phebe would ever say to her... I love you, Fela.

Phebe shook her head. Some of what Felina said was almost like she was saying good-bye to her rather than Rosa and the girls. Suddenly, Phebe felt an icy chill run down her spine, and she felt the same foreboding of impending death. She shuttered and then spoke in a whisper, "Damn, Felina. Now you've got me spooked. And of course, it has to be dark outside. Why couldn't we do this at noon?"

Instinctively, Phebe checked the babies.

There were hugs, congratulations, and tears of joy and several toasts. They talked at length and laughed and wished one another well. One of the girls said that because Phebe and Felina had done so well, it gave the rest of them hope for their own futures. Then Rosa told Felina that it was time for her to go home to her man and her son.

Felina agreed, she said her last good night, and started for the door. Then it happened.

A wild, young cowboy came in. He was as wild as the west Texas wind, and he was so young that he just turned nineteen a few weeks ago while on his first cattle drive. He walked through Rosa's swinging doors whooping and hollering and holding his sweat-stained hat as high as he could reach. For the first time in his young life, he truly felt like a man. He had done a man's job, and he had done so well on the drive that he had already been hired for another. His name was Allan.

Allan looked at all of the girls and said all he wanted was just one drink with each girl. Felina was almost at the door when the young, innocent man pleaded for her to have just one drink. After all, his next drink would be with another girl.

Felina smiled and shrugged. "Well, this will be my last farewell drink."

She was happy and glowing. Therefore she was smiling wide and beaming with joy.

Felina and the ever-so-young cowboy sat down. They had just sat down at a table. It had not been so much as a full minute since they sat down.

It was absolutely the worst time imaginable for Will to walk in and see Felina sharing a drink with a cowboy, regardless of how young he was. Will has been looking for Felina for over three hours, and his raging jealousy has been running wild. Before anyone could speak, something inside of Will snapped.

Will saw Felina before she saw him, and he totally misinterpreted her glowing face and wide smiles. With his own eyes, he saw her beaming with joy. Will refused to believe it was because of any love for him. It was already too late; the situation was beyond recovery.

Will grabbed Allan with his left hand and punched him hard in the face. Then Will backed up.

"I see you're wearing a gun. Now is the time to use it. Pull it, or I will kill you where you stand."

Felina and a couple of the girls desperately tried to explain nothing had happened and that Felina was leaving when the young man came in. Even Rosa tried to tell Will that the young man was having one drink with each of the girls. But it was too late. It was too late for Allan, and it was even too late for Will. What happened next was inevitable and had been destined for some time.

Will screamed at Allan. "Pull your gun, or I will kill you. You are getting more than fair warning. Now pull your damn gun or die."

Allan shook his head. "You don't understand, sir. Please let me explain. I meant no harm, and I don't want to cause any trouble. Please, sir, let me explain. You don't understand. Let me show you."

Again Will screamed at him. "If you're old enough to wear a gun, you are old enough to pull it. Now pull leather or die. This is your last chance. Pull your damn gun, boy, now."

Allan shook his head all the more. "You don't understand. Please let me show you. I need to show you something, sir. Please let me explain. I will buy you a drink, and I am sorry. I will leave and never come back."

"You should have thought about that before you walked into a saloon wearing a gun. Now for the last time…pull your gun or die where you are standing."

Allan continued to shake his head. "I can't. Please let me show you something. You need to see this. Please, sir." Then the young man made a fatal mistake by slowly reaching down for his gun.

In less than a heartbeat, Will pulled his gun and shot the kid just over his heart.

Allan's face instantly reflected his imminent death, and his knees started to buckle. Just before he fell forward, Allan held his gun up, sideways, for Will to see. "It's not even loaded, sir. I only wore it to feel like a man." Allan then crumpled and fell to the floor. The ever-so-young cowboy was dead within seconds, his twitching body violated by the violence and evil of a fatal bullet that tore a hole all the way through him.

Just for a moment, Will stood there in silence, shocked and unmoving by the foul evil deed he has done. The magnitude of Will's crime has yet to be absorbed by his paralyzed mind.

Many thoughts raced through his mind as the growing reality of his unchangeable act has shattered his entire life and several others. The Railyard is gone, Felina is gone, and all of their wealth is now meaningless. His son will be fatherless, and all that he has done was destroyed and lying beside Allan's dead body. His life is now as devastated and lifeless as the young cowboy's body. Felina had cast no spell, and he now realized that his behavior and actions changed because he himself changed.

He cannot yet comprehend what he has done and the hideous crime he has committed.

Then his numbed mind awakened enough for a single word to echo throughout his mind and soul—murder. Suddenly, he realized that he didn't kill the young cowboy; he murdered him.

Will now examined his innermost soul, and all too late, he now realizes in horror and terror. "Oh my God, it is not Felina who is evil...it's me."

Will looked around the saloon and to a man and woman he saw the same shocked and stunned faces and the look of his guilt. He knew the same word went through their minds as well as his own—murder. And there was no question that every person in the room thought him guilty. Even Felina's beautiful face reflected the evil and the guilt of his crime.

Will now realized he has but one chance and that is to run. And he has to run, now.

A fleeting last glance at Felina and out through the back door he ran, out where the horses were tied. Will caught a good one that looked like it could run. And he did run, as fast as he could, from El Paso all the way out to the badlands of New Mexico.

It took ten seconds for Allan to die, and when Allan died, so did Will's life of wealth and honor and his life with Felina. Will was now living an entirely new life, a life of fear and running and desperately trying to stay alive. Every moment, he fears everyone and everything. Even in the badlands, he was far from peace. Will was startled by the sound of a snapping twig, and he pulled his gun. Trembling and breaking out in a cold sweat and searching for nonexistent threats, he was ready to shoot. Then he slowly lowered his gun and his head. It was his own footstep that snapped the twig. He shook his head and thought that maybe the sheriff doesn't need a posse, he is not far from shooting at himself. How could he be so scared of his own footsteps?

His mind is flooded with equal parts of horror, terror, and crippling guilt. Will has never been a fugitive before, not on the scale of murder. *Oh God in heaven, is it possible to wake up and find this to be the spawn of all nightmares?*

Back in El Paso at Rosa's, the mind-shattering disaster has left Felina in catatonic shock. She is terrified of Will returning to get her and her not being there. Her son is in good hands, and Felina will not leave Rosa's. But Phebe cannot risk putting herself in danger of the ferocious gun-fire that is certain to occur when Will returns. Felina has seen Phebe... and her son... for the last time.

After five agonizing days in the badlands with his own insanity tearing at his mind, he could no longer endure the pain—not pain in his body but the excruciating, merciless pain in his heart. How could he have possibly been so incredibly stupid and so brutal? He had everything, he had the world on a string, but he destroyed everything, all for nothing. And adding insult to injury, he was totally wrong about his internal accusations of Felina. He was wrong about everything.

Back in El Paso, his life would be worthless. Everything was gone, and nothing was left, except for Felina. It's been so long since he had seen her that his love for her was now stronger than his fear of death. Will grimly made his decision; without much hope of getting to Felina, he was going back to El Paso anyway.

In his cruel but self-inflicted loneliness, Will spoke aloud, "Felina might not even want me anymore. Maybe she's the one who will fire the bullet with my name on it. But I have got to see her, and as soon as it gets dark, I will—"

Suddenly, two gunshots rang out in the distance. Will instantly realized from the sound that the gunshots were fired in the air. Someone was trying to get his attention, but he was still very wary and cautious. Will has camped just below the peak of a small hill that gave him an excellent view to see anyone approaching from the east. Will waited, and twenty minutes later, two more gunshots rang out, but much closer. The rider was either someone he knew, or it was a setup. Right now, he was figuring fifty-fifty. But friend or foe, how could anyone possibly have found him?

Will could now see the rider, and he soon recognized the Indian blanket under the saddle. Now it made sense. If anyone could find him, it was Jake. Will fired two shots in response. Then he could hear the rider, hopefully Jake, shouting but could not hear what he was saying.

Just in case, Will kept his rifle at ready until he recognized Jake.

Will told Jake to have Felina ready to leave at five o'clock tomorrow afternoon from Rosa's back door. He had to pick her up at Rosa's because Rosa's Cantina was at the very edge and outskirts of town, but the Railyard was almost a mile into the city. Each day he had been gone, Will had moved closer back to El Paso. Jake left, and Will waited until dark. He rode all night and intended to pick Felina up at Rosa's back door and be gone before anyone knew he was there. Will arrived at the hill overlooking El Paso at noon, but agonizingly, he must rest his horse for several hours. Two riders would be far too much for the exhausted horse to carry. Will intended to ride in quickly, pick Felina up, and then flee to Mexico until they can get to Europe.

An old rival, Oliver, spotted Will at the base of the mountain pass and reported him to the sheriff.

The sheriff feared Will greatly, so he asked Jake to lead the posse, but Jake declined. Then the sheriff pleaded with Jake to join the posse, but Jake refused. Then the sheriff demanded that Jake join them, but again Jake was unwavering and refused. Then the sheriff threatened Jake, but again, Jake did not waver.

The sheriff only had two hours to prepare, but a very large posse soon awaited Will near Rosa's Cantina. They remained hidden, waiting for Will to make his move and try to get to Rosa's back door. Then Will came riding in at a full gallop, but the posse had him surrounded before he even knew they were there. The posse was shouting and shooting, but Will was determined to make it to Rosa's back door. Felina heard a rifle shot, and she began to cry, and Will knew he had but moments to live.

Then Will knew something was dreadfully wrong as he felt a deep burning pain in his side. He was unspeakably weary, and he desperately tried to stay in his saddle, but he could no longer hold on, and he fell from his horse. Suffering the depths of exhaustion from a dying body, Will half-staggered and half-ran toward Rosa's back door, but he could no longer move in a straight line. His sight was almost gone, but off to his right, he saw five mounted cowboys and off to his left ride a dozen or more. Will saw that he was so close, and he must make it to Rosa's back door.

No longer able to run or move and as he stood there, he suddenly felt the quiet calm of impending death, and everything moved ever so slowly. The shouting, shooting, and thunderous hooves of the horses all faded into silence as Will looked around, now helpless and unable to so much as lift his arms. He was growing cold. It was well over a hundred degrees, but Will was getting colder with each heartbeat.

Then he saw the white puff of smoke from a rifle, and he felt the searing hot bullet go deep in his chest. The sickening sound of the bullet smacking and tearing into Will's body carried back to the shooter, who will be emotionally scarred for life. Will's shooter had tears flowing down his cheeks and he was crying. Just as Will's dying body failed him and he started to crumple and fall forward, the shooter lowered his rifle, and even though he was all but dead, Will was stunned to see who the shooter was; it is Josiah, the telegraph operator's son who helped so much when Ben was shot. Josiah was nineteen by a month, and Will had given Josiah his first steak dinner for his birthday.

Felina knew the posse was there, and now she ran out the back door screaming that Will never fired back or so much as drew his gun.

Will had but a moment left to live, barely enough for one little kiss good-bye and then he died in Felina's arms. Felina then grabbed the still holstered six-gun Will wore, and she pressed it against her breast. Then as she screamed curses at them and as she screamed for them to bury them together in hell so they can get some peacc, she pulled the trigger that instantly stilled her young, shattered heart, and she fell forward onto Will's lifeless body. Will was carrying the same six-gun Felina herself bought shortly after running away from home. And in all of this and with so many shooting at him, it was as Felina accused them; Will never fired back or so much as pulled his gun.

Even though it was technically illegal, the sheriff put Jake in jail for thirty days for contempt. The sheriff was extremely friendly and accommodating and allowed Hannah to come and go as she pleased. The sheriff did not even lock the jail cell door. Jake even swept the front walkway just to stay busy. Jake and the sheriff talked, played cards, and even joked. The sheriff also allowed Hannah to bring Jake anything he wanted to eat or even drink. The sheriff explained that he needed to do this to at least appear that he was setting an example with no exceptions.

However, on the eve of his release, the sheriff locked the cell door. The sheriff's entire demeanor changed radically, and then he began telling Jake a story. "There was a sheriff who would mark men for death, mostly for not doing what they were told. The sheriff would then politely put them in jail and then treat them like a king for the term of their sentence—"

Jake interrupted. "I know this story, sheriff, and I know what you are getting at. The sheriff that you speak of would then kill the unwary and unsuspecting prisoner on the eve of his release."

The sheriff pulled his gun and then opened the cell door to get a clear shot. Jake was shot in the back and killed. But Jake won the final battle. A bullet in the back while in jail cannot be rightfully explained, and Jake knew he had people who would not settle for the sheriff's explanation.

The sheriff had pulled his gun and told Jake that he would not tolerate Jake's refusal to lead the posse. Jake humiliated him, and he will not tolerate that. He is the sheriff, not Jake, and he told Jake that he should have done what he was told. But Jake knew he was going to die, so he lunged for the sheriff's throat, and the instant Jake heard the click of the hammer, Jake spun around as fast as he could. The sheriff tried to stop himself, but it was too late. He couldn't stop in time, and he pulled the trigger and shot Jake squarely in the back. This could not be explained, but the arrogant sheriff thought that everyone would simply accept what he said because he said so. But a bullet in the back inside a jail cell cannot be justified, and Jake knew the sheriff could not explain it. Jake died knowing he would be avenged, and he was right. But he never would have guessed it would be Alexander who would take vengeance for him.

There was no meaningful investigation, and the killer was never caught, not officially. But Jake was killed by an unusual caliber bullet from an unusual gun, the same as the sheriff carried. A few months later, Alexander sent Nathan and a backup man to ask the sheriff a few questions. But the sheriff disappeared and was never heard from or seen again. The overly arrogant sheriff knew his gun was unusual, and he was sending a message to those who would cross him. Alexander sent his own message—Jake was family, and if you kill a member of Alexander's family, you will die. Someone spread a rumor that the sheriff was killed by a grieving widow with no mercy. Alexander would not allow Hannah to kill, but he did let her watch the sheriff die.

The scene and focus returns to the gunfighters' table in the saloon in Agua Fria. Texas Red concluded telling his life story to the ranger. Texas Red casually glanced around and glowed inside when he saw that everyone in the nearly packed saloon was totally mesmerized and captivated by every word he had been saying. Some of the women even had tears in their eyes. Moreover, several reporters wrote and recorded every syllable of every word of Texas Red's entire life story.

"My mother, Felina, left a third of their wealth and legal custody of me to Mama Phebe and Papa Ben. And the bulk of Mother and Father's wealth was left to me when I reached legal age. Mama and Papa reared me as if I was their own, but they did not hesitate to tell me about Mother and Father in great detail. They told me many times that if my mind could formulate a question, then my mind was able to accept the answer. They hid nothing, and they did not glorify my parents, neither did they speak ill of them. They simply told me what happened, as best they could."

The ranger was a much simpler man. He was an Arizona ranger with a duty to perform, and he was a man with a brother to avenge. The ranger was one thing and one thing only, he was a gunfighter.

THE RANGER AND TEXAS RED

1882

A rizona ranger Kyle Lawton was not only the fastest gunfighter alive, he was among the fastest gunfighters who have ever lived. However, this supreme achievement came at what very well could be the ultimate price.

The ranger is the fastest gun alive…except.

He is one of the fastest, best, and most deadly gunfighter who has ever lived…except.

Becoming the best gunfighter on earth was his dream and driving ambition from childhood, and he has achieved it…except. Except for his secret injury.

The ranger has a fatal secret, not fatal to his opponent, but fatal to himself. The ranger has a hidden but severe injury that both sleeps and awakes with no warning, an injury that turned him from the best into the most helpless gunfighter alive.

Texas Red just might face the fastest gun alive on Saturday. However, he might, he just might, face a gunfighter as helpless as a twelve-year-old child. The price for being the best could cost the ranger his life, and the price for being the best had already cost him every other aspect of his life. The ranger is thirty-one years old, and he knows that he will never get any better and certainly no faster. He knew that he had to work much harder and practice much harder, not to get better but to simply maintain the skills he has, or as much of them as he can. Most of all, the ranger did not know for sure if he was at, or past his peak, and if he was past his peak, he did not know by how much, and worst of all, the ranger had a demon that haunted him mercilessly, even in his restless, tortured sleep. The longer the ranger stayed in one place, the stronger his internal demon became. The ranger had his chance to leave town and walk away, but he himself was the one who made the decision that now trapped him in a prison that became a little more of hell every day. The ranger cannot leave town without facing Texas Red's threat to hunt him down and kill him.

Part of the price of being the best is constant, never-ending practice and constant never-ending attention to every conceivable detail. The ranger, as well as Texas Red, had more hours perfecting the size, shape, angle, flexibility, and feel of his holster than most gunfighters put into all aspects of their gun fighting combined. However, like a razor-sharp double-edge sword of Damocles hanging over his head, the never-ending practice and pulling a four-and-a-half-pound Big Iron so many thousands, nay, tens of thousands, of pulls that made him the best are the very things that are now beginning to turn against him. It is almost unbelievable, but very likely, that the ranger has pulled the Big Iron half a million draws. What was required of him and was indispensable for him to do in order to be the best are the very actions and physical limits that could now pull the ranger from the best in the world to his grave.

The ranger desperately wanted to leave town, not to run, but to practice and hone his skills, but he did not want to practice where Texas Red can watch him. To be sure, the ranger wanted Texas Red to see his blinding speed, but what if his potentially fatal injury reared its ugly head and Texas Red learned the ranger's greatest weakness? The ranger made his choice to stay in town to arrest Texas Red and then face Texas Red in a gunfight. However, Texas Red had made it very clear that the ranger cannot leave town without facing a clear threat of death. Ironically, the ranger was in fact a prisoner—a gun-carrying prisoner free to go anywhere in town he wanted, but a prisoner nonetheless.

It was already past time for the ranger to practice and maintain his matchless skills. The ranger's draw was so incredibly fast that he cannot go more than a few days without diligent and extensive practice that included several hundred draws. The ranger must repeatedly fire the very powerful and equally loud Big Iron. Firing the weapon was part of the draw and part of the *feel* to maintain his speed, accuracy, and skills. However, the ranger's blinding speed magnified the slightest error in his draw.

There were four steps to a fast draw, and the ranger's speed was so great that each step must be flawless with no room for the slightest error. The first step was waiting to begin the draw with gun hand, holster, and body in perfect position for the fastest draw possible. The second step was starting the draw and simultaneously fanning or thumb cocking the gun and closing the gun hand around the gun handle. The third step was bringing the gun in line. The gun was now fully cocked and ready to fire. The wrist of the gun hand started to pivot to bring the gun in-line with the target. The index finger entered the trigger guard in preparation for pulling the trigger. The final step spoke for itself—firing the weapon and hitting the target.

The ranger sent a message to Texas Red that he needed to see him immediately about an urgent matter. The ranger waited impatiently in the saloon at the *gunfighters'* table but did not have to wait long. Texas Red was already on his way into town when the messenger met him on the south road about a mile out.

Everyone in the saloon was giving the ranger a wide berth. They had not seen him so anxious or edgy in the short time they have known him, and they do not know him well enough to know what to expect. It was very clear the ranger was very apprehensive about something, and they did not like what they were seeing.

Texas Red walked quickly into the saloon and was very concerned about any potential problem with the ranger. Texas Red would not tolerate anything interfering with his greatest moment of glory or his savoring of every minute of the weeklong buildup to the once-in-a-lifetime gunfight. He sat across the table from the obviously uneasy ranger.

"Is something wrong, ranger?"

The ranger looked away for a moment and then back at Texas Red. "I need to leave town for a day…you know I will be back."

Texas Red thought for a moment and then slowly shook his head. "A day out of town means half a day out and half a day back. There is nothing within half a day's ride that you could possibly need."

The ranger closed his eyes and let out a long sign as he rubbed the back of his head. "Yes, there is. I only need to go a mile out of town, but I need some open space to be alone and a place to practice. I need to get the hell out of here for a while. You can have me followed or put guards with rifles a mile and a half out of town. I need some quiet open space to pull leather and regain my focus and concentration."

The ranger abruptly turned his head away, and he clenched and opened his left hand repeatedly. Still looking away, the ranger spoke through clenched teeth. "Red…"

Texas Red instantly became alert. "Yes, ranger."

The ranger looked straight into Texas Red's eyes. "This is not a request. I am not asking."

Texas Red held his gun hand up, well away from his holster. "Okay, okay. Let's think about this and work something out."

Both men sat for several minutes without speaking, and then Texas Red stood up to leave. "Okay, let's do this, ranger. Ride out of town on the south road, the way you came in, and follow it for three miles, and you will come to a small clay road on your left. Follow that for about half a mile to the house. You will be my guest, and you can stay in the guesthouse, and we can practice together. And I will make sure it is just you and me." Texas Red chuckled. "Besides, I have been very curious to see you pull that Big Iron. We both know it's not the same, but we can pull leather against targets instead of each other. Good enough?"

The ranger was hesitant but nodded. He knew this was the best deal he was going to get. "Yeah…that's good enough."

Texas Red then turned to leave but stopped and spoke without turning around. "Will you give me your word that you will come to my ranch and not leave town?"

The ranger nodded. "You have my word, Red."

"Okay, I'll trust you. There will be no guards with rifles, and if anyone follows you, feel free to deal with them as you see fit." Texas Red turned and looked at the ranger and then touched the brim of his hat. "See you at the house, ranger."

The ranger kept his word and followed the directions. He rode up a small hill, and when he looked down at Texas Red's house, he froze. The ranger let out a breath and scoffed in disbelief. "Damn." Then he looked away for a moment and then looked back at the house and spoke his thoughts aloud. "It's not a mirage. Red's house is a mansion. Whew. I've never seen a house that big in my life. There are train stations smaller than—"

Texas Red's *ranch house* totals nine thousand square feet and sits three stories tall facing east. The guesthouse sits at the left rear of the main house and appears to be much older than the main house. Without question, the main house made a statement, and it sits in the sun like a jeweled crown that dwindles its surrounding. The wraparound porch grounds the house in addition to providing a cool place to sit on hot, arid New Mexico days. The six double chimneys topping the third floor attest to the cold winter winds that punish northern New Mexico pastures.

The ranger casually rode up to the house and, as he dismounted, tried to be nonchalant but wasn't very successful. Standing in front of the house, the house was too large to see all at once. His eyes were like a camera trying to put a huge picture together from many smaller ones.

The ranger started to walk up the wide steps when he realized he was still holding his horse's reins. Embarrassed to himself if none other, he quickly tied the reins to the hitching post in front of the porch and then walked up the wide front steps to the eight-foot-high double mahogany doors. As he drew his right hand back to knock, the right door opened, seemingly of itself.

Texas Red stood in the darkened area of the right hand doorway and smiled. "Come on in, ranger. I'll show you around." Again, the ranger shook his head as if to clear a dream. The ranger could not remotely have been prepared for this, which is exactly what Texas Red intended. He was doing everything in his power to distract, confuse, and overwhelm the ranger. Texas Red was after every advantage, every edge, any ploy, any angle, any position, and any upper hand he can gain. He knew his mansion can be overwhelming, and he made sure the ranger was uninformed and unprepared. No one in town dared to refer to Texas Red's mansion by anything other than, the *ranch house*.

With his life at risk, there was no blame for Texas Red wanting every possible advantage. Yet neither man could possibly know that within an hour, perhaps a bit more, both men would stand crushed and humiliated before the other. Within an hour, perhaps a bit more, both men would stand in fear for their own lives in the gunfight Saturday…and justifiably so. Either man can win this gunfight, and both men, even after practicing together, have learned that they cannot know who will win this historic, legendary gunfight until they actually draw leather, and one of them stood while the other lies in the dirt of Main Street. Both of their lives depended on the same thing—the ranger's gun hand.

Despite his maneuvering and posturing, Texas Red was quite willing to give the ranger a tour of his home, not only because he was so proud of it, and enjoyed showing it off, there was just… something…about the ranger that made Texas Red want to impress him. He started the tour as soon as the ranger walked through the door.

The entrance to the house led into a two-story foyer with a five-foot-wide handmade staircase winding up the left wall to the second floor gallery. The ranger could see doors leading off the gallery to what he thought would be the bedrooms. He could not see how to access the third floor, perhaps an unseen hallway and staircase. The third floor was Texas Red's personal bedroom, private bath, a small office, and a spectacular view.

The second floor ceiling in the foyer and entrance hall consisted of figured, engraved copper. Solid teak floors ran the length of the house upstairs and down. There were jewel-colored imported rugs to anchor the rich, warm-toned furniture in all of the rooms. The woodwork throughout the house was made of exotic and semi-exotic woods from all over the world. Except for wood that was necessarily thinner, no wood in the house, no matter how expensive, was less than an inch thick. The textured walls gave off a soft white light that contrasted with the richness of the natural darkness of the handcrafted woodwork and furniture.

The foyer has a number of doors. The immediate door on the left opened to the morning room. The ranger could see it was modest size and more intimate. The largest object in the room was the fireplace with overstuffed chairs and a small sofa hugging it. A lady's desk and chair filled one corner of the room, and a harpsichord filled the other corner. It was a pleasant setting to welcome the morning sun. The next door, further down the left wall, led into a formal dining room and was a very large and opulent room. Although seldom used, it was another statement about Texas Red. The furniture was ornate with rich tones to the wood, and the fabrics chosen for the chairs and window dressings were vibrantly colored silks.

To the right of the foyer, the first door opened into the grand salon, which centered on a massive stone fireplace with a very large rosewood mantle. The furniture, arranged in a number of more intimate groupings, included a Steinway grand piano at one end of the room. Although Steinway's manufactured in the United States since 1853 began with serial number 483, Texas Red's Steinway, imported from Germany, carried the serial number 037. This again was another statement. The carved cornice crowning the room highlighted the coffered ceiling. The double doors on the right, across from the staircase, opened into the library. Further down the hall on the right, past the staircase, was a third door that opened into the ranch office.

The ranger shook his head. Golden thread bordered blue, green, and purple curtains that lined many of the room but still allowed sunlight in. There were handmade furniture and coffee tables, chairs, doors, crown molding, textured walls, ceilings of handmade figured copper and handmade one-of-a-kind exquisite staircases. It was overwhelming and exceeded the ranger's personal dreams of wealth and splendor.

However, the most incredible and stunning thing the ranger has ever seen in his life is that half of the huge house has some degree of indoor plumbing, running water and gaslight. It was almost another world, and merely looking at it was incredibly surreal. The wide-eyed ranger looked at Texas Red and scoffed. "Red, I've seen towns smaller than this house. You could have a rodeo in here."

Texas Red winched at the thought of hooves, sand, and spurs on his prized teak floors. "I will pass on that one." Then looking around, Texas Red patted the ranger on the back of his left shoulder. "It took me over five years to build this house. William designed it, and Texas Red built it."

The ranger kept his eyes on the textured walls and copper-figured ceiling. "William?"

Texas Red nodded. "Yes, that is my birth name, William Travis Jr."

Still looking around at the house and focusing on an ivory doorknob, the ranger remarked almost absentmindedly, "You have flaming red hair, and your birth name is William." The ranger glanced over at Texas Red. "Were you named after William the Conqueror?"

"Touché, ranger, once again I am impressed. Yes, I was. My father's assumed name was Will, but it was expanded to William so I could be named after William the Conqueror."

The ranger then looked at Texas Red and gestured around at the large sitting room. "I don't mean to be abrasive or rude, but I didn't realize there was so much money in robbing stagecoaches and small-town banks."

Texas Red laughed. "There isn't." Then Texas Red gestured at not only the room but inclusive of the entire house. "All of this is honest money. Both of my parents were very wealthy, and my adopted parents used the money as my birth parents wished and invested it wisely. This may surprise you, ranger, but I have far more honest money than outlaw money…unless you count the gold."

The ranger echoed, "The gold?"

Texas Red nodded. "Yes, it was a secret shipment in a standard stagecoach on a standard route with standard security. Who knew there was a fortune in gold on the stage? We didn't know about the gold, had no idea. The only reason we hit that particular stagecoach was because we didn't have anything else to do that afternoon… it was our lucky day. I paid my men triple and hid the gold. I am the only one who knows where it is. I do not count it as part of my wealth because I haven't used any of it, not a dime of it. Actually, I get quite a kick out of knowing it's there and that I am the only one who knows where it is…but this is getting too serious, ranger."

Texas Red smiled and gestured with his hand. "Come on, ranger, there is something in the kitchen I think will interest you."

The ranger shook his head. "Something in the kitchen will interest me? Not likely, I don't think so unless it's food."

Texas Red stopped and sighed. "I get this mixed up now and then. Dishes in the kitchen are for cooking only, and the dishes for eating and general use are in the butler's pantry. Okay, ranger, you are safe. We are not going to the kitchen. We are going to the butler's pantry."

The ranger looked at Texas Red. "Exactly what are *general purpose* dishes?"

Texas Red laughed a good laugh. "Well, at least for the afternoon, you and I are partners, and we have vermin to vanquish."

"What does that have to do with general purpose dishes?"

"Come on, ranger, I will show you."

The ranger followed him into the butler's pantry where Texas Red opened a cabinet door and took about twenty shot glasses, and then he gestured with a nod of his head. "Grab some more, ranger, as many as you can carry. How many bullets do you have for that Big Iron you are so proud of?" It was obvious that Texas Red did not take the Big Iron seriously and certainly did not take it as a threat.

The ranger got another twenty or so shot glasses and chuckled. "I take it these are the vermin that won't live to see sundown, vermin made out of *general purpose* dishes."

Texas Red spoke in a gravelly voice, "That's right, partner. They are as good as dead." In a rare token of genuine respect, Texas Red stood still long enough for the ranger to get the shot glasses and then take the lead on the way to the back door. The ranger nodded his appreciation.

They walked through the dining room on the way to the back door, and the ranger looked around at the dining tables and the exquisite chairs and kitchen furnishings and even more running water and gaslights.

Once again, the ranger shook his head to clear his mind. "Why in the hell are you an outlaw?" Texas Red's only answer was a scoff.

"I'm serious, Red, why are you an outlaw? I'm as bone-curious about why you are an outlaw as you are about my Big Iron. Fess up, Red."

Texas Red rolled his eyes. "Get the back door, will you, ranger?"

THE RANGERS SECRET INJURY

The ranger leaned against the wall so he could hold the shot glasses as he quickly opened the back door, albeit with a bit of difficulty. He was careful not to drop any shot glasses, but once the door was open, the ranger saw a sight, a greeting, with which he was much more familiar. The ranger smiled and looked back at Texas Red. "This is more like it, Red."

Just outside of the back door was a shooting range, a well-used shooting range. There was a very solid wooden wall about fifty feet long and ten feet high with targets on the wall and metal pedestals at varying distances in front of the wall. Four-inch-by-four-inch wooden posts three feet long were buried sideways flush with the ground as markers that were also at varying distances from the wall. Thousands of empty brass casings littered the ground like a brass carpet.

For the first time in a while, the ranger was actually happy. There were no illusions or misunderstandings whatsoever; the ranger would get a fair chance in a fair gunfight with Texas Red, but the ranger had to play Texas Red's game, or the ranger faced death where he stood. The ranger easily pushed it all from his mind; the ranger was the best gunfighter in the world, the fastest man alive, and he was excited to be at a shooting range where he can practice and hone his skills. He no longer cared that Texas Red watched his every move. The excitement in the ranger's voice and in his actions was not lost on Texas Red, and there was no doubt that the ranger was in his element. However, the ranger had to face the truth deep down inside of himself. Death threat or not, he was beginning to enjoy some of Red's lifestyle. On the other hand, was it simply his joy and excitement from being in a place he could practice his gun-fighting skills? The lines were beginning to blur, but on the eve of the gunfight, the ranger will face a full test as to where he stood and what he stood for—a test few men could pass.

The ranger was grinning like a child at Christmas as he walked up and down the wall looking for the right spot at the right distance. The ranger looked at Texas Red. "What's your flavor, Red?" Texas Red gave a sweeping gesture with his right hand at all of them, but his favorite distance was forty feet.

Texas Red was a bit disappointed when the ranger chose two wooden markers, one for each of them, fifty feet from paper targets nailed to the wall. Then the ranger started looking at the pedestals, and finding two he liked, he set them just about ten feet from the wall. There it was, forty feet between them. Today, it was forty feet between them and the targets. Saturday, it would be forty feet between each other, but that was still five days away.

The ranger picked a third pedestal large enough to hold all of the shot glasses. He put the large pedestal to the side of their shooting lanes and then stacked all of the shot glasses on it. Texas Red continued to chuckle and even laugh at the excitement that he did not think the ranger had. However, Texas Red's chuckles and laughter would soon turn into a deep fear bordering on terror and for just cause.

The first thing Texas Red realized about the ranger, even before seeing his first draw, was this man was an elite gunfighter, a gunfighter from head to toe. Texas Red was about to see skills and speed he did not think existed, and Texas Red was about to be schooled by the best gunfighter alive.

But the ranger's worst fears will happen, from one blindingly fast draw to the next; the ranger's dreaded secret will be openly and undeniably exposed and lying in the dirt at the feet of Texas Red. The only person in the world who will know the ranger's vital secret is the very man the ranger will soon face in a gunfight to the death.

The ranger brought out his kit to clean and load the Big Iron and ensure that it was in perfect operational condition. The ranger even spent a lot of time on his holster and made sure he oiled the leather just right and the angle was right and the gun felt good in several dry practice draws. Texas Red watched with intense interest and then prepared his own weapon.

While Texas Red prepared his six-gun, the ranger was excitedly placing shot glasses in two pyramid-shaped targets, one on each pedestal. There were three shot glasses on the bottom row, and then two shot glasses stacked on top of them, with a single shot glass at the peak of the pyramid. Each man's gun held six bullets, and each target had six shot glasses.

Texas Red drew first and decided to try a couple of psychological ploys to put doubt and concern in the ranger's mind. Texas Red's draw was at full speed but pretended to be practice speed, and he hit the top shot glass dead center, which instantly shattered into dust. The explosive bullets Texas Red was using were very impressive on brittle glass, with intentions of intimidating the ranger. However, when used on a human gunfighter flooded with massive amounts of fear and adrenalin, the explosive bullets most often left the wounded gunfighter enough time to get one, possibly two, shots off. However, the ranger totally ignored the ploys and explosive bullets and the full speed practice draws; he was ready to pull leather. Speaking in total honestly without ploys or games, the ranger stopped and looked at Texas Red with a puzzled look. Then the ranger nodded to himself and then said, "You must be holding back or you have a minor injury."

The remark caught Texas Red by surprise. "What do you mean by that, ranger?"

"I realize this is just practice, but I was wondering why your draw was so slow. I really don't think you are afraid of me, Red. So you must have a minor injury." The sincerity and unshakable, total confidence of the ranger made Texas Red's heart skip a beat. Texas Red wasn't sure if he really wanted to see the ranger draw the Big Iron after all. Texas Red has felt fear a number of times, but for the first time in his life, he felt the un-tasted fear of foreboding, and he did not like it.

"Show me what you've got, ranger."

The ranger stood at ready and glanced over at Texas Red. "Say when, Red."

Texas Red responded instantly, "Draw…"

Texas Red then saw something with his own eyes that he did not think was physically possible. He was completely, utterly unprepared for what he saw. To his human eye, a muzzle blast with a tongue of fire and a cloud of blue-white smoke simply appeared out of nowhere. The ranger was so fast that Texas Red could not see the ranger's gun hand move nor could he see the gun itself move. He could not see the ranger's Big Iron at any time during the draw. During the rangers draw, the Big Iron was not visible to the human eye.

Texas Red shook his head to clear his mind and thought to himself, *That was impossible. I must be imagining this, or I must have missed something. I have got to see him draw again.*

Texas Red moved closer to the ranger's gun hand and stood as close as the ranger would allow before waving his hand waist high for Texas Red to move back. "Try that one more time, ranger."

The ranger smiled and chuckled. "I hear that a lot, say when."

"Draw…"

Once again, even though he was prepared, Texas Red could not focus his eyes on the ranger's gun hand or any part of the draw or the Big Iron. Once again, to Texas Red's human eye, the muzzle blast of a gunshot with a tongue of fire and a cloud of blue-white smoke seemed to appear from nowhere. Now Texas Red stood wide-eyed in total awe.

Texas Red spoke barely above a whisper, "I have heard about the legend for many years, even before I turned against the law. Even a few people I knew back east had heard of the legend, but I have never seen it nor have I ever met anyone who has ever seen it with their own eyes, until this very day. It was always a legend, something out there that people talked about but no one has actually seen. However, you have got it, ranger, and I have seen it with my own eyes. You possess the legend."

The ranger shrugged, "Sorry, Red, what legend?"

"A legend that only extremely rare, elite gunfighters can attain, elite gunfighters so rare there has never been two at the same time. Gunfighters who are so fast, they alone possess the legend—an invisible draw. The legend of the invisible draw was thought to be impossible for any man to attain and has never been documented or proven...until today. And of all things, you have attained the legend drawing a damn Big Iron."

Then Texas Red tried standing in different places and changed angles, and once he even stood no more than two feet from the target and looked backward at the ranger's draw. Twelve times, two cylinders of bullets, the ranger drew with invisible speed, and Texas Red tried in vain to find a place or point of view where he could clearly see the ranger's draw, but one thing was now undeniable, and the unthinkable was now a fact, and there was no longer any doubt in either man's mind. Texas Red did not stand a chance in hell against the ranger pulling a Big Iron with the legendary invisible draw. Texas Red hid it well, but internally, he was emotionally devastated and humiliated.

Still in shock and disbelief, Texas Red shook his head and looked at the ranger. "Achilles...without the fatal weakness."

Texas Red was surprised, even puzzled, when the ranger broke eye contact and looked away.

Then Texas Red displayed his greatest strength, which was superb, flawless accuracy. Texas Red turned his back to the shot glass pyramid, and as he was turning around, in the middle of the turn, the ranger would call out two numbers that corresponded to individual shot glasses. Texas Red never missed, but the ranger's supreme speed rendered Texas Red's skill almost meaningless. However, it is clear that since the ranger used his thumb to cock the Big Iron rather than fanning the hammer, he will only get one shot. If the ranger missed, Texas Red won't. As fast as the ranger is, his second shot is not nearly as fast. Although the ranger missed a few shot glasses, both men realized the ranger did not miss them by more than a fraction of an inch, and at forty feet, the ranger isn't going to miss a target the size of a man. Besides, perfect, pinpoint accuracy has nothing to do with the ranger's fatal secret. By now, the ranger was relaxed and supremely confident, and if possible, he was perhaps a bit overconfident.

"Red, I've been watching the way the shot glasses break, and I think I can break all six of them with one bullet."

Texas Red set them up, waited for the ranger to get ready, and then shouted, "Draw."

The ranger came close, but the bottom left shot glass was still standing. "You left one, ranger, fire at will."

The thought crossed the ranger's mind that maybe he showed Texas Red too much. Perhaps he should not have shown his full speed and skills. Then the question went through his mind if his life was now in danger. He drew to take out the last shot glass, but something...then it happened...then *it* happened.

Texas Red again watched intently to see the ranger's invisible draw and was shocked when he instantly realized something was going wrong. Texas Red could clearly see what was happening, and he could easily follow the ranger's moves and actions. The ranger's gun hand started to close around the gun handle, but when he cocked the hammer with his thumb, he lost his grip on the gun handle, and the Big Iron started to point straight up. Then the ranger pushed the Big Iron forward rather than gripping the handle and firing it. Texas Red realized the Big Iron was totally out of control, and the ranger was no longer holding it; he was pushing it. Texas Red was watching with such intensity that everything was in slow motion. The Big Iron hit the ground right in front of Texas Red's feet and hit hard enough to slide two feet and plow slightly into the dirt.

Texas Red glanced over at the ranger as he picked up the ranger's cherished Big Iron and held it out toward the ranger as he laughed. "Are you going to shoot me with this or bludgeon me with it? It's a good thing it didn't go off."

The ranger had his back turned to Texas Red and was holding both hands in front of his chest. Texas Red was laughing. "Everybody drops their hardware once in a while, ranger, guns have been slipping out of our hands for as long as there have been guns and gunfighters. But you don't want to be dropping *this* one very often."

Texas Red was still holding out the Big Iron to the ranger, but the ranger still had his back turned. Then Texas Red realized something was wrong. "Ranger?"

The ranger knew it was now impossible to hide his secret injury any longer, so he turned around for Texas Red to see. Texas Red let out his breath with an audible sound. "What the—"

The ranger was holding his right wrist with his left hand, and his right hand, his gun hand, had seized up into a nonfunctional claw. The seemingly invincible ranger was now helpless, helpless as a child. Texas Red grabbed the Big Iron and put it under his belt and immediately grabbed the ranger's hand and rubbed the muscles hard as he forcibly straightened each finger one by one. It hurt like living hell, and the ranger let Texas Red know it. However, without his gun and with his gun hand cramped into a claw, the ranger was helpless. In fact, without his gun, the ranger was helpless before the far larger and stronger Texas Red in any condition, even with a knife.

The ranger kept his hand stretched out and did not dare close it. After several minutes, he felt his hand relax inside, and whatever had locked up the muscles in his hand let go…for now.

Texas Red spoke almost to himself, "It appears the mighty Achilles does have a fatal flaw."

Then a new, un-tasted bloodlust began forming in Texas Red's soul—the most powerful bloodlust Texas Red had ever felt, but he pushed it aside for now. He would let it grow later.

Now it was the ranger's turn to be humiliated and emotionally shattered. The only person in the world who knows of his fatal weakness is the man he will soon face in a gunfight to the death. Although truth be known, knowing of the injury will not affect the gunfight.

When the ranger regained the full use of his gun hand, Texas Red handed him the Big Iron. The ranger nodded his thanks, but he could not look Texas Red in the eyes.

The ranger looked away and spoke in a flat voice, "Just seconds before that last draw, I was asking myself if I had shown you too much, and perhaps, I should not have shown you my full speed and skills. I wondered if my life was now in danger." The ranger then laughed at himself. "The answer is certain. I did indeed show you too much, and my life is very much in danger. But not in the way I was thinking."

Texas Red put his right hand on the ranger's left shoulder. "Let's go to the library and see what we can find out."

They reentered the house through the back door and went past the office door to the library. Books lined the library from the floor to its twelve-foot ceiling on every wall except where the fireplace stood. Two deep leather chairs faced each other in front of the fireplace. A large desk and chair sat in the middle of the right half of the room and a large library table with a few straight back chairs sat in the middle of the left side of the room. Each side of the room had a ladder attached to an iron rod that ran around the top perimeter of the bookshelves. The thick Turkish carpet grounding the two leather chairs drew the two men into the warm, inviting room. However, the ranger was too humiliated to be impressed with the massive library containing several thousand books, but he did note that he had not made enough money in his entire life to pay for half of the books in this library. Then he wondered what Red meant about seeing what they could find out. The ranger wasn't sure if his condition, if even known, is treatable. As it turned out, the ranger's condition is well known. Texas Red sat at his desk, and the ranger sat in one of the plush leather chairs.

Texas Red looked through an extensive catalog of his books and then concentrated on several individual books. "How often does this happen, ranger?"

The ranger still could not meet Texas Red's gaze, and it was a long moment before he answered, "It's different between each time, but it has gotten noticeably worse, much worse. It used to be so rare I didn't think anything of it. Then it started happening every few months, then about once a month, and now it's every couple of weeks or so."

Texas Red spent about half an hour looking back and forth at three books. "Do you ever feel a tingling or burning sensation?"

The ranger looked up in surprise and then said a bit more than he intended to, "Yeah…it's mostly a tingling sensation, sometimes just a little and sometimes a lot, but every now and then there is a burning sensation. The burning sensation doesn't happen very often but is more painful. And the outside edge of my gun hand is slightly numb all the time, but it doesn't affect my draw, at least not yet."

Texas Red closed the books and leaned back in his chair. "Let me tell you what I saw and see if you agree. You're thumb and trigger finger are fine. It is your three outside fingers that lose their grip, and you then push the Big Iron forward totally out of control, and the more you try to recover at this point, the more you push the Big Iron forward. It starts when you cock the hammer with your thumb. Your three outside fingers lose their grip, and your thumb pulling on the hammer tries to pull the Big Iron straight up. Then your hand loses its grip and control of the Big Iron, and the only thing you can do at this point is push the weapon forward, totally out of control, until the Big Iron ends up in the dirt."

The ranger quickly stood up and faced the fireplace. Then he pulled several easy draws and tried to remember exactly what happened at each step of the draw.

"Slow it down, ranger, and draw as slow as you can."

The ranger chuckled. "It feels funny trying to slow my draw down." The ranger slowed his draw, and he followed every split second of the draw in his mind and then realized for the first time exactly what happened and exactly when he loses control.

"That's it, and what you said is exactly what happens. What's going wrong, Red?"

Texas Red scoffed. "Far be it from me to help you with your draw, but you have permanently damaged your right side ulna nerve, and every time you pull serious leather, you risk further damage. The ulna nerve runs from our shoulders to our fingers and controls the outside three fingers on each hand. It is also the nerve in our elbows called the *funny bone*. There is nothing either of us can do to help or hurt you, and there is no reason for anyone else to know about this. I have seen the matchless speed of your invisible draw, and I have seen your own gun hand turn against you. Everything depends on which Achilles shows up Saturday, the invincible Achilles or the fatally flawed Achilles. We won't know, we can't know, which one you are until we pull leather. Ranger, we now know each other's greatest strength and greatest weakness. And one thing is for certain…we are both fully justified to fear for our lives, and no gunfight can ever be fairer than that."

Texas Red thought for a long moment. "I normally do not talk like this, but I think you will understand what I am saying. If your gun hand is working Saturday, then you have already won this gunfight…but if your gun hand is not working, then I have already won this gunfight. This gunfight is already over, and fate has already decided who will live and who will die…we just don't know what that decision is yet."

The ranger looked at Texas Red and shook his head. "I understand what you are saying clearly, and you make a lot of sense, Red. I really appreciate your offer to let me stay in your guesthouse, but I need to get back to town. I still haven't recovered from you seeing my gun hand turn into a misshapen claw. You saw me go from the peak of my skills and ability to the bottom of hell within a matter of seconds. I really need to go—"

"Will you give me your word you will be back in town by sunrise?"

"Unless something goes wrong, I'll be back in town within an hour."

Texas Red shook his head. "Ranger, don't you go drinking yourself into a stupor now."

The ranger shook his head and looked down, his voice laced with discouragement. "No, I don't need that at all. Thanks for the good advice, but alcohol is not what I need or want right now. And what you said about fate and the gunfight already being decided… that was very impressive, Red."

Texas Red walked the ranger to the door. "You need any company on the way back to town?"

"No thanks, Red, I need the time to clear my thoughts and get my mind back together."

The ranger got on his horse and, for the first time, looked down at Texas Red. "Has the thought crossed your mind to call off the gunfight?"

"Sure it has. The odds are still stacked way against me, but we both know that we cannot do that, and we both know we won't."

Texas Red realized the ranger had something specific in mind but had no idea what it was, at least not yet.

The ranger nodded. "I guess what we want doesn't matter much to men like us. We are stuck with what we are and what we do. What we want doesn't figure in much."

"We can have a few of the things we want, ranger, but not the things we think we want the most. To be the kind of men we are, we have to want what we are the most. Everything else is secondary, even a good woman and a family."

"I don't know, Red. I can stop pretty much any time I want to."

"Ranger, if you were able to stop, I would be facing a different ranger this Saturday. Every time you draw, that Big Iron could end up in the dirt at your opponent's feet. You can't stop, ranger. As long as you so much as think you can pull leather, you will keep on until you finally stand helpless before a merciless killer who will laugh as he blows half of your head off. You can't stop, ranger, if you could, you already would have. If you could stop, you would have a couple of sons and a daughter by now."

"Maybe you're right about the Big Iron, Red, and maybe it's time I drop down on the weight of my hardware."

Texas Red scoffed at the ranger's denial. "It is far too late for that ranger, and you couldn't hold a coffee cup when your gun hand goes wrong. Maybe it is time for you to drop your badge in the dirt instead of your Big Iron."

The ranger started to say something but stopped. He drew in a deep breath and sighed. "See ya in town, Red."

Texas Red also started to say something but stopped. "See you in town, ranger."

The ranger touched the brim of his hat and turned his horse into the night and back to town. The ranger had more to think about than he realized. *Could Red be right about not being able to stop?*

There was something else pulling at the ranger. It was pulling him like a powerful magnet, and it was scary, even scarier than facing Texas Red in a bare knuckles fistfight. One of the saloon girls has caught and captivated the ranger's eye, and for some strange reason that he cannot explain or understand, he wanted to see her... he *needed* to see her.

His greatest enemy knew his greatest secret, now torn from him and ripped from his soul. With his own horror-stricken eyes, he saw his secret injury plow his Big Iron into the dirt at the very feet of Texas Red, who is by far the last person on earth the ranger wanted to know about his gun hand that betrays him and turns into a useless claw. The ranger had never felt so humiliated and so disgraced in his entire life. His self-inflicted humiliation was so vicious that it constituted an injury in itself, an emotional injury, a psychological injury.

If only he can see her and talk to her, *she* can make things better.

LYNDA

As the ranger rode back toward town, he was crushed and humiliated. Red was the first person to ever see his gun hand go bad, and his hand was getting noticeably worse. Thinking about the gunfight five days from now, his hand had not gone bad twice in the same week before, but it has gotten bad enough to worry about when it will happen twice in the same week. The ranger was wondering what will happen next Saturday. And to top it all off, Texas Red owned a fabulous library and was able to figure out why his gun hand goes bad. Oddly, the ranger never thought of such wealth actually serving a useful purpose. And the ranger certainly did not like how much how much he was beginning to like Texas Red. He not only had a commission and a duty to fulfill, but he also had a vow to his dead brother. But the ranger believed Red when he said it was a fair fight, and that affected the ranger deeply. The idea that it was a fair gunfight blunted the hate toward Red, and the ranger had already seen a whole side of Red that was rarely displayed to those close to him and never to strangers.

But the ranger had to push that to the side of his mind. He was hurting so bad inside, and he knew he was less than an hour from making the biggest fool out of himself he ever has in his entire life. There was a saloon girl he met and talked to—well, they talked for thirty seconds, but her smile did something to him inside that he did not understand. Her smile was etched into his brain, and he could clearly see her smiling face even with his eyes closed. What did she do to him? She must have done something to him when he wasn't looking or paying attention.

The ride back to town seemed like a few minutes rather than the hour it took. The ranger casually walked into the saloon and nonchalantly looked around with his eyes searching only for her. Several men were standing at the bar and turned to look when he came through the swinging doors. All of them acknowledged his presence with a nod and even a smile. Most of them who spoke called him ranger. But a few of them actually called him by name; they called him Kyle. The ranger was taken back, and he tried to remember the last time he walked into a saloon, or anyplace else, and had people call him by his first name. He was stunned to realize that he couldn't remember the last time he walked into an establishment and was called by name, especially by five or six different people. The ranger felt an unfamiliar but a good feeling inside when everyone in the saloon recognized him. They instantly knew who he was, and all of them acknowledged him. Even those who did not speak at least nodded or touched the brim of their hats. As soon as they recognized him, they greeted him and then went back to their business with no concerns. It was friendly and personal, almost as if he was…accepted.

The ranger was further amazed when he walked up to the bar, and before he could speak, Sam asked him, "What's your pleasure, ranger? It's on the house. Everyone in town has been told to let you have anything you asked for." Then Sam chuckled, "Except for a way out of town. Texas Red will pick up the tab." The ranger was too preoccupied to answer Sam about what he wanted to drink, so while they talked, Sam fixed a drink of mild strength and held the top of the bar glass as he slid it across the bar to the ranger.

The ranger tipped his hat slightly. "Thanks, Sam. I know Red can afford it, but why would he do that?" Sam considered his answer before he spoke. "Some of it is because you can't leave town, so he is compensating you for that. But mostly, it's because he really respects you, and we have never seen that before. And I for one think he likes you, which is very much a first."

All this time, the ranger was trying to be casual as he continued to look around, but Sam was too knowledgeable and too experienced not to very quickly realize the ranger was looking for someone. A girl named Anita also noticed the ranger's head was on a swivel and walked over.

She looked at the ranger and said, "I guess Lynda is right. You are kinda cute."

The ranger looked over at Sam and then at Anita. "Excuse me, ma'am?"

"Her name is Lynda, and you made an impression on her too."

"Lynda?"

Anita smiled. "Yes, night before last. Lynda is the girl you made eyes at all night, but when you finally stood next to her, you spoke about a dozen words."

"I made an impression on her?"

"Sure did, ranger, she said it's a shame you're facing Texas Red in a gunfight next Saturday. She thinks you are nice and even cute."

"I uh…she…is she here?"

"No, but I sent a girl over to the hotel to get her."

"Someone is getting her and bringing her over here because of me? What if she gets mad?"

Anita scoffed. "She would more than likely get mad if I *didn't* tell her you were here."

The ranger was baffled, which was very rare. "How…how can you say that?"

"Because she said you were nice and that you are cute."

"That doesn't mean she wants someone to wake her up to tell her I'm here."

"Well, when she told us you were nice and that you are cute, I didn't think much of it. However, after she said it about fifteen or twenty times, then I got the feeling that—"

"Wow…fifteen or twenty…wow. I don't know what to say."

Anita chuckled and nodded. "We can tell, ranger."

"I can't stop thinking about her. I even think about her when I make a batch of bullets or clean my six-gun. And you're not supposed to think about anything else when you make bullets and clean a weapon, but I can't help it."

Anita stopped for a moment. "Is that...like a supreme compliment or something?"

"It sure is...nothing has ever distracted me before while I was doing those things, never."

Anita looked at Sam who was smiling and shaking his head the whole time. "Sam, this is getting more interesting by the minute."

Sam scoffed. "That is the understatement of the year."

Lynda walked through the swinging doors and the ranger got up and walked over to meet her.

Anita looked at Sam with a serious look on her face yet with a smile. "She laughed. Sam, did you know that Lynda laughed?"

"No, what do you mean, Anita?"

"In those few seconds they spoke night before last, Lynda laughed. Within those few seconds, the ranger said something that made her laugh."

"Maybe it wasn't what he said, maybe she was just responding to him."

"This is going to get very complicated, Sam." Then she sighed. "Okay, it already is."

"Sam, what do you think will happen when William finds out?"

Sam shook his head. "It will be one way or another with no middle ground. He will either have no problems with it, after all, Lynda is a grown woman, or there will be an argument that quickly builds up to pulling leather on the spot."

Anita then asked, "Didn't the ranger go out to the ranch today, and wasn't he supposed to spend the night, or longer, in the guest house?"

Sam nodded. "Yes, the ranger did go out there, but for some reason, he came back. But nothing about the ranger indicates anything serious went wrong. If they had pulled leather, the ranger would be either dead or gone. And if they had pulled leather, this is the last place the ranger would be."

Anita agreed. "I feel a lot better, Sam. You're right about this being the last place the ranger would be."

Both of them then looked around, wondering why it was taking so long for the ranger and Lynda to get there. But the ranger and Lynda were already sitting at the gunfighters' table, and Lynda was laughing. Lynda had not truly laughed in a very long time.

When the ranger saw Anita and Sam looking at them, he pointed at them and quickly said something to Lynda. Lynda then acted snooty and put her nose up in the air and turned her head away from then. Then Lynda looked back at them and scowled, and they could just hear Lynda say, "Give me your gun, quick, give me your gun before they get away." And then she giggled.

No one in Agua Fria had ever seen Lynda act like this. Anita had tears in her eyes, and she softly cried. The crusty, ole bartender was not far behind. Lynda was coming back to life.

The ranger and Lynda talked. Some of it was giddy, some happy, and some of it was even nonsensical, but they talked for a long time. And they quickly became more and more serious.

Then Lynda wanted to get more serious yet, and there was one question she really wanted to ask him more than anything else. And she especially wanted to see his reaction to the question.

"Kyle? May I ask you a serious question?"

"Sure."

"What do you think of and what goes through your mind when you look at my scars?" Lynda has never so much as acknowledged her scars to another man, let alone discussed them. But she had to hear the ranger's tone of voice when he answered and his face when he heard the question.

The ranger did not look away or hesitate but answered calmly and straightforward, "I think my scars are worse than yours. Even with your scars, you are still a beautiful woman, and don't ever think otherwise. But my scars are ugly, and they go deep, all the way to the bone. When I look at your scars, I think they are not self-inflicted but were forced on you by someone else's evil. My scars are all self-inflicted with no one else to blame. Make no mistake, we humans can be as savage as a meat ax, and we kill quickly. But at the same time, there is something inside of us, most of us anyway, that is damaged when we kill. And the more we kill, the more damage is done internally, damage that can never fully heal. Maybe that's what our soul is. It is what's left after all of the self-inflicted damage is done. I have nightmares about the men I've killed, Lynda, and I have a vicious recurring dream..." The ranger's voice trailed off.

Lynda reached over and held his hand.

"Kyle, please tell me what your recurring dream is. I still have nightmares and a recurring dream too. Sometimes my biggest fear is going to sleep, and sometimes it's even terrifying."

The ranger nodded with understanding. "My recurring dream is so real that I can actually feel the recoil of my Big Iron. I feel the weight of my footsteps, the warmth and brightness of the sun, and see extremely vivid colors that do not exist in nature. I dream that every morning at sunrise they all come back to life and I have to kill them all over again before sunset. In my dream, I spend my whole life killing them over and over again. There is no end, and there is no reward. This dream is so real that I actually relive the events, and emotionally, it's exactly like killing them in real life. Even waking up doesn't stop the emotional trauma."

Lynda looked into the ranger's eyes. "How can this be happening? I did not think it was possible for anyone on earth to ever understand what I have been going through and what it's like to endure daylight nightmares when I think myself mad and insane. I thought there was no hope for me, and yet here you are, living in your own nightmares and reliving your own terror, just like me. How is it even possible to meet someone who knows and understands exactly what I am going through?"

The ranger's eyes became soft and caring as he put his hand on top of hers. "If my nightmares and recurring dream end up helping you in any way, then I am glad for them and count them a blessing instead of a curse."

Sensing that someone was staring at her, Lynda glanced toward the bar and saw the last person on earth she wanted to see right now. He was standing back, out of the way, but he was there. And she did not know how he was going to react to this. She loves him dearly but does not want to damage this life-changing moment that no one else can possibly understand.

Lynda reached out, and holding the ranger's hand with both of her own, she gently squeezed his hand. "I will be right back."

The ranger smiled and held her hand as he politely helped her up. "I will be right here."

As she walked toward the bar, the power of Lynda's glare and her subtle but forceful gesture convinced the intruder to back away as he gestured toward her hotel room. Lynda nodded in agreement that she would talk to him later, but not now.

The intruder looked at Sam. "This sure complicates things."

Sam looked at the intruder incredulously and held his arms out and then let his arms fall to his sides. Sam then uttered something in his native Russian language that no one else could understand.

The intruder then asked, "Do I want to know what you just said?"

"Have a blessed day and may your grandchildren be blessed by your long presence."

The intruder looked at Sam. "I don't think that is what you really said."

Sam smiled, which was rare. "You're right, that isn't what I said. What I said could get me shot."

The intruder looked around and said, "Sam, I better get out of here before Lynda beats me senseless. Tell her I will see her in her hotel room." The intruder shook his head. "This sure does complicate things."

Sam nodded in agreement. "Yes, it sure does. Good luck."

The intruder started to leave but stopped. "Sam, I have to ask, what did you really say?"

"May God dissolve this madness before the bloodshed inflicts eternal wounds." Sam looked at him and shook his head. "Time does not heal *all* wounds. There are wounds that go beyond the flesh and embed themselves into the soul. Are you willing to face a lifetime of hate?"

The intruder nodded, "Worthy sentiments, Sam, and very appropriate ones. Let us see what happens."

The saloon was becoming busy and noisy. Lynda and the ranger soon agreed to meet again the next day, and then Lynda was gone. However, the ranger had not missed much. He saw Lynda's glare and gestures to ward off the intruder, and he saw the shadow of the intruder's gestures toward Lynda's hotel room. He saw the conversations between Sam and the shadowy intruder. The ranger missed very little, and many times his life has depended on noticing details in a swirl of activity. The only thing the ranger missed was the identity of the intruder. The intruder stood just out of sight, and the ranger could not see him.

Lynda sat on her bed looking out the window. She saw the intruder walking her direction, but she was not as concerned as she was. If there was going to be trouble, it would have occurred in the saloon, and it would have been quick and violent.

Lynda opened the door and allowed the intruder in, albeit with a long hostile glare and a most decidedly unfriendly demeanor.

The intruder looked down and sighed. "Lynda, you know very well that no other man loves you as much as I do, and will he take care of you like I do? Come on, Lynda, talk to me."

The ranger reached the door soon after the intruder, and he feared what he was going to hear as he listened through the door. He felt like it was a cheap shot, and he didn't like it, but he already cared too much not to. Besides, the ranger still did not know how Lynda got her scars or who gave them to her. Part of him strongly hoped that whoever did it was still alive.

The ranger could hear Lynda's voice, and he could tell she was moving around the room. Then he could hear her crying and sobbing. The ranger instinctively reached for the doorknob with his left hand, and he reached for the Big Iron with his right, but then he realized her crying was not a fearful or threatened cry. She was talking rapidly between sobs, and the intruder was listening intently to her and didn't make a sound or utter a single word.

Then Lynda moved closer to the door and apparently sat down.

Now he could hear what she was saying. "He said…he said even with my scars I am beautiful and that his scars are worse than mine. He said my scars were not my own evil but the evil of someone else that was forced on me. I never had any man talk to me like that even before my scars. I want to tell him the truth about me, and I want to tell him everything…and I want to tell him who you are." And then Lynda cried hard and could not stop sobbing.

The ranger heard enough. He took a deep breath, and not wanting to catch a bullet, he lightly knocked on the door and then opened it slowly. He quickly looked around as he stepped into the small room. Then the ranger stopped dead in his tracks. The intruder was…Texas Red.

Lynda didn't care; she grabbed her ranger and clung to him, and she buried her face in his chest, and she stood there hugging him and cried.

The ranger was about as stunned as he has ever been. "Red?"

Texas Red slowly, ever so slowly, shook his head, and he too was about as stunned as he has ever been. "I know you two have talked, but I do not know if you have been properly introduced. Lynda, this is Kyle Lawton, an Arizona ranger. Ranger, this is Lynda… my sister."

With fire in his eyes, the ranger glared at Red. "Your sister is a saloon girl?"

Despite everything, Lynda laughed and shook her head emphatically but kept her head buried in the ranger's chest with her head turned and the side of her face resting against him. Then she looked at her beloved brother and nodded for him to answer the ranger.

Before Texas Red could explain, the ranger asked, "What about Anita?"

Red looked at the ranger with surprise. "I will answer that, but why do you ask about Anita?"

The ranger shook his head as he answered, "She doesn't act like a saloon girl, and she doesn't fit in as one."

"Thank you, ranger, Anita hasn't been a true saloon girl for over three years."

The ranger understood. "You two are a…"

Texas Red shrugged his shoulders. "It is a closely guarded secret that the whole town knows."

Lynda raised her head and giggled. "Anita is carrying William's child."

It was Texas Red's turn to glare. "That was supposed to be confidential information."

The ranger grinned. "That's okay, Red. Knowing things like that makes me feel like part of the family."

Texas Red looked away with gritted teeth and let out a long sigh. "Ranger, have you ever heard of decimation?"

"You mean when the ancient Romans would kill every tenth soldier in their own army as punishment or to *motivate* them? Or just because—"

"I am impressed to the bone with you, ranger, but to no avail. You see, you are the tenth member of the family. Now stand up."

The ranger laughed. "That's a good one, Red. Have you ever wanted a big brother?"

"*Older* brother, ranger, I am the *big* brother, and you are the older…" Texas Red rolled his eyes and looked around the room. "Now you've got *me* referring to you as family."

Then the ranger was serious. "This sure complicates things."

Texas Red had no idea what he meant. "What does?"

The ranger's smile was thin. "The girls."

Texas Red scoffed. "Yes, to be sure, they do indeed complicate things, especially when one of the girls is my sister."

The ranger put his arms around Lynda and tightened his hug. "Red, you were going to say something about Lynda not being a saloon girl."

Red nodded. "Lynda is not now nor ever has been a saloon girl. When she was beaten and scarred, she felt like she was damaged and inferior. Lynda felt more comfortable and more at ease around saloon girls who many say are damaged and inferior. I think 'tainted' is a term often used. She dresses like a saloon girl and spends a lot of her time with them. She will serve drinks and mop the floors, but she has never so much as danced as a saloon girl."

The ranger asked, "What about misunderstandings from outsiders?"

Red chuckled. "That is why she has a big brother. I clarify certain issues and rules. By the way, ranger, do you remember the mansion you were so awed by?"

"How could I forget it?"

"Lynda owns half of everything you saw and half of a lot of things you didn't or couldn't see."

The ranger was almost embarrassed. "I've seen life pull some funny tricks. Life will put a rock in a snowball and send it your way once in a while, and life will even smile on you when you least expect it, but I never saw that one coming." Then the ranger laughed. In fact, he laughed enough for Texas Red to pull out his six-gun and set it on an end stand next to the bed. "Okay, ranger, whatever you are laughing about better make me laugh too. What is so funny?"

"Maybe we can have a rodeo on Lynda's half of the teak floor."

Lynda's eyes got big, and she waved her hands in front of her. "No, Kyle, we can't ever do that. You don't know what William went through to get that teak floor. William sweated blood to get that floor. When he ordered the flooring he specifically said he wanted teak and nothing else, and the man charged us for teak, and everything was fine. Except when the flooring got here, it was knotty pine instead of teak. Well, the foreman of the construction crew told his men to get that pine flooring down as fast as they could. That way, William would have to pay the labor twice. And you have never heard such cussing and fuming and threatening as when William looked at hundreds of pine knots in his *teak* floor. The foreman told William he would take care of it right away, but since it wasn't his fault, William would have to pay for the freight and any damage and labor for putting the pine floor down and taking it back up."

Lynda shrugged her shoulders and grinned. "I was shocked when William didn't say a word. But I understood it when the construction crew left for the night. William went into the gun room and got ten boxes of shotgun shells and two double barrel shotguns. And each box had twenty-five shotgun shells. William commenced to blowing holes all over that pine floor. William said it was easy to put holes in it because it was a cheap, soft, wimpy pine. And William fired every one of those shotgun shells into the floor. That floor looked like a team of prospectors was dynamiting for gold. The next morning, smoke was still coming out the windows, and you could smell burnt gunpowder halfway to town. Well, that foreman got so mad he yelled out for William to get his ass down there right now. When the foreman said that, I am already laughing, 'cause William is six feet two inches tall and almost 250 pounds while that foreman was about five feet six inches tall, and he didn't weigh no more than 125 pounds carrying a bucket of mud. Plus William is a fighter and the foreman ain't. When the foreman and three of his men walked around in the house, they started cussing and threatening William something fierce. But when William came charging down the stairs faster than a train and with pure fire in his eyes, they cussed a lot less. Then William looked at one the bigger men and asked him if there was something he wanted to say. As soon as he opened his mouth, William turned his day into night with one punch. Then William asked everybody else if they had anything to say. Then William went outside and walked into the middle of about ten men and asked them if any of them had anything to say. They stood around and looked at each other, but they decided they didn't have anything to say. Then William grabbed the foreman and pulled him straight up until they were eye to eye. Then William told him that he was charging the construction company 50 dollars an hour for every hour their floor stunk up our house. William had six shot glasses set up before they got there and then William drew his gun so fast that half of them couldn't see him draw, and William shot every one of those shot glasses in less than two seconds. Then William asked the foreman why his floor was still stinking up his house."

"Since William had to use his legal name to the construction company, everyone called him sir, or boss man, or Mr. Travis. I wish that you could have seen the look on their faces when they found out that Mr. Travis was Texas Red. That was the funniest part of the whole thing. I didn't dare tell William I was enjoying the stew out of this."

"From that moment on, there was nothing but cooperation and smiles. It was like giving milk to a kitten, and there was nothing but 'yes, sir' and 'boy howdy.'"

Lynda took a deep breath. "So you see, Kyle, we can't ever mess with William's teak floors cause even I'm afraid to do anything to those floors. Boy howdy."

The ranger marveled at the story and laughed. "I can see Red challenge those ten men so clear it is like I was there. Red wasn't born in the woods to be scared by an owl."

Lynda looked puzzled. "What does that mean?"

Texas Red answered, "The ranger is saying that I am an experienced fighter and unafraid."

Lynda cackled. "That foreman was about to become a lot more experienced himself."

The ranger smiled and continued, "That is a great story, and it changes the whole perception of the house. Instead of being just a collection of expensive wood and furniture, that story about the teak floors gives the entire house an aura of history and almost makes the house legendary. That is an incredible story…and we will indeed be most careful with Red's teak floor."

Texas Red thought to himself, "*Ranger, you've got five days left to live, yet you are worried about my teak floor? When I come home Saturday after our gunfight, I will put a large notch right in the middle of the floor in your honor.*"

Then Texas Red asked, "By the way, ranger, when are you going to officially arrest me?"

"I didn't think I needed to. I thought the gunfight was set, and that was it."

"Well, it would make folks happy, and it would give everyone something to talk about if you were to officially arrest me in public so everyone could see it happen."

"You want something to talk about? Okay, I'll arrest you Thursday night in the saloon, and if you don't cooperate, I will confront you again Friday night. Are you going to cooperate?"

"Not likely."

Texas Red glowed inside. Nothing would attract more attention than knowing in advance when he would be arrested and even greater if he was confronted twice. Everyone would be on pins and needles waiting to see what would happen.

Lynda glared at her brother and then smiled and asked the ranger, "Will you take me to Santa Fe tomorrow?"

The ranger looked at Red. "Do you have an extra man too—"

Red waved his left hand away from himself in a sweeping motion. "Go, just go."

Texas Red realized that he was no longer the one keeping the ranger in town. Besides, it would be easier without the ranger around to spread the word about his arrest Thursday night and the inevitable second confrontation on Friday night. Then he thought to himself, *I am going to be a legend among the great ones, maybe the greatest.*

THE RANGER AND LYNDA

The ranger and Lynda soon outgrew talking at the gunfighters' table in the saloon. Lynda has not wanted to go anywhere in public for a long time, but now she wanted nothing else. The ranger did not yet know how shocking it was to Texas Red for Lynda to ask the ranger to take her to Santa Fe, even though they may have to spend the night. Texas Red was equally shocked at himself for letting the ranger leave town.

But for the first time in five years, Lynda was excited, and she was all dressed up, and she was glowing and happy, and most of all, she just might have met the one man in the whole world who was right for her. Texas Red acknowledged that the ranger may be the only man she had ever met that can truly understand her and the only man who can make her happy. Perhaps he was even the only man who can love her and the only man she can love back. One thing for sure, even Texas Red never thought it possible for Lynda to meet a man like the ranger. In fact, Texas Red didn't even think such a man existed.

As the two of them rode off in her buggy, Texas Red stood on the boardwalk watching them disappear into the western horizon. He thought to himself, and his thoughts were not good, *Damn, Too bad I have to kill Lynda's ranger Saturday. Part of me would like to see how things worked out for them.* Texas Red chuckled internally. *I love my sister, and I might even take a bullet for her, but nothing can stand in the way of my fame and my status as a legend, not even the one man in the world who may be right for her. If it was anything else, anything at all, I would do it, or allow it, for both of them. But I will not give up what fate has decreed for me and my future.*

Texas Red was intoxicated with imagined power. "*Fate has already decreed that I am the one to have the fame, the glory, and the highest magnitude of greatness. I am the one who will be the legend of this gunfight, and nothing will stand between me and my fame. All I have to do is kill yet another ranger in yet another gunfight. At least one good thing will come out of this for Lynda, and that is she will be happy and will have met her man, even if only for such a short time.*"

As the buggy rode out of sight, Texas Red had another thought. "*I have just realized that fate has also decreed that I am going to be the hero and the good guy, and I will be thought of as being magnanimous, and I will be part of history, and I will be a great legend. But I have to be careful so nothing spoils or tarnishes my image and the perception of me. Letting them go to Santa Fe alone after forcing the ranger to remain in town at all times was a very good decision. That makes me look good to everybody. Not that it is a problem, but I cannot appear to be arrogant or egotistical. I can let them go to Santa Fe because I know that I am no longer the one who is keeping the ranger in town. The ranger is wearing the most powerful handcuffs in existence, handcuffs not for the wrists, but for the heart. Besides, the ranger has a duty to perform, and he actually believes that he has a chance to win this gunfight.*"

Without realizing it, Texas Red nodded and shook his head according to his internal thoughts. Then he chuckled out loud, "The ranger actually thinks he can outdraw me. Now that is arrogance."

Texas Red smiled and turned to walk over to the saloon to have a happy evening with Anita. But he stopped in his tracks as another thought flashed through his mind. *Yes, that is a good idea, William.* Then he shook his head and thought. *No, this idea did not come from William, this one is pure Texas Red. How would I act and what would I do if I actually believed the ranger had a chance to win our gunfight? I will act, and I will treat the ranger accordingly. I will even wait until the right time, and I will talk the ranger into demonstrating his invincible speed to a packed saloon, and I will make sure all of the newspaper and magazine reporters are there.*

A wagon going moderately fast bore down on the distracted Texas Red. When he realized the wagon was coming straight at him, he could have easily gotten out of the way in plenty of time, but instead of moving, Texas Red drew his gun and killed both horses that were pulling the wagon. No one dared to stop and look. Everyone kept going about their business as if nothing was happening. With the ranger gone, Texas Red felt free to be more like his real self. Besides, he has been *nice* for about as long as he could. A passing thought crossed his mind that perhaps he feared the ranger more than he realized. But he scoffed internally and ignored the thought.

Texas Red then grabbed the driver with his left hand and pulled the driver to the ground. He put the barrel of his six-gun an inch into the driver's left eye and then cocked the hammer. The driver was in excruciating pain, but he dared not move. Fully intending to kill the driver, Texas Red demanded, "Give me one good reason why I don't kill you right here in the street. You want to die here lying in the dirt? Tell me why I shouldn't kill you, and I will let you go. You have ten seconds to save your own life."

The driver stammered but could not think of anything to say that would not get him killed instantly. Then with just a few seconds left, the driver answered, "Sir, there is no good reason for you not to kill me."

Texas Red scoffed. "Have you been hanging around the ranger? I am impressed, driver." He actually kept his word and did not kill the driver. He pulled the barrel away from the driver's eye and holstered the weapon. He then nodded at the driver and said, "The death of your horses will suffice. Have a good day, sir." Then he continued walking toward the saloon.

The driver had a .45 caliber Winchester 1876 Centennial rifle in the wagon, and he had a fleeting thought of going for it. But he rightly concluded that Texas Red saw the rifle and knew how long it would take the driver to get to it. So again, the driver saved his own life, this time by standing up but not moving as much as an inch toward the wagon.

Texas Red turned around prepared to draw, but the driver stood well away from the wagon.

Texas Red was more impressed this time than the first time. He saw Sam standing at the swinging doors. "Sam, tell Elijah that I will replace this very smart man's horses."

With great relief, Sam nodded and proceeded to do what Texas Red told him.

Sam got word to Elijah that Texas Red needed two horses. Elijah was a blacksmith, carpenter, and owner of a livery stable and delivery service. He fought his way out of slavery, literally with his fists. He was a heavyweight bare knuckles boxing champion and never lost a fight. He was a quiet man who kept to himself yet bore a heavy cross. Sometimes his cross was heavier than even his immense strength could bear. He was such a good fighter, there was no meaningful competition, and he was forced to retire. In an act of counterfeit mercy, he was given his freedom and $500. Elijah did well and made the most of his freedom, but he was forced to leave something behind that tore a permanent hole in his heart… his family. He bore his grievous cross in silence and never shared his painful secrets. Elijah would take his secrets to his grave.

They have been on the trail to Santa Fe for about an hour. The ranger once again looked over at Lynda as if to make sure she was still there. "You know we might have to spend the night in Santa Fe."

Lynda giggled mischievously. "Why do you think I waited so long to get packed and ready? You can count on us staying the night."

A few minutes later, a much more serious Lynda took a deep breath and sighed. "By the way, Kyle, are we out in the middle of nowhere?"

The ranger looked around. "Sure looks like it. I reckon you could say that."

Then Lynda leaned against the ranger's shoulder. "Can I ask a personal question?"

The ranger smiled and kissed her on the forehead. "Lynda, you can ask me anything about anything."

"How can a US marshal afford such an expensive, custom-made Big Iron? And your clothes and boots are very nice and cost a lot more than most can afford. Not to mention your very expensive horse and saddle. Even your rifle has engraving and gold inlay."

The ranger was both surprised and impressed. "You don't miss much, do you? You're beautiful *and* intelligent, now that's a scary combination. I'm beginning to fear you more than Red."

Lynda cackled but was surprisingly hesitant. "I've learned a lot being around the girls. It's amazing how smart they are, and they are the ones who don't miss a thing. By the time a man ties up his horse and walks in the saloon, the girls already know his life story just by watching him." Lynda became nervous, even a bit fearful, and she could not look the ranger in the eyes.

The ranger stopped the buggy and looked at Lynda with a broad smile. "Lynda, you can always say or ask what's on your mind straight out. What are you really asking me?"

Lynda gestured to her face and her scars. " These scars put the first notch on William's gun handle. Kyle, you already know that William is wanted in El Paso for killing a deputy. What you don't know is that the deputy is the one who beat me severely and raped me several times. William killed the deputy who put these hideous scars on me. But, Kyle, please don't make me talk about that right now. I can't. Please wait awhile, and I will tell you all about it, but no more right now, please, Kyle. But what I'm really asking you is if you are a corrupt lawman who hides behind his badge but is a bigger outlaw than the men he puts in jail. You have a lot of money for a US marshal, Kyle, and that scares me."

The ranger was almost scolding. "That is a very dangerous question to ask out here in the middle of nowhere. You ask questions like that when you have protection and safety, not out here where you are helpless and defenseless. You would have just forced a corrupt lawman to kill you even if he really didn't want to. If my money was from corruption and you figured it out, I would have to kill you. I am so well known in my profession that I would have to protect my secret. Don't you see how dangerous this question could be?"

"That's the same thing the girls told me, but they said if I had protection and safety, you would simply lie. I have to know if you are real, Kyle. If you are not the man I have been dreaming of, and aching for, then the rest of my life is already worthless. If you are not real, Kyle, then it doesn't matter what you do to me. The man I ache for doesn't exist. I only know that if I make it to Santa Fe alive, I will have a life worth living. And I am willing to risk my life on it."

Then Lynda brushed the side of the ranger's face with the back of her hand. "I have to know, Kyle, even if the knowing kills me. I set it all up so we would be alone in a situation where I would be helpless, and then I would ask you a question that would force a corrupt lawman to kill me. It's the only way. In my heart, I know you are the man for me, but I have to know for sure."

The ranger was stunned, and a sickening knot quickly formed in his stomach. He has seen far too many criminals use a badge as a shield for greed and worse. The ranger has even hunted a few of them down. But for now he pushed that aside and focused on Lynda.

The ranger nodded and looked at Lynda with a calming smile. "You asked me two excellent questions, Lynda. Two questions with two good answers. First, our dad had two Big Irons custom-made for my brother and me without us knowing it. They are a matched pair but not identical. Dad presented them to us as part of a belated celebration."

"He had a belated celebration?"

"Dad struck a fairly decent silver lode. Tragically, a few months after the official celebration, he was working the mine alone, drinking heavy, and using dynamite, which was a fatal combination. Dad was killed by his own lifelong dream. My brother was a Texas ranger, and I was a US marshal, and we were given two choices. We could work the mine or take a settlement. Since we don't cotton much for digging in the dirt, we did a little investigating and found that top dollar for Dad's mine was $50,000, but it could take awhile to sell. We settled quickly for $40,000, which gave us $20,000 each. My brother's share went to his wife and children, and I still have my share in investments. I've lived off my salary, and with no expenses to speak of, I have saved a thousand dollars in ten years just from my salary. Plus I keep some cash handy just for situations like this."

"What do you mean situations like this?"

"A situation where I have to take the most beautiful woman I have ever seen to Santa Fe."

Lynda's smile came from her heart. "So even if I wasn't so wealthy, you could take good care of me for the rest of my life."

"Well, we sure couldn't live in a mansion like you have now."

Lynda smiled and spoke the most endearing and most heart-melting words he has ever heard, "Kyle, I have a feeling that if I lived in a tent with you, it would be a mansion."

The ranger lightly slapped the backs of the horses with the straps to get the buggy back on the road.

A thought flashed through the ranger's mind, and he looked at Lynda. "Besides everything else, Red can spot an honest man or a criminal in a heartbeat, and I have spent far too much time with Red to fool him. If Red had the slightest doubt, we would have a chaperone, or more likely, we wouldn't be making this trip."

Lynda nodded. "That's what Anita said. But I still had to find out for myself, and I had to know for certain how a US marshal had so much money."

The ranger took a deep breath and looked away, "Speaking of money."

Lynda did not hesitate. "We have 1.6 million dollars deposited in six bank accounts covering five states invested in twenty-seven different investment funds from cattle to wheat to lumber to new homes to a lot of different things. You'd have to ask William to be sure, but I think we even invest in ship building. The ranch house cost us $240,000 and took five years to build. And we have an estimated half million dollars in range cattle, open land, buildings, and houses. Our total net worth is about 2.8 million dollars. And you can feel free to tell William that I decided to tell you all of this."

The ranger looked at her and grinned. "How much were the teak floors?"

Lynda laughed and clapped her hands together. "Actually, I don't know. William and I have an open book policy where all we have to do is ask. I have my own investment bankers and attorney. We share some, and we both have our own. We have three safes, and we both know the combinations to all three, and house policy is that either of us can open them any time we please. And we do not handle, invest, or spend more than $25,000 without advising the other, and that is accumulative. But with all of this, I have never asked William how much the teak floors cost us."

The ranger shook his head. "My question was going to be if you knew how the money was being used and if you were sure Red was being straight with you. Are you sure Red won't get mad about what you've told me?"

"William himself arranged everything in such a way that we cannot hide much from each other. And I know for a fact that he has never even tried."

"Well, I would bet that Red got a very steep discount on the teak floor."

"Oh, how steep do you think?"

The ranger thought for a few seconds. "I would say 50 percent or more."

Lynda shook her head. "No, I don't believe even William could get a discount that big."

"William didn't...Texas Red did."

"How much are you willing to lose, ranger?"

"Oh, I will take a thousand from you."

Lynda spit in the palm of her hand. "Put 'er there and weep."

The ranger laughed and spit in his hand, and they clasped hands and sealed the bet.

They rode for another hour or so alternately talking and sitting in a comfortable silence. Then they would talk some more. With each passing minute, their talk became more serious and intimate, and they bonded together exceptionally quick.

"Kyle?"

"Yes?"

"How can things happen so fast between us? It's sort of confusing. I can't possibly imagine this happening with any other man I have ever met or even dreamed of. Yet with us, I can't imagine it happening any other way. What takes months for most people only takes hours for us, and yet it seems and feels so right and proper. I don't understand how this can be happening."

The ranger chuckled. "I am sitting here thinking and wondering the exact same thing. And the only way I can reckon it is that life changes, molds, and shapes us into what we are. And where most people have to spend time to fit together, and some never do, life has shaped you and me so that we fit together right off. It doesn't take much time for us to fit together because life has already shaped us for each other. I can't see it any other way."

"See what I mean, Kyle? I can already tell when something is bothering you, and something is bothering you, so out with it. We never laid eyes on each other until three or four days ago, and already you can't hide things from me, and you can't lie to me. I sort of like this part, so tell me what you are thinking and what's bothering you."

The ranger nodded and looked at her with a thin smile. "I would like to ask you about your recurring dream, and I would like to know what your thoughts are about this coming Saturday. But I don't know how to ask you about such important, tender things."

"Kyle, do you know what I mean when I say *walk the horse?*"

"Sure do, you get off the horse and walk beside it and talk to the horse and spend time with the horse. That's why they call it walk the horse because you're walking beside it instead of riding it."

"Kyle?"

The ranger grinned. "Yes?"

"We've only known you since Friday, and you know what? A couple of times now, William has come home all fussing and fuming about that ranger. William said he is going to shoot that ranger dead, right where he stands. You know why William says that?"

"No, I have no idea."

"Because William says you are the most aggravating and infuriating man who has ever lived. And do you know what?"

"No, what?"

"I'm beginning to believe William is right, because I am ready to shoot you right here, myself. Here I am thinking of you in terms of being my man, but I am still ready to shoot you right where you stand…or sit. A minute ago, you wondered what I thought about next Saturday. Well, right now I'm thinking that you won't live long enough to worry about next Saturday."

The ranger laughed and then grinned as he looked at Lynda. "Actually, I don't know what you mean by walking the horse. Although I do realize it is a term that doesn't literally mean walking beside a horse as I might have unintentionally implied."

"Unintentionally implied? That much right there with you admittin' it is enough to shoot you for, and no jury in the world would convict me. Besides, all I have to do is ask William to shoot the ranger, and William would say hell yeah, I'll shoot the ranger right now."

The ranger chuckled and looked straight ahead.

Lynda looked at him suspiciously. "What was that chuckling all about?"

"And here I thought we were worried about *your* safety and well being."

"That was an hour ago, and you answered that. Now it's your safety that is in question."

The ranger was very much aware of how good it was for Lynda to talk like this. Life has been bottled up inside of her, and she has not been able to talk with humor for a very long time. This was doing her a lot of good, and Lynda was rejoining life and basking in the bright sunshine.

The ranger became somewhat more serious but still smiled. "Okay, what does it mean to walk the horse?"

Lynda shrugged. "Maybe this is just a family custom that nobody else does, but the first part of it is to actually walk the horse…as you unintentionally implied."

The ranger stopped the buggy, and they got off and walked up to the horse. Almost immediately, the horse responded and seemed to enjoy their company. The horse stayed beside them as they walked together without having to be held by the bridle.

The ranger then asked, "Is this a serious matter?"

Lynda looked at him without smiling, probably the first time she's done that. "Yes, it is very serious, and there are rules. Everything we say, every word, falls to the ground and is absorbed by the dirt. And by doing this, you make a sacred vow never to discuss what is said to anyone at any time again. And according to our tradition, only the horse can talk about it. We can say or ask anything we want of each other, but we can never discuss what is said here again. The only way we can speak anything said here is to dig the words back out of the dirt. The only way we can hear what is spoken here is to have the horse speak it. And if this is done without a horse, you can designate any object to symbolize the presence of a horse. This tradition has been in my mother's family for generations and has never been known to be broken. Kyle, do you swear before God and vow to us to keep and follow the rules of our tradition and custom?"

"Are you required to answer every question asked no matter what it is?"

"No, but you are expected to answer any severe questions to some degree and say more than you normally would."

"Does Red abide by this tradition?"

"Yes, he most certainly does. As does Anita, Sam, and another individual, and so will their unborn child."

"Can Red nullify and cancel this agreement?"

Lynda shook her head. "He could have disapproved, but he approved of you, as did Anita and I and as did Sam and the other individual who cannot be named at this time but will be named later. And one more thing is that you cannot use anything you hear in a court of law. Murder and treason excepted."

The ranger had to think about this for a while, and Lynda remained silent as he pondered it.

"Okay, I swear before God and I vow to you and the family that I will never break the sanctity of this tradition, and I will forever abide by the rules."

Lynda held his hand and interlocked fingers. "This makes you part of the family, Kyle."

The ranger kissed her hand tenderly. "I have a powerful interest in becoming your man. Will you allow me the chance to learn, to grow, and to develop into your man?"

Lynda had tears in her eyes as she brushed the side of his face with her hand. "You're already there, Kyle. You are already my man if you want me, and let me explain how I can say that so soon."

"Please do, Lynda. But I can say that as fast as things are going for us, it feels right, inside, and I know it's working for us, and I know we have a future."

"Some folks would say it can't be real this soon, and others would say it's just a physical attraction that will soon burn out. But I say that even if it is a bit fast, I already know deep in my heart that when the dust settles, it will be you and me standing together for the rest of our lives. I can say that because we are not going to grow further apart, Kyle, we are going to grow closer together. Because we are going to become the people that are right for each other, so in a way, it is not too soon for us because I know in my heart that we will be together from now on. And like you said, life has shaped us for each other, so we are already years ahead of most. We are more right for each other right now than some people will ever be. And we can't ignore the nightmares and horrible dreams we both have. Nobody else can ever understand us as well as we already understand each other. And people will swear that it is too soon for us simply because it was, or would have been, too soon for *them*. Those nightmares and recurring dreams are life changing in the wrong direction. So who else can put up with us but us?"

The ranger chuckled.

Lynda looked at him. "There goes that chuckle again. Fess up, Kyle."

"Some folks would say we are crazy, and let's agree with them."

Lynda looked at her new man with her head tilted a little sideways. "Why would we do that?"

"Because if we are crazy, then we are not accountable for our actions, so no matter what we do, it can't be wrong. And Red will have to pay the bills."

"Kyle, that comes so close to making sense that it's spooky and downright scary."

After a few minutes of silence, the ranger was serious again and asked her, "Since we are walking the horse, will you tell me about your recurring dream?"

"I couldn't even describe the dreams or talk about them until I heard you talk about your recurring nightmares. They are so severe and real that I didn't know how to talk about them. I tried to talk to William about the dreams, but I couldn't put any of it into words even when I tried. But my dreams don't have anything to do with walking the horse. We can talk about the dreams now or later and at will. I don't mind that. But there is something else I want to say to you, and discuss with you, that absolutely cannot ever be discussed again, and you can't even think about it real strong."

Back in Agua Fria, by pure chance, Texas Red walked in front of the telegraph office. He took about five or six steps past the front door when the telegraph operator came tearing out of his office. "Sir. Sir. I have an urgent top priority telegram, sir."

Texas Red was puzzled. "You have an urgent telegram for *me?*"

The telegraph operator looked around and waited for a few people to walk past.

"No, sir, it's for the ranger, and he needs to read this immediately. This is critically urgent, and the message was sent top priority. He really needs to read this, sir. I've heard he is out of town. Will you see to it that he gets this pronto?"

Texas Red was reading the telegram as the operator spoke, "Whoa, this *is* extremely urgent. You are right about him needing to see this. And you are also right about the ranger and my sister being out of town. But they didn't tell me when they would be back."

The operator's eyes involuntarily widened. "They left town without telling *you* when they would be back?"

Texas Red chuckled and then shrugged his shoulders. "They sure did, and there's not much I could do about it. The ranger has a gun, my sister is a grown woman, and I wasn't invited."

The operator laughed. "Thank you for taking care of this for me." Then the operator patted Texas Red on the shoulder. "You are a good man, sir." The operator smiled broadly. "Yes, sir, you are a good man."

Texas Red cringed to the bone when this lowlife, no-account, worthless one...dared to touch him. The telegraph operator probably would not have lived anyway because not only did he know about the vitally urgent telegram, he understood what it meant and how important it was. Texas Red then swore the doomed operator to secrecy until the ranger got back in town, and the telegraph operator readily and heartily agreed that this was classified government information.

Texas Red then made a very fast trip to the ranch house, where he opened a personal safe, and he took a small amount of powder from a box and put the powder in a small envelope. Then he went back to the telegraph office and gave the operator a brand-new ten-dollar bill and then asked if the message was complete. Texas Red casually glanced around and saw a steaming cup of English tea. Then Texas Red, ever so friendly-like, asked to be alerted if another telegram came in. Texas Red then walked over and patted the telegraph operator on the shoulder and told him he too was a good man. Then the telegraph operator looked up from his chair at Texas Red and thanked him.

Four hours later, the telegraph operator sat at his desk with his visor on and a pencil in his hand. He had opened the front door hoping for a cooling breeze, and the cup of English tea had cooled to room temperature. The telegraph machine insistently chattered with busy activity, but the telegraph operator did not acknowledge. The miraculous machine was insistent, but the telegraph operator did not respond. The metallic chatter continued, but the operator did not answer.

The telegraph operator was dead at his post. A painless, instant death was about as much mercy as Texas Red was capable of.

The ranger and Lynda stopped for a moment, and Lynda looked up into his eyes. "How can our own minds turn so viciously against us? How can our own brain trap us in such terror night after night? Why can't our own minds and our own brains protect us instead of attacking us with such savagery? Sometimes I want to end it with a bullet so bad."

Then Lynda smiled and brushed his cheek with her hand. "But then, if I had ended it, I would have never met you, and maybe that's the answer, or some of it. It is because of our individual suffering that we can be there for each other and help each other when we really need it. You know something, Kyle? If either one of us had never suffered so much, we wouldn't be right for each other. We could never understand each other."

The ranger smiled at her as he had never smiled at a woman in his life. "You make so much sense, and I am so very impressed with you. You might be onto something, because if having those nightmares is what it took to be with you, then they are good things, not bad. You are already starting to erase the bad parts, and you are replacing them with good...with yourself."

The ranger held her close to him with an embrace that warmed her heart and gave her hope. He spoke tenderly to her, "If that is what it took to be here at this time, in this place, with you, then it was all very much worth it. There is already a place in my heart for you that no one else could ever take. You are the first person in my life that I have shared my nightmares with, and you are the first who can understand. There isn't a woman alive who can take your place, my sweet, never."

That he called her my sweet was not lost on Lynda, not for an instant, but it was time to tell her ranger about her nightmares.

Lynda took a deep breath and closed her eyes. "My recurring nightmare always starts after he is gone. Oddly, the places on my face where he beat me burn like fire rather than pain from being hit. It is so hard to breathe because he hit me so hard in my ribs. And even though he is gone, I can still feel him. I cry and scream and do everything I can think of, but he is still there inside of me, and he is still in me, violating me even after he is gone. I scream for help, but my screams are no more than whispers, and I cannot get up or run. I can't move, and all this time, he is violating me even though I can't see anything there. It hurts so much, and I have never felt so totally, completely helpless in my life. It is almost as if he is more powerful than God, and he laughs like a maniac, and he taunts me ceaselessly while he is raping me to fulfill his pleasure, and he enjoys inflicting pain and torment. And all this time, he is still violating me and taunting me even though he isn't there. Then I hear knocking at my door, and then I can get up, and I answer the door. When I open my door, all of my neighbors and friends are there. They are not friendly to me at all, and they merely glance at me and then tell me that nothing is wrong and nothing happened and all of my lies are delusions. Then I go outside, and everything has changed, everything is a doctor's office. No livery stable, no store, no blacksmith, no restaurant, and no hotel, nothing...everything and every building, every home, office, and every business are now doctor's offices. All of the doctors look identical, and all of them do and say the same thing. They refuse to examine me or look at me. All the doctors do are hold up their stethoscopes and say... 'See, there is nothing wrong. It's all in your mind, and everything you claim is just a figment of your imagination.'"

Lynda held her ranger tight and laid her head on his shoulder and sobbed. Then she continued, "Then there is a shred of mercy when I wake up and realize it was another nightmare. But it is exactly like you said when you told me about your nightmare, the emotional trauma is so great that I actually relive the real event and waking up doesn't stop the emotional part of the nightmare. Hold me. Please hold me, my dear ranger. I have never been able to talk about it before. I could never find the words, and I didn't know how to talk about it until you told me about your own nightmares. It's an enormous freedom, and I don't feel as trapped and helpless as I did a few hours ago. Do you see it, my ranger? You have already made my life better."

The ranger nodded. "And none of this would have happened if it wasn't for the bad times we had to endure alone until it was time for us to meet up. Does that make sense?"

Lynda nodded. "Yes, that makes a lot of sense. And now we can spend the rest of our lives replacing the evil we've endured with the good we can now develop and share together."

They walked beside the horse in silence for a while, digesting the new life and the new reality that now reaches out to them, a life neither of them dared to dream of just a short time ago. The adjustment to each other is happening quick and easy, and they both wondered why it couldn't have happened long ago. But after pondering on it, both of them concluded that it could not have happened before now because they weren't ready for each other until now. And they both eagerly awaited the future that now beckoned to them, but they did not yet know there was one last gigantic hurdle, the most hurtful hurdle of their lives.

Sheriff Pratt and Doc Wilson stood in the telegraph office looking for anything they could find that would explain the sudden death of a very healthy man, not to mention a dead man still sitting in his chair and still holding a pencil. The doctor pointed at a brand-new ten-dollar bill with a paperweight on it. "I don't have to ask where that came from. Are you thinking the same thing I am thinking?"

The sheriff nodded. "I'm thinking that since the ranger left town, Texas Red has been on a terror spree. The ranger's influence seems to have restrained Texas Red a bit. And I'm thinking that with the ranger gone, Texas Red has no restraints and is running wild. Either that, or Texas Red has killed the ranger, maybe Lynda too, and feels free to do as he pleases. I sure hope the ranger is still alive. He may be our only hope to take out Texas Red. But I have to admit that I am fretting some. I can't see Texas Red letting the ranger and Lynda leave town. Well, we'll know soon enough."

Texas Red was in the library at the ranch house reading the critical, top priority telegram over and over. Then he spoke aloud, "This complicates things far more than the women."

Then he held the telegram up and tore it into a hundred pieces and then burned the unreadable pieces. Again, he spoke aloud, "This un-complicates things. Sorry, ranger, but you will never know what was in that telegram. This proves that providence is on my side. If I had not let you and Lynda leave town, you would have gotten this telegram, and that just wouldn't do."

Lynda looked at her ranger and then looked ahead. Then she looked back at him. "We are now walking the horse."

The ranger nodded his understanding of what she meant. "Okay, ask me anything you want."

Lynda shook her head. "It's more of a discussion than asking questions. Awhile ago I said I had something to discuss with you that can never be repeated or shared.

Again, the ranger nodded. "I remember, and I agree to it."

"Sometimes good people do bad things, and sometimes bad people do good things."

The ranger looked at her and smiled according to her seriousness. "I have seen examples of both cases, and yes, it does happen, quite often in fact."

"I know that William is an outlaw, or at least, Texas Red is. And he has done some bad things. I play the fool a lot, Kyle, and pretend that Texas Red does not exist. Only William exists, and he is a good man who does no wrong. But I know his temper, and I know... Kyle. I know that he is obsessed with fame, with glory, and with becoming a legend. And he thinks this gunfight will give him all of that and more. He believes this will be one of the greatest fast-draw gunfights in history, and he wants fame and legendary status more than anything or anyone else in his life. But since our childhood, William has always been good to me and has taken good care of me. Every day of my life, William has been the best brother a girl could have. If William is a bad man, he has done a lot of good things, especially when it comes to me. And he is so good with a gun, Kyle. I have seen every one of his gunfights, and no man has ever come close to beating him. But I have got to ask you, Kyle, and I have to know. You spent most of a day with William, and you two spent that time at the gun range just outside of the back door. I know you two pulled a lot of leather, and I've got to know, Kyle...who is faster, you or William?"

"Lynda, I am a gifted and specially trained gunfighter. For ten years, I hunted down the best of the best. I hunted and faced outlaw gunfighters who thought they were the fastest on earth. But when I faced them, they never cleared leather. I am a highly trained professional, and I possess what some legends call the invisible draw. My draw is too fast for the human eye to follow."

"You are faster than William?"

"You call him William, and I call him Red, but either way, I am an order of magnitude faster than he is. But I do have an injury, which Red was able to identify and explain in the library. I have permanent nerve damage to my hand. Every now and then, my gun hand goes bad, and I cannot grip my gun handle during a draw, and the Big Iron ends up in the dirt. When it happened at the ranch and

Red saw it, I was crushed and humiliated. We went to the library, and Red figured out what went wrong. But I had to leave, and I had to come back to the saloon to see you. Somehow, I knew that I had to see you and that you would make it better, and you would make me better. Hell, you would make everything better. I knew that I needed you, and I knew you would be there. I needed you so much, and you were there."

"Now I know what William meant. He said fate has already decided that he is going to win this gunfight no matter how fast you are. He truly believes that fate has already decided that he is going to win. He is so sure of it, and he won't even think of it any other way. He's almost obsessed. But if you are that fast, William doesn't have a chance. How often does your gun hand go bad? What kind of chance does William have? What chance do you have?"

"My hand has gotten a lot worse in the last year, and it goes bad every few weeks. My best guess is that Red has no more than a 10 percent chance, and I know how convinced he is that fate has already decided in his favor, and you are right. He won't think of it, or hear of it, any other way. But my biggest fear of all, and by far, is you."

"Me?"

"If I win, how are you going to feel about me after the gunfight?"

"At this point, I don't know, Kyle. I honestly don't know. Is it possible to call the gunfight off?"

"Considering how much Red wants this gunfight and how much he is convinced that fate is on his side, it will be nigh onto impossible to convince Red to call it off. But I promise and swear to you that if it is possible, I will find a way to call it off."

"Will you still arrest him and take him back to Phoenix, and what about your brother?"

"I don't think Red will allow himself to be arrested or taken back to Phoenix. That's not going to happen. As for my brother, you have seen all of Red's gunfights. Was it a fair fight?"

"I don't know which one your brother was, but they were all fair fights, all of them. In fact, William has always let the other man pull first."

"That makes a huge difference, sweetie, especially coming from you."

Lynda stopped and looked up at her ranger. "I've had some things bottled up inside me for a long time, and I needed to say them. Thank you for listening to me, Kyle."

"You are so very welcome, and I hope there is a way to work everything out, but don't forget, my sweet, that I have a duty to perform. But let's think about this and see what we can do, at least half of it will work itself out. It's amazing how many times things work themselves out no matter what we do."

Lynda smiled warmly. "Are you ready to get back in the buggy and go to Santa Fe?"

"Let's go, my sweet, you have some shopping to do."

Lynda cackled. "I sure do."

Back in Agua Fria, events are compounding and moving at lightning speed. Texas Red is out of control and has killed two horses and almost killed the wagon driver. Then a very healthy telegraph operator was found dead at his post, and the ranger and Lynda have suddenly disappeared on a mysterious trip to Santa Fe. Yet Texas Red has repeatedly made it crystal clear to everyone that the ranger would be hunted down and killed if he tried to leave town. The entire town was absolutely ablaze with gossip and rumors. The whole town was buzzing and saturated with questions and with worry. And the number 1 question on everyone's lips and the topic of every discussion is…where are they? Where is the ranger and Lynda, and an equal question is, are they dead or alive? The latest news is that Texas Red has punched out two men who were standing too close to him and nodded at him. One of them has a busted jaw, and the other has a cracked orbital socket.

Because of Texas Red's presence, it only took a few hours for the small town to attract a lot of attention. Agua Fria was the most scrutinized small town in the country. Sheriff Pratt told Texas Red that territorial authorities were both ready and eager to become involved, and that was not good. True to form, Texas Red denied all responsibility and blamed everyone else including the ranger. The sheriff met with Texas Red in the private room in the saloon and bluntly asked him if the ranger and Lynda had fallen into harm's way. Texas Red gestured for the sheriff to follow him as he walked back out to the saloon. Texas Red then asked the twenty men or so if they had any fear that the ranger had been harmed.

Texas Red grabbed the first man that nodded. "I am going to burn your farmhouse and your barn to the ground."

"No, please…God, no. That's all we've got to our names."

"Well, there is a way you can stop this."

"Yes, sir, anything, what can I do to stop this?"

"I am *telling* you, and the sheriff, and everyone else, that the ranger and my sister are in Santa Fe having a great time while I am here fighting for my life with all of these hideous false accusations and innuendo. I'm sorry but I didn't hear you. Did you say that you would like to keep your farmhouse and your barn?"

"Yes, sir, I sure did. Anything, just tell me what to do."

"Okay, here is what you can do, and actually, it is fairly simple. The short route to Santa Fe is less than ten miles, but we will call it ten miles, which means you can make it in about an hour. You have four hours to ride to Santa Fe and find the ranger and my sister. She will be shopping, and they will be staying at the nicest hotel in town, and they are in her black buggy. Then all you have to do is ride back here and report to the sheriff that they are indeed alive and well. And you might want to bring back some proof. That is all you have to do to save your farmhouse and barn."

The farmer calculated the trip in his mind and came up short. "I need more time, sir. Four hours isn't enough because it will take time to find them. I need five hours, sir, that's all I ask—five hours. There is so much at stake, please allow five hours. I won't even go home. I will leave from here and go straight to Santa Fe, and I will find them, and I will talk to them, and I will bring back proof that I am not lying just to save my barn."

"Okay, now we're getting somewhere. Since you are being so cooperative, I will not only give you your five hours, but it is fourteen minutes till 2. Your five hours will start at the top of the next hour, which is 2 p.m. And by the way, I would like the ranger's watch as proof."

The farmer headed for the door and his horse. As he was leaving, Texas Red glared at him. "Do not say or do anything that will cause them to come home early. Be relaxed and no excitement, just tell them some people question that I let the ranger leave town."

"Yes, sir." And he was gone.

Three hours and forty-seven minutes later, the farmer came back grinning from ear to ear. It did not take long for everyone to gather at the bar.

The farmer reported to the sheriff that indeed all was well. Then the farmer looked at Texas Red. "Sir, do you know about them?"

"In what respect?"

"Well, they are…they are a couple. They are glowing and hugging, and they are together. All you have to do is look at them, and you know they are a couple."

Texas Red nodded. "That's why I let them go to Santa Fe, because they were beginning to get disgusting. Then he looked at the farmer and smiled. "Where is the ranger's watch?"

The farmer again smiled. "The ranger said that Red is well aware of the fact that I don't have a watch."

Texas Red looked at the sheriff. "The ranger is alive and well, and a man dying on the job is neither a crime nor a territorial matter. The two horses were replaced, and there are no issues here that are of territorial concerns. Everything is under control thanks to you, sheriff, and I will swear to that if need be. Right, men? And the sheriff is buying a round for everyone in here."

Texas Red gestured to the sheriff and to Sam that he would take care of the tab for the sheriff.

A choirs of voices saluted the sheriff and several offered toasts. "Hear. Hear. Here's to the sheriff. The sheriff took care of everything. Good job, Sheriff Pratt."

The sheriff nodded in amazement. "I will notify the powers that be."

"Thank you, sheriff."

The ranger and Lynda waited in a short line to get a room. When their turn came, the hotel clerk was extremely rude. "I am not impressed with the fake badge, sir. Perhaps you should leave quietly before I call security."

The ranger looked around and then glared at the clerk. "Are you talking to us?"

"Sir, and I use the term loosely, your badge is a territorial ranger's badge, which was used by the Arizona rangers twenty years ago. Sir, there are no Arizona rangers nor have been since. And even if you were an Arizona ranger, what are you doing in New Mexico Territory?"

The ranger was angry. "The best thing you can do is find someone who knows what they are talking about. I was a US marshal for ten years, and I am now currently an Arizona ranger on special assignment at the request of the territory of New Mexico."

The clerk held his right hand up and snapped his fingers to alert security. "That is a lie, sir, and you are a liar."

The ranger looked at the clerk with a cold glare and spoke slowly, "Are you calling me a liar right in front of my wife?"

Lynda glowed inside unlike anything she has ever felt before in her life.

The clerk pointed sharply and accusingly at Lynda, and he spoke loudly with intentions of embarrassing them. "I know what you are trying to do, and I cannot be deceived. That trollop is not your wife. She is a common adventuress and a lady of the evening. I refuse to allow you to expunge the essence of your lust with that tramp of a woman within the walls of this righteous establishment. I will not tolerate or allow your evil to be—"

The clerk should have never opened his mouth about Lynda. The ranger reached over and grabbed the clerk and pulled the two-hundred-pound man over the counter with ease and threw him to the floor. The ranger drew his Big Iron and turned it backward and handed it to Lynda, and she handled the Big Iron so well it looked as if they had done this for years. When the clerk attempted to get up, the ranger kicked the clerk in the side of his head so hard that as dim as the internal lights in his brain already were, they now instantly went black.

The second man was also taller and heavier than the ranger, but as he reached out to grab the ranger, the ranger moved his arms in a sweeping motion and pushed the security man's arms to the side. The ranger instantly drew back his right hand and, with the palm of his hand, hit the security man squarely and solidly on the nose, which instantly broke, and his nose gushed blood like a water spigot. He was staggering, disorientated, and out of the fight.

The third man was the biggest of the three, but he ignored Lynda and concentrated only on the ranger as he came up behind him. Holding the Big Iron by the end of the barrel, Lynda swung it like a club and caught the third man right between the eyes with the butt of the handle. The third man's internal lights fared no better than the clerk's.

The ranger quickly turned around in a complete circle, but he had no other challengers. Then Lynda joined him at his side and handed him the Big Iron. She whispered, "Where did you learn how to fight like that?"

The ranger smiled and whispered back, "I spent some time with a tribe of friendly Apaches."

Lynda chuckled. "I'm glad they were friendly."

The manager of the hotel, who recently became a part owner and a distinguished-looking middle-aged man, who was a banker, walked up at about the same time. The banker asked, "Would you like to file and press criminal charges? I am a witness who saw and heard everything that just happened. I will be glad to testify in court."

The manager responded instantly, "Thank you, sir. We are absolutely going to file and press criminal charges to the maximum extent of the law. Thank you for off—"

The bankers laugh was mocking. "The best thing you can do is shut up, step back, and remain quiet. I was not talking to you. I was talking to Lynda. This woman who you insulted, embarrassed, humiliated, slandered, and called a whore can write a check and pay cash for this entire *righteous* establishment at will. And on top of everything else, you called her husband a liar and then attacked a duly authorized Arizona ranger, who is an official governmental agent of the law. Mister, since you are new here, I don't know who you are or what your name is, but you are having one of the worst days of your life. By the way, if you are wondering who I am, I am Lynda's chief investment banker."

Within a very short time, the ranger and Lynda were given the presidential suite on the top floor for two nights and unlimited access to the restaurant menu with twenty-four-hour room service, all at no charge.

As they entered the suite, even Lynda was impressed, and she gasped. "Honey, I have been all over the world, and I've been to Europe half a dozen times, but I have never seen a room like this before. And here it is, ten miles from home. Ain't that a kick?"

Then she smiled at her ranger. "I would dream of a handsome prince who would take me away, and we would live happily ever after. And here my real prince literally rides right up to my front door and stays in my town. Of course, a *real* prince would have made sure I was home when he rode up to my front door instead of pulling leather with my brother."

The ranger chuckled. "Okay, so what happened with the handsome prince?"

Lynda gestured with her hand. "Aw…there were a lot of handsome princes, to be sure, but they were all taken or spoken for. The only ones left were ugly and broke. And most of them were looking for new money to save their castle or their imagined empire."

They were silent as they looked at each other. Lynda walked up to her ranger and hugged him for a long time. Then she stepped back and slowly disrobed herself. Lynda was truly the most beautiful woman the ranger has ever seen in his life. The moon shone brightly through the open breezy window and cast a strong blue hue to everything it touched. The blue tone made Lynda even more beautiful, and the ranger found it difficult to breathe. With tears, she caressed the man who now held all of her hopes and dreams for a lifetime. He looked at her and was unable to see all of her womanly glory at one time. There could nevermore be any question or doubt that he was now helpless before this goddess among women. Merely touching the sheer softness of her skin elevated Kyle to a new level of existence.

Then she slowly disrobed her man, her ranger, and they stood embraced together in the soft blue glow of the moon that seemed to be created just for them.

Lynda not only stood before him physically naked, she stood before him in the nakedness of her heart and her very soul. She has made herself totally vulnerable to him, and she has put her entire emotional life in his hands. She has given him the emotional power to destroy her, and she has given him the power to save her.

She gave herself to him with the fullness of undiluted passion, passion fueled by years of nightmares and years of heart-paralyzing and soul-crushing loneliness. Trodden upon and overwhelmed by life while fighting alone for an unseen purpose. She now gave him all that she had to offer, and he took her. With his own undiluted passions and unspeakable loneliness, he both took her and accepted her for all time. Just as she had, he accepted her.

The heart and core of the source of their terror, their nightmares, is now being replaced with each shared heartbeat. The terror of sleep is being replaced with hope, love, and a new life. Already fading is the life where the very act of existence was a source of pain.

In the past, they were alive but were not living. Tonight…they lived. The power of their passionate bonding exceeded the physical and soared into a spirit realm that is reserved for the elite of heart and only for those bonded with the purity of souls.

At some point in the early hours, the ranger got up and walked over to the window and was quickly joined by the woman who now owned his heart. Their loving embrace was now as natural as breathing. Still unclothed and standing in the fading blue light of the lover's moon, Kyle Lawton got down on his knees. He did not get on his knees before her; rather he got on his knees in front of her.

Her ranger looked up at her and hugged her around her stomach. "On my knees before God almighty, I swear to you, my love, that you are already my wife."

Lynda cried softly and shed soft tears. But her tears were not from her eyes; they were from her heart.

The ranger looked at her and shook his head in disbelief. "My love, you are the most beautiful woman that I have ever seen in my life. Above all others, you are a goddess among women, and as long as there is a breath of air in my body, you will be treated as such."

The ranger and Lynda settled out of court with the hotel for a large sum of money that was, finding them worthy, distributed among several territorial charities. The hotel management was informed that every dime of the money from their grievous error helped a lot of down and out people who desperately needed help. The hotel responded with a special thank-you card, signed by the manager and his nephew, the errant but wiser clerk. It seemed that the hotel had received over two hundred heartfelt thank-you cards expressing the deepest gratitude. Some of the cards are priceless artwork handmade by children. Showing her elegance and true class, Lynda gave the hotel credit, by name, for the funds she distributed to the charities. Lynda can be elegant and refined if you let her, but she can be otherwise if you force her. The sheriff's final report had an interesting entry, an entry that somehow found its way into Texas Red's hands.

THURSDAY NIGHT

The ranger and his lady got back to Agua Fria Thursday afternoon. The gunfight was less than forty-eight hours away but, at the moment, was the furthest thing from their minds. Events were about to develop in such a way that cancelling the gunfight seemed so nigh on hand that it was knocking on the door. But Texas Red had already sealed such a door shut, forever. And Texas Red had already guaranteed that the gunfight cannot remotely be cancelled. And the legendary gunfight was about to get very personal. There was much the ranger was not yet aware of.

However, there was to be one last happy time, one final round of laughter and smiles and one final round of counterfeit hope.

The ranger suggested they stop at the saloon before going across the street to their room in the hotel, and Lynda readily agreed.

When they walked in, both were surprised at how many people were in the saloon. They wondered how many people knew about the ranger arresting Texas Red, who stood at the middle of the bar. And as soon as they walked in, everybody and everything became totally silent. It seemed that everyone was expecting trouble.

As soon as the patrons saw them, it was apparent and undeniable that the ranger and Lynda were a couple. No one had to ask; all they had to do was look at them. Also apparent is that Lynda has changed in many ways. No longer quiet and shy, she was confident and glowing and no longer looks down. Just the way she looked around at everyone was different.

Everyone knew what had happened in Agua Fria, but nobody knew what had happened in Santa Fe.

Texas Red filled everyone in on the details of what happened in Santa Fe. The crowd was stunned. Lynda was directly involved in a fistfight? It was a fight that involved five people, and Lynda knocked a very large security agent out cold?

Texas Red gestured with a circular motion at the patrons and then shook his head at length. "I let them go to Santa Fe, and within a few hours, they become the terror of New Mexico Territory. But most of all, my meek, quiet, little sister bludgeoned a large security agent with the ranger's Big Iron. Pray tell, sis, how in the world did you end up with the Big Iron?"

Before she could answer, Texas Red challenged her, "All by yourself, you singlehandedly knocked out a security agent with the ranger's Big Iron with no help whatsoever from the ranger?"

"That is correct, and I did indeed put his lights out. And to the letter, we followed the rules of fair play."

Texas Red looked at the ranger who nodded that she did indeed singlehandedly take out a security agent, but he shrugged and shook his head about the meaning of following the rules of fair play.

Texas Red looked at his beloved sister. "I would have never believed it, but I have two questions. First, what do you mean by following the rules of fair play?"

"They started it, and we finished it, fair enough?" And then she cackled.

Everyone laughed, and then Texas Red took a step back and held his hands up at shoulder height. "Sorry I interrupted you before, but how on earth did you end up with the ranger's Big Iron in the middle of a fistfight?"

Lynda looked around at everyone and shook her head. "It wasn't a fistfight because nobody hit anybody with a fist. When that loudmouthed bellhop called—"

The ranger interrupted, "Honey, it was the desk clerk, not a bellhop."

Lynda grinned. "I'm betting he is a bellhop now. And that reminds me, ranger, you owe me a thousand dollars." Lynda looked around at everyone and spoke with a singsong voice, "I done skinned the ranger for a thousand dollars."

The ranger shook his head. "Sorry, Red, but it's like taking candy from a baby, but I hope this lady can cover a thousand-dollar bet she made with me."

There were humorous chuckles from the patrons, and Texas Red smiled. "It might take her awhile to scrape up that much money, but she can probably handle it. What is the bet?"

Lynda spoke up, "Now, don't tell William what side of the bet you or I are on. Just ask the question as plain and simple as you can, and then he will answer it, and then I will collect my thousand dollars."

The ranger smiled. "And what if I win?"

Lynda giggled. "If you win, you can present William with an invoice for a thousand dollars for consultation fees."

Everyone noticed that Lynda was openly calling her brother William, which she had never done before. This was, to be sure, a different person than the Lynda who rode off with the ranger some two days and a handful of hours ago.

The ranger looked around at everyone as he thought about the question. "Okay, was the final discount you received on the cost of the downstairs teak floor greater than or less than 50 percent? We are not asking how much the floor cost, just the final discount."

Texas Red shook his head sharply. "How in the living hell did the two of you go on a buggy ride to Santa Fe and end up making a thousand-dollar bet about the final discount I got on the cost of my downstairs teak floor?"

Lynda answered without hesitation, "We talked about a lot of things, William, and I do mean a lot of things. We talked about life and death and the meaning of the in-between. And we figure the thousand-dollar bet is part of the in-between. So was the final discount over or under 50 percent?"

Texas Red was still stunned at the question. He was not prepared in the least for the new Lynda. What could the ranger have done to her in less than two and a half days? They left on Tuesday at 1:00

p.m. and came back on Thursday at 5:00 p.m. How can anyone change so much in two days and four hours?

Texas Red concluded that Lynda had been changing internally for a long time, but the changes were bottled up inside of her and could not get out. And boy howdy did the ranger ever pull the cork out of that bottle.

Then Texas Red felt Lynda staring at him. "Well?"

He laughed. "The final discount percentage for the downstairs teak floor was 80 percent. All we had to pay was the cost of materials. The freight and labor were gratis. Who won the bet?"

Lynda shook her head. "Are you two in cahoots on this?"

"No, it was good business on the contractor's part because he has been able to tell prospective buyers that he built a house for the famous outlaw named Texas Red. That knotty pine floor was only down there for a day, but word of it will live forever, and if it was me, I would keep it for display. Besides, after he found out who I was, he was afraid not to discount the teak floor by a substantial margin. Especially after he saw 250 shotgun holes in the knotty pine."

Looking at Lynda, the ranger grinned. "I'll have breakfast in bed for the next month if you please."

"Kyle Lawton, if I bring you breakfast in bed, you won't be eating it, you'll be wearing it."

The ranger was milking it for all it was worth. "But I won the bet."

"You forced yourself on me, and I agreed to the bet under duress. You took advantage of a helpless, little girl."

Again, the townsfolk voiced their approval of Lynda. The people of the town loved the new Lynda, and they liked the ranger for bringing her back to life.

Then one more time, Texas Red asked Lynda, "How did you get possession of the ranger's Big Iron in the middle of a fight?"

Lynda looked at her ranger and batted her eyes several times. "As I was saying before I was so rudely interrupted, when that bellhop called my ranger a liar with a fake badge and then called me a whore, Kyle took exception to his language and pulled him over the counter and threw the bellhop to the floor and then kicked him in the head. Well, Kyle realized he was still packing the Big Iron, and he didn't want any gunplay, so he pulled the Big Iron and handed it to me. While Kyle was taking out the second man, I saw the biggest man of the bunch sneaking up behind Kyle and was going to ambush my new boyfriend. So I held the Big Iron by the end of the barrel and swung it like a club as hard as I could. Well, I guess he heard me and turned around because his forehead and the Big Iron ended up in the same place at the same time, and he went down like a felled ox. And he didn't move a muscle or even twitch an eye. He might have been skiing on the Alps or sunning himself on a beach somewhere in his dreams, but he sure wasn't fighting anymore. He was done for the day."

Everyone in the saloon cheered and applauded, and those who were seated stood up. Lynda responded with a full curtsey in three directions.

Texas Red had one more thing to add. After all, any glowing reflection on his sister also reflected on him. "Don't ask me how I got this, but I was able to get part of the sheriff's report in Santa Fe. And apparently, the sheriff has deep respect for Lynda and her ranger." He then read the partial report.

> The assailant knocked out by Mrs. Lynda Lawton, the ranger's wife, glared at her in a threatening manner upon regaining consciousness, so she spat at him. Then he took a step toward her, and she jabbed him in his left eye with her right forefinger, which had a long, hardened fingernail. As the errant security agent was being handcuffed, she issued an additional challenge. "When you mess with a woman's man, don't ever ignore the woman, especially when she has a Big Iron in her hands. Do you want to step outside and do this again? There's already too much blood on the carpet to do it in here."
>
> Mrs. Lawton's challenge wisely went unanswered. At this point, the Arizona ranger's only involvement was

to keep Mrs. Lawton at bay and to expend a significant amount of effort to regain possession of his firearm.

Again, the townsfolk laughed and applauded Lynda with cheers and toasts.

Shaking his head, Texas Red looked at the ranger. "What? You had to expend a significant amount of effort to regain your firearm?" Then he looked at both of them. "What's this part about Mrs. Lawton? Did you two get married?"

Lynda shook her head. "Not by law, but my man got down on his knees and swore to God Almighty that I am already his wife. Besides, we can't get legally married without inviting the town. Plus the fact that Anita and I have a gunfight to stop." Texas Red scoffed and shook his head thinking that trying to stop the gunfight was futile.

But once again, the crowd voiced their approval of Lynda as Texas Red realized something for the first time. "My God, she reminds me so much of Mama Phebe. And she's got this whole town eating out of her hand. All this time, I've been going about things the wrong way. But then, who else but the ranger could have brought Lynda back to life?" Texas Red looked around, and even he was surprised at how many people showed up to watch the ranger arrest him. Then he went back to the ranch to get Anita. The ranger and Lynda went to their room across the street.

The saloon was crowded to capacity, and it was barely sundown. Word has reached far and wide that tonight could be the gunfight of all times, the legendary gunfight between the ranger and Texas Red. Everyone knew the gunfight was set for Saturday at noon, but when the ranger faced Texas Red and officially placed him under arrest, there was no telling what would happen. This situation could come unraveled within a heartbeat.

Newspaper reporters arrived from over a hundred miles around but were clearly staying out of everyone's way, and they were reporting on the town as much as the gunfight. There was no actual time set for the arrest of Texas Red by the ranger; it would occur when both men felt like it. With the whereabouts of both men known to all, no one dared approach them. Texas Red was with Anita at the ranch, and the ranger was with Lynda in their room across the street from the saloon.

In the den out at the ranch, Anita walked up behind Texas Red and put her arms around him. "Is there going to be a gunfight tonight? I don't want anything to happen to you…or Kyle either. Don't you understand that no matter what happens both Lynda and I lose? Either way, not one of us but both of us lose."

Texas Red shook his head. "In a gunfight, there is a winner and a loser. One of us will win, and the other will be dead. That's how gunfights work, and there is no changing that. You have a winner, and you have a loser. What do you mean both of you girls lose either way?"

"The ranger and Lynda are right for each other. If you win, she loses Kyle, and if Kyle wins, she loses you. If you win, I will watch Lynda die inside as certain as if she caught the bullet, and if Kyle wins, then Lynda and I both will lose *you*. There is no winner here, William. Nobody wins, and everybody loses in this one…I know how much you want to be remembered in history as a legendary gunfighter, the best who ever lived. But, William, nobody wins this gunfight and nobody can."

"What are you saying, Anita?"

Anita took a deep breath and let it out slowly. "Call it off, William. Work something out, and call it off. I don't care what you say, you and the ranger have become more than friends in just a week. This is a sad and twisted thing to say, William, but I believe either of you would take a bullet for the other on the way to the gunfight. Kyle doesn't want this either. Maybe both of you do not want this, but you won't admit it to each other, or even to yourselves. William, it still isn't too late to call it off."

"I am an outlaw, and the ranger was sent here to arrest me or shoot me. He cannot change that." Texas Red hugged her and sighed. "I realize how this sounds, but there really is a matter of honor here and a matter of us living with ourselves for the rest of our lives."

"Living with yourselves for the rest of your lives? After one of you kills the other? After one of you kills someone who has become like a brother. Is the honor you speak of going to heal the hearts that this gunfight guarantees to shatter and scar for life? One of you is going to die, and that will torment us for the rest of our lives. I found you, and you found me. Kyle found Lynda, and Lynda found Kyle...William, we could all be so happy for the rest of our lives. I am begging you, my love, find a way to stop this and call it off."

With historic and legendary fame at his fingertips, there was no way Texas Red would even consider calling it off, but Anita had a valid point about everyone losing no matter who wins the gunfight.

Texas Red did not want to spend the rest of his life with his sister's hatred for him growing stronger every time she looked at him. He knew that Lynda would suffer grievously, and her grief would strongly affect Anita, and that would permanently change his relationship with her.

However, there was no way possible he would give up his fame and legendary status as the best gunfighter alive. Just when Texas Red got to the point where he decided to accept the hostility and hate and live with it, he got an idea, something that would look like he was nearly begging the ranger and would look like he was bending over backward to the breaking point but something he knew the ranger could not and would not accept. It would make him look like the good guy instead of the outlaw.

Lost in their thoughts, Texas Red and Anita ended up in different rooms, so Texas Red called out to her, and he sounded excited and happy at the tone of his voice. When she came to him, he looked at her and smiled. "I have an idea that just might work. Let's hook up the buggy and go see the ranger."

In the ranger's room, there was a similar discussion between the ranger and Lynda. "One of you is going to kill the other, violently and horribly, and the memory of that will be etched in my mind forever and in Anita's mind as well. Call it off, Kyle, think of a way, and make a way to stop this gunfight. Put a stop to it, Kyle. If you slam a bullet into my brother's body, part of me will still love you for the rest of my life...but part of me will also hate you for the rest of my life, and both of us will have to live with that."

"It would have to be something Red agrees with too. You know what would happen to me if I simply tried to leave town...and don't forget that I am a ranger and he is an outlaw."

Lynda nodded. "Yes...you're right. It has to be something William will agree to."

Then she walked over to him, hugged him, and buried her face in his chest. "I know that you are a ranger and William is an outlaw. I can't get that part out of my mind, so I will make you a deal, Kyle, and it is the best I can do."

The ranger brushed her hair back with his hand. "Anything, Lynda. I will do anything to keep you and to keep you from hating me if I win."

She nodded. "Okay, then do the very, very best you are capable of doing to get William to agree to stop this evil madness. If you really do the very best you can to stop this, I will know it and see it...I can live with that without hating you, Kyle."

"Are you sure you could live with that?"

"Yes, I know I can, and I hate to say this, but William forcing you to stay in town and William's threat to hunt you down and kill you if you leave makes it a lot easier. In a way, it is William's fault. Besides...oh God, I will make any excuse I can to love you and not hate you."

The ranger smiled softly. "That's a first in my life, Lynda. But I swear to you that I will do my best to think—" The ranger interrupted himself and smiled.

"Did you think of something already?"

"Let me work on it. It's an incomplete thought, but I have something to work with. What is the greatest gift anyone could give to Red? Something of such supreme value that even he cannot buy it. Something that is beyond his wealth, and something he cannot attain, but something that would change his life for the better."

Lynda became excited and hopeful. "Okay, I will leave you alone and let you work it out. I will wait for you in the saloon, but there is no hurry, Kyle."

The ranger nodded. "The more I think about it, the more I like it…it just might work. The greatest gift Red could possibly receive, yet he does not have the power or money to attain it. But I have the power to give it…yes."

An hour later, just as it was getting dark, Texas Red and Anita parked the buggy and walked into the saloon. As soon as they walked in, they saw Lynda and couldn't miss how excited and smiling she was. When she saw them, she waved and blew kisses at them. Texas Red wasn't sure what to think of this, but his instincts told him that he didn't like it. However, it didn't matter what it was, nothing is going to stand in the way of what he thought of as his rightful fame. However, Texas Red and Anita noticed that Lynda was alone, and the ranger was nowhere in sight.

At any rate, Texas Red was prepared to make the ranger a deal that would stop the gunfight. He knows the ranger will not accept the deal, so he intends to make the offer publicly and in front of everyone in the saloon. In his mind, Texas Red was already practicing his shock and dismay at the ranger declining his *irresistible* offer. Texas Red was very much aware that every man in the saloon, except the ranger, would instantly accept his offer that is literally life changing. However, there is a critical fact Red does not know.

He has no idea that the ranger is finalizing his own offer to stop the gunfight that is even greater and even more life changing than his own offer. Texas Red has no idea that the ranger has an excellent reason to decline his offer. But Texas Red cannot justify declining the ranger's offer. Many people will soon realize that Texas Red has a hidden agenda and has no intentions of stopping the gunfight. If both men reject the other's offer to stop the gunfight, then the gunfight is inevitable. But even the devil himself could not resist the offer the ranger is about to make to Texas Red.

Again, there was no set time for the official arrest tonight, but everyone knew that at some point tonight, the ranger was going to place Texas Red under arrest, and everyone knew the *understanding* is to settle the matter in a gunfight to the death at high noon Saturday.

Even the ranger did not yet know that he will soon change the time of the gunfight to 11:20, but for the first time in his life, he understood why he would do such a thing. The same question was on everyone's mind, including Texas Red and the ranger—Will the situation degenerate into unintended anger, unintended hostility, and unplanned gunplay?

The town was buzzing and talking about nothing else, and many strangers were in town to watch the historic, legendary gunfight. Even a few known outlaws risked being there but were quietly tolerated for the duration of the event. Almost everyone liked the ranger, and everyone agreed that the ranger was a natural match for Lynda, a good match that probably would have lasted a lifetime. However, all of the betting, talk, and speculation was the same. Even with his impressive résumé, the odds were 10 to 1 that the ranger was about to meet his death. No one other than Texas Red knows how incredibly fast the ranger is, but neither does anyone know about the ranger's secret injury that may well cost him his life.

The ranger's hand had never gone bad twice in a row, so he practiced pulling leather on and off all day. However, every draw was flawless and precise, and he could not get his hand to turn into the fatal, treasonous claw even after several hundred draws. Now the ranger was concerned about burning out his hand with fatigue, so he had to go with his hand as it was, devil may come.

After much thinking, the ranger walked into the saloon and was happily greeted by Lynda, and they hugged. Then Texas Red saw them and stood up and looked around to get everyone's attention.

As soon as everyone was looking at him, Texas Red gestured toward the ranger. "The ranger is here to arrest me." There were murmurs and head shaking from the crowd, and the subdued response left no doubt who they believed was going to win the gunfight, but the ranger was totally undaunted, except for the nagging fear about his gun hand.

The ranger whispered something in Lynda's ear, and she left his side to speak to Anita. They exchanged whispers at length, and then Lynda returned to the ranger's side. "You are not going to believe this, but William wants to make *you* an offer to stop the gunfight."

The ranger looked around and shook his head. He had not realized how much the gunfight had taken on a life of its own. The sheer momentum would make it very difficult to stop, and it certainly would take the full support of both of them to call it off. But he was glad that Red had an idea to stop it and that at least Red tried.

Then something got everyone's full attention. Three of Texas Red's best men, meaning the toughest and meanest, walked into the saloon with a small iron box, and they were armed to the teeth. Each had a loaded rifle at ready, and each had twin holsters with fully loaded pistols. As they walked to the end of the bar, the men standing there peeled off and cleared the bar immediately, giving Texas Red's men all of the space they wanted.

The ranger stood up and started to walk over to Texas Red, but he waved the ranger off and gestured for the ranger to sit down at the gunfighters' table. Not knowing what was happening or what else to do, the ranger complied and Lynda joined him.

Anita also joined them at the table and explained. "William has a lot of money in that little iron box. He wants to make an offer to cancel the gunfight and give you two a whole new life."

The ranger shook his head to clear his mind. "What? That doesn't make any sense, and it's a lot easier for Red to shoot somebody than to pay them off."

Anita shook her head emphatically. "No. This is not any kind of payoff. Two new critical issues have occurred that have changed

William's mind. William wants to terminate the gunfight. And since you are a ranger and he is an outlaw, he has an offer that you and Lynda can both accept."

The ranger was suspicious, something wasn't right. Then he asked, "What are the critical issues?"

Anita looked down and then at Lynda and then looked at the ranger. "Something that only William and Lynda knows…I am carrying William's child, and William now realizes this is a fight neither of you can win. Nor does he want his own sister to hate him for the rest of her life should he win. William thinks there will be less pressure on you, and it will help you if he makes the offer public. William will explain everything."

Then Lynda asked Anita, "Do you agree with this? Do you believe this, Anita?"

"If it would call off the gunfight, I will believe the devil himself."

The ranger looked at Lynda, and she nodded in agreement. Then he looked over at Texas Red who was standing at the end of the bar, and the ranger nodded. Texas Red smiled instantly, but for the first time, the ranger truly did not trust Red; something wasn't right. However, at this point the ranger did not have much choice.

Nothing was lost on the townspeople and reporters. Every move and every gesture was noted and thoroughly discussed. It was beginning to look like there would be no gunfight, at least not tonight.

Then Texas Red stepped away from the bar and held his hands up to get everyone's attention, which he already had. No one was remotely prepared for what Texas Red said next.

The immediate and abrupt silence was eerie. Anita and Lynda thought it not possible for so many people to be so quiet. Texas Red had carefully rehearsed this many times in his mind.

"Some new information on vital issues has just now come to my attention. As you know, my beloved sister and the Arizona ranger have met and grown into a couple, and as they now stand, they are a couple who are either in love or fast becoming such. And when it comes to my sister, I find the ranger worthy of her." There were a lot of murmurs and quick comments about Texas Red's open approval of the ranger.

When it concerned Lynda, Texas Red always remained William, and she never saw or dealt with Texas Red. She heard the name Texas Red but never saw the reality. The toughest and most dangerous men in the state stood at attention and said "yes, sir" and "no, sir," and they said "yes, ma'am" and "no, ma'am" while in her presence. Beards were trimmed and baths were taken. In addition, every man on the ranch had clean clothes readily available. The most feared men in the state knew how to bow properly when she curtsied, and they drew water for her and helped her adjust her bonnets and hats. William truly loved his sister and never abused her in any way, and she never wanted for money or anything she desired. If she so much as mentioned a new dress, within a few weeks, she was wearing it. If she mentioned London or Paris more than twice in the same week, she was gone within a few days, along with two of Texas Red's most trusted men. If William could have taken her horrible nightmares in her place, he would have done so without hesitation. In addition, she owned half of the mansion three miles north of town. She often teased William that her half was the half with the indoor plumbing. Lynda was the only direct, living link Texas Red still had with William. Texas Red was a model brother. However, it was the rest of the world he had problems with.

Texas Red continued, "I have decided to once again give the ranger a chance to walk out of here alive...and he can take Lynda with him if she is willing, which I think she is. Lynda owns many things, such as half of the ranch house, half of the cattle, and half of the land thought to be mine is hers, and a lot more. However, it would take time to sell anything of substance for cash, but we have a situation here that to be honest, I do not think would remain stable long enough to do that. In addition, I insist that Lynda has the same standard of living that she has had since birth. Here is my offer to the ranger and his lady. First, all that she owns is still hers. I will maintain all that she wants to keep, and I will pay her the full value, with no discounts, for anything she wants to sell. Simply stated,

I will pay Lynda full price. This is not about money. However, in order to maintain her current lifestyle, I offer the ranger a dowry."

Texas Red nodded to his trusted men guarding the small iron box. They quickly opened the box, and there were gasps from all who could see what was in the box, and word quickly spread that the box was stacked full of 100-dollar bills laid flat. Judging from the size of the box, there was a minimum of $200,000 in the box, most likely more.

Texas Red looked at Lynda and the ranger and then motioned for them to come up to the bar. As Texas Red's eyes met the rangers, he could see the anger in the ranger's eyes, which was expected. Texas Red knew the ranger would decline the offer, and he knew the ranger had to decline it. Yet the ranger realized he had to hear the offer before he could decline it. In fact, he could not decline it too quickly, and he had to *think* about it. The ranger now understood that Texas Red was doing a very good job of making himself look like a towering hero by making a magnanimous offer that Texas Red knows the ranger must decline.

Looking around at the crowd more than the ranger or Lynda, Texas Red explained, "For her dowry, my sister can have as many 100-dollar bills as she can fit in her right hand, and she can use her left hand to help pack her right hand to be sure she has as many 100-dollar bills as her right hand can carry. All she has to do is carry them about thirty feet to the gunfighters' table." Texas Red was almost intoxicated from the attention and the increasing excitement of the legendary gunfight Saturday at noon. Knowing the ranger could not accept the money and knowing the ranger still had to arrest or shoot him, Texas Red was making a game out of the dowry, and to be sure, he was enjoying himself. And he fully intended to make the ranger look bad.

That is not how it went down at all. Texas Red and his men may be feared elsewhere but not by Lynda. How could she fear men who have escorted her and protected her all over the world for many years? She didn't follow *William's* rules, she made up her own. She packed every 100-dollar bill she could fit into her right hand, then clinched a stack of bills with her teeth, and then grabbed a handful of bills with her left hand. Before Texas Red could respond, she scurried as fast as she could to the gunfighters' table and dumped the bills on top of the table. Then she bounced up and down and clapped her hands like a schoolgirl. Then she brought the house down in laughter when she said, "Texas Red, you have just been robbed."

This was going much better than Texas Red had hoped for. Now there would be enormous pressure on the ranger to accept his offer, and it sure will make the ranger look bad when he had to refuse. Not to mention how much this pressure will affect the ranger tomorrow.

Texas Red was doing everything he could think of to distract the ranger, break his concentration, put pressure on him, slow his draw, and Texas Red was doing everything he could think of to build the legendary status of this gunfight. However, he was very serious when he said that he found the ranger worthy of his sister. By now, Texas Red was totally convinced that fate will provide him with whatever it will take for him to win the famed gunfight.

Then Texas Red thought to himself, *too bad the ranger isn't going to live much longer. Those two may well have lasted a lifetime.*

Then Texas Red made his plea to the ranger as he gestured toward the gunfighters' table now swollen with 100-dollar bills. "Ranger, it is all yours. You can ride out of here on tomorrow's stagecoach, and you can take my sister with you as well as all"—Texas Red stopped, shook his head, and chuckled—"as well as all of the money stolen from me by the dreaded raven-haired bandit." Again there was much laughter but mixed with caution. No one has ever seen Texas Red act like this before, and no one knew exactly what to expect or how long it would last, but they all knew the vicious killer was not gone. He was still there in Texas Red's back pocket.

Then Texas Red added another level to his offer. "I will sweeten the pot even further, ranger. Let's count the money on the table, and six months from today, I will send the two of you an equal amount and then one more time six months beyond that. And that, ranger, is the best I can do."

The ranger shook his head. "Why are you being so generous, Red?"

Texas Red acted uncomfortable, but it was just an act. "If I win the gunfight Saturday, my own sister, who is beloved, and you know that, will hate me for the rest of her life. And who knows, she may hate me into the next life as well. I will do anything in my power to keep her from hating me. And don't forget, ranger, you were not invited here."

The ranger shook his head. "Not true, Red. I was duly and legally invited here, not by you but by the Territory of New Mexico via special request to the Arizona rangers."

Texas Red had not thought of that. He was embarrassed, and somehow, it dampened his inner feelings of invincibility. It was yet another warning sign that Texas Red was not in total control of the situation, and it is yet another warning he chose to ignore.

The ranger decided not to wait and *think* about the offer; after all, he needed to respond now. "Red, you know damn well that I cannot accept this offer. In fact, I can't even consider it. As I told you before, and as you have seen with your own eyes, I am a specially trained gunfighter commissioned to extract outlaws no one else can face, and now, that outlaw is you. I must stay on mission, Red, and I cannot allow anything to distract me or divert me from my mission."

Texas Red glared at the ranger with the coldness of death. "Then I guess you and I have said all there is to say to each other."

Again, the ranger shook his head. "Not quite yet, there is one more thing for me to say that would interest you."

Texas Red was ever so tempted to pull leather at that very moment, but he rightly suspected the ranger was fully aware of it and was ready to draw. Again, Texas Red spoke with the coldness of death, "Then say it, ranger, and get out…while you can."

Then the ranger also spoke with anger and in deadly coldness, "You want to pull leather with me, Red? Do you want to pull right now? Let's trash the fame, the glory, and the game playing. Let's get down to business right here and right now."

Sam stepped in-between them. "The gunfight is Saturday, not tonight. I'll stand here between you two all night if I have to. I know neither of you will shoot an unarmed man who is no threat to you. Now both of you back off and cool down. What is it you have to say to him, ranger?"

"I don't know if I want to say it now or not."

Texas Red looked away as he spoke, "Say it, ranger, it is your last chance. What is on your mind?"

The ranger kept his gun hand clear of the Big Iron and walked over close to Red. He then spoke so that only Red could hear, "As I said, I must decline your offer...but I have a counteroffer."

"Let's hear it."

The ranger shook his head. "Only in private with just the four of us, five if you want Sam in on it and six if you add your most trusted man."

Texas Red scoffed. "You are full of surprises, ranger. Okay, the saloon has a back room made just for private meetings, and it will be the six of us, including my lead man, Frank."

Within minutes, the six of them were in the back room with a trusted friend running the bar for Sam.

Sam looked around and saw that everyone was settled. "Okay, ranger, you have the floor. Let's hear what you've got in mind."

The ranger looked around at each of them. "Red, I offer you what you offered me, a whole new life. No one expects any of us lawmen to bring back a body we may have for five or six days, and no lawman would do it. There are provisions to document the death of an outlaw. Therefore, my offer is this...Red, I will *kill* you right here in this room tonight in front of all of these witnesses. Our words became heated, and one thing led to another. Red, I offer you a complete new life with no past, no crimes, no wanted posters, no endless stream of want-to-be gunfighters, and no more looking over your shoulder. I offer you a complete new life with a clean slate. With the help of a few ranking men in this town, I can document your death and even put up a grave marker." The ranger shrugged his shoulders. "Sometimes they double-check things, which is a high probability in a major case like this without a body."

Texas Red scoffed. "Too easy, ranger, what is the catch?"

"Well...I have wrestled with my own conscience for a while now, and I am an Arizona ranger with a duty to perform. I do not mind if William lives, but Texas Red *must* die."

"Thanks for clearing that up, ranger, now what in the hell are you talking about? I can tell there is something you do not want to say, which means there is something I do not want to hear."

"William does not have to die, but Texas Red *must* die."

"We have already covered that, ranger. Next sentence please, the hard part."

"Anita carries a small caliber derringer with her at all times. Well...if you were to shoot yourself in the middle of your gun hand with her derringer, you would no longer be able to pull leather, and that would *kill* Texas Red yet leave William alive, and that would probably save your life. If not this Saturday, then another day when *your* hand turns into a claw."

Texas Red nodded. "And my grieving sister could then liquidate all of our assets and then split the cash, and then we all live like kings for the rest of our lives in a foreign country, or maybe Europe. Is that it?"

The ranger nodded hesitantly. "Yeah...that's...that's about it, that's the idea. You could even supervise and direct the liquidating of your assets yourself...personally...you know...be in charge."

Texas Red laughed mockingly. "Go to hell, ranger, that *ain't* gonna happen. I'll be damn if I am going to deliberately emasculate myself so you can take the easy way out."

Then Texas Red looked around at everyone. "Does anyone else have any ideas?"

With the only answer being silence, Texas Red looked each person in the eyes and then glared straight at the ranger. "A worthy effort, ranger, but you do not have much time for a plan B. Saturday noon, ranger, bring your gun."

Knowing the gunfight was now inevitable the ranger returned Texas Red's glare squarely in the eyes as they all stood up. "I made you an offer that stretched my limits to the breaking point, but you declined. I have no further options, Red. I have to take you back… dead or alive."

"Okay, ranger, but you can arrest me tomorrow night. I am coming too close to killing you tonight, and I need to get away from you for a while."

"That boat floats in both directions, Red. I'm getting real tired of the games and the glory hunting. And I've heard that some things happened while Lynda and I were in Santa Fe. And you have no idea of how close you came to dying a couple of times yourself tonight. And then you refuse the offer of a lifetime. No matter how much fame and glory you get, you will be a hunted man for the rest of your life, and what are you going to do with Anita and the baby? It doesn't matter who lives or dies Saturday…either way you lose, Red."

The ranger started to say more, but Texas Red put his hands up. "Let's call it a night, ranger, and let's do what we need to do tomorrow."

The ranger rubbed the back of his head in frustration, but he nodded, and each quickly went his way.

When Texas Red got back to the ranch, Anita was waiting for him.

"What's the matter with you, William? What is wrong with you?"

Anita shook her head in disbelief. "Don't you realize that the ranger has the power to change our lives…and our baby's life?"

Texas Red poured a drink and held his hand up to her as a warning, but she was beyond that. "We can have a brand-new life with no one looking for us. We can have the best of everything including a fortune in money, and we can have a lot more than we deserve. The ranger has power that our money can never buy, and he can erase the past and give us a clean slate. Don't you care about our baby and the life he will have?"

Texas Red threw the whiskey glass against the wall and it shattered into thousands of pieces. "What about what I want? What about me?"

Undaunted, Anita grabbed him by the shoulders. "What is wrong? What is going on, William? Why didn't you take the ranger's offer?"

Texas Red's eyes were glazed as he spoke, "Fame, glory, being a historic legend is all right in front of me, and all I have to do is reach out and take it. Normal men never get the chance to be as great as I can be. Greatness eludes them, but all I have to do is take it. It is right there. Don't you understand that it is all right there in front of me? Normal men live and die in the backwater of life, and no one ever knows their name, but I can be famous and a renowned legend, and people will speak my name for centuries. Only Achilles can be compared to me."

Texas Red almost ran out of the house to the guest house, leaving a shocked and stunned Anita standing in the middle of the quite room. "He's mad, William is mad with the lust for fame and glory."

An hour later, Texas Red was lying down, trying to attain an unreachable sleep. He felt Anita crawl in bed with him, and she half laid on him. "There is something else going on, I know it, William. There is something else, and I know it. What is it that I don't know, William?"

He then told her in detail what he had done in the last two days, and he even told Anita how he killed the telegraph operator to keep the ranger from reading the telegram. Being sick with child for those two days, Anita did not know what William had done.

Anita closed her eyes. "Oh, God, the ranger will never make that offer if he finds out about the telegraph operator. I love you more than my own life, William, and I will help you any way I can that does not endanger our child."

"What? You will help me?"

"You are the father of my child, and I love you more than life itself. But we only have one hope. You have to agree to the ranger's offer as fast as you can, and then we have to get the ranger and Lynda out of town as fast as possible. If we can buy enough time for the ranger to fill out and file the papers of your death, then it doesn't matter what he finds out. We probably need more time than we have, but it's our only chance."

Texas Red looked into her beautiful eyes. "I would have never believed that anyone, even you, could ever love someone like me that much. I am not easy to love, maybe there is a God."

FRIDAY NIGHT

The six of them—the ranger, Lynda, Texas Red, Anita, Sam, and Frank—met in the private room in the saloon just after dark. Lynda and Anita insisted they meet to discuss any new offers or ideas to stop the gunfight. Anita cleared her throat and even kicked Texas Red in the shin under the table, but all he did was stare at his folded hands, which were on top of the table.

Anita then blurted out, "William has something he wants to say."

Texas Red shook his head no. "I am pondering an idea, but I have nothing to say at the moment." Then he looked at the ranger. "I may or may not have something to discuss with you later."

The ranger looked at the clock. "What do you mean later? Later is now, Red."

Texas Red shrugged. "Is your offer of a new life with a clean slate still valid?"

"It is."

"Perhaps we will discuss it and come to terms."

"There are no terms, Red. The offer stands as stated."

"I will not emasculate myself by putting a bullet through my own hand."

"It is the only way, Red. I absolutely insist that Texas Red dies, and there is no other way I can think of where Texas Red dies and William lives."

"Perhaps there is nothing to discuss."

"Would you like to hear what I really, deeply think is going on with you?"

Texas Red shrugged. "Let's hear it, ranger."

What the ranger said next staggered and shocked everyone in the room, especially Texas Red.

"I believe you have what is called double consciousness or split personalities. William has the master's degree and sanity, but Texas Red is the strong, gun-slinging outlaw who cares for little else other than satisfying his own grandiose delusions that borders on, if not crosses into insanity. At first, William was the dominant personality, especially in college. But Texas Red became the dominant personality after El Paso. I have no illusions that a bullet through the gun hand will truly kill Texas Red, but it will reestablish William as the dominate personality, and that is close enough. William will do the rest. I absolutely will not give Texas Red a clean slate because he will simply do it all over again. But if William is your dominant personality, I will give him a clean slate. That is what I mean when I say that William can live but Texas Red must die."

Texas Red laughed mockingly. "Ranger, you are just smart enough to be stupid. That is the greatest display of ignorance I have seen in a very long time. I have a master's degree, and guess what my major is…it is in psychology. And who in the hell do you think you are to throw around loose theories like they are substantiated fact?"

The ranger smiled and shook his head. "William has the master's degree, not you. And your retort is pure grandiose delusions. Now, if you are the one with the degree in psychology, then defend yourself against my accusation and tell us about grandiose delusions and explain what they are and how I am wrong. You can't because you do not have William's knowledge. You share his intellect, and you've learned to speak very concise and correct English, to be sure, but that is just part of your charade."

Texas Red's only response was a glaring silence.

"Again, you might share William's intelligence, but you do not have his knowledge and education. That is why it is called *double* consciousness."

Texas Red seethed inside with hatred of the ranger. No one, at any time, has even suspected, let alone come close to realizing that the ranger is right. He is Texas Red, but he is not William.

Sam called an end to the meeting and suggested they take time to cool off before the ranger officially arrested Texas Red.

As everyone else walked out of the private room into the saloon, the ranger pulled Red aside and spoke to him privately.

"Red?"

Texas Red spoke through gritted teeth, "Yes, ranger."

The ranger sighed and wondered if he was being too weak, but he was going to say it anyway, and he will say it because he *wanted* to, not because he had to. "I know that I am the only one who calls you Red, but more especially, you will not tolerate anyone, other than the girls, calling you William in private, let alone in public. Even they do not call you William openly very often, and some people don't even know that you're given birth name is William, so I will…"

Texas Red rolled his eyes. The pressure and strain were beginning to show. "What…is…your…point, ranger?"

"I am about to speak in the official capacity of an Arizona ranger, which is legally binding. I will not call you Red or William. I will use your preferred name of Texas Red."

Texas Red let out a long breath, shook his head, and closed his eyes. "I am sure that means something to you, and somehow, it is important to you, and for that, I thank you. But you need to get away from me, ranger, because right now I cannot stand the sight of you or the sound of your voice."

Texas Red had to get away from the ranger, so he quickly stepped in front of the ranger, walked into the saloon, and stood at the bar. No one approached him or spoke to him, not even Sam, but the ranger had triggered a thought, and Red was working it out in his mind.

The ranger was surprised at the abrupt change in Red.

Realizing that Texas Red needed a few minutes to himself, the ranger took his time walking out of the private room into the saloon.

In fact, the ranger took an extra moment to look at the private room. It was only then that the ranger realized he had not taken the time to look around, not only at the private room but at the saloon as well. The private room was nondescript and was about thirty feet long and some twenty feet wide with a long conference table about fifteen feet long and six feet wide in the center of the room. There were no other tables but plenty of chairs lined the walls. The walls were light-blue with dark paneling covering the bottom three feet of the walls with matched chair rails running across the top of the paneling. The ten-foot ceiling is painted light-gray. The private room was neither elaborate nor dirty and dingy, which allows the focus of meetings to remain on the meeting rather than the room.

As the ranger walked into the saloon, he glanced over at Texas Red, who obviously was in no mood for talk or company as he stared at his drink. It was also obvious there was something Texas Red had not yet come to terms with. There wasn't anyone within ten feet of where Texas Red stood at the bar, perhaps a bit more than ten feet.

The ranger took a few more moments to look around at the saloon.

The saloon was rectangular shape and looked to be some 120 feet long north and south and about 60 feet wide east and west. The obligatory swinging doors were almost center of the east wall facing the street. Typical of the times, the saloon never completely closed, and the floor was usually covered with a mixture of sawdust and peanut hulls. The stairway to the girls' living quarters and the pleasure rooms was about 40 feet from the south end of the saloon, and the stair steps were 10 feet wide to allow plenty of room for patrons who were less than sober.

Bumping into someone at the wrong time, even if a genuine accident could cause a fistfight or even gunplay, so the steps were as wide as reasonably possible. The bar itself was about one hundred feet long with a large break in the bar to access the areas behind the bar; such as the back door, which is to the left of the stairway, and then for the stairway itself and then for the door to the private room, which is on the right of the stairway. The break in the bar spanned perhaps ten feet and centered about thirty feet from the south end of the bar.

The bartender personally served the patrons at the bar on the north side of the stairway, and there was interaction of a much more social nature at the north end. The bar section to the south of the stairs was for those who preferred quiet solitude, and the saloon girls quietly and quickly served them. There was little, if any, interaction or talk at the south end of the bar. However, there was plenty of talk, noise, chatter, gambling, poker, and some music at the north end. The north end also had many more tables and chairs than the south end.

Suddenly a booming voice filled the room. "Is there a ranger in the house?"

The ranger smiled. Whatever Red was working out in his mind has been resolved. The entire room very quickly became quiet and tense. The ranger faced Texas Red who had not yet turned around. "Yes, sir, there is a ranger in the house, an Arizona ranger."

Then the ranger walked up to the bar where Texas Red stood as the silence became ominous. Still without turning around, Texas Red asked, "Do you have something to say to me, ranger?"

No one had any trouble hearing the ranger as he nodded and answered, "My name is Kyle Lawton, and I am an Arizona ranger commissioned by the territory of Arizona and sent here by special order at the request of the great territory of New Mexico. I am here to extract an outlaw named Texas Red. Sir, are you Texas Red?"

Texas Red then turned around with his arms and hands nonthreatening on top of the bar. He did not intend to threaten the very dangerous ranger. It was not time. Then to everyone's amazement, including the ranger, Texas Red shook his head no. "No, sir, my name is not Texas Red. My name is Travis…William Travis Jr." Texas Red correctly realized that giving his birth name would humanize him in the eyes of the public and make him appear to be more of an average, likeable person rather than a vicious killer. The ranger triggered the thought in Red's mind when the ranger told Red in the private room that he would not refer to him as Red or by his birth name of William.

The ranger was beginning to grow tired of Red's game playing and glory seeking. The ranger responded immediately, "Are you the persona of William Travis Jr. who is known as, referred to, and *called* Texas Red?"

Red was surprised at the ranger's quick thinking and mental skills. Red then nodded slowly. "Yes, sir, I am the persona of William Travis Jr. *called* Texas Red, and I am proud of both names."

The ranger shrugged and shook his head. "Texas Red, you are charged with high crimes against the territory of New Mexico, Arizona, and the State of Texas. These high crimes, some of which are punishable by hanging, include bank robbery, stagecoach robbery, train robbery, and murder of no less than twenty individuals and possibly more. In addition, these charges include being wanted for questioning in El Paso, Texas. I am hereby officially placing you under arrest, and I will escort you back to Phoenix, Arizona, where you will face a federal judge in a lawful court, and you will be given full, unobstructed opportunity to disprove these charges."

Red shook his head and scoffed. "Ranger, you make it sound downright scary. The words you used and the way you phrase everything makes me scared to go with you to Phoenix. You want to know something, ranger? I think I will stay right here. Not only did you make Phoenix sound like a place where lot of bad things can happen, you even threw in El Paso. Now *that* is a scary place."

Texas Red rubbed his chin as if seriously considering what the ranger said. "No, ranger, I have to decline your ominous, official-sounding proclamation. Taking trips with you just sounds too dangerous and scary. Besides, I have a better idea."

Fully knowing he has done everything he can possibly do, the ranger was surprisingly relaxed, even at peace. "Oh, just what would your better idea be?"

"We don't have to go to all of those dangerous and scary sounding places to settle our differences. We can settle everything right here without all of that traveling."

Texas Red was shocked and was so stunned at what the ranger did next, that for a moment, he did not even resist.

The ranger took out a pair of steel handcuffs, walked up to Red, took Red's left arm, and started to clasp the handcuffs on him. The five-foot-ten-inch, 180-pound ranger was actually trying to handcuff the six-foot-two-inch, 240-pound *Texas Red*. Nothing, but nothing anyone could think of could cancel a man's birth certificate any quicker than trying to clasp handcuffs on Texas Red while he was still alive, unbound and packing a loaded six-gun. If any other man on earth did that, he would be dead before he started to fall.

Texas Red pulled back and snatched the handcuffs out of the ranger's hand. Then Red pushed the ranger hard in the middle of his chest with his left hand, and Red was reaching for his gun with his right hand.

As hard as Red shoved the ranger, it was surprising that the ranger had to take but a single step backward to regain his balance. Seeing Red reach for his gun, the ranger was at ready almost instantly and was only a fraction of a second from pulling leather.

Red very quickly put his hands up at shoulder height. Had they pulled leather at that precise moment, the ranger's errant gun hand would not have failed him. Forever unknown to Red, this was the second time since he met the ranger that he had come within a tenth of a second from death.

Red raised his hands shoulder high because he very quickly realized that the ranger was not seriously trying to cuff him. The cuffs came out of the ranger's hands far too easy, and there was no resistance when Red pulled them out of the ranger's hand. The ranger could not have handcuffed a child with the amount of strength he was using. The ranger well knew that Red would die before allowing anyone to handcuff him, but he had to go through the motions.

The two of them stood there glaring at each other, breathing hard, and both broke out into a sweat.

"That was a little too close, ranger. I don't want to kill you yet." Red tried to laugh, but it didn't work; his throat was much too dry.

Everyone could now see that the pressure and stress was wearing more on Texas Red than it was the ranger, but the talk was much in Red's favor.

The ranger shook his head, ever so slowly, and he had the look of an angered predator, a dangerously angered predator with no fear and was very frustrated. "I am sick and tired of your games, Red, and I am sick of your bull and your delusions of grandeur. I am sick of your glory hunting and you playing games with a life or death gunfight. Most of all, I am damn sick and tired of your cavalier attitude about killing and even about dying. Let's pull leather right now, Red, and let's get this circus over with."

Texas Red glared at the ranger about as hard as he has ever glared at a man in his life. It is certainly the hardest glare of Texas Red's life without pulling leather. However, he desperately wanted and ached for the glory and the legend he will become tomorrow at noon. He was even willing to put up with the ranger's attitude for a few more hours. It was no longer Friday night. It was very early on Saturday morning.

For the final time, there was a last-second emotional cool down between Texas Red and the Arizona ranger who was there to take him back to Phoenix, dead or alive.

Red stood at the bar, looking around at the faces in the crowd, but he did not look at the ranger who stood close by.

"I respect and honor your lack of serious physical effort to handcuff me, but this is not a request, ranger. Do not attempt to put those handcuffs on me again."

"I insist, Red. I am either going to handcuff you or kill you, and you know I can do it."

"I refuse, ranger. If you attempt to restrain me, cuff me, or put me in jail, I will kill you where you stand. We have a date with destiny tomorrow at high noon, so let's keep it. By the way, ranger, it does not matter how fast you are. Fate has already decreed that I will win the gunfight tomorrow, fair and square, with dozens of witnesses. Perhaps even a couple of hundred will show up. Like it or not, ranger, it is a legendary gunfight with a lifetime of glory for the winner."

The ranger scoffed. "Red, you are as stuck on fame and glory as I am my Big Iron."

The ranger took a deep breath and sighed. Without question, the gunfight was now inevitable beyond any shadow of doubt. "I'm changing the time of our gunfight, Red."

Texas Red shrugged. "Anything *reasonable* is fine with me, what time do you want?"

"11:20 in the morning."

Texas Red scoffed. "That will shorten your life by almost an hour. Tell me, ranger, why such an unusual time?"

The ranger thought for a second. "I had a hunch you would figure it out instantly. I'll let you figure it out, and it is something very close to you."

"I do not feel like riddles and puzzles right now, ranger, I am not in the mood."

"I assure you that you will laugh when you figure it out."

"What if I do not laugh?"

"You can shoot me twice."

"What is that supposed to mean?"

The ranger chuckled. "In order to shoot me twice, you have to shoot me the first time, and that's the tough one."

Texas Red smiled. "You just gave me another idea, ranger. Let's stir up so more legend for our legendary gunfight."

The ranger shook his head. "You don't ever quit or give up, do you, Red?"

"Nope, there's no future in quitting and giving up, so I don't."

Texas Red turned from the bar, looked around at everyone, and then held his hands up to get their attention, which took about four seconds. Again, the saloon became almost eerily silent.

"When is the last time any of you saw me show such respect for a gunfighter?"

Several men started to speak, but it was Sam who gestured for them stop, and he spoke. Being the town bartender, he knew more than anyone else what was going on and what everyone felt, believed, and thought.

"You never have. No one has ever seen you show such respect, and some say they can even see a slight bit of fear in you for the ranger."

Texas Red then responded. "Sorry, Sam, but let me clarify something here. You say that I have a *slight* bit of fear of the ranger. No, I will tell you the truth and admit that I have a *lot* of fear of the ranger. I know several things about the ranger that no one else in town knows. I am the only one who has seen the ranger draw that Big Iron he is packing. If I told you the clean, pure truth about how fast the ranger really is, not one of you would believe me. The speed of the ranger's draw is something that cannot be believed from the telling of it. The ranger's draw has to be seen to be believed, but that's just it. The ranger's draw is too fast for the human eye to follow."

Speaking for everyone, only Sam dared to interrupt and ask, "Sir, how can we see the ranger's draw if it's too fast to be seen by the human eye?"

Texas Red nodded. "That is an excellent question, a most intelligent question. The ranger's draw is too fast to see but his draw can be demonstrated. I watched the ranger draw over a hundred times in my own backyard, and I watched from every angle, but I only saw one."

Every person in the saloon has heard some form or version of the legendary invisible draw but not one person in the room has ever seen it. Nor has anyone met or seen any known gunfighter who can fulfill this legend. The legend of the invisible draw is something that everyone has heard about, but no one has seen.

However, this crowd, on this day, in the local saloon in the small town of Agua Fria was about to witness history. Even the seasoned, veteran newspaper and magazine reporters will stand both astonished and in disbelief. They will indeed write history but will write carefully for fear of disbelief and fear of those who would count them among fools. Nevertheless, on this day, there are too many patrons, too many townsfolk, too many notable leaders, and too many credible reporters from too many places to deny the unanimous and astounding eyewitness reports. On this day, the proof and confirmation were not only undeniable but also overwhelming. Lastly, the glory-creating and legend-making machine that Texas Red has assembled and produced in just seven days is now turning its powerful focus onto the ranger.

Texas Red put a shot glass down moderately hard on the bar top and then gestured with his hand. "Come on, ranger. Show everyone in the saloon what you have got."

The ranger pointed at the very expensive one-piece mirror behind the bar. "Red, if I hit that mirror, it would take me the rest of my life to pay for it."

Texas Red laughed. "Ranger, the rest of your life is about nine hours from now. Do you honestly believe that breaking a mirror will bring you bad luck worse than facing me in a gunfight?"

The crowd laughed hard. Then Texas Red picked up the shot glass and set it on the stairway about five feet up. He then gestured to the shot glass with his hand. "Ranger, if you miss, can you replace a board?" Again, the crowd laughed.

The ranger looked around. "I don't know, Red. I'm not comfortable showing off. I really don't know." As the ranger looked at everyone, he saw two beautiful eyes looking right back at him. The beautiful eyes were none other than Lynda's, and her smile encouraged him.

Still looking at Lynda, the ranger smiled back and nodded. "Okay, Red. I'll give it a shot, so to speak. Pun not intended."

Following the ranger's eyes back to the source of his smile, Texas Red was not surprised to see that it was Lynda. In fact, he would have been surprised if it wasn't Lynda. Then Texas Red stopped and looked down for a moment. Something had started working in the back of his mind. He could not identify it, but suddenly, something was on his mind about Lynda and the ranger, but he couldn't figure it out yet. It was really bothering him.

The ranger nodded to the crowd and held his hat up. They applauded and cheered.

An unknown voice shouted, "Show us what you've really got, ranger. Nobody can be as fast as Texas Red just told us you are."

Just as the ranger squared up on the target, Sam spoke up, "Stop, stop. Don't shoot." With everyone wondering why, Sam walked over to the target. He laid a cleaning cloth on top of the shot glass so the glass would not shatter and end up embedded in the patron's skin, or eyes. Then he laid a dozen or so cloths on the staircase within easy reach.

Sam walked back to the bar, looked at the ranger, smiled, and gestured toward the shot glass.

The ranger squared to the shot glass and glanced at Texas Red. "Say when, Red."

He did not hesitate. "Draw…"

Just as in Red's backyard at the gun range and as Texas Red personally witnessed, the blast of a gunshot and the tongue of flame from his barrel and the cloud of blue-white smoke seemed to appear from nowhere with no discernible movements by the ranger.

The saloon remained as quiet as a tomb long after the booming sound of the ranger's Big Iron dissipated into the walls.

There were no sounds, talk, or even murmurs from the crowd. Stunned into silence, no one knew what to say. Not to mention that no one was sure what had just happened. Moreover, like Texas Red at the gun range, they wanted to see it again. Then many of the patrons wanted to look at it from a different angle and then from yet another. After two dozen earsplitting, heart-pounding shots, the crowd realized that the ranger was every bit as fast as Texas Red said he was.

Lynda was smiling with pride at her ranger when her face suddenly froze in fear that approached terror. She fought through the crowd to get to Texas Red. Lynda was frantic.

"William? William!" When she got to him, she grabbed him by the shoulders and spoke in desperation without taking a breath. "William, you can't fight Kyle. You can't match his speed. No gunfighter alive is as fast as Kyle is, and I believe you already know that. When you two practiced together at the ranch that day, you must have seen him draw, and you must have known all along how fast he is." Lynda glared at the ranger. "I will not let you take William back to Phoenix, or any place else. Kyle, if you try to shoot William, you will have to shoot me first." Then she glared at Texas Red. "William, I will not let you fight him. You can't fight Kyle. William, I have seen all of your gunfights, and no one, but no one on this earth is as fast as Kyle is, and you know it. This is suicide, William, sheer suicide."

Lynda stood there, out of breath, looking back and forth at them. "The gunfight is off."

Then she reached out with her last hope. "Kyle, we will accept the dowry. Shoot William in the hand if you must, but we will accept the dowry. I still have the money, and we will get two more stacks just like it." Lynda then glared at both men with all of her strength and power. "Gentlemen, this fight is over...this gunfight has been canceled."

Texas Red looked down at his beloved sister. "No, sis, it's one or the other. You cannot have the dowry *and* shoot me in the hand. It is one or the other, but not both, right, ranger?"

The ranger ignored the rhetorical question and hugged Lynda. "You've only heard half of the story. There is something else no one but Red knows about me."

The ranger then got everyone's attention.

"With everything that has been said and done and with everything that has happened, there is one more thing for you to know. I am going to put everything on the table. The speed of my draw has come at a very high price. I have, what was up until this minute, a secret injury known only to Red. Red and I practiced our skills out at the ranch with just the two of us. We learned each other's greatest strength and each other's greatest weakness."

The ranger gestured toward the stairs where he shot the bar glasses. "You have seen my speed and my strength, but Red has seen my *other* draw. When my gun hand works, my draw is fast and sure, just as you've seen. Not to mention that when my gun hand works, my draw is too fast for the human eye to follow. However, when my gun hand goes bad, I am as helpless as a child. Red is right. My Big Iron may yet get me killed. I have pulled this very heavy Big Iron countless tens of thousands of draws, and in so doing…I have permanently injured and damaged a major nerve in my right arm and hand. Without warning, when I try to grip my gun handle, my gun hand seizes into a useless, misshapen claw, and my prized Big Iron ends up in the dirt at my opponent's feet. When this happens, if my opponent is a target, I live. If my opponent is a man, I die." The ranger gestured toward Red. "Even we do not know who is going to win this gunfight, and we can't know until the moment we actually pull leather. You can ask Red."

Texas Red nodded. "Every word the ranger just said is true. The ranger's damaged nerve, called the right side ulna nerve, runs from our shoulders to our outside three fingers. When the nerve goes bad, we lose control of those fingers, and it is impossible to grip a gun handle. The muscles cramp up and freeze his right hand into a claw, and it happened to the ranger while we were practicing, and I did a stupid thing."

The ranger looked puzzled and shrugged. "What stupid thing?"

Still looking around at everyone, Texas Red answered, "I grabbed his seized-up hand and forcefully straightened out his fingers one by one."

Again, the ranger looked puzzled. "How was that a stupid thing?"

Texas Red looked around at everyone and laughed. "I should have been *breaking* his fingers, not straightening them. How ironic would it be if the very fingers that I rubbed and straightened out end up killing me? I think of how many times I have held the Big Iron in my own hands. Was I holding my own harbinger of death?"

Texas Red did not really believe for one second that he was in any danger. He was incorrigibly convinced that somehow, fate would allow him to kill the ranger. Everything he did and said was intended solely to increase the fame and strengthen the legend. In his own mind, it was utterly impossible and totally unthinkable for him to lose this gunfight. Fate has already decided in his favor, so nothing else mattered, not even the ranger's invisible draw. In fact, the ranger's invisible draw would only enhance and magnify his fame and legendary status as the greatest gunfighter alive. He will be the first man to beat the invisible draw.

Texas Red then held his hands up. "One last thing about the ranger's gun hand, and that is you should have heard this man cuss me out while I was straightening out his fingers. You should have heard the threats he made and the things he was going to do to me. However, I wasn't worried about his cussing and threats because the first thing I did was to pick up his Big Iron and put it under my belt. I didn't have to fear the ranger because he had a cramped up gun hand, and he was unarmed. The biggest thing I had to fear at that point was that the Big Iron still had a hot barrel." Texas Red was somewhat exaggerating about the hot barrel, but the humor worked.

Almost everyone laughed hard and at length. However, Anita and Lynda were not laughing.

Almost without hope, Lynda confronted the only two men she loved. "You mean the two of you practiced together for a gunfight, where you shared your greatest secrets, and you practically became brothers, and William takes you into our library and figures out what's wrong with your gun hand...and then you set a date to face each other on a dirt street with full intentions of killing each other."

Lynda shook her head at both of them, then despondently remarked, "We humans still aren't much more than animals, are we?"

Their personal lives have become openly public. Everything they were saying, they said openly and, at times, loudly. They have talked, argued, and acted as if no one else was there. However, the whole world was there, and even fame, history, and legendary greatness was there. It would not be easy to claim a place in history as a legend, but it was there for the taking, and everyone in the saloon was aware of it. Something else everyone realized was that half of any legend was created *after* the gunfight.

Then Texas Red began laughing, and he slapped the ranger on the back. He just realized why the ranger set the gunfight at such an unusual time. As the ranger said, it was indeed something very close to him. Although Texas Red was hard pressed to believe what the ranger did.

With the ranger standing beside them, Texas Red looked at Lynda, then looked away, and then looked back at her and scoffed. "Your ranger has changed the time of the gunfight. He set the gunfight for 11:20."

"At 11:20? No one in his right mind would set a gunfight for 11:20. What's the matter with you, Kyle? That time doesn't make any sense wha—" She looked at the ranger and drew in her breath with an audible sound. "For God's sake, Kyle, tell me that you didn't set the time of this gunfight because...because of me. Tell me you didn't do that, Kyle...tell me."

Texas Red answered, "I'm afraid he did, sis. He has it real bad for you, and this is his way of honoring you and showing you how much he cares. The ranger doesn't know what else to do, but he did it, sis, he really did it."

"Did you, Kyle? Did you change the time of the gunfight? Did you set the time of your gunfight with my brother at 11:20? Does 11:20 stand for November 20th? Did you set the time of your gunfight according to my birthday?" Lynda hugged her ranger. "I don't know whether to kiss you or shoot you. What am I going to do with you, Kyle?"

The ranger smiled. "Keep me."

The ranger has fallen so hard for Texas Red's sister that he did set the time of the legendary gunfight to a time that represents her birthday. This indeed is the fuel of legendary greatness.

The newspaper and magazine reporters were writing furiously.

THE GUNFIGHT

IT IS TIME TO KILL...

The ranger looked around and asked Lynda, "Where did Red and Anita go?"

"Anita had to lay down for a while, so they went back to the ranch house."

Then yet another shocking event occurred. It is 4:00 a.m., and the sheriff's deputy was walking straight toward them with full eye contact.

When the deputy approached them, he spoke quietly, "The sheriff would like to see you in your room across the street. He is waiting for you, and of course, this is confidential and most urgent." The deputy did not fully stop, and he touched the brim of his hat in a token of politeness and kept walking.

As the ranger and Lynda walked into their hotel, the desk clerk pointed toward the upstairs rooms. "The sheriff is waiting for you in your room. He just got here, and the sheriff said that as the ranking law officer, the ranger needs to hear what he has to say."

The sheriff was barely a full minute ahead of them and had not yet sat down. As they entered, he took his hat off and the expression on his face reflected an unspoken regret for what he was about to say.

The sheriff offered that Lynda may want to leave as he had some very strong and incriminating things to say about Texas Red. But there was no way she was going to leave, and she would make up her own mind concerning any guilt or innocence after hearing what the sheriff had to say. Besides, anything that directly involved her man, now involved her. Even Lynda did not yet know that every woman in town was being contacted, and many were already actively involved in planning the biggest wedding this town had ever seen. They believed that Lynda's miracle of renewed life is nothing short of an emotional resurrection. They were planning an event that was not only a wedding but was a tribute to the ranger and Lynda, a tribute to the town…and to God. For the ranger to swear on his knees to God that Lynda was already his wife was tolerable, but for Lynda to openly state there could be no wedding without inviting the town, that opened their hearts to her.

But now is the time for bad news and time for the beginning of Texas Red's swift collapse, a collapse that will prove to be fatal within hours.

The sheriff explained that within minutes of them leaving sight of town, Texas Red killed two horses in the middle of the street and inflicted permanent damage to the wagon driver's left eye with the barrel of his gun. Twice within a matter of minutes, the driver's life was perilously in danger. Then the sheriff told the ranger of the bizarre and sudden death of a very healthy telegraph operator who was still sitting at his chair, still holding a pencil, and still had his left hand resting on his left leg. Texas Red was clearly seen at or near the telegraph office within an hour before the operator's dead body was discovered.

The ranger quickly looked at the sheriff and let out a breath. "The telegraph operator was poisoned."

The ranger broke eye contact and looked away. Chills ran up and down Lynda's spine at her ranger's reaction. No one had to say anything more. Texas Red was the prime suspect, the only suspect, in the premeditated murder of the telegraph operator due to an insignificant, senseless motive to prevent the ranger from receiving a top priority telegram. The ranger held his hands out to his sides and let them fall. Then he sat on the bed.

The ranger said aloud what the sheriff and Lynda were thinking within their minds, "Somebody sent me a telegram that Red didn't—"The ranger took a deep breath and started over. "Someone sent me a telegram that Texas Red does not want me to read." He looked at Lynda and shrugged. "Please prove me wrong. I have never wanted to be wrong so much in my life, so please prove me wrong, my love."

Lynda shook her head. "I don't think I can, Kyle." Then she cried. "I don't think I can prove you wrong. In fact, I was thinking the same thing, the very same." Lynda hugged the ranger very close and looked up into his eyes. "You were right about Texas Red and William, and now that I understand what has been going on since El Paso, I don't think Texas Red is ever going to allow William to be the dominate one again. He will die rather than give up control."

The ranger walked over and stood at the window. Looking outside, he asked the sheriff, "Do we have another telegraph operator yet?"

The sheriff nodded. "A temporary operator came in on the morning stage, and since this is urgent, the stage was even running a bit early. He was here at 9 a.m. and went straight to work sorting through the messages. He is sorting both the live messages on wire and those that were written down. We do not expect to find a written copy of the telegram we believe was sent to you."

The ranger then decided. "We need to know what that mysterious telegram says. Sheriff, will you have the new operator get us another copy of that telegram whenever and however he can?"

"Yes, sir, it is already his first priority."

The ranger shrugged. "We will go back to the saloon and see what happens."

The sheriff nodded. "Okay, and the telegraph operator is working through the night, so if he finds something, we will let you know immediately."

When they got back to the saloon, Texas Red and Anita had returned, and Red was standing at the bar with his back to the mirror facing the swinging doors. When the ranger and Lynda walked in, Texas Red ever so subtlety gestured to the ranger.

They would mix small talk with fatal talk. They could barely look each other in the eyes, and the ranger's voice was somber.

"What do you have in mind, Red?"

Deep down in his gut, Red could already tell by the ranger's voice and his demeanor that the ranger knew something. Maybe not everything just yet, but he was sure the ranger knew enough. An extremely rare cold knot of fear was forming in the pit of Texas Red's stomach.

The hesitation in Red's voice was almost indiscernible, but it was there. "Anything left of that offer you made about a whole new clean slate? I've got a child on the way, ranger, and I have a woman waiting to marry me—a woman, truth be known, who is too good for me. You know ranger, it will not be long before you will need to think about a ring for Lynda."

"I've got one ordered from San Francisco. Be here in a week. I hope you get to see it, Red."

"You have money, ranger? I never thought of you as having money."

"Compared to you, I am a pauper, but compared to the average man, I have a pocketful of rocks."

"Do you have more than $5,000?"

"With my investments, many times over, why do you ask?"

"If I had known you could afford to replace my teak floor, I would have let you have your rodeo."

The ranger scoffed. "At another time, that would have been funny, Red. Very funny."

"Were you serious about ordering Lynda a ring? Are you two that serious?"

"I am very serious about ordering her a ring, and yes, we are that serious. And I was serious when I said that I hope you get to see it."

"Maybe you should not say that if there is not anything left of that offer you made me."

"Look, Red, let's dump the bull. If we face each other, I will kill you, and we both know it. If you see Lynda's ring, that will mean the gunfight did not take place."

"That is a likely outcome, I admit that. But do not forget about your hand, and we both know about that too. And there is always fate."

"There might be a certain amount of fate in a man's life, Red, but I have never won or lost a gunfight based on fate."

Texas Red scoffed. "You have never lost a gunfight for any reason, ranger. We only get to lose one. Second place is a grave marker, so the fact you are still alive means you are undefeated."

"Never quite thought of it like that, but I reckon it makes sense."

Texas Red looked around several times, fidgeted with his fingers, and then looked square at the ranger. "I realize you are waiting for something, ranger, and you are waiting for something that is mighty important. While you are waiting, tell me something. How did you figure out the double consciousness? No one else has even come close or so much as suspected such a thing. So how did you figure it out?"

"A couple of things stuck in my mind, took root, and grew until I realized there were two personalities in the same body and mind."

"What could have happened that stuck in your mind like that?"

"It wasn't what you said as much as the way you said it. When I asked you if you had a college degree, you nodded yes. Then you changed your mind and said, 'No, it was the *other guy* that got the degree.' It was strange how you said it, like there really was another person. Then, to add to that, at the ranch house when my gun hand went bad, it was William in the library, not you. You never could have found the information that William did. I saw William looking around and smiling like he hadn't been there in a while, and he kept looking at everything. It was almost like he had come home from a long trip. Another thing is that his voice changed just a little too much within a matter of seconds for no reason."

Instinctively, the ranger looked around to make sure Lynda and Anita were okay. They were sitting at the gunfighters' table undisturbed. So the ranger continued, "There were a few other things, both significant and insignificant here and there, such as it was clear to me that you have never been to college, yet I saw the master's degree on the wall with an excellent grade transcript pinned on the wall next to it. But it all grew together until I realized it was double consciousness, which I not only learned about in college,

I had an aunt who had double consciousness. So I had personal experience with it for a number of years. But even at that, it still took some time to put it all together. It is a very rare condition, Red, but as you well know, it does exist. What made it tougher to figure out is that you have William's cooperation, but my aunt's double consciousness fought each other like a bad marriage getting worse. That, added to your very high level of intelligence, made it a lot tougher."

Texas Red scoffed. "You figured it out in a week, and you say it was tough?"

The ranger was looking intently at the swinging doors. Red followed his eyes to the doors and to the deputy who, unlike last time, was walking with purpose. The deputy saw Lynda and Anita at the gunfighters' table and quickly joined them. Red then saw Lynda point in their direction. The deputy nodded at the ranger and stood at the gunfighters' table and waited for the ranger. As the ranger approached, the deputy handed him an envelope. Anita already knew what it was, and she got up and walked over to Texas Red at the bar.

Everyone watched the ranger stare at Texas Red as the ranger handed the envelope to Lynda. She opened it, unfolded a telegram, and then nudged the ranger to get his attention.

The ranger broke eye contact with Red, and then he and Lynda read the telegram together. It was indeed the mysterious, undelivered telegram. The ranger instantly understood why Texas Red did not want him to see it. When the ranger and Lynda looked at Texas Red and Anita, the expression on their faces told Red and Anita that what they feared most has just occurred. And now, Texas Red will face an enraged, highly skilled gunfighter who was on a mission. And they are only a few hours away from their legendary gunfight.

The ranger said something to Lynda, and then he sat down in a chair with his back turned to Texas Red, which was the ultimate and greatest insult possible.

Texas Red glared hard at the ranger from across the room, which went unseen, but Red did not approach or challenge the dangerous ranger. The saloon was still sparse of reporters, visitors, and patrons, and Texas Red had decided in his mind that he will not kill the ranger until every person in town was watching.

Lynda spoke to Sam who in turn spoke to Texas Red and Anita. Lynda then walked over to someone sitting in the corner, but the ranger could not see who it was. The ranger then turned his chair and again faced Texas Red. The ranger had made his point but did not want to press it any further. Within a few minutes, he would be speaking to Texas Red.

Everyone nodded in agreement to Sam. Sam then nodded in agreement to Lynda and Lynda then returned to the ranger.

Lynda's smile was encouraging. "Okay, my love, everything is set, and everyone is agreeable to meet in private under the terms of the tradition called walking the horse. It is customary for the one who calls the meeting to be the first to enter the room. Sam is the eldest, so you will nod to him, and he will explain the rules and purpose of this tradition. And make no mistake, my love, this tradition has saved many, many lives and has saved unspeakable suffering. When Sam is finished, then you will speak first."

The ranger stood up and looked around. He then walked to the door to the private room and walked in. The ranger remained standing, and he quickly saw that Frank was the final member of the family tradition.

When everyone was seated, the ranger nodded to Sam who stood up and held a horseshoe in one hand and a handful of sawdust in the other.

"All of our words fall to the floor and are absorbed by the sawdust. You can only repeat the words spoken here if you extract the words back out of the sawdust. This horseshoe is the symbolic presence of a horse, a most faithful animal, and as such, only the symbolic horse can speak anything said here. If you wish to speak any words that are spoken here, you must first extract them from the sawdust and then speak them. If you wish to hear any words that are spoken here, you can hear them only from the horse who heard them or the symbolic presence of a horse. If you stay here in this room, then you promise and swear before God to keep this oath of silence. This is an extremely serious and critical matter. There are lives, marriages, and families at stake here as well as the future of an unborn child. If you do not agree with the oath, then you must leave right now." Sam held his hand out and let the sawdust fall back to the floor, and he placed the horseshoe in the center of the table.

Sam paused, and everyone stayed seated. Then, he continued, "I think everyone here realizes that the true meaning and purpose of this tradition is to provide a last chance for combatants to work things out peaceably without gunplay, bloodshed, and death. This tradition is intended to give you a last chance to say things that you would not normally get to say to each other and to give everyone a solemn and equal place to say it."

"There is a deadly and most certainly a fatal contention between two men among us. Ranger, outside of your official purpose here, what is your grievance with Texas Red?"

Holding the telegram in his right hand, the ranger looked Red squarely in the eyes, and the ranger talked slow and ominous, "There are so many important pieces of paper, Red. A lot of babies get a piece of paper when they are born now. And there is a piece of paper called a death certificate when we die. A piece of paper when we get married, a piece of paper for a divorce, a piece of paper called a deed if we own land. A piece of paper called a bank statement, another piece of paper that says we have a college degree. You and I both have one of those pieces of paper. Yours is a master's degree, and mine is a bachelor's degree, but we have the pieces of paper, Red. We get many pieces of paper in our lives, some more important than others. But then there is that one piece of paper that transcends all others, a piece of paper that means life or death…a piece of paper that you murdered an innocent man for, Red."

The ranger tossed the ominous telegram on the table in front of Texas Red, and it spun around moderately fast and slid six or eight inches and then stopped. Texas Red followed it with his eyes and then looked up at the ranger. Red ignored the sixty-three-word telegram that has just destroyed his new life and all hope for him and

Anita starting over. But Anita did not yet realize that ensuring the gunfight occurred rather than calling it off was Red's all-consuming goal. If it required the death of a mere telegraph operator to ensure the historic, legendary gunfight, then so be it.

Then Lynda lashed out at Texas Red, and her words were born of fear as much as anger. "You have imprisoned my *real* brother and made him helpless, and you only allow him to be active when it suits your purpose or you need him to do things you cannot do. You have always been there. I understand that now. But you did not take control of my brother's life until El Paso. And you did not kill the deputy in El Paso for me. You did it because you enjoy killing. You are not my brother, you are a vicious killer. I am so glad Mama isn't here to see this. And I hate you, Texas Red, and I hope you rot in hell."

Texas Red was stunned. "Lynda, every word you said stings like a bullet, and every word hurts to the bone. But you are wrong about one thing. I am not the one who killed the deputy in El Paso. That, my dear, was William's doing. He did it for you and because of what the deputy did to you. Let's be realistic, even William is a killer in the right circumstances, and any man alive would have killed the deputy for what he did to you. William was the dominate one when he killed the deputy, but it was William's own hate that allowed me to become dominant. And don't forget that part of William is in me and part of me is in William. I am not 100 percent Texas Red, and he is not 100 percent William. It does not work like that. Am I right or wrong, ranger?"

The ranger answered, "You are right, Red, but I've been thinking about something. Even though you are the dominant one, William can cause you a great deal of grief, so why doesn't he? What has made William so cooperative with you for the last five or six years now? Have you truly been a good brother to Lynda…or have you been holding her hostage? All you had to do at any time of your choosing was to arrange an accident that no one would question, and everything was yours. But then you would have to spend the rest of your life with an enraged William inside of your own mind who would no longer care about anything except tormenting you. It was a standoff, and William was content with taking care of his sister, and he protected her from you."

Texas Red scoffed. "Either way, ranger, Lynda has had an incredible life that is far above others. But, ranger, you and I have a gunfight in a few hours, and I am going to kill you. And I will indeed take full pleasure watching you die as you bleed to death inside of your own body. They say that bullets are very hot, so I will ask you about that as you lay dying at my feet. I will burn every second of your agony into my memory forever, and I will think of it often."

The ranger tapped the folded telegram several times with his forefinger. "Red, why did you murder a man just to prevent this telegram from being delivered to me?"

Then Sam stood up. "Sorry to interrupt, ranger, but what does this mysterious but critical telegram say? It would be most helpful if you shared it with us."

The ranger nodded his apology and then recited the telegram from memory.

Flash—Flash—Top Priority—Flash—Flash

Flash message for Arizona Ranger Kyle Lawton. All Arizona ranger units have been disbanded. All offices closed for further business. You may complete or cancel current mission at your discretion. Further actions are at own expense. You remain an authorized Arizona ranger for length of current mission. At end of mission, you have been approved to revert to US marshal.

Good luck, ranger.

Texas Red shook his head and sneered. "So you really were a US marshal. Until I read the telegram, I wasn't sure if you were telling the truth or just trying to be bigger than you are. I am very impressed, ranger, or should I say, marshal?"

Before the ranger could respond that he was still an authorized Arizona ranger, Anita got up crying and actually grabbed and hugged the ranger. "Let's all just go home now. Your mission is over, Kyle. You are the only ranger left, and all you have to do is call an end to your mission, and everything will be all right. It's over, Kyle. Let's all just go home, and everything will be fine." Then she reached over and picked up the telegram. In vain, she tore the telegram into pieces and then tore the pieces into smaller pieces. Then she tried to burn the small pieces, but Sam would not let her, but he did put the shredded telegram in a trash can out back, and he quickly burned it for her as she watched.

With all hope now shattered, Anita looked around at everyone and spoke in a mournful voice, "Can't we just go home and let everything be all right?" Then she took the ranger's hand and put it to her stomach. "There is a baby in there, Kyle. Let's go give the widow of the telegraph operator more money than she ever dreamed of. In a way, his family will actually be better off. Kyle, you are in charge and almost like God. If you say it's over, then it's over, and all you have to do is say everything is all right, and everything will be all right. I beg you, Kyle, please make everything all right, and let's go home. I am so tired."

The ranger kissed her tenderly on top of her head. The ranger has figured out and now realized Red's true motive and the one thing Red will never agree to. "Okay, Anita. With two very easy, simple conditions, I will declare my mission at end. It is no longer required for Red to disable his gun hand. We can all go home, and everything is all right, and everything is okay. As soon as Red does two things that are well within his reach, I will give the sheriff my badge, and Lynda and I will leave town immediately."

Texas Red smirked. "I already know that I am not going to like this, but for the sake of my fiancée and my sister and my unborn child, I will hear your two conditions before I mock you, laugh, and decline." Texas Red already knew what one of the conditions would be, and he already knew it was a condition that will be an instant deal breaker. "But for the sake of others, I will play your game, ranger, what is the first condition?"

The ranger glared at Red. "I really don't care whether you like it or not, these two conditions are not negotiable. The only possible answer to these conditions is either yes or no."

"First, give the widow of the telegraph operator you murdered $100,000."

Texas Red shrugged. "Okay, that's easy enough. If I agree to the second condition, his widow will have the money before sundown. Okay, ranger, this is it, what is the second condition?"

"The second condition consist only of words, Red, only of words. All you have to do is go into the saloon and announce to everyone that the Arizona rangers have disbanded and the ranger's mission is at end…and then announce our gunfight has been cancelled."

The ranger even removed his badge and handed it to Sam. Sam looked at the badge resting in the palm of his hand knowing he will have to give it right back. Anita grabbed Kyle and cried so hard. "Thank you, Kyle. How can I ever thank you? Our baby will live in peace now. Our baby will never know. Oh, I am so happy, Kyle. You did it, and you really made everything all right. We can go home now and get the widow's money. I will bring it back myself, but I am so tired."

Anita grabbed Texas Red's left hand and tried to go into the saloon to make the happy announcements, but Red would not budge. Red glared at the ranger with hostility that bordered on hate.

"Why are you trying to turn everyone against me? Why are you trying to steal my rightful greatness, my fame, and my status as a great legend? We *must* have our gunfight, ranger. Nothing can stop that. Fate has already decided that I will win this gunfight, no matter how fast you are. So why are you trying to blemish my name and lower me before my friends and loved ones? You are trying to humiliate me and make yourself better than me. Why are you trying to destroy me, ranger? You know, don't you? You know I am going to win this gunfight. Is that why you keep trying to stop it, so you can pretend to be better than *me*? Well, it isn't going to work ranger."

Even Frank, Texas Red's most trusted man, shook his head and thought, *The ranger ain't tryin' to take anything from the boss. The boss ain't thinkin' right. All the ranger is doin' is tryin' to stop the gunfight. The boss's lady begged the ranger to stop the fight, and he did. The boss… the boss he is wrong on this thing.*

Texas Red's words were shocking even to the ranger, and he said a lot more than the ranger expected. "What's the matter with you, Red? Don't you see what a golden opportunity you have? Nobody is going to question or double-check any paperwork I submit. Nobody is even going to read all of it. Anything I turn in will automatically be processed as approved with no questions asked, can't you see that?"

Texas Red retorted, "The only thing I can see is you trying to take my fame and glory from me. But it's already been given to me, and God has chosen *me* from among all men for greatness and to be known for the rest of time. I cannot let anyone take that away from me, not even you. Understand, ranger?"

The ranger responded, "Yes, I understand, Red, and now so does everyone else. You have openly shown your true colors, and you have made it crystal clear to everyone that you care for nothing else except your fame and glory and chasing your own grandiose delusions. You live in a fantasy world of your own making, Red, and you have openly admitted that you put nothing first except your perceived calling from God to self-imagined greatness. You even murdered the telegraph operator so the telegram would not interfere with your gunfight of delusions. Your lifetime of fame and glory and your game playing and your counterfeit self-importance have come to an end, Red, enough is enough. You have killed and murdered far too many people, all to feed a self-induced fairytale."

Red mocked him. "A tin badge and ten years of hunting inferiors does not make you a judge over me. You will feel my power and my wrath. I do not have to explain myself to you, but I did what I did because it was necessary to keep you from stopping my masterpiece of eminence and fame. This gunfight is a once-in-a-lifetime chance for true greatness and supreme legendary status. If you had gotten the telegram before I did, you would have tried to stop the gunfight and that I could not allow. Fate will not allow you to diminish my greatness. It has already been decided."

The ranger was incredulous. "This is not make-believe, Red. Why do you think I am here? All you had to do at any time was simply state that you are not going to call off the gunfight for any reason. No explanation or details needed. I think your arrogance has affected your judgment. If you insist on a gunfight, that is fine with me. But you are the one who has to explain yourself to Lynda and Anita. I was sent here to arrest you, not to pacify or appease you and certainly not to glorify you. If you want a gunfight, you got it, buddy. You murdered a man over a telegram that was sent to *me*. But now I am the one who will not call the gunfight off. You are a vicious, mindless killer, and murdering the telegraph operator, a man with a family, is inexcusable and cannot be overlooked or forgiven. It's 5:17 a.m., and one of us has about six hours left to live. So *you* better live them. This is no longer official business. This is personal, *Texas Red*. I am going to kill you, you son of a bitch."

Sam slowly stood up, and his regret was obvious before he spoke, "We have exceeded all reasonable boundaries and efforts to end this in peace, and we have failed. Gentlemen, you need to attend to your personal affairs until the appointed time. Reason has been exceeded by wrath, and peace has been exceeded by the call for blood. This matter cannot be settled with words or settled in peace. It will be settled with loaded guns in the street."

As they stood up, Lynda cried and hugged Texas Red. "Despite everything else and despite what I said, I still love you, William."

Texas Red's voice was surprisingly calm and soft. "I love you too, sis. I am not William, but I am still your brother, both of us are. You dealt with William a lot more than with me because you would have figured me out a long time ago. But in my own way, and as much as I can, I really do love you and care about you. I always have. Now take care of your ranger. He only has six hours left to live."

The ranger and Texas Red did not glare at each other as they walked out of the private room, but they exchanged a look of deadly coldness, a look of two predators ready to kill. They had less than a dozen words to speak to each other before one of them lies dying on the street with perhaps two minutes left to live.

Texas Red and Anita went to the ranch house, and the ranger and Lynda went to their room across the street. It was now 5:30, and one of them had less than six hours to live.

When they walked in the hotel, the desk clerk smiled and crossed herself.

Lynda smiled and nodded her thanks.

As soon as they cleared the door, Lynda put her left hand on the ranger's shoulder. "I don't understand, my love. One minute you're almost screaming at him to save his life, and the next minute you're cussing him and ready to shoot him."

"I had to get Red to admit out of his own mouth that he will not even consider stopping the gunfight. If I win this gunfight, I am so scared of you hating me or a part of you hating me. So I had to get Red to openly admit that he will never agree to cancel the gunfight. And I needed everyone to see that even with the greatest offer I can make, he has no interest in cancelling the gunfight, even for a clean slate and a new life for Anita and their baby. But I couldn't just accuse him of it. I had to get Red to say it and say it openly."

Then Lynda asked, "Could you have really done what you offered him? Could you really have given him a clean slate and a new life?"

The ranger nodded. "Oh yeah, I sure could, especially now that the rangers are disbanding and closing down. Red knows I could have and so does Sam."

"This may sound strange since we are about to do everything in our power to kill each other, but I'm afraid for Red. Not only is he obsessed and delusional, but he no longer has any reasons to hide it, so it will get so much worse. And any traces of William are probably gone for good. But in all of this turmoil and bloodlust, with the loaded guns, threats, and anger and with a dirt street waiting to absorb our blood, there's one thing that sticks out in my mind more than anything else."

"What could that be?"

"The baby, Anita's baby."

"With everything that's going on, Anita's baby sticks out in your mind?"

Despite the situation, the ranger smiled. "Yeah, when Anita put my hand to her stomach, I felt the baby move, and when Anita hugged me, I felt him kick me. It's like I was pressing in on his territory too much, and he actually kicked me. He's already fighting for what's rightfully his. That boy needs his father to teach him how and when to fight. He's not even born yet, and he's already a fighter. He will need to learn to control it properly."

"Oh? Texas Red is vicious, and he's a killer, and he's only twenty-four years old. He murdered a man over a telegram, he has double consciousness, he's obsessed with his own importance, and he's delusional. Do you really think he's the right man to teach a growing child how to control himself?"

"Lynda?"

"Yes, my love."

"Honey, I've…I'm thirty-one years old, and I've never felt a baby move or kick before."

Lynda held the ranger tight, and she gave him a long kiss, and then she laid her head on his shoulder and whispered, "We can have a baby of our own. It's usually part of the deal."

With all of the pent-up emotions and with passion he did not know existed and with the unspoken truth that he could die within a matter of hours, he took his woman into his very soul.

As they laid together in the glow of the aftermath of their passions, combined with unspoken fears, the ranger started laughing.

Lynda raised herself up on her elbows and slightly glared at her ranger. "This had better be good, Kyle. For you to be laughing like that at a time like this, you better have something extra funny to say."

"I was just thinking if Red wins the gunfight."

"No wonder you understand all of those things wrong with William so well, you've got them yourself. I will give you one chance to tell me what is so funny. You have ten seconds, and the clock is ticking."

"The mortician will never be able to get this smirk off my face."

"Why would you have a smirk…Kyle Lawton, when I am finished with you, you won't have to worry about the gunfight because you're going to be hurting so bad that you wouldn't be able to feel the bullet anyway. I am so embarrassed. You are so naughty."

Within a minute, Lynda chuckled herself, and the ranger said, "Okay, now it's my turn. What is so funny?"

"If the mortician can't get the smirk off your face, won't that make every man in the territory chase me down and want to marry me?"

The ranger laughed even more. "You didn't say that. Now tell me you didn't say that."

Lynda giggled. "Yes, I did. I didn't think I had it in me, but I said it all right, and I said it out loud right in front of God and everybody."

The ranger had to stifle his laugh. "Now that was not funny, sweetie, not even a little bit."

Lynda could not help herself. "I know, honey, it was terrible, wasn't it?"

Then the ranger became very serious and somber. "I can't lose you, baby, I just can't. I will win this gunfight if I have to crawl on my belly and use my teeth. I cannot leave you, and I will not leave or lose you. I can't, I just can't, baby. I'll will myself to win this fight, because I just can't lose this one. In all my other gunfights, I had nothing to lose. Now I have everything to lose, and I just will not lose this one."

Lynda sat up and held his face in her hands. "What is it, Kyle? There is something you want to tell me, what is it?"

"I've been practicing a new move…just in case. When my gun hand goes bad, I cannot grip or hold the gun handle, but I can push the Big Iron. And even if my hand goes bad, I will still be much faster than Red in the first half of the draw. With practice, I have learned to control the Big Iron enough to push it to my left hand, and I should be able to get off at least one shot. Honey, if Red takes me out, he is going to get everything I've got, and everything I have. If all I can do is spit at him, then I will spit at him. If all I can do is pinch him with the cheeks of my ass, then I will leave the biggest bruises I possibly can. But I will not lose this one, because to lose this gunfight is to lose you, and that is unthinkable, for I am a loved man." Lynda held the side of his face to her breasts and hugged him for a long time. Neither of them said a word as she held him ever so tenderly and lightly rocked back and forth. The only sound in the quiet, still room was Lynda softly crying. And in their shared silence, their hearts bonded even more, and they reached a whole new level.

Back at the ranch house, Texas Red was a raging emotional storm. He could not stay still or concentrate or settle down. He sat down and then got up, and in a few minutes, he would sit down again and immediately get back up. When he sat down, he wanted to get up, and when he got up, he wanted to sit down. All he could think about was that arrogant ranger. Anita attempted to comfort him and love him, but Texas Red would yell at her saying that having any kind of last rites would be against fate and would be saying that the ranger had a chance.

Anita tried to talk to him, but again, Texas Red yelled that she was acting like the ranger had a chance and that she thought the ranger could actually win. For the very first time, Anita feared her beloved man. But Texas Red was collapsing internally, and she did not know who he was anymore, and this is a man she has never seen before.

"You do not understand, Anita. We cannot perform any kind of last rites or do anything that looks like we think the ranger has a chance. Fate has already decided. We don't need any rituals."

"But, William, don't you want me anyway, just like any other day or night?"

Texas Red let out a hard breath. "Let's get this straight, and I will explain it one more time. I…am…not…William. William is gone. I am Texas Red, and you barely met William anyway. I am the one you met and talked to and got to know and the one you fell in love with, and it is *my* child you are carrying. You would not even like him."

Anita was so confused and so exhausted. "That may well be true, but William is the only name I know you by, and the other William is a stranger who happens to have your name."

"Okay, okay. Until I get this business with the ranger settled, you may call me William, but William is not the name that will become the living legend, so you must get used to calling me Texas Red, perhaps even Red, and the sooner the better."

Anita walked up to him and pressed her body against his. Then she smiled seductively and giggled. "Would Texas Red be interested in a good time?"

Texas Red rubbed the back of his head and glared at Anita. "Okay, let's have a good time." Then he grabbed her and all but threw her to the floor, and then he ripped her clothes off and ravaged her and hurt her. When she reminded him that she was carrying his child, he scoffed and got rougher. When he finished with her, he then grabbed her by the neck and pulled her face within a few inches of his. "How come I don't feel any better, saloon girl?" Then he shoved her to the floor. Words cannot describe how badly it hurt her when he spit out the words *saloon girl*.

Anita felt cheapened and used, perhaps even defiled, but she still attempted to show her love and be there for her man, but he rejected and humiliated her at every turn. Texas Red was out of control, and he no longer cared. He kept yelling that she did not understand that fate had already decided the gunfight in his favor. He was in a downward spiral into unrecoverable destruction. And within the past few hours, Texas Red had driven away and estranged all who cared for him. All save one. And even the woman who carried his child paid a severe price for her loyalty and faithfulness.

At 7:30 a.m., Anita could endure no more, and mercifully, she collapsed on her couch by the sewing table in the den.

Texas Red sat on the couch next to her, and resting his chin on his chest, he dozed into a shallow pseudo-sleep.

At 10:30 a.m., Texas Red saddled up and told Frank to get the buggy ready and take Anita into town. At a gallop, it would take Red but fifteen minutes to cover the three and a half miles to town.

Lynda likewise drifted into a shallow sleep while the ranger alternately lay on the bed, sat on the bed, and stood at the window while darkness turned into daybreak, which turned to dawn and then sunrise.

The saloon, the streets, and the town were swollen and crowded by 9:00 a.m. As Texas Red rode into town, he looked up and saw the ranger standing at the window. They looked at each other for a long moment but did not acknowledge each other; they just looked.

Texas Red rode up to the saloon, and Elijah was there and took his horse. Coincidently and ironically, the ranger's and Texas Red's horses were stabled together, and they got along far better than their owners.

The ranger gently woke Lynda and then went down to the saloon. As expected, the bar cleared when Texas Red walked up to it and, a few minutes later, again cleared for the ranger. The ranger stepped up to the bar about ten feet from Texas Red, and the bar quickly cleared between them.

The ranger looked over at Red, but Red ignored him and looked straight ahead. The ranger wanted to say something, but there were no words that could say it. The ranger could not translate his thoughts into words, so the upshot was silence. Then Red looked over at the ranger, and the ranger ignored him and looked straight ahead.

Texas Red took a very deep breath and sighed. "I guess this is it, huh, ranger?"

The ranger nodded and looked at Red, and they made eye contact. "I reckon it is, Red."

Without a word, both took a coin out of their pocket, and the ranger slapped his coin on the bar next to Red's drink, and Red slapped his coin on the bar next to the ranger's drink, drinks that neither man had touched.

It was now 11:15 am, and they turned and walked toward the swinging doors, which seemed to open themselves. The gunfighters then went to their chosen spot to begin the walk of death.

In the small town of Agua Fria, New Mexico, history wrote a new page, and a legend was forged. Two of the fastest, most deadly, and most feared gunfighters alive, Texas Red and an Arizona ranger, were pacing off the final steps that one of them would ever take. Within minutes, a fatal bullet would be, must be, fired. Only one will survive. There was eighty feet between them as they walked toward each other on the wooden boardwalk on either side of the street. They had not yet stepped out of the shade and onto the dirt street that would soon claim and absorb the blood of the second fastest.

As they paused for a moment, both men tipped their hats ever so slightly to the other and nodded with the last remnants, the last vestiges and last thoughts of friendship or respect. The past week of their lives must now be forgotten and pushed aside; it is time to kill.

They know each other's greatest strength and greatest weakness. Both men knew they had just cause to fear for their lives, and both know without question that the other man could win this gunfight. They know that they may well lose their life, and both gunfighters are too skilled to risk mercy and aim for an incapacitating wound. They *must*, and they will, aim for an instant kill.

One of them had a draw so blindingly fast that gun-fighting legends refer to it as an invisible draw, a draw so rare there had never been two such elite gunfighters alive at the same time. However, this master gunfighter had attained such legendary speed at a potentially fatal price. An erstwhile secret injury, openly known since just last night, could render the fastest gun alive as helpless as a child.

They resumed their slow but fatal walk with death. With sixty feet between them, they stepped out onto the dirt street, at the appointed time, to take those final steps that one of them would ever take. With fifty feet between them, they could no longer see the other as human nor could they see anything except what was directly in front of them as both men were so intensely focused, their sight compressed into a tight scope of tunnel vision.

Texas Red chose the appointed day, and the ranger chose the appointed time. It was exactly 11:20 Saturday morning, and there was forty feet between them when they stopped to make their play.

Both men reached for their guns at exactly the same instant. There were two gunfighters and two guns, but there was only one blast from a single gunshot, and there was only one tongue of flame, and there was but one cloud of blue-white smoke. The second fastest gunfighter now lay in the dirt street, dying by the second. He had perhaps two minutes to live, and he lived them with the ultimate humiliation feared by all gunfighters—the dying gunfighter never cleared leather.

In an instant, the gunfight was over. The outlaw called Texas Red lay dying on the very street and in the very dirt where he had put so many others. Everyone looked at one another in disbelief of the ranger's speed and swiftness. Twenty men tried to take Texas Red, and all twenty were dead. Everyone in town just knew that Texas Red could not be beat, and they *knew* that the handsome, easy smiling ranger they all liked would be just another notch on Texas Red's gun handle. But it was now certain that the ranger is one of the fastest guns who had ever lived. But it was all over in a mere eye blink. It happened so fast that no one knew the gunfight occurred until it was over. And everyone tried to understand what their eyes had just seen.

The reason it all seemed to happen so fast is that no one saw or experienced this legendary gunfight through Texas Red's eyes. For Texas Red, it was a far different perception.

There was forty feet between them when they stopped to make their play. Both men reached for their guns at exactly the same instant. To both gunfighters, everything moved in extreme slow motion. Their perception of time was on a level very few could understand, and fewer still would ever experience. It was physically impossible for their movements to match their perception of time. They were almost spectators to their own actions.

Texas Red could clearly see everything that happened, as it happened, in precise detail.

The ranger nodded ever so slightly to begin the gunfight. Then he hesitated for the slightest fraction of a second, and then both gunfighters reached for their guns at the same instant. Texas Red was already thinking that the slight hesitation, while insuring a fair start, was a fatal mistake. In the first few milliseconds, the draw was even as both gunfighters touched their guns and both began gripping the handle at the same time. At this point, there was no advantage to either gunfighter.

Texas Red could feel the inertia as he pulled on his gun, but in shock, he could see that the ranger had already moved his Big Iron about three inches. In panic, Texas Red pulled harder and faster, but his Navy Colt was still unmoving while he could see the Big Iron was not far from clearing the ranger's holster. Texas Red pulled leather as hard as he has ever pulled in his life, but now panic gave way to sheer terror as Texas Red could now see the entire Big Iron but his own gun had moved no more than a few inches. Texas Red saw the ranger raising the barrel of the Big Iron parallel to the ground, and the end of the barrel was now even with the core of Red's body. He now knew it was hopeless. If the ranger's gun hand had gone bad, the Big Iron would be lying in the dirt, or at least falling to the dirt, rather than pointing at the center of Texas Red's body.

Texas Red's Navy Colt was about halfway out of his holster, and that was as far as it ever got.

All of the fame, glory, legendary status, and lost love transformed into a lethal cocktail of fear, panic, and terror. All too late, Texas Red realized he never had a guarantee from anyone that he would win this gunfight, and he had no calling of greatness from God. On the pain of death, Texas Red realized that just because he won all of those gunfights in the past did not mean he will win gunfights in the future. One had nothing to do with the other. The ranger was right, and all of Texas Red's fame and glory was just a self-created delusion, a delusion for which he will now pay the ultimate price.

Texas Red saw the hammer of the Big Iron slam forward, and he saw the Big Iron fire. He saw the tongue of fire come out of the barrel straight at him, and he watched the flame expand outward from the barrel, and he heard the blast from the powerful Big Iron. Then he saw the cloud of blue-white smoke very quickly expand and churn in the turmoil of expanding gases conflicting with each other.

As soon as Texas Red saw the barrel of the Big Iron parallel with the ground, he had a choice. He could either pull his six-gun another inch out of the holster or he could move his body a fraction of an inch. Texas Red decided to move his body that small fraction of an inch, and that decision made the difference between instant death and two more minutes of cognizance.

Texas Red screamed within his own mind. *God, help me. Don't let him kill me. I want to live. Let him wound me, but, God, don't let me die. I will let him shoot me in the gun hand or my legs and arms, but let me live, oh God. Please let me live. I have a baby on the way and a woman who loves me. I will take care of them, oh God, let me live.*

Then Texas Red turned his attention to the ranger. "You aren't really going to kill me, are you, my friend? Wound me and hurt me real bad, but don't kill me, ranger. I am helpless before you, and you know it, so you're going to wound me, aren't you? You are good enough and fast enough to take the chance, so wound me, ranger. We will fill out the paperwork, and I will never break the law again."

No one would believe the telling of it, but Texas Red saw the huge bullet leave the barrel of the Big Iron, and it was going to slam into the center of his body. He felt the calmness, the utter quiet, and the peace of impending death. Within his own mind, Texas Red then cried out with the only prayer that would ever be answered in his short life.

God, we both know I deserve the bullet I can see coming straight at me. I have this coming to me, and we both know it. I yield to that, and I plead that you watch after my boy. Make sure he doesn't end up like me, and make sure his mother—

Instantly, everything went totally pitch-black. There was no sensation of impact from either the bullet or the ground. But Texas Red was vaguely aware that he was lying on the ground on his back.

To everyone's amazement, Texas Red stirred and slowly looked around and tried to clear his vision. Then as he regained most of his sight, he realized that he did not have long to live.

He looked around and spoke weakly, "Ranger? Where are you, ranger?"

The ranger was right beside him. "I'm right here, Red."

"Am I hit as bad as I think?"

"Yeah, you're hit bad."

"Where's Anita? I have to talk to her even if I don't do anything else."

Anita cried but controlled it. "I'm right here, my love."

Texas Red's weak smile and ghostly voice alluded to eminent death. "I beg your forgiveness for everything wrong I have done. I love you more than everything else in life put together, and I treated you badly, and I did not spend enough time with you. I am so sorry, Anita, and I ask you to forgive all of my many wrongs to you. And I acknowledge to you that I was so wrong, and you are such a special, special woman, and not just a woman, you are a special person. Take care of our boy, and make the ranger pay for everything. I am about to make him very wealthy."

Anita cried but fought it off to speak her last words to her man. "How can there be a need to forgive you when I love you so much? I will take care of our child, my love, and I will be glad to make the ranger pay for everything. You made me so happy, and you pulled me out of the saloons and saved me from a life of horrible nightmares. I don't need to forgive you. I thank you, and I love you."

Then Texas Red asked for Lynda.

"I am right here, my brother."

"Did the ranger really order you a ring?"

"Yes, he did. I was with him when he sent the telegram to San Francisco."

Texas Red scoffed. "Telegram? Do not use that word. It will be the death of me."

There were weak smiles and subdued chuckles from those who stood around. Some folks said that Texas Red deserved a bullet, but seeing him lie in the reality of it with his blood pouring into the dirt, they lost the joy of it.

"Ranger, I want to give you an early wedding gift. I need to tell you something but only you can hear." Everyone backed off a few feet, and the ranger put his head close to Red. Everyone could hear Texas Red talking but could not understand what he was saying. He had to stop a few times because of the pain. The ranger straightened up but stayed on one knee.

"Ranger, do you understand what I said?"

The ranger shook his head. "I heard everything you said, but I don't know what it means."

"I just gave you the directions to my gold and a cache of other wealth."

The ranger struggled to figure it out and thought quickly. "Directions?" Then he nodded. "Okay, what is the reference point?"

Texas Red then knew the ranger understood. "It is the door knob of the back door to the shooting range."

Anita always carried a small derringer with her. Texas Red subtlety gestured for her to give him her gun. She quickly pulled it out of her handbag without being seen and was able to cock it without attracting attention. Then she held Red's hand with both of hers and slipped him the small but deadly gun.

"Ranger, I want to give…give Lynda an early wedding gift… too. The greatest gift I…I can give her…something money cannot buy…but I need you to do it."

It was very obvious from Texas Red's voice and glazed eyes that he was at the very door of death.

"Sure, Red, anything, you name it."

"Swear that…you will love and protect my sister…above… all else."

The ranger readily nodded. "Yes, I swear to—"

It took supreme effort for Texas Red to shake his head. "No… raise… raise your right hand."

"Sure, Red."The ranger dutifully raised his right hand. "I swear—"
Bam!

The small blast from the derringer had people looking for cover. The ranger started cursing and screaming at Red. "Damn you, Red…that hurts like hell. You shot a hole all the way through my hand. The bullet put a hole through some bones. Damn you, Red. It hurts so bad I am going to shoot you again as soon as I can pick up a gun."

Lynda rushed to her ranger's side. "What happened? What is going on, and what does shooting you have to do with my wedding gift?"

The ranger showed Lynda the hole in his hand but could not stand still as the pain was agonizing. "Red just forced me to retire, and I can't even be a US marshal again…I am no longer a gunfighter. Red just ruined my gun hand."

Lynda looked down at her brother and then at the ranger. "That is the greatest wedding gift he could have possibly given me. He gave me you, Kyle. I would much rather you have a hole in your hand than in your head."

"Damn you all to hell, Red. Oh God, my hand hurts so bad, and there are bones sticking out of the back of my hand. I've never had anything hurt so much in my life. I am going to—"

The ranger walked up to Red briskly and drew his foot back as if to kick Red in the ribs. But when the ranger looked down at Red, he stopped…and slowly lowered his foot to the ground. Somehow, the excruciating pain in his hand stopped, and he knelt down on one knee and put his left hand on Red's chest and shook him. "Red? Red?"

The gaze of Texas Red's unblinking eyes was focused on the heart and essence of eternity. The ranger heard his erstwhile friend expunge his lungs of the last, gasping breath of air he would ever take.

Texas Red...was dead.

TODAY

And the swiftness of the Ranger is still talked about today.

—From the ballad "Big Iron"

I n a modern city in the US southwest and in a modern top-of-the-line museum of the old west, a local middle school history class, due to their exceptional essays about the old west, had the special honor of being conducted on a rare tour by the museum's celebrated and renowned curator. The young, single curator had devoted himself to his career and elected to forego a family or children for the near future. The curator's specialty is gunfighters, gunfights and their weapons. So much so that pretty much everything known about gunfighters and gunfights in the old west was in this museum. In addition, many original artifacts and all types of items surviving from the old west were on display, and some could even be gently touched.

The class entered the last room of the tour, which was by far the largest room they had seen, a room filled with artifacts. The curator had ensured that his museum had by far the most artifacts and had more genuine slivers of history than any other old west museum. The curator personally owned many of the artifacts, and the curator was a *very* wealthy man, born of it.

The students fanned out into the huge room in awe of the irreplaceable artifacts with both complete and partial objects. Everything from shovels, wooden wagon wheels, clothing still containing color, bridles, harnesses, old horseshoes, and many guns were on display. Eventually, almost every student gathered in the center of the room.

At the center of the room, in a spotlighted sealed glass case is an old, fragile gun belt still containing the actual rounds of ammunition placed in the belt by its original owner in 1882. The well-worn holster contained one of the most prized possessions in the entire museum—a customized, one-of-a-kind 1847 Colt Walker, better known as…a Big Iron. Although worn ever so thin and fragile, the blackened gun belt was still intact and was carefully laid out in a circle and buckled. At the very center of the gun belt was a badge, the badge of an Arizona Ranger.

At the bottom center of the circled gun belt, just outside of the circle is another surprising artifact. It is another gun; it is a highly modified, finely tuned handgun used only by highly skilled gunfighters. It is a .36 caliber 1851 Navy Colt black powder revolver, with twenty notches carved in the handle. It is the very gun owned and used by Texas Red. Somehow, in some way, the curator was able to pull off a major miraculous feat and display not only the rangers badge and gun belt but also both of the actual guns used by the ranger and Texas Red in their famed, legendary gunfight.

Most of all, the four priceless, irreplaceable artifacts have been thoroughly examined, documented, and confirmed to be authentic. Yet the source of these artifacts was a closely held, inviolate secret the curator stanchly refused to discuss. Above all else, gunfighters, gunfights, and the old west were the curator's deep abiding lifelong passions. His PhD in history, acquired at a relatively young age so he could pursue his driving passions, was a necessary tool in order to achieve his true goal.

The curator had no desire for fame, glory, or publicity. His driving passion was to find, obtain, maintain, and preserve as many old west artifacts as he possibly can, especially anything to do with gunfighters, gunfights, and their weapons. Otherwise, he would display another gun, a gun that was such an extremely rare historic artifact that it would make it impossible for him to display five such rare, historic artifacts without appearing to be a fraud. Although he was the legal and rightful owner of these supreme artifacts, it would require explanations he did not care to give or share. The curator values his privacy, but with all of this, there is yet a sixth artifact residing in the curator's safe. All six artifacts date back to a common focal point, the legendary gunfight.

The curator was comfortable with only himself knowing where the last two artifacts are, and he rather enjoyed being the only one who not only knew *where* they were but *what* they were. They were artifacts of inestimable value and were irreplaceable. Beyond that, the ranger was a US marshal for ten years before becoming an Arizona ranger, albeit for only one mission, and the curator even had the US marshal's badge worn by the ranger.

As if drawn by a magnet, the students gathered around the glass-encased treasures.

There were several brass plaques, as well as pamphlets, describing and explaining the events leading up to the historic, legendary gunfight.

One boy looked up at the curator and asked, "Do the guns still work?"

The curator nodded. "I have been told by expert gunsmiths who examined the guns that there is a 95 percent chance that both guns are still fully operational."

Then a girl asked a two-part question with a very surprising second question no one asked the curator before, "Can you trace the owners of these artifacts back to the ranger and Texas Red?"

"Yes, I can, and that part was actually very easy…at least, for me it was."

"Are these artifacts cursed? Do bad things happen to the owners?"

The curator only had to think for a few seconds. "No, there is no curse or evil spirits or toxic karma suffered by the owners of these artifacts. No such things were ever pronounced on the artifacts or any claims of a curse on owners of the artifacts. A lot of bad things happened to the owners of this gun, but it was due to their own actions and decisions, not a curse."

Then the class teacher looked up at the curator and asked, "With all of your records and everything you know, can you tell us who the fastest gunfighter was?"

The curator answered without hesitation, "There are rumors and legends about a small number of extremely rare master gunfighters who achieved and attained a level of skill unmatched by others. However, one and only one master gunfighter ever had credible witnesses and had his superb skills documented by a credible newspaper plus a dozen reporters. Only one master gunfighter proved and documented that he possessed the greatest gun-fighting skill attainable. It was a draw too fast for the human eye to follow and a legendary skill proven only once in the history of the old west, a skill known as…the invisible draw."

"It is said that to the human eye, the blast of his gunshot, the tongue of fire from his barrel, and the cloud of blue-white smoke seemed to appear from nowhere with no discernible movements by the gunfighter. Even today, the invisible draw is a skill mastered only by a few fast-draw artists and professionals. In the old west… it was virtually nonexistent and only once proven."

The curator gestured to the blackened gun belt and the customized Big Iron. "Notice the badge in the center of the display. One 1860 Arizona ranger's badge was reissued in 1882 to one ranger. The 1882 Arizona rangers only existed for about two months, from March 8 to May 20, 1882, and they were formed for the sole purpose of fighting Apaches within Arizona Territory. However, within that short time, Arizona commissioned a ranger to extract one of the most feared and deadly outlaws known. The ranger traveled to the town of Aqua Fria. The outlaw's name was William Travis Jr., better known as Texas Red, and he lived in Agua Fria, New Mexico Territory. The Ranger's name was Kyle Lawton, and he was the only gunfighter in the old west ever documented and proven to possess the skills to pull leather with an invisible draw. In addition, you have to consider the fact that the Big Iron the ranger pulled weighs just over four and a half pounds, while Texas Red's firearm weighed but two and a half pounds, perhaps an ounce or two less. But to answer your question, I do not believe there can be any doubt that Arizona Ranger Kyle Lawton was not only the fastest gunfighter in the old west but one of the fastest gunfighters who has ever lived."

The curator thought for a moment and added, "And for personal reasons, it is a bit difficult for me to accept that, or like it. But that is what happened, and the ranger was man enough to prove it." When asked about that comment, the curator politely declined to elaborate. It was, perhaps, a rare slip of the tongue by the curator. On the other hand, perhaps it was the children. The curator did not realize how likable children could be, and they were so spontaneous and asked intelligent questions. The children made the curator think of sponges that soak up knowledge rather than water, and they caught the curator somewhat by surprise and put him slightly off balance. In fact, the curator was very impressed and much more at ease than he thought he would be. He actually enjoyed conducting the tour and even extended it somewhat.

Then the curator gathered the children around the glass case and proceeded to tell them the entire story of Texas Red and the ranger. He started the story with Texas Red's father becoming wealthy when he was mistaken for an heir of a rather large fortune. Then he told of Texas Red's father meeting Felina in El Paso and their love, and he told them of the tragic end to their lives. He ended the story with Texas Red reverting to William as he lay dying in the street. He also told of Texas Red shooting the ranger in his gun hand with the small derringer, which doubtless saved the rangers life. The curator then ended the story with the point that you cannot have everything in life and that the ranger and Texas Red's sister, Lynda, for whatever reason, could not have children. The ranger swore to Texas Red that they would take good care of his secret love and of his son. The ranger kept his word, and he treated and reared Texas Red's son as if he were his own.

The children were totally mesmerized and captivated by the curator's story. They sat in awe and wonderment, but the teacher both smiled and frowned, and she shook her head through much of the story, especially toward the end. His story was too detailed, and he knew too much personal information, and he just had too many artifacts, and all of this was just too good to be true. She would have words with the curator. She admired him for the way he talked to the children, but something just wasn't right, and this whole situation pointed to a fabrication or a fraud. It was all just too convenient.

The teacher walked up to him, and looking up at him, she only now realized how tall the curator was, but she brushed it aside. "I would have a moment with you to have words."

The curator looked down at her and smiled knowingly. He had been challenged before. "Of course, but let's take care of the children first."

She was a bit embarrassed but undaunted. "Certainly."

The curator looked around at the still wide-eyed children. "What do you think is the most important thing for a gunfighter to do?"

A small girl raised her hand and answered at the same time. "Practice the draw?"

"Yes, excellent answer. Not many people know just how demanding it is to be a fast draw expert, whether in the old west or today. A top-level fast draw expert will pull leather as many as ten thousand draws a month. Some even more."

The same girl asked, "Is that how the ranger got injured because he practiced so much with a heavy iron?"

The curator smiled and chuckled. "Yes, it is. That is exactly how the ranger got his secret injury. He practiced thousands of times a month with a heavy iron, and it damaged a nerve in his arm."

Another little girl spoke slowly as she asked, "What would have happened if the ranger's hand went bad when he had the fight with Texas Red?"

The curator smiled approvingly at her, and she smiled back at him as he answered her with a melting heart, "Then the name of this display would be Thunderbolt instead of Big Iron."

She then looked at him questioningly. "What do you mean Thunderbolt?"

"That is the nickname Texas Red gave his six-gun."

The curator did not want to answer the next level of her question, which doubtless would involve discussing someone getting killed, so he nodded at her and asked the class the next question.

"What do you think is the second most important thing a gunfighter should do?"

An excited boy blurted out, "Buying bullets?"

Everyone laughed, and the curator shook his head. "I cannot say no to that answer. That is a very good answer, so we are going to say yes, the second most important thing for a gunfighter to do is to buy bullets. In fact, a very important part of practicing is to fire the weapon many times in order to get the feel of the recoil and the feel of the weapon itself. So bullets it is."

The curator did not want to delve any deeper into the guns and their real purpose, and it was about time for them to leave, so he asked the class, "Does anyone have anything they would like to say?"

One of the larger boys bolted to his feet. "If I had lived back then, I would have been the fastest, and I could beat anybody. I would have been faster than Texas Red and the ranger. I know I would have been the best. I would beat all of them."

The curator smiled and responded, "No, you would not—"

"Yes, I would have."

"No, you wouldn't."

"I would too, and I would be the best ever."

The curator shook his head no, and the boy nodded his head yes.

The curator got down on one knee, put his forehead against the boy's forehead, and scowled, "You couldn't have been the fastest or the best, and you could have only been the second fastest and second best."

The boy scowled right back and pushed against the curator's forehead. "How do you know that?"

The curator wrinkled his nose. "Because *I* would have been the fastest and the best."

The boy laughed and then did something that shocked the curator. The boy grabbed him, gave him a big hug, and said, "I like you, and I had lots of fun. Your museum is the best one in the whole world."

It was so unexpected. The curator had to subtlety rub his eyes, and then the children had to leave.

As everyone began to clear out, the teacher walked up to the curator. "I cannot believe how good you were with the children and how they responded to you, but I would be remiss in my responsibilities if I did not at least ask a few questions of you."

The curator chuckled. "You mean interrogate me?"

The teacher scoffed. "I don't have my bright lights and thumbscrews."

The curator nodded as he realized the teacher was being very serious. "You are wondering how I could possibly have so much detailed and personal information about so many people who lived so long ago, and you are at least slightly suspicious about how I could possibly have so many appropriate artifacts. You do not object to my language or actions or how I interacted with the children, but you question the accuracy and validity of what I said to them. You are uncomfortable with this situation because it is supposed to be a factual history lesson not a creative literature class. How am I doing so far?"

The teacher looked up at him. "You left out the fact that so much of what you said is not available in any other history class, history book, or old west museum that I know of."

"Yes, you are concerned about credibility of exclusive knowledge, which is usually nil, and you question why I have so much detailed information while other sources have so little, and—"

The teacher sighed. "Yes?"

"And you are probably wondering if there is a well-planned and well executed-hoax or fraud involved here."

The teacher took a deep breath and sighed. "Yes, the thought has crossed."

"Okay, I really think you would like to see what is in the safe in my office."

"You can't mean more artifacts…"

"Yes, I have two more artifacts in the safe, but more importantly is the documentation I have."

She followed him into his office and politely looked away as he opened the safe. He reached in and picked up two objects, one somewhat larger than the other. He turned around held out his hands that were clinched. "Pick a hand."

She gestured with her eyes at his right hand. He turned his hand over and opened it. He was holding a large caliber mushroomed bullet. The teacher backed up a few steps, shook her head, and gasped. "That's not—"

The curator slowly nodded. "Yes, it is. This is the very bullet that killed Texas Red."

The teacher was incredulous. "What's in your other hand, a blood sample?"

He scoffed. "Pretty close." He opened his left hand, and she saw a small caliber derringer.

Recovering somewhat from the shock, she asked, "Is this the derringer Texas Red used to shoot the ranger in his gun hand? Why did he shoot the ranger in the hand instead of shooting the ranger in the head or someplace vital?"

"The derringer is one and the same, but here is what you are really looking for." With that, the curator handed her an official-looking envelope. Inside was a complete list of the artifacts and the authenticity of each item.

While she was looking at the documentation, the curator explained that Texas Red shot the ranger in the hand as a wedding gift to his sister that ended the ranger's gun-fighting career, which doubtless saved his life. He then explained that different members of the family wrote the detailed information he had in a set of journals and diaries at different times.

The teacher handed the envelope back to the curator. "This means all of the artifacts are genuine, but how could you possibly obtain all of them for yourself? How could you buy, find, steal, or track down all of these artifacts? How is it possible to obtain such an entire collection?"

The curator chuckled. "I did not buy them, find them, steal them, or track them down."

"Then how could you possibly have obtained such a treasured, one-of-a-kind collection of artifacts, not to mention the personal journals?"

The six foot two inch, 240-pound curator removed his cowboy hat, revealing his flaming red hair.

"I inherited them."

LYRICS

"EL PASO"

Out in the West Texas town of El Paso
I fell in love with a Mexican girl.
Night-time would find me in Rosa's cantina;
Music would play and Felina would whirl.

Blacker than night were the eyes of Felina,
Wicked and evil while casting a spell.
My love was deep for this Mexican maiden;
I was in love but in vain, I could tell.

One night a wild young cowboy came in,
Wild as the West Texas wind.
Dashing and daring,
A drink he was sharing
With wicked Felina,
The girl that I loved.

So in anger I

Challenged his right for the love of this maiden.
Down went his hand for the gun that he wore.
My challenge was answered in less than a heart-beat;
The handsome young stranger lay dead on the floor.

Just for a moment I stood there in silence,
Shocked by the foul evil deed I had done.
Many thoughts raced through my mind as I stood there;
I had but one chance and that was to run.

Out through the back door of Rosa's I ran,
Out where the horses were tied.
I caught a good one.
It looked like it could run.
Up on its back
And away I did ride,

Just as fast as I

Could from the West Texas town of El Paso
Out to the bad-lands of New Mexico.

Back in El Paso my life would be worthless.
Everything's gone in life; nothing is left.
It's been so long since I've seen the young maiden
My love is stronger than my fear of death.

I saddled up and away I did go,
Riding alone in the dark.
Maybe tomorrow
A bullet may find me.
Tonight nothing's worse than this
Pain in my heart.

And at last here I

Am on the hill overlooking El Paso;
I can see Rosa's cantina below.
My love is strong and it pushes me onward.
Down off the hill to Felina I go.

Off to my right I see five mounted cowboys;
Off to my left ride a dozen or more.
Shouting and shooting I can't let them catch me.
I have to make it to Rosa's back door.

Something is dreadfully wrong for I feel
A deep burning pain in my side.
Though I am trying
To stay in the saddle,
I'm getting weary,
Unable to ride.

But my love for

Felina is strong and I rise where I'd fallen,
Though I am weary I can't stop to rest.
I see the white puff of smoke from the rifle.
I feel the bullet go deep in my chest.

From out of nowhere Felina has found me,
Kissing my cheek as she kneels by my side.
Cradled by two loving arms that I'll die for,
One little kiss and Felina, good-bye.

"FALEENA"

Out in New Mexico, many long years ago
There in a shack on the desert, one night in a storm
Amid streaks of lightnin' and loud desert thunder
To a young Mexican couple, a baby was born;
Just as the baby cried, thunder and lightnin' died
Moon gave it's light to the world and the stars did the same
Mother and Father, both proud of the daughter
That heaven had sent them, Faleena was this baby's name.

When she was seventeen, bothered by crazy dreams
She ran away from the shack and left them to roam
Father and Mother, both asked one another
What made her run away, what made Faleena leave home;
Tired of the desert nights, fartherly grieved to strife
She ran away late one night in the moon's golden beam
She didn't know where she'd go, but she'd get there
And she would find happiness, if she would follow her dream.

After she ran away, she went to Santa Fe
And in the year that she stayed there, she learned about life
In just a little while, she learned that with her smile
She could have pretty clothes, she could be any man's wife;
Rich men romanced her, they dined and they danced her
She understood men and she treated them all just the same
A form that was fine and rare, dark shining glossy hair
Lovely to look at, Faleena was this woman's name.

Restless in Santa Fe, she had to get away
To any town where the lights had a much brighter glow
One cowboy mentioned the town of El Paso
They never stopped dancin' and money like whiskey would flow;

She bought a one-way, a ticket from Santa Fe
Three days and nights on a stage with a rest now and then
She didn't mind that, she knew she would find that
Her new life would be more exciting than where she had been

The stage made its last stop, up there on the mountain top
To let her see all the lights at the foot of the hill
Her world was brighter and deep down inside her
An uncontrolled beating, her young heart just wouldn't be still;
She got a hotel, a room at the Lily Belle
Quickly she changed to a form-fitting black satin dress
Every man stopped to stare, at this form fine and rare
Even the women remarked of the charm she possessed.

Dancin' and laughter, was what she was after
And Rosa's Cantina had lights, with love in the gleam
That's what she hunted and that's what she wanted
Rosa's was one place, a nice girl would never be seen;
It was the same way, it was back in Santa Fe
Men would make fools of themselves at the thought of romance
Rosa took heed of, the place was in need of
This kind of excitement, so she paid Faleena to dance.

A year passed or maybe more and then through the swingin' doors
Came a young cowboy so tall and so handsomely dressed
This one was new in town, hadn't been seen around
He was so different, he wasn't like all of the rest;
Faleena danced close to him, then threw a rose to him
Quickly he walked to her table and there he sat down
And in a day or so, wherever folks would go
They'd see this young cowboy, showin' Faleena the town.

Six weeks he went with her, each minute spent with her
But he was insanely jealous of glances she'd give
Inside he was a-hurtin', from all of her flirtin'
But that was her nature and that was the way that she lived;
She flirted one night, it started a gun-fight
And after the smoke cleared away, on the floor lay a man
Faleena's young lover, had shot down another
And he had to leave there, so out through the back door he ran

The next day at five o'clock, she heard a rifle shot
Quickly she ran to the door, that was facin' the pass
She saw her cowboy, her wild-ridin' cowboy
Low in the saddle, her cowboy was ridin' in fast;
She ran to meet him, to kiss and to greet him
He saw her and motioned her back, with a wave of his hand
Bullets were flyin', Faleena was cryin'
As she saw him fall from the saddle and into the sand.

Faleena knelt near him, to hold and to hear him
As she felt the warm blood that flowed from the wound in his side
He raised to kiss her and she heard him whisper
"Never forget me—Faleena it's over, goodbye."
Quickly she grabbed for, the six-gun that he wore
And screamin' in anger and placin' the gun to her breast
Bury us both deep and maybe we'll find peace
And pullin' the trigger, she fell 'cross the dead cowboy's chest.

Out in El Paso, whenever the wind blows
If you listen closely at night, you'll hear in the wind
A woman is cryin', it's not the wind sighin'
Old timer's tell you, Faleena is callin' for him;
You'll hear them talkin' and you'll hear them walkin'
You'll hear them laugh and you'll look, but there's no one around
Don't be alarmed—there is really no harm there
It's only the young cowboy, showin' Faleena the town.

"BIG IRON"

To the town of Agua Fria rode a stranger one fine day
Hardly spoke to folks around him didn't have too much to say
No one dared to ask his business no one dared to make a slip
for the stranger there among them had a big iron on his hip
Big iron on his hip

It was early in the morning when he rode into the town
He came riding from the south side slowly lookin' all around
He's an outlaw loose and running came the whisper from each lip
And he's here to do some business with the big iron on his hip
big iron on his hip

In this town there lived an outlaw by the name of Texas Red
Many men had tried to take him and that many men were dead
He was vicious and a killer though a youth of twenty four
And the notches on his pistol numbered one an nineteen more
One and nineteen more

Now the stranger started talking made it plain to folks around
Was an Arizona ranger wouldn't be too long in town
He came here to take an outlaw back alive or maybe dead
And he said it didn't matter he was after Texas Red
After Texas Red

Wasn't long before the story was relayed to Texas Red
But the outlaw didn't worry men that tried before were dead
Twenty men had tried to take him twenty men had made a slip
Twenty one would be the ranger with the big iron on his hip
Big iron on his hip

The morning passed so quickly it was time for them to meet
It was twenty past eleven when they walked out in the street
Folks were watching from the windows every-body held their breath
They knew this handsome ranger was about to meet his death
About to meet his death

There was forty feet between them when they stopped to make their play
And the swiftness of the ranger is still talked about today
Texas Red had not cleared leather fore a bullet fairly ripped
And the ranger's aim was deadly with the big iron on his hip
Big iron on his hip

It was over in a moment and the folks had gathered round
There before them lay the body of the outlaw on the ground
Oh he might have went on living but he made one fatal slip
When he tried to match the ranger with the big iron on his hip
Big iron on his hip

Big iron Big iron

When he tried to match the ranger with the big iron on his hip

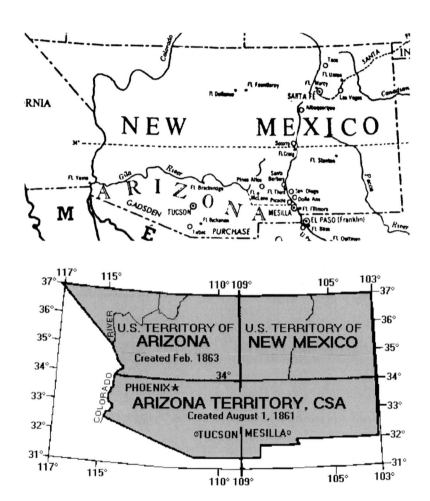

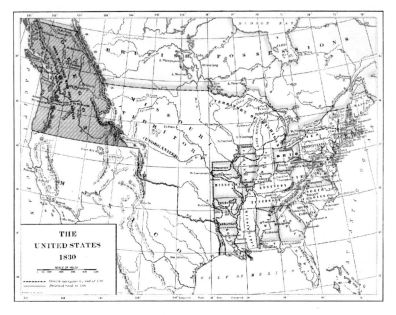

The United States, 1830
Dixon Ryan Fox, *Harper's Atlas of American History* (New York, NY: Harper & Brothers Publishers , 1920) 38
Downloaded from *Maps ETC*, on the web at http://etc.usf.edu/maps   [map #3303]

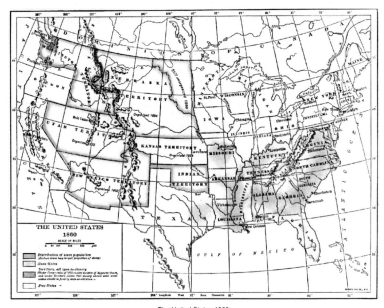

The United States 1860
Dixon Ryan Fox, *Harper's Atlas of American History* (New York, NY: Harper & Brothers Publishers , 1920)
Downloaded from *Maps ETC*, on the web at http://etc.usf.edu/maps   [map #03339]

The United States in 1870, 1870
Albert Bushnell Hart, L.L.D., *The American Nation Vol. 22* (New York, NY: Harper and Brothers, 1907)
Downloaded from *Maps ETC.* on the web at http://etc.usf.edu/maps   [map #02851]